A Tangle of Gold

ALSO BY JACLYN MORIARTY

A Corner of White (The Colors of Madeleine, Book 1)
The Cracks in the Kingdom (The Colors of Madeleine, Book 2)

Feeling Sorry for Celia
The Year of Secret Assignments
The Murder of Bindy Mackenzie
The Ghosts of Ashbury High

The Spell Book of Listen Taylor

A Tangle of Gold

THE COLORS OF MADELEINE

BOOK THREE

JACLYN MORIARTY

ARTHUR A. LEVINE BOOKS
An Imprint of Scholastic Inc.

From Queries to *The Opticks*, by Isaac Newton (1721):

Eggs grow . . . & change into animals, Tad-poles into Frogs & worms into Flyes. All Birds Beasts & Fishes Insects Trees & other Vegetables, with their several parts, grow out of water . . . And among such various & strange transmutations why may not Nature change bodies into light & light into bodies?

From Queries to *The Opticks*, by Isaac Newton (1721):

For some colours are agreeable as those of Gold & Indigo, & others disagree.

From *Letter of Mr. Isaac Newton, Containing His New Theory about Light and Colours* (*Philosophical Transactions of the Royal Society*, number 80, 1671–2):

[B]ut if any one [colour] predominate, the light must incline to that colour; as it happens in the blue flame of brimstone; the yellow flame of a candle; and the various colours of the fixed stars. . . .

From *The Prelude*, Book 3, by William Wordsworth
(1799–1805, published 1850):

And from my pillow, looking forth by light
Of moon or favouring stars, I could behold
The antechapel where the statue stood
Of Newton with his prism and silent face,
The marble index of a mind for ever
Voyaging through strange seas of Thought, alone.

The Cello Winds

The Winds of Cello are a hoot. I mean that literally. Sometimes they sound exactly like a cross between a car horn and an owl. No, it's more like a car horn and an owl engaged in chat:

> *Toot hoot.*
> *Hoot toot?*
> *Toot.*
> *Ho-o-t?!*

Then, just when you're not expecting it — just when you're sniggering and turning to your books — the Cello Winds switch. Something surges forward like a sailboat on a wave; springs at your heart with claws of gold. The Wind finds its feet — or its wings, or its voice — and the music that it sounds! How to describe it? *Exquisite* does not even come close!

Try this. I have a friend (Albert) who once suggested that the music of the Winds is *"that elusive thing that lies beyond all beauty; the aesthetic heart and soul of grief and love."* I'll be honest, I often find Albert quite insufferable, but here, somehow, he almost hits the mark.

Of course, the Cello Winds do more than play their music:[1] They also blow away disease. In our Kingdom, no pestilence takes hold.

No doubt you'll arrive in Cello determined to hear the Wind. Your determination counts for nothing. Indeed, you could spend a lifetime in Cello and never hear it once. (On the other hand, I am acquainted with a woman [Sophia] who has only ever *been* to Cello once — and that, very briefly, in transit — yet for the entire fifteen minutes she was regaled by the Winds. So. You know. Go figure.)

[1] In the seventeenth century, instrument makers in Bologna, Italy, the World, modified the bass violin to create a large, stringed musical instrument. Someone who had once visited Cello observed that the instrument's melancholy tone resembled the Cello Winds. Hence, the instrument was named the violon*cello*. These days, it is simply known as "the cello."

A Tangle of Gold

PART 1

1.

*W*hen Elliot Baranski came to Cambridge, England, he only stayed for just over two weeks.

Which was preposterous.

He was from the Kingdom of Cello, he had stumbled into the World when he fell into a ravine and landed in a BP petrol station, he'd walked from this petrol station to Cambridge so as to find his friend Madeleine Tully, but, unexpectedly — a real bonus — the first person he'd run into was Abel Baranski, who was only Elliot's long-lost dad.

All of which was perfectly reasonable.

Brilliant, even.

But this! Leaving after just over two weeks!

Well, it was preposterous. It was so preposterous it was making Madeleine's nose bleed.

Madeleine was standing on the platform at the Cambridge railway station with a bleeding nose. Around her, the others were talking about flight times, and how Abel and Elliot felt about turbulence, and whether Abel had remembered to drop off the key to his flat, and where the dog, Sulky-Anne, would live now, and whether her new owners had been informed about Sulky-Anne's fear of marshmallows. And so on.

Abel was taking each of the questions in mild, thoughtful turn. Elliot, meanwhile, was standing apart, watching the tracks.

That was Elliot Baranski in his overcoat and his woollen hat. That was Elliot's bare hands and wrists. That was Elliot kicking a suitcase lightly with the toe of his boot.

He glanced towards Madeleine. She caught his glance and held it, trying to convey a lot of things — well, primarily one thing: *This is preposterous!* — in her expression. But Elliot scratched at the edge of his wool hat and turned away again. She hadn't conveyed anything. The blood-soaked tissues pressed against her face had probably interfered.

Madeleine ran through the events of the past just-over-two-weeks. Fiercely, she counted them. There were eight.

First, Abel held a party to introduce his long-lost son to everyone.

Everyone consisted of Madeleine's friends, Belle and Jack, and their assortment of home-schooling teachers: Madeleine's mother, Belle's mother, Jack's grandfather, and Darshana Charan, who taught them Science and Mathematics in exchange for the babysitting of her daughters. Abel himself was their ICT and Geography teacher. He lived in the flat downstairs from Madeleine and her mother.

Madeleine came down early, to help tidy, but Belle and Jack turned up while the place was still a mess.

"So, this is Elliot?" Belle said.

"It is," Elliot himself agreed.

"From the parking meter."

"From the Kingdom of Cello," Madeleine corrected her. "We just wrote to each other through a crack inside the parking meter. Remember, I told you —"

"Shut it. I'm trying to appraise him."

There was a pause while Belle stared at Elliot.

"He's hot," she concluded, turning to Madeleine. "Respect." She offered Madeleine a fist bump, which was not Belle's style. It might have been ironic.

"Nice aura too," Belle tossed back at Elliot as she moved into the flat, looking for food.

"Well, thanks," Elliot said.

Jack said, "Hiya!" and asked Elliot if he'd ever visited Cambridge before.

"You tosser," Belle said from the kitchenette. "He's from another *dimension*."

Jack shrugged. "In a former life, then? Have you got memories of your former lives, Elliot? And did you ever, in a former life, live in our dimension and visit Cambridge?"

Elliot was still considering this when the others arrived — everyone was early, wanting to meet the long-lost son — and things became a chaos of pouring drinks, opening biscuits, pulling trays of chocolate-pecan brownies from the oven, clearing spaces on Abel's workbenches, tripping over the dog, and trying to prevent Darshana Charan's little girls from electrocuting themselves. Someone switched on some music, but Abel reached out and turned it off.

"Hang on," he said. "I have to make my speech."

He had already decided not to mention the Kingdom of Cello. It was true that Belle and Jack knew about Cello, but if he tried to explain it to the adults, it would only end in —

"Tears," Madeleine offered.

"Scepticism," Abel said. "And if there's one thing I can't abide, it's scepticism."

So, instead, he announced to the room that he'd been suffering amnesia the whole time he'd known them (which was true), and that his name was *not* Denny, as he'd thought, but Abel Baranski, and that here was his lost son, Elliot, all the way from the U.S. of A.

"Stand up, Elliot," he said, "so they can see you."

"No need," somebody pointed out. "He'll be the only stranger in the room. There. That one."

"Ah, he's proud of his son," another voice put in indulgently, and Elliot obliged them by standing so everyone could continue smiling at him.

"Our plan is to see if we can figure out how to get ourselves back home to the U.S. of A.," Abel continued.

"You could buy plane tickets," someone suggested. "That'd be your best bet."

Abel switched the music on again, and it turned into a party.

Elliot was friendly and shook people's hands and smiled at their jokes, but he didn't say much. Once, he turned towards the sound of Belle's mother, who was making fun of Belle's earrings, reaching out to touch them and pretending they sizzled, which made no sense. His face was carefully blank as he watched this, but Madeleine caught the tiny crease of a frown, just above his eye. He turned away again. Another time, she saw him look down and find Darshana's little girls crouched by his feet.

"You've got a scab here on your ankle," the girls told him. "We're just picking it off for you."

He laughed and crouched down to chat with them, shifting his ankle away from their fingers as he did. But Madeleine didn't hear what they said.

Next, Madeleine, Belle, and Jack showed Elliot around Cambridge.

This was the day after the party. Jack had drawn up an itinerary and he led the tour, reciting a lot of historical facts, most of which he invented. Elliot listened, gazing at the architecture. He shook his head in slow admiration sometimes, which made Jack happy.

They went punting on the Cam that day, and Elliot asked if he could try steering. He stood up on the slippery platform and followed their instructions: You lift the pole out of the water, raise it hand over hand, then let it fall down to the riverbed. At first, Elliot concentrated hard, but then a calm fell over him and you could see it become part of his body, the action of the pole rising and falling, and everything about him seemed to move quietly and smoothly, and he disappeared in thought. Madeleine watched him while the punt moved with its *plash*, quiet, *plash*. There weren't many people on the river, but Elliot nodded, friendly, every time they passed another punt. He never once got the pole caught on a snag.

Third, they invited Elliot to play tennis with them.

Elliot watched them warm up. "I've played a game something like this before," he said, half to himself.

Then he stepped onto the court and returned Belle's shot with a beautiful, swift, unexpected backhand. He laughed when he heard the scoring — "forty-love," "deuce" — then he stopped laughing and figured out how it worked.

He often went quiet, Madeleine noticed, figuring things out. He seemed laid-back, easy-going-farm-boy — like he should be chewing on a piece of straw — but if you looked close, you'd see flickering frowns, and you knew he was studying things from all sorts of angles, trying to piece it all together.

Fourth, most nights, Madeleine went downstairs to Abel's flat and hung out with Abel and Elliot, drinking cocoa, eating muffins, and talking about how to get them home. Abel was spending his days reading quantum physics, writing copious notes, and studying the parking meter. He liked to talk things through with Madeleine, and to quiz her about the experiments she and Elliot had done when the two of them had tried to solve the crack.

"Electricity and magnetism jostled it," Madeleine said, "but we think a mirror and a light is the best." She glanced over at Elliot. "Right?"

Elliot nodded.

"Only, the crack in the parking meter here is too small for people, so we never actually got it open. You need a *bigger* crack, a people-moving crack, and then we think a mirror and light will work — but we don't know for sure." Again, she looked at Elliot.

"Right," Elliot agreed, but said no more.

Some nights, Madeleine's mother, Holly, joined them too. She was doing a fashion design course by correspondence, and she'd bring down the samples she was sewing and work on zips or buttons while they talked. She thought their conversation about the Kingdom of Cello was a game or a story they'd invented.

"This is better than TV!" she said. Then she reflected, "Well, in all honesty, it's not. TV's great these days. Such high production values. But still. This isn't bad!"

Fifth, everyone decided that Elliot may as well join in their home schooling while he was here.

So he came along to a History class with Jack's grandfather, Federico Cagnetti.

The class was in an office above the porter's lodge at Trinity. Federico was crouching by the fireplace, warming his hands, when they arrived. His hands were long and craggy, with sprouts of white hair on the knuckles, and these hairs glowed in the gaslight.

Elliot sat beside Madeleine.

"It is the turn of Belle," Federico said abruptly, pressing his hands onto his thighs to raise himself and scowling around, light from the gas fire eerie in his eyes. "Lucky for Belle."

Madeleine was conscious of Elliot's profile. His shadow was blending with the shadow of his chair. His legs in their jeans stretched themselves out, then changed their mind, and moved back closer to the chair legs. One shoelace was tied in a knotty double bow; the other had come loose and was trailing on the floor. His hand reached up and touched a long, fine scar that ran down the side of his neck.

"In this class," Federico said to Elliot, "we have the hat. Also, welcome," he added, remembering himself with a sudden blink.

"The hat?"

Federico's eyes widened. The new kid was an idiot! "The *hat*," he repeated, and he gestured towards his own bowler hat, sitting face up on the desk.

"Ah."

Federico relaxed. He held the hat towards Belle.

"He puts historical names in here," Belle explained, "and then we choose from it and we have to do a presentation on the name. So it's like his hat is destiny."

"That's true," Jack agreed, interested. "The papers in the hat are like tea leaves or coffee grinds, only the future they predict is assignment-specific."

Federico began muttering to himself, low and fast, in Italian.

"He's cursing us," Jack translated for the others. "That's wasteful, Nonno. You should save those insults for when we spray-paint gang symbols all over the office. This is more your general-chitchat-among-students-while-teacher's-hand-gets-tired-holding-out-a-hat situation."

"Just put on an ironic voice," Madeleine suggested. "And say: *Fascinating, people, but let's move on.*"

Federico's muttering rose and accelerated until he sounded like factory machinery with a wrench loose in its workings.

"All right, all right," Belle said. "Keep your hat on."

Then she laughed so hard at her own joke that she almost knocked the hat out of Federico's hand. The others laughed too.

Belle breathed in the last of her laughter, tears in her eyes, and finally reached into the hat. She rustled papers for a while, still smiling to herself, and withdrew a folded slip. She opened it.

"Leonardo da Vinci."

Federico beamed. "*Leonardo da Vinci,*" he repeated with relish.

"He was the blue ninja turtle," Jack said.

"That's all right, then," Belle said. "I look good in blue." She spoke to Elliot again. "We have to *become* the people we do the projects on. One time, Jack got the poet Byron and Madeleine got Isaac Newton, and they both became obsessed. Are you still obsessed?"

Jack began to recite at once:

"Did ye not hear it? — No; 'twas but the wind,
Or the car rattling o'er the stony street;
On with the dance! let joy be unconfined."

He paused. "That's just a few lines. I can do the whole thing if you like."

"I read about Isaac Newton every day," Madeleine put in. "Did you know he was an alchemist? They say maybe the mercury sent him mad."

"So, yep, they are still obsessed. I don't get like that because I have a more reasonable turn of mind." Belle looked back at Federico. "So you want me to become Leonardo da Vinci?"

"To become him? This is impossible!"

Belle raised a shrewd eyebrow. "Now you're being inconsistent, cause it was impossible for Madeleine to become Isaac Newton, and yet she did. Or anyway she didn't. She's still Madeleine."

Federico nodded slowly.

"Ha," Belle said. "I get you. Touché, and that. Or maybe that slow nod is more confusion than you being wise. Either way, I *could* become Leonardo if it's helpful to you, Federico. Everyone knows that if you believe something strongly enough, it comes true. Like, I once knew a guy who saw a billboard with a picture of peanuts on it and he went into anaphylactic shock."

"Who was this?" Jack asked.

"Because he was allergic to peanuts."

"Who?"

"It was an ad for a financial institution or something. *You can buy a house with peanuts*, it said. Or you can't. Either way, that's why the picture."

"You don't know anyone that happened to at all," Jack decided.

"Nah," Belle agreed. "I don't. But imagine."

"You can't believe a word she says," Jack told Elliot. "Although she's actually completely honest."

"It is the time for me to sleep," Federico announced. "As you are speaking more nonsense than the people I meet in my dreams. So! I will visit my dream friends instead."

He folded his arms, closed his eyes, and bowed his head.

There was a thoughtful pause.

"That's quite good, Nonno," Jack said eventually. "You've got our attention. But open your eyes soon or we'll lose interest and entertain ourselves again."

Federico grimaced, eyes still closed. He pressed his chin into his chest.

They waited. The fireplace hissed. Federico's breathing slowed.

"He really is asleep," Belle whispered.

Federico's shoulders rose and fell comfortably, in time with his breathing.

"So this is home schooling," Elliot said.

The others laughed.

"You can't believe a word *he* says," Belle said abruptly, pointing at Elliot. "Talking about believing."

The others looked from Belle to Elliot, who seemed surprised but not offended.

"It's not so much you can't believe him," Belle clarified. "It's more *he* doesn't believe what he's saying. You don't even have to look at his aura, you can hear it in his voice. He's play-acting. He doesn't believe that the Kingdom of Cello exists, let alone that that's where he's from."

Elliot smiled in a pleasant, neutral way.

Jack raised an eyebrow. "You're right."

Sixth, that very night, at their regular nighttime meeting, Abel announced that he had news.

His voice made Holly pause in her sewing. Madeleine bit her finger instead of the muffin she was eating.

"I was at the parking meter today," Abel continued. There was a faint wheeze behind his words, which seemed like an effect, designed to heighten tension. "And a *note was there from Cello*."

"Oh, nice!" Holly resumed sewing.

Madeleine looked across at Elliot, but he was leaning over, scratching Sulky-Anne's head.

"Here's what the note says." Abel's hands trembled. He read.

This is a message for Madeleine Tully. Are Abel and Elliot Baranski there with you? If so, we want to bring them back to Cello. Meet us here Monday, midnight, to discuss. Keira

"Who's Keira?" Holly said. "New character?"

Madeleine reached for a paper and pen. She angled the paper towards her mother and drew three circles.

"Okay," she said, writing in each circle. "Here are the three most powerful organisations in Cello. The royal family. The Hostiles. And the WSU."

"Oh, *I* see," said Holly.

"No, you don't. You don't even know what I'm talking about." She pointed to the circles in turn. "The royal family are in charge. The Hostiles want to take them down. The WSU is the World Severance Unit, and its job is to stop any contact between Cello and our world." She looked over at Abel and Elliot. "Is this right so far?"

Elliot walked into the kitchen and opened a can of dog food for Sulky-Anne.

Abel nodded. "Perfect. Carry on."

"Abel was on the royal side. The Hostiles chased him over a ravine and he fell through a crack into our world."

"Lucky," Holly said.

"So that's how Abel ended up here. He lost his memory and thought his name was Denny. Meanwhile, back in Cello, the Hostiles kidnapped the royal family and sent *them* through to our world, where they also forgot who they were."

"Huh."

"But one princess was left behind. Princess Ko. She ran the Kingdom secretly, without telling anybody her family was gone, and she formed a Royal Youth Alliance to help her bring them back. Elliot was part of the Alliance. He worked with me, talking through the parking meter, to try to find the royals and solve the cracks and send the royals home."

"So you had a big responsibility, Madeleine," Holly said. "I'm proud."

"Thank you. But talking to me was risky for Elliot because it's illegal. The WSU found out, chased *him* over the same ravine, and he also fell through a crack into our world."

"Symmetrical!" Holly said. "Or too much of a coincidence?"

"Anyhow, there were three other teenagers also on the Royal Youth Alliance with Elliot. Their names were Sergio, Samuel, and Keira."

There was a pause. Holly was threading a needle. Madeleine waited.

Holly looked up. "*Keira!* The one who wrote the note we just heard! The new character! Great. I'd forgotten we were trying to place her. Thank you, Madeleine."

"You're welcome," Madeleine said. She looked at Abel. "I don't know much about Keira, except what Elliot told me."

Elliot was now at the sink, refilling Sulky-Anne's water bowl, his back to them.

"I think she was from Jagged Edge," Madeleine continued slowly. "That's a sort of high-tech province in Cello," she explained to her mother. "And I think she had some connection to the Hostiles. Her mother was a Hostile? So. Do we trust her?"

Abel studied Keira's note again, then looked at Madeleine's diagram.

"You've got the three most powerful organisations in Cello," he said. "But you're missing a fourth. Each province has its own council. Mostly, they're just for show, but in Jagged Edge, the provincial council is controlled by a group called the Elite. And a lot of people think they actually run everything — the whole Kingdom, I mean. They've got links to the criminal underworld, which helps."

"Oh, then, for *sure* they're the most powerful," Holly put in. "Crime lords always control everything, because they've got lawlessness and tattooed thugs and sinister men in hats and shadows with scars — they've got all that on their side. So if you're saying that this Keira girl is from the Jagged Edge place, *and* has Hostile connections, well, I wouldn't trust her to pick up the milk, let alone to bring you home to Cello."

"She's also beautiful," Madeleine reflected. "I remember Elliot telling me that."

"That settles it, then. Never trust the pretty ones. Well, I'm tired. Shall we go up to bed, Mads?"

"Uh," said Madeleine. "I have to go with Abel to the parking meter? It's Monday today. We should go hear what this Keira has to say."

"Wow." Holly stood. "You're really *invested* in this thing, aren't you? I guess, as long as you stay warm and don't get chased over any ravines." She took an extra muffin, "for the road," and she headed upstairs.

Seventh, Madeleine and Abel put on their coats, ready to go talk to Keira at the parking meter.

Elliot said he was "beat" and he'd turn in.

"Let me know what goes down," he said, grinning, and Madeleine smiled back, and stepped through the door after Abel.

She remembered her umbrella. She swung back around. Elliot startled, seeing her, and he grabbed at his grin again. But it was too late. She'd caught the expression on his face. It reminded her of those selfies older women post of themselves sometimes without makeup: You'd get accustomed to seeing them all shiny and glossy, and then wham! Here was the truth. A ravaged, exhausted, colourless old face. Elliot's expression was that, but also more: It was utter despair.

"You coming, Mads?" Abel called to her from the staircase.

Elliot held her gaze and his careful smile.

Madeleine closed the door and followed Abel.

And finally, eighth, she and Abel arrived at the parking meter.

The mist hunched along the road as if the air itself was huddling, cold.

Abel was wheezing. He shouldn't be out on a winter night with that chest of his. She could see he was forcing himself to slow his breathing.

She was holding a notepad and pen. Staring at a parking meter. In an empty laneway.

It was exactly like the nights she used to come here to talk to Elliot, except that Elliot was now in a flat ten minutes from here and Elliot's father was beside her.

Also, she was going to speak to a beautiful stranger named Keira.

"It's exactly midnight," Abel said, shining the torch onto his watch and then onto the parking meter.

A slip of white appeared along the crack.

"Punctual," he said.

Madeleine pulled out the paper, and Abel leaned close and read with her.

This is Keira. Are you there, Madeleine?

Abel breathed in with a sharp rasp. Madeleine wrote a single word.

Yep.

Are you in contact with Abel and Elliot Baranski?

Yes. Abel's right beside me. Elliot's home in bed.

There was a long pause, then another note appeared.

So Abel and Elliot are alive?

Well, Abel's right beside me like I said. I'd have mentioned if he was a corpse. I can't swear that Elliot's still alive cause I guess a pirate could've broken in and cut his throat in the last ten minutes. Still. That seems doubtful.

There was another break, then another note from Keira:

Okay, here's the deal. The nearest people-moving crack to you is in a city called Berlin, Germany. Based on the maps I have, it looks a reasonable journey for Abel and Elliot to take. Do you know it? If not, I can give you the coordinates. If I give you the precise location of the crack in Berlin, can you direct Abel and Elliot Baranski to be there on Wednesday night? And we'll bring them across.

The torchlight wavered. Madeleine looked up, but Abel's face was in shadow. She wrote a reply.

Who is "we"? Are Princess Ko and the Royal Youth Alliance organising this?

No. It's me, Keira, and also Elliot's mother, and a bunch of Elliot's friends, plus the local Sheriff and Deputy, plus two secret agent guys. Can you get the Baranskis to Berlin?

Yeah, it's not too far. And I already know exactly where that people-moving crack is — I'm the one who worked with Elliot trying to get the royals back to Cello, remember? But I didn't know if it was sealed now or not. And I never knew if the mirror-light thing worked. So did it? And is it safe? Are the royals safe home?

As she sent this reply, she brushed her hand against the parking meter. It was cold like a shot of flame.

Keira's note was brief.

I can unseal the crack. Light-mirror trick does work. We got the King and younger prince home to Cello using it.

Madeleine frowned. Beside her, Abel was trying to hold the torch-light under his chin while he reached into his pocket for his inhaler. She wrote:

Only the King and the little prince? What about the rest of the royal family?

The WSU found out what was happening. They put guards on the other cracks and sealed them, so we had to quit.

"Ask her what time we need to be in Berlin," Abel said, but Madeleine was already writing.

Are you saying that if the other royals went to the places I told them to go, at the times I told them to, they'd still be waiting now???

Sure. If they're morons. That was weeks ago. Can you confirm you can get Abel and Elliot Baranski to Berlin by Wednesday night?

"Tell her you can," Abel said. "But ask what time. And ask if the crack's being guarded on their side."

Madeleine was writing fast, but another note from Keira was emerging. Abel grabbed it and read it to himself.

"She's already answered my questions. She says the guards are still there, but they're arranging a diversion for midnight while we come through. She says timing is vital."

"Does she?" Madeleine said. "And does she even know there's a time difference between here and Germany?"

She folded her own reply while Abel was still trying to read her handwriting over her shoulder:

This is too dangerous. The last time Elliot was in Cello, the WSU chased him over a cliff — if there hadn't been a crack thru to the World he'd be dead. You're going to "divert" the guards? You screw up the timing and Elliot's dead. And even if you get him thru safe, how's he going to STAY safe? They'll hunt him down and kill him all over again.

Keira's reply was scribbled.

Can't talk much longer. Agree that Elliot's in danger here. We have that sorted — he'll go straight into hiding with a Hostile branch. Friends of mine arranging that. He can stay w/them till we get his name cleared.

Madeleine's eyes widened. She wrote again:

Wait, are you saying there'll be Hostiles there too?????? It was Hostiles who nearly killed ABEL, and they DID kill his brother. Basically you have executioners lined up waiting to take both Elliot and Abel down the moment they arrive!!

"Madeleine." Abel spoke her name in a space between wheezes. She ignored him and sent the message. Keira's reply came quickly.

You need to stop worrying about this end of things. We've got that. You just need to get them to Berlin.

Abel was holding the torch high. "Madeleine," he said again. She was vaguely aware that his shoulders were rising and falling. She wrote in giant scribbles.

Keira, listen to me, Abel and Elliot are alive and well in my world and nobody's hunting them down with guns and dogs and choppers. Whereas, last time they were in YOUR world they were basically dead. With respect, you haven't "got" that end at all. You couldn't even transfer the whole royal family w/o everything going to hell??? So half the royals are still trapped, alone in the World?? Princess Jupiter is right there in Berlin — why don't you get her thru first? And set up transfers for the Queen and the other prince at the same time?

Keira's reply arrived a few moments later.

Are you serious? Now you want to throw in a royal or two? You have no clue what has been happening here. It's total chaos. Princess Ko has been arrested. Hostiles on the rise. Elite taking power. Anyway, I can't have this conversation. Great that Abel and Elliot are alive and well but I don't think you or "your World" can take the credit for that. Cut out the commentary and let me know that this is going to happen. Once they're thru, I'll seal this crack and cut off all communications with u and the World — it's way too dangerous.

Madeleine clenched her fists so her nails cut into her palms. She turned the page in her notebook so fast it tore in half. She raised her pen to think — and felt a hand wrap around her own hand.

It was Abel.

She looked up at him and thought about how noisy asthma made the world. It was not just a regular wheeze, it was a cacophony of rattles and odd, tiny squeals.

"Madeleine," he said for the third time, and she realised that his tone had been the same for each. Loaded with certainty. "I haven't seen my wife or my home for over a year."

He paused, looking at her in the darkness.

"For most of that time," he continued, "I have not been myself. I've believed I was somebody else. You remember we once talked about the concept of displacement?"

Madeleine nodded.

"To not remember your own self," Abel said, "is the greatest displacement that there is."

Madeleine stopped halfway to another nod.

"To be *dead*," she argued, "is greater. I don't trust this Keira. Who knows what she's up to? And there's no way she can guarantee that you'll be safe. We need to think about this."

Abel shook his inhaler again and took a deep drag.

"Cello is already starting to seem more theoretical than real. I could lose myself again, any time. As for Elliot, he says he knows who he is, but I suspect he just thinks we're all insane. He's playing along until he figures what to do."

"No." Madeleine shook her head and right away remembered Belle that morning: *He doesn't believe that the Kingdom of Cello exists, let alone that that's where he's from.*

She bit her lip.

"It's still better that he's here," she said, "and safe," but she was thinking of that pleasant, neutral smile on Elliot's face, and the despair that she'd glimpsed behind that smile.

Abel watched her, waiting, then he spoke her name one more time: "Madeleine," he said, "we're going home."

She wrote.

Abel and Elliot will be in Berlin at midnight on Wednesday.
What else do we need to know?

So that was it.

Eight events and here they were at the station, saying goodbye.

She pulled the tissues away from her face so she could hold up her fingers and see exactly what the number eight looked like, in terms of fingers.

There was a rush of blood from her nose. She replaced the tissues.

Ah, she knew what eight looked like anyway.

Sure, maybe you could split some of those events into pieces and thereby increase the number, and there were probably a few minor incidents in between that she'd forgotten, *plus* there'd been the frenzied packing up of a flat and a business in the last two days — but *still*. Still.

She'd had Elliot for a total of eight events, and now he was leaving.

Since the day he arrived, they had not had a single conversation on their own.

The train approached. Abel touched her shoulder.

"Thank you," he said, "for everything."

"A pleasure." Her voice was muffled by the tissues.

Other passengers were stepping around their group, pressing closer to the edge of the platform.

Elliot looked at her uncertainly.

"Are you okay?" he said. He had picked up a suitcase. The train doors were opening, passengers pouring out.

Madeleine nodded. "Yeah, this happens a lot. It'll stop. It's probably stopped now."

She pulled the tissues away. Elliot frowned.

"It's still bleeding," he said. "I think something serious is going on there."

He looked sideways along the platform, thinking, but Abel had stepped onto the train.

"Let's go," he called.

The automatic doors began to close.

Elliot swivelled, grabbed the door, and wrenched it open again. He glanced back at Madeleine, raised a hand at the others, and jumped aboard. The doors slammed. She could see him through the glass, still with that vague frown.

A whistle blew, then another.

The shapes of them, Abel and Elliot, made their way down the aisle, looking at seats, not windows.

The train was moving.

"There go ICT and Geography!" sang Darshana.

"That is *not* their names!" shouted her daughters.

Maybe that was Elliot's hand now, pressed to the window waving, or maybe not.

The train picked up speed, and fled, thrusting a storm of empty air behind it.

The blood rained down her mouth and chin, the empty air stormed, and the tracks, the platform, the station — everything — disappeared.

2.

*I*nstead, there was a marketplace.

A boy, about twelve years old, was running. He slipped and slid on cobblestones. His eyes and nose were creased by an angry scowl, but his mouth was loose and childish with fear. Bigger boys were chasing him. They ran through the crowded marketplace: sudden sideways darts and awkward elbowing. People stood about watching the chase, or not watching it, their backs turned to reach for apples or figs.

Shadows overtook the boy. A shoe was flung, a wooden pail. Water flew, the boy cried out —

Now the boy was in an office.

An elderly, bearded man was seated at a desk. The man gazed in mild surprise at the boy. The boy panted noisily, his shoulders heaving. Water patched his shirt, and his face was as white as yoghurt. Behind the boy, a floor-to-ceiling window looked out onto high-rises, cables, and oddly shaped contraptions, a little like helicopters, flying sedately by.

A sensation like reality tearing itself along a perforated line, and everything was back.

3.

"What *was* that?" Madeleine's mother demanded.

The train had gone. The platform was almost empty now, and the others were staring at her.

"You went all spacey," Jack told her.

"I was just about to slap you," Belle declared. "Quite hard."

"Everything disappeared! And I was in a marketplace and a kid was running, and then I was in an office, and there was this old guy with a beard, and weird things were flying by the window!" Madeleine looked down. The bloody tissues were on the ground. She could feel dried blood on her chin.

"It'll be all the blood that you lost," Darshana said, laughing. "You see, it takes your brain cells with it! There are your brain cells all over the platform! Get away from Madeleine's brain cells, children!" Her daughters were crawling around on the platform, studying the blood splatters.

Holly offered Madeleine water and told her to sit down a minute, and then they all set off towards home, away from the station. A small crowd swaying along, everything swaying as if Madeleine was on the train herself. The others glanced at her as they walked, checking on her, chatting about the sudden departure of Abel and Elliot, giddy smiles, wild smiles, everyone pretending to be happy.

4.

That night, Madeleine lay on her couch-bed and felt the silence rising up from the flat downstairs. It joined the darkness in her own flat, injecting it with shots of deeper darkness.

A thread of burning colours was coiling through her veins. A hot-oil rainbow. It smelled like ink spilled from permanent markers, the high, poisoned sweetness of it.

She was going mad.

She got up to wash her face and tried to close the bathroom door quietly. But you couldn't. The door had swollen with damp, so to close it, you had to shove hard. It slammed.

She stood, breathing heavily, staring at the sound of a slamming door.

The door is closed. The story is done.

Then a crack of light ran through her. *The story is not over!* There were Cellians still in her world! The stranded royals!

She sat at the computer — Abel had given them a stack of computer equipment before he left — and she opened a new document. Her mother slept across the room. She tried to type quietly.

Dearest Royal Cellian,

You might remember me as the girl who wrote to you about the Kingdom of Cello?

I have no idea if you ever believed me. Probably not. You probably still think you're someone else. (Don't blame yourself for the amnesia. It happens to all Cellians.)

BUT, if you did believe it, well, you might have gone to the meeting place I told you about, ready to be taken home. In which case, I am very sorry, because I now know that didn't happen. You would have just stood there. You might have got cold and hungry. And depressed.

The good news is that two people from your family DID get home: the King and the little prince. So, if you remember who they are, you can rejoice, knowing they are safe. (Or you can feel jealous and bitter that they got home and you didn't. It depends on your character.)

(If you don't remember who they are, you can just be like, "whatever.")

The bad news is that things went wrong, and now there are issues with getting you home, so you're still here, stranded.

I hope our World is treating you okay, and that the contrast between being a royal in Cello and a regular person here is not doing your head in.

Hopefully the issues will get sorted soon. In the meantime, if you want to talk to someone who knows a bit about where you're from? You can talk to me. Anytime.

I plan to do what I can to help you.

Best wishes,

Madeleine Tully

She found the addresses she had for Queen Lyra, who was in Taipei, Taiwan, and for Prince Chyba, who was in Boise, Idaho, and printed copies for them. She would post these the next day. She had an email address for Princess Jupiter, who was in Berlin, Germany, so she pasted the text into an email.

She hit Send so hard her mother startled in her sleep.

5.

They were in Madeleine's flat for their English lesson with Holly. Rain fell steadily outside, and the room was golden lit and shadowed. There was the usual clutter of fabric, tape measures, and pattern books, but there was also a crowd of extra furniture.

Abel had brought this upstairs before he left. As well as the computer equipment, there were two new armchairs, a standing lamp, and a rice steamer.

The heat was turned high, and the room was warm with baking.

"It smells like muffins," Jack said.

"No, it doesn't," Belle argued.

"Well, it does. Abel gave me some recipes before he left," Madeleine explained.

Jack sighed. "I wonder if they got home okay?"

"Oh, I'm sure they did." Holly spoke from the lamplight. "We'll hear from them eventually. They'll email."

Her three students glanced at one another.

"Did Abel *say* he'd email you?" Jack asked.

Holly was holding a threaded needle in the air while she frowned down at a sheet of paper. She transferred the frown to a square of fabric, then took it back to the paper again. She looked up.

"I don't know," she said. "But he will. Why wouldn't he? I never called him Abel, you know. I kept saying Denny right up until they left. I don't cope when people change their names. Even if I *technically* respect their decision, I feel like it's a bit of a joke, like I'm humouring a kid who's decided that his name is now Ultra Spidermonkey."

"Has anybody moved into Abel and Elliot's flat downstairs?" Belle asked. "Oh, yeah, and my mother says she doesn't want to be one of our home-school teachers anymore."

Madeleine was in the kitchenette, peering through the dark oven glass. She looked up. "Seriously?"

"I said, has anybody moved into the flat downstairs?"

"We heard you," said Jack. "We're considering the collapse of our home-schooling system. Why doesn't she want to teach anymore?"

Madeleine looked from Belle to Jack. A silence formed between them. It widened and stretched. Eventually, Belle spoke.

"She says it's starting to get boring. So, has anybody moved in or not?"

"No," Holly said. "The flat downstairs is still empty."

6.

$\mathcal{T}$wo days later, an email arrived.

Madeleine was alone in the flat, sitting at the computer eating a biscuit. She picked out a tiny crumb from between the *H* and the *J*, and when she looked up again, the email was there.

Ariel Peters.

Who *is* that? she thought, but she knew the answer.

Ariel Peters was Princess Jupiter. A member of the Cello royal family.

Hi Madeleine,

LOL. I can't believe I'm hearing from u "Cello" guys again. This is the maddest thing that's happened to me EVER, only it's totally not. Cause I think a lot madder things happened in my life, only I fried my brains like scrambled eggs and so they're gone. The memories of mad things, I mean, not my brains. Tho not sure that's true either, how do u know if your brains are gone or not? Get a scan of some kind I guess. But who can afford that?

Drugs! Don't do them!!! Unless you're already off your face, so then you might as well do more.

Okay, I'm happy to be Princess Jupiter again, but if u want me to be a pole dancer/stripper Princess Jupiter? No. I'm taking pole classes at the moment but that's totally my choice, my body, not yours, and there's a lot of fitness and ingenuity that goes into pole, which you just cannot take for granted.

You are wicked lucky to be hearing from me cos I waited on the corner of Friedrichstrasse and Unter den Linden for SIX hours!!! Cause I BELIEVED there was a Kingdom of Cello and that I was the Princess Jupiter and I was going to be collected and taken home! LOL. You totally got me. I was so excited about meeting my own castle and my lady-in-waiting (what's she waiting for? ME, I thought!) and having my own personal royal tattoo artist! (I love getting ink, it feels insane & that was going to be my first royal maneuver: employ my own tattoo artist and get him/her a special wing of the castle, maybe even a castle of his/her own? for his/her equipment and to draw designs esp. for me all day long.)

Anyhow, v. happy to hear more about your plans for taking me to Cello and my life as a princess, but I am NOT STANDING ON ANY STREET CORNERS MISSING SHIFTS AT WORK AND NEARLY GETTING FIRED AGAIN!!!!

Best wishes,

Ariel (Princess Jupiter)

P.S. I work at a bar. I live in a room upstairs from the bar. That's sorta part of my pay. So do you see what I'm saying here? If I lose my job, then i ALSO lose my HOME!!!! & I don't know anyone else in Berlin, and I don't even speak German!!! (But I've learned a bit since I got here), and not everyone believes me when I say I'm 18 (LOL, coz I'm NOT!! — i don't think — i'm a lot younger — but can't really remember), and it's TOO COLD TO SLEEP ON THE STREETS AT THE MOMENT!! So, just don't nearly make me lose my job again, OK?

P.P.S. But you told me about that mad trick where if I squeeze lemon juice into my inner elbow it makes a colourful pattern. And u said it meant I was from the Kingdom of Cello cos that's the only difference between "Cellians" and "Worldians." Remember?

So i tried it and it made the colourful pattern! I love it more than I love Comets and Tornadoes, which I totally do, both the cocktails and the actualities. I was gonna get the pattern tattooed there, like a reminder, but then I realised it'd be cheaper just to carry a lemon around.

P.P.P.S. I do the trick all the time now, in the bar, with the lemon and people love it. One lady said I must've got struck by lightning once and it's the residue of light making the pattern. LOL. And NOBODY ELSE CAN DO THE COLOURFUL SPECKLES THING (everyone always tries). So I want to thank you for that. I have no idea how you knew I could do it, but if you know anything else I don't know about me (e.g., can I make my ears light up by rubbing watermelon into them?), well, TELL ME!!!! BYEEEE.

Madeleine gazed at the screen.

After a moment, all she could see was exclamation marks. She looked away. Somewhere, someone was drilling.

She wrote a reply.

Dear Princess Jupiter,

I'm very happy to hear from you, and to hear that you forgive me for sending you to a street corner for six hours while you nearly lost your job. (I THINK you're saying you forgive me, anyway.) Now I feel guilty about that, and I also feel guilty for writing to you at all, cause maybe it's given you false hope that I can get you home, and I'm actually sorta useless to you. I'm not in contact with people in Cello anymore. You could easily be like, who even IS she? And what's the POINT of her?

And you're right: I don't know how to help you, but I promise I'll keep thinking about it.

And in the meantime, at least I could tell you what I know about you? Maybe I can help you remember who you are.

I've never been to Cello (not properly anyway — I've seen glimpses of it), and I've only ever met two people from there. One was Elliot Baranski. He lives in a country town called Bonfire in the province of the Farms. He and I were writing to each other through a crack in a parking meter for a long time, before he "stumbled" through to Yorkshire. ("Stumble" is a technical term — people fall between Cello and the World sometimes, in situations of absence and strong emotion.) He ended up here in Cambridge for a couple of weeks. He's gone back now.

So everything I know about you and Cello comes from my late-night starlit conversations with Elliot. I'll try to remember what I can.

Your name is Princess Jupiter.

You disappeared from the penthouse suite at the Harrington Hotel, Ducale, in Golden Coast.

Your father is King Cetus, your mother is Queen Lyra. You have a sister, Princess Ko, and two brothers, Prince Chyba and Prince Tippett.

I think you mostly lived in the White Palace, which is in the Magical North, but you travelled a lot, like to boarding schools and to the different palaces — I can't remember what the other palaces were called, but I think there was a Cardamom Palace in Jagged Edge.

And finally, no offence, but I remember Elliot once told me that you're the princess with the reputation. For being wild, out-of-control, and a troublemaker. I hope you don't have me executed or something for saying that. I thought it might help. And actually it's sort of consistent with the identity you've created for yourself?

The only other Cellian I've met is Elliot's dad, Abel Baranski. He used to live downstairs from me and my mum. Actually, he was the first person we met when we came to Cambridge. We were sitting in a café counting our money (not much) and possessions (hardly any, just a sewing machine really) and wondering what to do, when this guy at a nearby table introduced himself (two-day-old stubble, cute accent, slight breathlessness, which made him seem sorta vulnerable). He said that he couldn't help overhearing we had nowhere to live, and that the place above him was currently vacant.

He had forgotten himself. He thought his name was Denny and that he was a computer repairman from Kentucky. He and my mum became friends, and he fixed stuff for us, and baked, and he even became one of our home-schooling teachers.

He only remembered himself when Elliot appeared at his front door. It was the emotional surge of seeing his son for the first time in over a year that snapped him back.

Which makes me think that all these words are a waste of time. You don't need a list of facts about yourself, you need something to shock you into yourself again.

I don't have a shock for you. All I can really tell you is this: I didn't believe in the Kingdom of Cello myself for a long time — even after I started writing to Elliot — but trust me, it's real.

Talk soon,

Madeleine

P.S. So, are the tattoos a recent thing — I mean, did you get them in Berlin? — or have you had them for a while? Cos I'm thinking you might be in trouble when you get back and they find out Princess Jupiter is covered in tattoos . . . but could be just the sort of scandal the Cellian tabloids like to print about you. LOL. M x

7.

$\mathcal{I}$t was so cold that Belle was doing her presentation wearing her coat and scarf. She kept pausing to unwind the scarf, shake it out, and then tie it more firmly around her neck. Now and then she cast hostile glances at the fireplace. It was failing to warm the room sufficiently.

Belle was talking about Leonardo da Vinci, but Madeleine's mind was wandering. She was wondering if Princess Jupiter was cold in Berlin, and whether she would reply to Madeleine's email.

She tuned back in.

"So he painted the *Mona Lisa*," Belle was saying. "Which, I mean, go, Leonardo. It's totally famous. But how much praise should we *really* give him for that, is what I'm asking, cause he hardly did any other painting, and what's quality without quantity? He only finished about *fifteen*, and the *Mona Lisa* might be great, but seriously, is it *that* great?"

"Well . . ." Federico began, but he let it go.

"Anyhow, that psycho dude, Freud, had this idea that Leonardo never finished his paintings because he had *issues*. To do with the tail feathers of a kite having once brushed his face when he was a baby in a pram. And I'm like, yeah, go for it, Freud, whatever does it for you.

But seriously, what? And besides which, Leonardo needs to take responsibility for his own behaviour, and not hide behind Freud or behind tail feathers. Am I right?"

Jack and Madeleine nodded sagely. Federico sucked on his teeth.

"As for the *Mona Lisa*, he totally forgot to label that, or, like, keep a record, so we don't even know if it *is* the Mona Lisa. Cause there are so many *others* it could've been besides Lisa, or so many Lisas if it *was* Lisa, or maybe it's an imaginary person, and what's with the landscape behind it? Did he make that up as he went along? And how did he get that freakish expression on her face? So that's too many questions, which is unfair to the historians. Some people say he got clowns to dance while he painted her, to make her do that little smile, which makes me think (a) what sort of model was she that she couldn't just do her own smile? and (b) how useless were those clowns that they couldn't get her to do a proper full-on laugh?"

Belle tugged hard on her scarf, then looked startled.

"Nearly strangled myself," she explained. She loosened the scarf.

"Anyhow, so if we don't know who the Mona Lisa is, then the painting doesn't exist, in my theoretical opinion, which means Leonardo did practically *nothing*."

Federico sighed deeply. "Belle. Go on."

"So that's the negatives about Leonardo, but on the plus side, he was totally smart." She consulted her notes. "He made fine efforts towards inventing submarines, parachutes, three-speed gear shifts, snorkels, hydraulic jacks, canal locks, revolving stages, water-powered alarm clocks, and helicopters. Here's a picture of his helicopter. Not a very good one, but as he was not a trained aeronautical engineer, I think a round of applause is on the cards."

She handed a printout to Federico, who nodded his approval, and then passed it on to Jack.

"I have nothing to say about this," Jack said.

He handed it to Madeleine.

Her thoughts had strayed again, so when the paper appeared in her hand, she was confused for a moment.

She glanced down, poised to return it to Belle. A wave of heat seemed to surge from her chin to her scalp.

"I *know* this helicopter," she said. "I've *seen* this helicopter."

It was the same odd conical shape. Cables linked the blades with the base.

"Remember when I had that weird — episode — at the station?" she breathed. "When I saw a boy being chased through a marketplace, and then he was in a high-rise office, and an old guy was at a desk, and strange things were flying by the window? It was *this*. *These* were flying by."

"Now she pays attention," Belle said. "Now that it's about her."

"Sorry."

"That's okay. I don't really listen to a word you say either."

Madeleine laughed, and then saw that Belle was serious. "You don't?"

"It's not personal," Belle offered.

"It's not," Jack confirmed. "She also never listens to me."

Madeleine glanced at Belle. There was that curious sense of a silence zinging back and forth between Belle and Jack.

She looked down at the sketch of the flying machine again. "Have you got a picture of Leonardo himself?"

"Of course I have. What sort of a presentation do you think this is? But I was saving it for the end."

"Show me now?"

Belle leafed through her notes resentfully, then held up a black-and-white printout. It was an aged face, a large nose, a grim expression. Swirls of hair poured from his head and chin.

"Well, that's him," Madeleine said. "The old guy sitting at the desk in the office. The one I saw when I hallucinated or whatever."

Jack swung around and looked at her. "Get out of here."

"It is."

Belle scowled. "You hallucinated my assignment. Hallucinate your own." She burst out laughing. "Ah, I don't care. You can share if you want."

Here, Federico growled and told Belle to get on with it, or he would make her *eat* the educational syllabus. He had a copy here somewhere, he warned. Then he looked around the office, vaguely. "I think," he added.

"That's all right," Belle said. "I'm not hungry. But I wouldn't mind a coffee." She looked at Federico's coffee pot. "You never offer us your coffee, Federico, which, wouldn't that be consistent with the egalitarian ideal of home schooling if you did?"

Federico poured himself a coffee, and sipped from it.

"I do not know this egalitarian ideal," he said. "And I do not care. Because what I want to know, Belle, is how you get anyplace where you are going? You must always be going from the path and climbing into people's houses through their windows and people must say, What? Who are you? Why are you here in my house?"

"You're sort of doing the same thing right now," Belle said.

"Ha, you are the funny one. Completely wrong because I was continuing on my path exactly as I planned, but still you are funny. So. To continue."

"Oh, well." Belle flicked through her notes. "After this, I just wrote seven random facts, yeah? Cause there's a *lot* around about this dude. You try to find out something these days, and you get drowned in information."

"I blame the Internet," Jack said.

Madeleine interjected. "Doesn't anybody care that I saw Leonardo da Vinci and his flying machine on the platform at Cambridge railway station?"

"No, they do not," Federico pronounced. "But the Internet, about this I can speak for hours. It is to blame for everything. Do you know this Silk Road? You use it to buy drugs. That is an example. But you must not do that. I think it is closed now, but still, you must not. It is a deep, dark otherworld of the corruption and the wickedness, this Internet. You must, all of you, stay away from it."

Belle frowned. "Well, I don't know I'd go that far."

"Just ignore him," Jack advised.

"I'll carry on about Leonardo, then, shall I? Okay. Here are my seven random facts.

1. He was left-handed.
2. He liked to draw cats. There's this picture of his that is all cats with a single tiny lion.
3. Also, dragons. He said the best way to draw a dragon is to do this: Give it the head of a mastiff, the eyes of a cat, the ears of a porcupine, the muzzle of a greyhound, the brow of a lion, the crest of an old rooster, and the neck of a tortoise.
4. That is bollocks. I tried it. It looked nothing like a dragon.
5. He loved animals. Whenever he passed places with birds for sale, he'd buy them, take them out of their cages, and set them free.
6. That is awesome, and you should now take a moment to smile out of respect for the awesomeness of a guy who'd do a thing like that for the birds."

Obediently, everyone smiled, including Belle herself, and then she continued.

"And the final random fact about Leonardo is this:

7. One day, when he was a kid, he was out walking and found this cave. He'd been abandoned by his parents when he was a baby, and lived with his grandparents. Anyhow, here is what he wrote about this cave. It shows conclusively that he went on a bit, and that he wasn't too sure how he felt about caves."

She turned to another sheet of paper, and read:

"I came to the entrance to a large cave and stopped for a moment, struck with amazement, for I had not suspected its existence. Stooping down, my left hand around my knee, while with the right I shaded my frowning eyes to peer in, I leaned this way and that, trying to see if there was anything inside, despite the darkness that reigned there. After I had remained thus for a moment, two emotions suddenly awoke in me: fear and desire. Fear of the dark, threatening cave and desire to see if it contained some miraculous thing."

Belle looked up. "That's it," she said. "His notes stop there, so we never know if he went into the cave or not. And that is a beautiful, mysterious, thought-provoking place for my presentation to end. You can clap now."

Federico and Jack applauded loudly.

Madeleine clapped too, but in a slow, significant, distant way, suggesting that her thoughts were being carried sideways, to a place that was far removed from here, and profound.

"What?" demanded Belle. "What now?"

A strange calm was descending on Madeleine, a calm that had the weight of syrup. She turned her head slowly, pushing through the syrup.

"He went to the Kingdom of Cello," she said. "Leonardo da Vinci must have gone there."

Automatically, Belle and Jack glanced towards Federico.

But Federico was relaxing, his hands clasped behind his head, eyes towards the ceiling, apparently lost in thought.

They returned their gaze to Madeleine, dubious.

She smiled.

"The cave must have taken him there," she said. "Why else would he know how to draw dragons? Dragons don't exist. Except in Cello."

The calm grew thicker and heavier. Madeleine felt drowsy with it.

Belle dragged a chair from across the room, positioned it right in front of Madeleine, and sat down. She clicked her fingers sharply just below Madeleine's eyes.

Madeleine blinked, then returned to her dreamy trance.

Belle clicked her fingers again.

"Stop it," complained Madeleine.

"Belle," Jack said. "Cut it out."

Belle swung around so she was facing Jack. "*Don't*," she spat, "get me started on *you*."

Jack flinched.

Federico sat forwards abruptly. "Where were we?" he said.

*T*wo weeks later, Madeleine heard from Princess Jupiter again.

She had started to wonder if she'd offended the Princess somehow. Or if something might have happened to her. Everything about Jupiter seemed precarious — the stories that Elliot had told about her, the fact that she was a teenager alone in a strange city. What if she *had* lost her job now and was living on the streets?

But late one night, another email arrived.

Hola!!

(Well, at least my Spanish is on fire. Too bad about my German. LOL.)

Tatsachlich mein Deutsch ist nicht so freakin' bad.

Can't be arsed doing an umlaut on that word. Can't remember where it goes. Tatsachlich. I think it means "actually." Could also mean "I hope you die a long painful death of the injuries you got when the avalanche took out your horse and carriage." Ha-ha. Nah. It doesn't.

Don't think so anyhow.

Anywayz, how are you? Thanks for your email.

I'm sorta stoked that I was the wild girl of the family. But I promise to reform and be supergood and always take my crown off at the breakfast table, and not make out with the peasants (only with hot visiting princes) if you can just get me home. I'm done with the wild life. I haven't touched a drop of booze/taken, inhaled, snorted, or injected a single Illicit Substance since you wrote (except a couple of Es, which don't count, cos u can't see Caljerlkj's Men Temps without dropping an E & they were playing here), I swear on my latest tat (and yeah, I've got all of them since I've been in Berlin). You want to know what I've got? I have a dragon carrying a basket of eggs, with its own espresso machine, I have a big sort of balloon-shaped monster hanging around in the air over a patch of swamp (that one came to me in a dream)(it's the only one i sorta regret actually)(swamp = not that pretty), SEVEN different butterflies in various states of undress (that's a joke, it just came out of my typing fingers, the butterflies are all completely nude, which is what you'd expect in a butterfly) (unless you count their wings as clothing, which I don't think you can, that'd be like saying a naked person wasn't naked because she had arms), and a teeny little cello, which I got yesterday, in honour of my Kingdom.

Tell me ANYTHING about my Kingdom. Anything to stop me scratching my freaking ankles! (Eczema.)

Bye for now,

PRINCESS JUPITER

P.S. Cardamom Palace. Best. Name. Ever.

Madeleine replied right away.

Dear Princess Jupiter,

Okay, guess what? These are three things that Elliot told me about Cello in our late-night conversations.

There is a terrible swamp where there are giant creatures, as big as whales, but gluggy like jellyfish, floating in the air.

There are dragons.

There's a teeny magical being called the "Butterfly Child."

So, look, I'm not a psychiatrist, but if you seriously have tattoos of monsters over swamps, dragons, and butterflies, well, if that's not repressed memories of the Kingdom of Cello, I don't know what is. I will eat my mother's sewing machine if I'm wrong. (Which would upset her. I'd cut it up very finely first.) See, your subconscious is going insane trying to get the message to you that you're from the Kingdom of Cello.

Maybe write down a list of tattoos you'd LIKE to get and by the end of the list you'll have the whole Kingdom of Cello mapped out for yourself. (Don't actually get them done, you might regret that once you get home. It'll be like your body's turned into a shopping list of things you've already bought.)

Okay, hope Berlin's fun and that your German's on fire,

Madeleine xx

Bonjour Madeleine,

You're funny. (: :)(How do you do a smiley face on this keyboard?) I just realised something. I don't know a single thing about you, which is sort of crazy cause you seem to know more about me than I know about me. Can you tell me about you?

Jupiter xx

Hiya Jupiter,

Thanks for asking about me. Well, I used to be selfish a lot of the time, and kinda wild. I don't like my previous self. I don't even want to think about her — I was about to tell you about some of the stuff I did, and the people I hurt, but then it was like these flames were coming out of the keyboard and running up my arms, into my face.

Anyhow, in the end, I ran away to Cambridge, and my mother came with me, and she got sick with a brain tumour, but she's okay now. And I really miss my dad.

I have friends here, Belle and Jack, and they're great, but sometimes I feel lonely. They've been best friends since they were really young, so they're sort of a complete unit. Jack once told me that sometimes they have these huge fights — Belle suddenly gets furious about something and they end up nearly killing each other. I have this feeling that they're on the verge of one of their fights now, and the strange thing is that this makes me feel even more separate than ever. There's all this tension zinging between them. And the other day they both had bloodshot eyes and I asked them what was going on, and they acted like I hadn't even spoken. It's like this impending fight is a giant secret. Or it's an electromagnetic field, and I'm not allowed through the gate.

I told you that Elliot and I wrote notes to each other at a parking meter? And then he was just here for a couple of weeks? Well, this might sound stupid but I think he was my best friend. Like the other half of me. I'm so scared something might have happened to him when he went back. I miss him so much I sometimes look at windows and I want to just walk right through them — like press myself through the glass. I want their sharp edges to fragment me.

Best wishes,
Madeleine

9.

 $\mathcal{M}$ adeleine woke early with a bleeding nose. She felt around for the box of tissues, the floor surged towards her — and then vanished.

She was somewhere new, a different room.

A small window glared with the white light of a cold afternoon. Outside the window, she saw a frozen canal, a long narrow boat on its side. People moved about, slipping and sliding, catching at one another or the boat. She could hear them laughing and shouting. Opposite, buildings pressed together, their facades an elegance of arched windows, balconies, and balustrades.

In the room itself was a fireplace, a violin on a stand, a man with dark orange hair. The man took no notice of her. He was lighting a candle at the fire. Now he straightened, placed the lit candle in his left hand, and reached, with his right, to unhook a mirror from the wall.

The last thing Madeleine saw before all this disappeared was that somebody else — a girl — was hiding in the shadows of a corner.

Then she was home again. Her nose had stopped bleeding.

Her mother was already up, working at the sewing machine.

"It happened again," she told her mother. "Like when we were at the station and everything disappeared and I saw a marketplace? Well, I just saw a room with a fireplace, and a man with a violin, and a hidden girl."

"Uh-huh," said Holly. "Crazy. Maybe it was a dream this time?"

"There was a frozen canal outside the window."

"Venice," said Holly.

The canal, the gondola, the balustrades.

"Exactly," Madeleine said. "Venice. But I don't think it was a dream."

She got up and sat at the computer. She opened Google and typed *Why am I hallucinating about Venice?*

Google paused at that, and then offered songs about angels in Venice, a blog on the reality of Venice (compare and contrast the effect of hallucinogens, said the blog), and information about classes of cruise tickets to Venice.

"Sometimes," she said, "the Internet is not all it's cracked up to be."

Her mother murmured agreement. The sewing machine buzzed.

Madeleine tapped her fingertips together. She thought of the frozen canal.

Very cold winter in Venice, she typed, and Google was prompt to offer travel sites on the best times of the year to visit.

She thought about the room she had seen. The fireplace and candle, the ornate furniture, rich and solid, both polished and rough, the elaborate clothing worn by the redheaded man and the hidden girl.

Historical very cold winter in Venice, she amended.

The third result was a Wikipedia entry titled "Great Frost of 1709."

She clicked on this. In 1709, she read, Europe saw the coldest winter in five hundred years. There was famine in France. A girl wrapped in furs by a roaring fire shivered so much she could hardly hold her pen. In Venice, there were dukes with red and dripping noses, frozen canals where people slipped and slid on the ice.

Okay, Madeleine decided, I have had a vision of Venice in the Great Frost of 1709. This seemed clear to her, and made her mildly proud.

So who was the man in the vision? she almost typed, but stopped herself.

She tapped the keys lightly for a while, not making any impression, then she tried *Do Italians have red hair?* and scrolled through the results, not concentrating, lost in absent-minded thought, until something caught her.

Composer, red priest, 18th century.

It was an article about a redheaded violinist who lived in Venice in the early 1700s.

Antonio Vivaldi.

She was suddenly strangely frightened. Her mother was singing softly. She searched for images of Vivaldi.

And there he was. The man she'd just seen. In the pictures, he wore a long, curling white wig and he had a self-satisfied expression, but that was his delicate, girlish face, the gentle play of his lips.

She sat back and stared. Seriously, she thought, *why* would I be hallucinating about Vivaldi?

She knew nothing about him! She cared nothing about him!

Well, the only thing she knew was that he'd composed that tune they played in shopping centres all the time, and at ice skating rinks. *The Four Seasons*. But she couldn't even remember how that went! She read a few short biographies of him and found out he'd taught violin in a sort of musical orphanage called the Ospedale della Pietà for years. Mothers used to place unwanted baby girls in the *"scaffetta"* of this orphanage: a revolving drawer set in the stone wall. They would ring the bell and run, and the assistant prioress would gather up the baby from the opening. The child's ankle would be branded with a *P*. If a baby grew up with musical skills, she'd be raised as a musician, and Vivaldi might teach her.

Bizarre.

Maybe the girl she'd seen in the shadows was one of these orphans? A young musician taking violin lessons from Vivaldi?

Madeleine decided she should find a YouTube clip of someone playing *The Four Seasons*, but she sat back in the chair and did nothing. She should get dressed. She should have breakfast.

She thought of the seasons in Cello, how they roamed around the Kingdom, sometimes lingering, and then she became aware that her mother had stopped sewing and was moving about the room, behaving oddly.

In fact, she was behaving like a series of seasons passing at high speed. She was rustling like dry autumn leaves, blowing sighs like winter winds, making thin, high-pitched bleating noises like little spring lambs.

Holly was circling the ironing board. Some item of clothing — a dress or skirt — was draped over her arm. As Madeleine watched, Holly unplugged the iron at the wall, plugged it in again, then lunged towards the ironing board.

"What's going on?"

Holly was frowning closely at the iron. Next she glanced at the front door.

"The iron's broken," Holly said.

"Huh." Madeleine couldn't think of anything more interesting to say.

"I need the iron."

"Okay."

"I cannot finish a piece of work without ironing it."

"Really?" Now she was interested. "I mean, I always see you ironing after you finish sewing but I didn't think it was, like, compulsory."

"It is. It's a thing of mine. I've tried everything. I've switched it on and off at least five times. I've shaken it. I've slapped it. Turned it upside down. Everything." As Holly talked, her eyes kept flying to the front door and then back to the iron.

Madeleine followed her mother's eyes. Holly seemed angry with the door. It seemed the door might somehow be culpable here. Maybe in the night it had climbed off its hinges, trundled over to the ironing board, and broken the iron?

Then she understood.

"You want Abel to fix it for you," she told Holly. "You want to run downstairs and ask for Abel's help, but he's not there."

Her mother flung the dress across the room. She raised the iron high, as if she might hurl that too. She stopped herself.

"I *need* to iron!" she half shouted. "I don't *care* that it might be pathological or obsessive or whatever. I don't have many needs. Look at where we live! But I *need* to iron."

Madeleine waited.

Her mother replaced the iron on the board.

"Denny could have fixed it," Holly said more calmly. "He knew about electronics."

Madeleine nodded. Of course he knew about electronics. Back in the Kingdom of Cello, he was named Abel and he owned an electronics repair shop.

"You know, he never gave me his email address?" Holly shook the iron lightly. "I didn't even think of asking him. I just assumed he'd email *me* when he got home. He knew *my* email address. He set it up for me."

What if Madeleine told her mother about the Kingdom of Cello?

Ah, pointless.

"I miss him too," she said instead.

Her mother was still glaring, and abruptly Madeleine understood.

It wasn't just that her mother missed the guy who could fix irons. She missed him for himself. She'd loved him. She'd let go of Madeleine's father: She'd even tried online dating, Madeleine knew. But all the time there'd been the man downstairs. He'd been there from the start, rolling his newspaper as he explained in that café that there was a place for them, right upstairs from him.

Meanwhile, he'd had a wife, a life, a son, a business back home far, far away.

So Holly was on her own now, with no place left to fall.

10.

Ahoy there Madeleine,

It is I, Captain Princess Jupiter! Hoisting the sails upwards! Or whichever direction it is the sails are supposed to go in.

They must go up. Where else'd they go. (I wrote "hoisting the SALES" first. Then I was like, that looks wrong.)

Thanks for telling me about how much you miss Elliot. I didn't realise that was the situation, and now I feel like I understand you better. And you had Elliot right there for a couple of weeks, in person? And now he's gone? That's like the universe messing with your mind. That's cold, man. No wonder you feel like walking through glass. (Don't do that, by the way. Don't hurt yourself. You think it'll make you feel better, but it just makes you bleed. And it sends signals to the universe that you're someone who deserves to be hurt, which I don't think that you do.)

Also, thanks for taking an interest in making me back into a princess. Cause I really want that: I'm sorta done with this life. It's, like, when I first found myself in Berlin, I was like, huh? But then I just went with it, and I was happy cause I'm into wurst. I love the noble sausage. But now, I'm so over this life here.

It's not like I was one of those little kids who play princess or wish they had a pink tiara, I threw rocks at those kids. One of my foster mothers got me a fairy dress once and I used it to line the hamster cage. And it's not like I even want to be pretty. I just want to have a hot bath without some douche pounding on the door, or busting in cause the lock's dodgy, and without having to wash muddy footprints off the bottom of the tub, and the line of grime around the edge, and the hair that's clogging up the drains, before I even get in.

And I've got an ear infection now cause this dude started kissing me right after I'd put my head under the tap to make the bad feeling go away, and I had water in my ear, which I wanted to shake out, or dry, but he's kissing me in this romantic way where he makes your head tip over sideways, so the water was running down, right into the ear, and it wouldn't've been polite to stop him in that moment.

I really liked that dude. His name was Ulrich, and he walked in this crazy way like he'd just got off a horse. His legs wide apart, I mean. I was never sure if that was a condition he suffered from, or if he was being funny. He had little rabbit teeth too, which a lot of people can't carry off, but he did, his face made me happy. He's stopped coming by now tho, and I never got his number, so there goes Ulrich.

Also, every time I start to think I've got German zorted, people come in the bar and start talking zuper fast at me, or in a different dialect or regional accent or whatever, and I'm done for. And I'm zorta sick of wurst.

BYE

Ariel

Dear Princess Jupiter,

Okay, I think we have to get you out of there and back to your Kingdom. It doesn't sound like you're having fun, and it's stupid, I mean, there are enough poor people around without you having to be one, when you've got perfectly good palaces just across the way.

But I don't know how.

I keep thinking about the idea of people changing themselves. Like you. You've transformed yourself into a girl called Ariel Peters. You've given yourself a new past, which is sort of based on your true past. Like, you talk about your foster mother giving you a fairy dress and that was probably a nanny trying to get you to dress up for a royal ball?

But this transformation, it's not real. You've shuffled yourself around, or taken a step sideways. And it's wrong. Maybe it's even why you're doing so many drugs and stuff?

I don't know if I'm truly myself or not. I know I've changed a lot since I got here — I'm much quieter, and I read and think all the time, and I'm obsessed with Isaac Newton. Whereas before I was always running, moving, dancing. So which one am I? The one from before or now? I keep staring at myself in mirrors and windows, thinking, is that me?

You are so right about the universe messing with me, by giving me Elliot and then taking him away.

He wasn't himself, though, not really. Not compared to how he was when we wrote to each other, or when we held each other in the space between. He was remote, and once I saw this rush of trouble cross his features.

You know, I look at the parking meter every single day, hoping Elliot might write to me? I mean, I know he was going into hiding for a while (with Hostiles!!!) but I think that must have been sorted out by now and he'd be back home. So I just keep looking, and hoping. Even though I know it would put his life in danger to write.

When I was saying goodbye to Elliot at the train station, I had this fantasy beforehand, that he'd look me in the eye and realise he loved me or whatever, and kiss me goodbye, but what actually happened was I had a bleeding nose — I keep getting bleeding noses all the time — so there's blood all over my face and I'm mad at him for leaving and he's frowning, like, what is WRONG with that girl?

M xx

Hey Madz,

Nah, he was frowning cause he was worried about you but he had to catch the train, so there was nothing he could do to help. Imagine if he'd been laughing, like, "Baby, you're bleeding & I'm jumping aboard the see-ya-later train!" or imagine if he'd been going in for the kiss when you're trying to deal with your situation? Those two things would mean he's an insensitive arse. He was frowning coz he's nice. He sounds hot.

I bet you hear from him soon.

Your friend,

the Amnesiacal, Maniacal Princess

P.S. I'm so tired today. Tell me more about my Kingdom?

Jupiter,

That's a nice thing to say, what you said about Elliot. Thanks.

Okay, here are some things Elliot told me about Cello:

They play a game called deftball, where they kind of jump over furrows in the ground. There's something called a Cat Walk in the province of Nature Strip, where cats of all kinds — lions, panthers, tabby cats — promenade at dusk. There are living Colours that fly through the Kingdom like weather patterns, forming mist or rain or darts or thunderclouds, and they can tear you apart or blind you, or make you sleep, or help you brew tea, or find the things that are lost.

It sounds like an amazing kingdom, but I don't think I'm ever going to hear from Elliot again. I think the Kingdom's door is shut and locked, and I'm so, so sorry that you got left behind.

Look after yourself,

Love,

Madeleine

11.

$\mathcal{M}$adeleine, Belle, and Jack were at Auntie's Tea Shop.

"Your nose is bleeding again," Jack said.

"Get any blood on the scones," Belle said, "and I'll give you a shiner to match. Tip your head back."

"No. Tip it forward."

Everything tipped and was gone.

She was in a room with sloping ceilings. Two small boys were crouched on the floor. They leaned towards each other, studying a patch of sunlight on the floor. Smudged black drawings covered the walls: She glimpsed a bird, a ship, a circle.

And then she was back. Her nose had stopped bleeding.

Belle was licking strawberry jam from a knife. Jack was examining the cream. Neither of them had noticed anything.

"I just had another hallucination," Madeleine told them.

"You what?" Belle demanded. "How'd you do that?"

"Well, remember I had that weird sort of vision on the station when we said goodbye to Elliot? The other day I had another one, and it just happened again right now."

She told them about Vivaldi and the musical orphanage. Then she told them she'd just seen two boys in a sort of attic room.

"And pictures of a bird, a ship, and a circle on the wall," she added.

A bird, a ship, a circle. That series of words was familiar.

A bird, a ship, a circle.

The words turned their own circle, and started again.

A bird, a ship, a circle.

The tablecloth was lace. She ran her palm across the patterns, caught her fingers in the holes.

A bird, a ship, a —

She knew where she'd seen those words before.

In a description of Isaac Newton's bedroom. When he was twelve, Isaac had gone away to school, and he'd boarded in the garret room of an apothecary. On his sloping walls, he'd drawn charcoal pictures: beasts, men, plants, triangles, mathematical figures, a bird, a ship, a circle.

"I think one of the boys was Isaac Newton," she said.

The others chewed thoughtfully.

"Do you know about the hypnagogic state?" Belle said after a moment. "It's this in-between point where you're sort of awake and sort of asleep at the same time. You go into a trance and journey *deep* inside yourself — like travelling to another world — and, if you're lucky, you feel yourself being torn apart, broken into pieces, which is unbelievable agony. Then you put yourself together again and you're enlightened."

"Do you think that's what's been happening to me?" Madeleine asked. "I've been going into an in-between trance?"

"Nah. I think you were dreaming."

"But I wasn't asleep. I was sitting here eating a scone."

"You mean she keeps falling asleep for microseconds?" Jack mused, getting interested. "Like narcolepsy?"

Belle slammed her knife onto the table.

"What?" said Jack. "What'd I say?"

All three were looking at the knife. The jam on it had smeared the white of the cloth.

Belle turned to Madeleine. "It hardly ever happens, that hypnagogic state. I've only seen that sort of enlightenment in an aura once. Guy was a parking inspector. Think about that."

There was another long quiet.

Abruptly, Jack pushed his chair back. He dropped a few coins on the table, and walked out of the café.

Belle watched him go, then reached across to his leftover scone.

"What's going on with you two?" Madeleine asked.

Belle let the scone fall. She looked at the window. "Don't worry about it," she said, twirling her hand vaguely, and then she also stood and walked from the café. The door thudded closed behind her.

Madeleine sat alone at the table.

If Isaac Newton was one of the boys she'd just seen, who was the other? She knew he'd been a loner as a child. His father had died before he was born, and his mother remarried when Isaac was three. He got left behind with his grandparents. He wandered streets and fields alone. He built windmills, kites, and water clocks. At school, other children teased him.

So who was the other boy?

She thought back over the image she had seen. The two boys were the exact same size and colouring.

It was not two boys, she realised. It was the same boy twice.

One boy alone, facing himself.

12.

After a moment, Madeleine took a notepad and pen from her backpack.

She ate the leftover scones, and she wrote a letter to her father.

Dear Dad,

The last time I wrote to you, you sent the letter back. Mum says we should leave you be, and not get in contact at all. But I'm disobeying her.

Because I want to tell you something about Isaac Newton.

I know, right? Weird. And yet maybe pleasing to you too! Cause look at me getting all scholarly on you!

Anyhow, you'll know Isaac was the greatest scientist ever, practically, or at least, one of the top three. He still hasn't been voted off the show. Ha. That's a reality TV reference. But listen.

HE WAS INTO ALCHEMY. Like, making metal into gold? Did you know this about Isaac Newton?

Nobody really knew it until the 1930s when Sotheby's put a lot of his manuscripts up for sale. There were thousands of pages in Newton's own handwriting, all about alchemy.

Look, I KNOW it's my own fault for running away in the first place, and bringing Mum with me, but we don't have much money right now. Practically none, in fact. And I can't even tell you how boring it is, being poor. So when I read that Isaac was an alchemist, I thought maybe that was the reason I'd got obsessed with him in the first place. Like, he was going to teach me how to get rich again! So I've been reading a lot about alchemy.

At first, I was like, okay, cool, I just need to get me a fireplace and a crucible and some Bunsen burners and, maybe, like a chemistry lab in a dungeon, and get down to some heating, distilling, grinding, dissolving, and so on.

But pretty quickly I started to see problems.

E.g., you need the Philosopher's Stone. I think that's a chunk of rock. I think it's red. And you need it to make gold. But where is it? Where?

Also, possibly bigger problem. There's not a single piece of proof that alchemy ever worked. So I might be wasting my time.

I guess if it DID work, it'd be daft for alchemists to go around shouting: "We've figured out how to make gold! You just do blah and blah and you've got it!" Cause then everyone would do blah and blah, and if everyone's got gold, it stops BEING gold. If you see what I mean. It's as common as blades of grass. Grass can be a very nice green but no girlfriend's going to go, "OMG, this necklace is pure blades of grass, this is the best birthday ever!"

So maybe it did work and they kept it secret. Which brings me to the next problem, which is that all the alchemy books are written in code. Those alchemists were into secrecy like Mum's into chocolate. They had secret clubs, they called each other code names (Isaac's was an anagram of his own name in Latin), they met at secret locations. They invented their own alphabets, they spoke in metaphors and riddles. Their alchemy books sound like someone tripping, or like a kid who's been given a list of random spelling words and told to make a story out of them. So they're all about frogs and toads, three-headed serpents, the green lion, the king clad in purple with a golden crown, the grey wolf, the unicorn, the white rose, the red rose, the black rose, butterflies, three-headed eagle, fire-breathing dragon, black raven, the phoenix, the moon gliding into the sea . . .

Very nice and poetic, I'm sure, but also a language I don't speak.

Anyhow, so I'm reading these alchemy books and slamming into problems everywhere I turn, and then I read that alchemy is not just about making gold. It's also about the elixir of life. An elixir is like a medicine, but the elixir of life is the key to immortality.

So then I felt stupid and ashamed for having thought that alchemy was a message sent to make me rich. In my last letter to you I told you I was scared about Mum, and that I thought she was sick. Turned out that was an understatement. She had a brain tumour. She's okay now, but you know, those things can come back. I'm living in this constant terror of it coming back, to be honest. I think she's okay — I mean she hasn't been acting weird (or not more weird than her regular self) or getting headaches or anything. But it could happen. And if alchemy can make an elixir of life, that's exactly what I need to cure Mum.

And then FINALLY (don't worry, this letter, which you are probably not reading — which you have probably sent right back to me — this letter is about to end) — well, I discovered something else about alchemy. Something sort of blindingly important. It's about the self. It's like, it's not just making an elixir for your body and transforming metal into gold. It's an elixir to cure your SOUL — it's transforming yourself into the best that you can be.

And that brings me to my point. I know I was wicked and wild, and I caused you a lot of stress, and cost you a lot of money. I've hurt people a lot by running away. So the question is, have I changed? Like cured my soul of the evil, and become a sort of gold version of myself?

In some ways, yes. I don't sneak out in the night, well, that's not true, I did that all the time for a while, but only to talk to a parking meter (don't ask, that's another story). But I'm not breaking laws or running away or partying, and I'm doing my homework, and reading a lot, and (I THINK, I HOPE) I am thinking about other people instead of just myself.

But in some ways, no. I have not changed. I think I've always been searching for something kind of amazing and magical. You know how I said that Sotheby's put Newton's alchemy papers up for auction? Well, the economist Maynard Keynes bought them all. I guess he was rich, being economically minded. He gave a speech about the papers, and here's a line from his speech:

"Newton was not the first of the age of reason. He was the last of the magicians."

If Isaac Newton, one of the greatest scientists of all time, was a magician — if he believed in magic, why shouldn't I?

Listen, Dad, I grew up thinking that YOU were a magician. I have never felt so alone in my life as right now. It's like all I do is stare at myself in the mirror. But, like I said, I still believe in magic. Please, prove me right and come and find us.

Love,

Madeleine

P.S. This sounds stupid, but I think maybe there's something wrong with ME now — I mean, physically wrong? I keep getting bleeding noses. I keep seeing weird things, like hallucinations. I mean, I've seen Leonardo da Vinci, Vivaldi, and Newton, so maybe this is just my subconscious telling me I should cut out all the reading, or I should pursue an academic career in history. But still. It's scaring me. A lot.

13.

After she posted the letter to her father, Madeleine felt a strange calm melting through her. She carried the calm around, and watched colours fade and pale. She still looked at the parking meter in the laneway each day, but it began to resemble any other meter. It was crooked and out of order, but it was no longer a gateway to the Kingdom of Cello. There were never any slivers of white paper there. Elliot and his Kingdom were sealed away, gone.

One Saturday afternoon, there was a flurry of snow, and she cycled down the laneway, concentrating on the slipperiness, without even considering her parking meter. She stopped when she realised what she'd done, and backed up. Then she gazed at it for a long time: at its bright white snowcap, and the fine tracings of white lining its seams and edges, and its damp metallic greys and blues, and at the absence of cracks of paper.

This was how you said goodbye.

Then, as she watched, a glimpse of white appeared, bright and defiant. It hesitated, then slid right out. She reached a gloved hand to catch it, her heart crashing like a drum kit.

Madeleine,
  Urgent. We need your help again. Speak here tonight at midnight?
  Keira

PART 2

1.

$\mathcal{T}$he blindfold caught in Elliot's hair while the girl, Chime, was tying it.

Her hands were gentle as they disentangled the hair, and then sharp again while tightening the knot.

Now it was just him and the blindfold. The deep blackness of it, the soft coolness, the close pull of its binding. It's all come down to this, he thought. It's nothing but me in a blindfold.

"Can you see?"

"No."

"Are you sure?"

"Can't see a thing."

He felt the light change as she moved from behind him. Now her voice came from the side. "How many fingers am I holding up?"

Elliot paused.

"Is this scientific?" he asked.

They both laughed.

A mild chuckle joined their laughter. It was the Assistant. That was the crowded smell of him: apricot-scented shampoo, leather coat, salted cashew nuts.

"It'll be fine," the Assistant said. "It's a first-rate blindfold."

The Assistant's hand fell on Elliot's shoulder.

"You know the rules?"

"I do."

"Blindfold doesn't come off until she tells you. Follow her instructions to the letter. Back here in under an hour?"

Elliot nodded.

"And keep a firm hold on *this*." Rope was pressed into his palm.

"Wrap it around your hand," Chime suggested.

He did so, liking the rope's dry roughness, finding the soft frayed end with the tip of his thumb.

"Stay close behind me," said Chime. "Don't make a sound."

Elliot nodded again. Each time his head moved, there were busy scritching sounds: the blindfold rubbing against his scalp and hair.

"Ready?" said the Assistant.

He hadn't seen the sky for over a month. "Ready?" he said. "You're kidding, right?"

The Assistant chuckled again. "Go on, then. Have a blast."

There was a series of beeps. A quiet rolling. The Exit door slid open.

2.

*F*ive weeks earlier, Elliot had woken into darkness.

The sounds of breathing. The turn of a body on a mattress.

He was on a bed. A thin pillow. He was wearing someone else's T-shirt and boxer shorts. These fell uncertainly against his skin. The room was deep in darkness. He propped himself up to look over the side of the bed at the floor, but too much darkness fell too far: a rush of vertigo.

It's a bunk bed, he told himself. You're on a bunk bed.

Abruptly, a light shone in his eyes.

He closed his eyes.

This is me, he told himself. *Elliot Baranski*, and right away he felt that as a physical weight. His own name was climbing onto him, clambering awkwardly onto his chest, waiting to see what he would do. He tilted, trying to tip it off.

Well, now, that's crazy, he thought.

As far as he recalled, he'd never had to shift under the weight of his own name before. Generally, his name — his *self* — fit him so fine he didn't notice it.

The light was still there. He could sense it from behind his eyelids. A fine pencil line of light.

He opened his eyes again.

Someone was shining a flashlight at him.

"You'll be awake now," murmured a girl's voice.

He squinted but could only make out a vague form. She was just across from him. On a bunk bed too, he guessed, only she was sitting up.

He tried to sit, but a surge of something else came over him. This was genuinely physical, only again he couldn't figure it. It was a mild throbbing, for a start, in his shoulders and his lower back. Also a dull pain in his gums and sinuses, and, weirdly enough, behind his ears. But it was more than just a catalog of aches, it was a sense of being totally, physically beat. As if he'd been working in the fields without a break for a week. Hammering for days, leaping endless deftball furrows, felling trees, sawing wood, partying all night.

"You are Elliot Baranski," said the girl.

There it was again, his name. He felt it press harder, dig its elbows into his kidneys.

"You've been in the World," she continued. "You remember that?"

He thought about it.

"I remember a gas station," he said. "I remember walking a long way. My dad in a doorway." He stopped. He stared into the darkness. He kept right on staring. "After that," he said, "I've got nothing."

"Well, that'll be you forgetting yourself," she told him. "A person changes, I am hearing, when a person goes to the World. Changes into another. If you return before that other you has set, you lose it all."

That was a Nature Strip accent, Elliot realized. The words turning in on themselves, an almost eerie remoteness, those skids into harshness. But her voice was also soft and low and —

"My name is Chime."

That was disconcerting. She'd spoken the exact adjective he was about to apply to her voice. Chiming. Now it seemed as if he, personally, had named her. He felt light-headed with the power.

"That's quite a name," he said eventually.

"My mother was from the Sjakertaat. It's common there."

"But you sound Nature-Strippian."

Now he saw the shape of her moving slightly, and the hand that was holding the flashlight waved, indicating the space of the room.

"There are eight of us here — nine now, for you also are here — and we are the regulars of this compound. We have come from all over Cello."

The thin thread of light moved around the room, and he caught glimpses of concrete floor. The room was rectangular, walls lined with bunks, a narrow strip between them. He saw rumples of blankets, mounds of sleeping people, some large and bulky, some curled and neat, now and then an arm or foot half slipping from covers.

"That is where we hang our jackets," Chime concluded. "Hooks on the wall."

But she had turned the light back onto him before he could admire the hooks.

There was an important question he had to ask, only — he got it. "Why am I here?"

"We are keeping you here for your protection, and if we are not, then the WSU would be finding out you are alive, and they would be after the killing of you, for that you were communicating with a girl from the World, and so you must be dead again."

Elliot waited. His mind was catching up with her words.

"These are the things that I know of you," Chime added.

But did Elliot know these things of himself? He'd communicated with the World? Seriously?

Of course he had.

The sculpture in the high school grounds. Late-night conversations in notes. Madeleine.

So, yeah, that part was true. He ticked that off.

And yes, he also recalled. The WSU had found out.

Choppers. A chase.

He'd fallen off a cliff's edge, and fallen through to the World.

Now he was here.

"What is this place?" he said.

"It is a Hostile compound. You are among Hostiles."

Everything froze, then instantly set fire. A *Hostile* compound? He grabbed at pieces in his memory: Hostiles were revolutionaries; they were stealthy, violent, heck, they were *killers*!

He was forcing this, he realized. His fear was mostly theoretical. The ache in his muscles and bones, the weird pressure of his own name on his chest — *those* were plenty real. As for terror about

Hostiles, who had the room, to be honest. He set that aside. He'd feel it later.

"We will not harm you," Chime added. "We are protecting you. Not that I think you are afraid."

Once again he flinched at the confluence of their thoughts.

"But *why*?" Elliot asked. "I mean, it's good of you and all, to keep me safe, but I'm just some kid from the Farms, and aren't you guys tied up bringing down a monarchy?"

That was maybe risky, saying that. Maybe disrespectful? He hadn't planned it; it sort of rolled out as he recalled what the Hostiles were about.

But the girl, Chime, answered his question thoughtfully.

"We are," she agreed, "but this is another thing I know of you. That you are friends with the girl, Keira. And it is Keira who has arranged for your protection here. You are the first non-Hostile ever to breathe between these walls, but Keira asked us to do it, and Keira is a person of much influence with us."

Here came another set of memories unfolding. Keira — the Royal Youth Alliance —

He was too weary to follow that path any farther.

"Where are we?" he asked.

"In a Hostile compound. As I said."

"No, I mean, where is the compound?"

"This, and I cannot tell you."

Elliot sighed. His mind was in that many pieces. He didn't see how he could put it back together without knowing exactly where his body was. You need a starting point, someplace to tether yourself.

"Well, what *province* am I in?"

"This, and I cannot tell you."

"I can't even know what province I'm in?"

66

"You cannot."

"As soon as it's daylight, I'll figure it out."

"You will not," Chime informed him. "We have no windows. And you will not be stepping outside of the doors."

"You want to put money on that?"

"You will not be stepping outside of the doors," Chime repeated. "Now that you are here, you cannot leave except in a state of unconsciousness. Artificially induced, of course — hopefully. A non-Hostile may never know the location of a Hostile compound. How are you thinking we got you here? You were injected with the maximum dose of seventh-level Green. Only now, three days later, you have woken."

Ah. Seventh-level Green. That explained his body feeling like it had been trampled by a team of oxen, then run through a spin cycle.

Something else was coming to him. The most profound ache in his body — he was about to identify it.

Three days he'd been out?

He must be *starving*.

The ache was hunger.

"I need to eat," he said, immediately beginning to panic.

"These are oat biscuits," she replied. "I had them ready. Eat slowly."

There was a rustling sound, and Elliot reached out to the space between the bunk beds and took a paper bag from her.

"Appreciate that," he said once he'd eaten the whole bag. He lay back down, his head on the pillow. Now he felt nothing except sleepy. "How long am I supposed to stay here?"

"This, and I cannot — ah, but I can say that the girl, Keira, she is working to clear your name with the WSU so that you may walk free and fearless. Once that is done, we will arrange for your departure. She is now with your family in your hometown. I believe this is somewhere in the Farms."

"Bonfire, the Farms."

"This, and it is the one. She will contact you at some future moment."

Keira in Bonfire?

Something seemed hilariously unlikely about that. Keira, the city girl, Night-Dweller, Jagged-Edgian, in the *Farms*? Keira with the Sheriff and the Deputy. Keira with his buddies back home. How would she even have *gotten* there?

Elliot in the World.

Also unlikely.

He closed his eyes and tried again to see it, his time in the World. But it was nothing but shadows and mists. There was a dim light amidst the mist, and he couldn't tell if that was Chime's flashlight, still aimed at his face, or a trace of memory trying to get through. It made him want to raise a hand to his eyes to shelter them, to squint into the shadows, to try to see that light. As if the shadows themselves were a glare, blinding him. He fell asleep.

3.

*T*he next morning, the room was empty when he woke.

Most of the beds had been made. A half-empty glass of water stood on the floor next to one bed. A boot lay on its side in the center of another, making a dip in the blanket.

At the end of the room, there was a basin.

He washed his face.

He looked up and there he was in the mirror.

Elliot Baranski.

He was about to consider why this perfectly ordinary fact kept stopping him in his tracks, when he noticed the yellow line crossing his forehead. At first he thought it was a mark on the mirror, but when he moved his head around, it stayed with him. He rubbed at his forehead with water.

"That will not disappear, no matter how you soap it," said a voice. "That will be your clearance level."

It was the voice he'd heard in the night.

He turned to look at her. She was dark-skinned, as you'd expect of someone whose mother was from Sjakertaat, although her hair was the orangey-black that was common to Nature Strip. His primary impression, however, was that Chime had a lot more *voice* than her body could carry. Even as it had murmured in the darkness last night, it had seemed so full and complex. But she herself was thin as a bunch of twigs. Her skin seemed cling-wrapped to her bones. There was no room for error, no space for wear and tear. It's all there, he thought, all of Chime. On display, without protection.

Then he saw that she was pointing to her own forehead, and that it was also marked with a horizontal line. Only hers was blue.

"It only shows up under the special lights of Hostile compounds," she explained. "Come. You must shower, and I'll find you some clothes. All of yours, as that you wore when you came from the World, have been burned, of course, as they've the plague there. And you were scrubbed and disinfected yourself while you were under the seventh-level Green."

She turned and led him from the room.

*　　*　　*

After he'd showered and dressed, Chime found him again and announced that she would take him on a tour of the compound, and then to breakfast.

"Let's reverse that order," he suggested, and she considered her fingernails a moment.

"No. Tour first."

It was larger than he'd imagined a Hostile compound to be, and also more neatly labeled. Corridors were lined with closed doors and each of these carried a small placard: Strategy. Medical Supplies. Recuperation. Communications. The doors responded to the stripes on their foreheads: His yellow stripe was the lowest clearance level, so he only had access to Bathrooms, Showers, Laundry, Kitchen, and Exercise Room A.

"Here, and you will see the weights, the stationary bike, and so on," she said, gesturing at this room. "When you are not working, you will enjoy these facilities."

"There are other exercise rooms?"

Chime stopped and looked at him. "This one is not enough for you?"

"Well, sure. I mean, I don't know. I've never exercised in a room like this in my life. I like to run. Outside. In the woods. It's just the A makes me think there's a B someplace, maybe a C."

She nodded. "You are right. But you only have clearance for A."

Somehow this felt personal. They could exclude him from Strategy, sure, but what, the gym equipment in B and C was too fancy for him? It seemed mean-spirited.

Chime carried on, passing doors labeled Briefing, Training, and, around a corner, Debriefing.

"They couldn't brief and debrief in the same place?"

Chime ignored him.

"You mentioned me working," Elliot remembered. "How can I work if you won't let me outside?"

She laughed as if he was teasing her.

"That wasn't meant as a joke. But okay if you find it funny."

"You will work in the kitchen with me. You're from the Farms, are you not? This, and I hear they can cook there."

At an Exit door, Elliot stopped.

"So this door won't open for me?"

"This, and of course not," she replied.

"What if there's a fire?"

"Come to me. I'll get you out."

"What if I can't find you? What if you're at another Exit, and everything between us is in flames?"

She laughed again. "Come to breakfast."

In the dining room, he was introduced to the other Hostiles. They didn't seem especially interested by him. There were four men and three women, and they were finishing up their breakfast, some of them already pushing back chairs as Elliot and Chime arrived. They glanced at him but then carried on with their conversations or with stacking used plates onto trays.

The only exception was the man whom Chime introduced as "the Assistant." He slowly scraped his knife across his almost-empty plate, gazing at Elliot, a slight smile forming.

"You've woken at last?" he said.

"Seems so."

"Why do you think—" The Assistant paused. "Let me rephrase that. What *was* it that finally woke you from a three-day slumber, do you think?"

Having asked this question, the Assistant leaned forward on folded arms, and scrutinized Elliot.

Elliot stared back.

"I guess I can't say," he replied eventually.

The man continued to gaze for several seconds, then nodded. "Okay. Welcome, Elliot. I've taken the liberty of outlining a program for you to follow while you're with us. Chime should be your point of contact for questions, but if there's anything else you need, ask for me — go ahead and ask for *the Assistant*!" The abrupt swing into cheer at the end was alarming. The guy was trying for a Farms accent, Elliot realized. Well, he'd heard worse.

"Is there a chief?" he asked.

"Excuse me?"

"Or, I don't know, a director or something? I mean, if you're Assistant."

The man studied him again, eyes alight.

"*I* see what you're up to," he said, and grinned broadly. "Nice try. I admire you already." He returned to scraping his plate.

Elliot was bewildered. It had just been a question.

Later that day, while she was showing Elliot around the kitchen and explaining what his duties would be, Chime answered the question anyway.

"I don't see as why you shouldn't know who the Director is," she said as she opened the pantry door and stepped back so he could see inside. "You know Keira already, and you know she has connections to the Hostiles, yes? Well, and you know her mother is a Hostile?"

"I do," Elliot replied. He studied the pantry. It was a mess of crowded and spilling food. Opened packets of flour sat in their own dust. Something wilted in a corner. Potatoes rotted. A container of tomato sauce had split, and the sauce had dripped from one shelf down to the next and then congealed.

"Mischka Tegan," he added.

Chime closed the pantry door.

"No," she said. "Mischka, yes, but Tegan is not the name."

She was opening a double-doored refrigerator now. Those blackish leaves that were pasted along a shelf might once have been lettuce.

"It's the name she used when she came to my hometown," Elliot explained, "and tricked my father and uncle into helping with the Hostile cause. They thought she was a Loyalist."

He stopped. The memories were coming back to him like rocks riding a slope, and he was speaking them aloud before he'd checked them. What was he thinking, telling a Hostile that his father was a Loyalist?

"Aaah." Chime nodded. "I recall this story. And that's how your father ended up in the World, and your uncle dead."

Elliot was silent.

"This is the deep freeze." Chime made no move to open it. "Well, and in any case, here's another truth. Keira's mother is officially Director here. Only, she is in prison now."

Another landslide of memories. He sorted through it cautiously.

"Keira told me that her mother was in prison," he said eventually. "And she only avoided execution because Keira agreed to help the RYA?"

Chime nodded. "Yes. It is our hope that Keira herself was secretly undermining the royals from the inside at that point. Was she?"

Elliot lifted the lid of the deep freeze himself. Cold misted up at him.

"I guess," he said.

But he was recalling that it was Keira who had calculated the locations of the royals in the world and who had given them each communication rings. Which was a lot more helpful than undermining.

"I don't know," Chime said thoughtfully. "This, and I think that Keira has never truly been Hostile. I think perhaps that Keira's her own person."

Elliot relented. "I think so too."

"I like people who are their own person. Are you?"

"I hope. I don't know. How do we know?"

Chime was standing with her back to the counter. Now she hoisted herself up so she was sitting there, heels thudding a cupboard door.

"This I also like. People who ask questions. Elliot, I like you," she said.

4.

Over the next few weeks, Elliot followed the Assistant's program. It turned out to be pretty simple: assist Chime in the kitchen from nine A.M. through five P.M. (with breaks as determined, erratically, by Chime); work out in the exercise room five thirty P.M. through seven P.M. Kick back on Sundays in the recreation room.

Turned out that working out in an exercise room was not so bad, once you got around the crazy notion of a bicycle fixed to the ground. He began to look forward to that part of his day, and felt agitated when the room got too crowded or was closed for repairs. His first couple of sessions, Chime explained how the equipment worked, and which was for "strength" and "cardio." After that, she ignored him, exercising separately. She was a whole lot stronger, he noticed, than those skinny arms and legs might imply.

It also turned out that the compound itself was more chaotic than he'd first imagined. There might have been only eight other regulars but it seemed like scores of people came and went. There were separate bunkrooms for the transients. So far as Elliot could figure, these were recruits coming in for training, envoys from other Hostile branches, sick or injured people who needed medical treatment, and delivery guys arriving with sacks of flour or rice, jars of honey or dried herbs, toilet paper, toothpaste, and news.

By listening to conversations, Elliot learned what had been happening in the Kingdom. It seemed word had gotten out that Princess Ko had been running the Kingdom on her own. People had gotten themselves in a real state about that. Didn't like to think they'd been duped. The Jagged Edge Elite had placed her under house arrest in her own palace, along with two other members of the Royal Youth Alliance, Sergio and Samuel (who had OQ poisoning). But not Keira? And not Elliot himself, come to think of it. He supposed he *would* have been arrested if the WSU hadn't already chased him over a ravine and announced that he was dead. Which was sort of funny and a jolt at the same time.

Anyhow, the idea of Princess Ko under arrest was even crazier than Keira in Bonfire, or himself in the World. That Princess had as much clue about being told what to do as he himself had about what "cardio" meant.

Another day, he heard that the King had been brought back from the World just in time to attend the Namesaking Ceremony in the Kingdom of Aldhibah. So the RYA had been successful. He felt proud. He'd been a major part of making that happen. But his pride clashed directly with the grave voices around him. Apparently, the King was now back from Aldhibah and was engaged in talks with the Jagged Edge Elite. He was asking for the release of his daughter, Princess Ko, the recovery of the remainder of his family from the World, and the restoration of the King himself to his rightful position. As King.

This all seemed fine to Elliot. Soothing. Order on its way. But the way these people talked it was a gloomy, dreary sigh.

At first, Elliot assumed he'd make friends with the regulars here — in addition to Chime — and then he realized that was about as likely as a Nature-Strippian flat-headed jaguar strolling up and shaking his hand.

The only time the regulars appeared from behind closed doors was mealtimes, or on Sundays in the recreation rooms, and then they'd engage in their own conversations, leaning over their meals or their board games, backs to Elliot. Now and then, one would glance pointedly his way, and their murmurs would stop, the others rolling eyes or twisting their mouths with impatience. He got it. There were things they couldn't say. He was stifling them. But still, it was a lot like grade school — except that, in grade school, this hadn't happened to him. He'd always had buddies. This was new. He wasn't keen on it.

Once, the man who slept in the bunk beneath him tapped on the side of the bed and said, "Hey, kid, I hear you were a deftball player."

"I was," Elliot said. "I am."

He waited, but the man — Ming-Sun was his name — was silent.

"You play yourself?" he said eventually, but the silence continued, and when he ducked his head over the side of the bed, Ming-Sun turned onto his side and was asleep. Over the next few days, he made a few attempts to engage Ming-Sun in conversation, but each time the man either completely ignored him, or else furrowed his brow, like he couldn't figure out what language Elliot spoke. So he gave up.

5.

*N*ights, Elliot would lie in his bunk bed in the total darkness and ask himself just who he thought he was. But he found it changed all the time. He couldn't get ahold of it.

So he changed his tactics. He figured he'd sort through his memories. Starting with his childhood. The month when he ate a boiled egg and a mini-cheesecake for breakfast each morning. His first crush, on the dentist's assistant. The complicated rules of the games he and his buddies used to invent. He even tried to dig up the games the *girls* played, their rhyming chants and the way they liked to spring up and down all the time. Over swinging ropes, elastic bands they strung between their ankles, or just on the spot, over nothing at all.

One night he caught an even earlier memory of himself as a small boy sitting up on his father's shoulders. There'd been some joke to do with his dad standing alongside Uncle Jon, to measure who was taller, and he, Elliot, had made his father the winner, by adding that extra height. His pride in this had made him twist his legs around his father's neck, tight, and his father said, "Easy there," but easily, gripping Elliot's ankles sure and firm, and then Uncle Jon's hands had reached up, "Give the kid here, I'll take him on *my* shoulders and we'll see what's what," and he'd tumbled into Uncle Jon's arms.

The memory ended there.

Some nights he fished for glimpses of his little cousin, Corrie-Lynn, and he recalled how she'd sit in her stroller as a baby, pulling out the ribbons that her mother, Auntie Alanna, used to tie in the child's hair. He remembered taking one from her little hand, seeing the fine hairs tangled in it, turning back to her cool, steady gaze as she wrenched the next ribbon away.

He took himself through grade school to high school, afternoons riding motor scooters with his buddies, going to Sugarloaf, falling in love, breaking hearts, working the farms, and the greenhouse.

He dragged himself through the night he found his Uncle Jon dead and his father missing, the year he spent hunting for his dad in Purple caverns. Getting snared by Princess Ko for her Royal Youth Alliance — the terrible day when he learned that his father was dead, and he himself was chased by choppers — finding his father alive in a doorway in the World, and then his memories hit darkness.

There was still a thin thread of light in that darkness. He saw it every night. But it was always too dark in *here*, in this bunkroom, to see it properly. Noisy, also. The clattering and clanging, toilets flushing, and a general sense of water running. There were constant leaks, buckets everywhere — and more distant sounds, sometimes he thought he heard a drumbeat, but he couldn't disentangle this from the thudding of his own heart. There were strange shrieks and distant howls, and now and then a sound like remote animals gargling, but again, that would be entwined with the noises in the bathroom pipes. . . .

Most nights, he'd find something bigger than his memories surging inside him, and he'd begin to twitch and turn, even to *writhe* in his bed thinking of closed doors, locked doors, whispers, codes and passwords, the cracks between Cello and the World tightly sealed.

He'd think of the tape that was embedded in his forehead and that lit up as a yellow stripe. *Stop it,* he'd think. *Stop embedding me. Making me into what you want. I am Elliot. I'm my own.* He thought of darkened rooms, blackened paper, blank faces, hunched shoulders, cold stares, and, most of all, he thought of Exit doors.

I'm from the *Farms*, he said, over and over, in his mind. I'm a *Farms* boy. Don't you get it?

6.

$\mathcal{I}$n the kitchen, Chime outlined the daily menus to Elliot, pointing out the various residents' food preferences and allergies. Mostly, it turned out, she wanted him to chop vegetables and wash dishes.

Each day, Chime disappeared for a couple of hours. When she returned, she'd be carrying buckets of onions, turnips, and carrots, roots clumped in dirt. Her fingernails would be black, and there'd be smudges on her cheek and neck. It was a blacker dirt than Elliot was used to at the Farms, but either way, he'd always been partial to a girl with dirty fingernails and smudges.

The more he worked with her, the more he saw that she wasn't slight and skinny at all; her body was rough and hard and muscle-bound, and she could rip things apart — packaging, raw vegetables — with her teeth or her bare hands. Like most Nature Strip girls, she'd make music by clicking her tongue and tapping her hands on the table, sometimes singing a strange verse or two, her accent riding roughshod over the soft thrum of her voice.

"Yes, I can tell you, I can tell you, sure," she'd say in response to a simple question he might ask, and he could almost see the twists of her accent, the way it swerved around corners.

He learned who she was in ragged bursts, as if she were ripping out handfuls of grass and handing these to him. Her mother had gone home to the Kingdom of Sjakertaat when Chime was still young, she told him, and Chime hadn't seen her since. "That must have been tough on you," Elliot said, but she was silent. Two days later, she explained that it was a Sjakertaatian tradition — mothers always returned to their tribes once their firstborns were four or five — and had not affected her in the slightest.

Her father had been a Color Bender, she told him another day, and she had traveled to Nature Strip with him, learning the art. Again, Elliot adjusted his opinion of Chime. To Color bend, even as an adult, you had to have the kind of reckless courage that stepped right up to insanity. College graduates would sometimes go to Nature Strip and sign up for three-month Color bending contracts. The pay was fantastic; you could make a killing in a short time. But they never lasted the contract.

Chime's father had joined this Hostile branch when Chime was ten, she explained, and he was now on a mission for them.

"You see much of him?" Elliot asked.

Chime added flour to the pan and stirred.

One day, Elliot picked up a newspaper that a transient had left in the rec room.

The back page reported a shock defeat in a champion deftball game, and he read that article carefully. It felt good, thinking about regular things like deftball controversies. Then he flicked the paper open at a random page.

A giant photograph of Keira stared up at him.

So that was disconcerting. He'd almost forgotten Keira — or, at least, she'd turned into a sort of minor celebrity in his mind, like someone he used to watch on a TV show. Her eyes, in the picture, seemed contemptuous, as if she was annoyed with him for being here in the rec room of a Hostile compound.

You're the one who *put* me here, he reminded the picture.

He'd forgotten how beautiful she was. The cheekbones, and the hair spiked as if in honor of her province, Jagged Edge, and the big mouth curling in that intense half smile.

He looked at the accompanying article. It was some kind of opinion column by a guy called T. I. Candle. Familiar name.

Perhaps I should begin by introducing myself.

Please, Elliot thought.

It is I, T. I. Candle! The *Cellian Herald* has kindly invited me to write a series of columns on the state of the Kingdom. And you, dear reader, now peruse my first!

But who am I? If you suspect that I am the author of the best-selling book, *The Kingdom of Cello: An Illustrated Travel Guide*, you are correct. I claim that honor.

Of course. That was the book his little cousin, Corrie-Lynn, was always lugging around. Elliot had always thought the guy was a total ass. He read on.

Perhaps you also believe that I currently hold the prestigious position of Chair of the Cellian Travelers Club, have postdoctoral degrees from the Universities of Brellidge and Yogurt, consider myself a foremost wildlife explorer, dabbler in politics, biochemistry, and viticulture, am a proud member of the Council of Elders in the picturesque hamlet of Lanternville, Magical North (where I reside, when not traveling) — and the (equally) proud owner of a cat named Patricia?

You do?

Well, in all that, I am sorry to say, you are wrong.

Ho-ho.

No. That was mere humor. Once again, you are spot-on, and I congratulate you on your encyclopedic knowledge of yours truly.

"Yep," Elliot murmured. "Still a total ass."

He skimmed the next paragraph. It was a summary of the recent events in Cello. The next paragraph took up the issue of the missing royals.

What of Cello's royal family? We know that the King is in talks with the Elite, and little Prince Tippett is safely installed in the White Palace with his nanny.

But what of the Queen? Prince Chyba? Princess Jupiter?

They remain trapped in the World.

Which begs the question: Should we retrieve them? Should the WSU send in a team and bring our royals home? Surely the cracks would only need to be opened a few seconds, then safely resealed, no harm done?

Here is Anders Jerome, Assistant Deputy Director of

the WSU, in yesterday's press release:

"We cannot and must not unseal any cracks through to the World. To open a crack, even for a fraction of a second, would be an invitation to the plague — that infamous disease of the World — to enter our Kingdom. Moreover, it would directly violate numerous treaty obligations owed to our neighboring Kingdoms and republics."

It breaks my heart to say it, but Mr. Jerome is right. For the safety of our Kingdom, the royals should stay RIGHT WHERE THEY ARE.

Look. The royal family are a hoot. I'm crazy about them! The King and Queen are personal friends, or at the least really jolly acquaintances. I have watched with delight, and occasional winces, as the royal children have clambered their way through childhood.

And yet we CANNOT tamper with those cracks.

As a traveler to distant climes, I have personally witnessed the plague in action. Women and children shriek from behind windows and doors. Streets that once thronged with people are left desolate. There is the stench of filthy linen, pus, blood, dust, vomit, vinegar. In the agony of swellings, people shoot themselves or throw themselves under steam trains.

It's just no cup of tea.

Certainly, the Cello Wind would blow the plague away from OUR Kingdom (or would it? I haven't heard a peep about the Wind for some time, to be honest....), but the plague would find its way to other Kingdoms and Empires, and for them, there would be no relief.

Indeed, if we so much as glanced toward a crack detector, our neighbor, the Kingdom of Aldhibah, would open fire. They'd launch missiles and storm our borders, in strict accordance with their treaty rights.

We CANNOT rescue the remaining royals. We must sacrifice them for the greater good.

Anyway, I'm sure they are cheerful in the World! They have no doubt forgotten their true identities, and don't even know what they're missing. And I hear that the World is a pleasant-enough place. (Assuming our royals have found a plague-free corner.)

Before I conclude, I will mention one other missing person. She is Keira Platter, of Tek, Jagged Edge [pictured, right].

She was a member of the RYA. She assisted the Princess in her deception of the Kingdom. She should be found, arrested, and face the charges against her.

It is only fair. The other members (excepting Elliot Baranski, who has already met his destiny, having perished in his hometown) are under lock and key. I invite all citizens to keep a careful eye out for the face in this picture.

Elliot looked back at Keira's photograph. He stroked it once with his thumb. He closed the paper.

Another day, Chime asked Elliot if he'd like a piece of Vermillion candy.

He didn't know what she was talking about.

"Vermillion candy," she repeated, unlocking a drawer and sliding it open. It was crammed with deep red toffees that were wrapped in cellophane and attached to wooden sticks.

"Someone brought these in with a shipment not long back," she explained. "They're always along with things we've not requested. Melons, umbrellas, olives. What are they thinking, and who in rightness of mind would eat an olive? Vile, disgusting pieces of all that is salty and dark."

"Olives are great. Especially those huge ones from the East Wapshire Hills in Golden Coast. You tried those?"

She ignored him, selecting two pieces of candy from the drawer, unwrapping these, dropping the paper back into the drawer, and locking it again.

"Whereas, these now," she said, and sighed into a smile.

Elliot looked from the candy in Chime's hand to her face. "Vermillion?" she said. "It's a Color?"

"Never knew it came as candy."

"It doesn't, but if you catch yourself a twist of Vermillion, it's wonderful, it is, infused in toffee. Suck it slowly and the effect will last for hours."

She handed him one.

"Don't chew it, though. You'll just turn stupid."

For a while, they worked side by side in silence, sucking on their Vermillion candy. Elliot was peeling potatoes — Chime was slicing these — and soon, a pleasant sensation slid from his right shoulder and down his arm. It reached his fingertips. It was remote, the sensation, then he realized what it was. It was calm. It's been a while, he thought, surprised. He found he could actually see the calm: He watched his hand passing Chime a potato, and there it was, in the veins, scars, and knuckles of his hand, a visible, physical calm.

He pulled the toffee from his mouth, looked at it a moment, then returned it and sucked harder. Immediately, the sensation careened along his left arm. It flowed down his spine.

"Set it down, now and then," Chime advised. "Take it slow. Make it last." She had placed her own candy on a saucer beside her.

"You have been to the World," she continued musingly. "What happens to *you*, d'you think, when you cross to another reality? Is it still you? If you go from Cello to the World, and back, who *are* you as you cross? Are you light? I mean, are you transformed into light and then back into yourself? And if you've once been light, is it still you?"

Elliot glanced at her and smiled. He saw no need to reply. Her questions, and their internal repetition, were like a soft brushing back and forth.

After a while, though, he found himself speaking.

"I reckon I'd have noticed," he said, "if I'd turned into a light."

He picked up the candy again, and there was another slide of serenity, this time in his shoulder blades, and skimming his calf muscles.

Chime sliced potatoes, slow and steady.

"I figure it's like this." Elliot decided he ought to take her seriously. What the heck. Why not. "There was the me I was when I was growing up. Hanging with my buddies, making trouble, going to school. *That* me seems embarrassing now, like I was an ant scooting up and down a leaf, never noticing the whole tree."

He paused. He watched the peeler in his hand. Before the Vermillion candy, the peeler had moved in jabs and bursts, but now it swooped like it loved this potato; it curved, following contours.

"Then there was the me when my uncle was dead and my dad had disappeared. That's just a bunch of pictures and feelings now. Blood on grass; my Uncle Jon like an animal someone had gotten halfway through gutting; and most of all the terror that my dad was somewhere looking the same way. The only thing kept the pieces together then was the fight. Searching for him, I mean, and fighting the rumors that he'd just run off on us. Fights with things that stopped me searching: a broken ankle, a Butterfly Child, Princess Ko. But next thing you know I'm in the World and there he is. My dad."

Again, Elliot paused so he could marvel at the beauty of the peeler's motion. Peeling this potato used to be a kind of violence, a vicious flaying. Now it was ballet. He'd never been all that into ballet: He remembered an old girlfriend, Kala, and he'd had to sit through her little sisters rehearsing in the living room. That had been cute, but mainly a chore, only now, well, if a potato and a peeler could dance the ballet, there must be something in it.

Actually, he saw, ballet was a crock. What he was doing was, he was *setting this potato free*. Releasing it from its binds. He felt the relief of the smooth white object as it slipped from its own skin. He weighed it in his hand, its damp coolness.

There was a heck of a lot of honesty here, he thought, in this potato.

"So, you see," he said. "The fighting's done. My dad is safe. It's like I've been set loose from a long, long fever. Now the clarity's back and I can see myself at last, but I don't know who the heck it is I see."

He reached for the stick of candy again. It was dwindling. He smiled at it with gratitude. This beautiful calm. He felt as if he'd been thudding up a flight of stairs, heavy grocery bags in each hand, and now he'd set them down. Or working in the greenhouse back home, hauling a potted quince for his mother while she hesitated, changing her mind about where she wanted it set, and she'd finally decided.

Was that the candy, or was that the relief of speaking those words about himself aloud? The words, he realized, had been tearing back and forth inside his skull these last weeks.

"And isn't it the strangest," said Chime, "that, in those days of fighting, you were also fighting things you could not see?"

"What do you mean?"

"When you were on the Royal Youth Alliance, under the command of Princess Ko?"

Elliot smiled. He hadn't thought of himself as under Princess Ko's command, but of course that's exactly where he'd been.

"Uh-huh."

"There was a traitor."

Elliot studied the empty stick of the Vermillion candy. Pieces of toffee were still caked around it. He scraped at these with his teeth. Then he turned to Chime.

"A traitor?" He smiled again. "What do you mean?"

"Somebody on the Royal Youth Alliance was working against your team. You surely knew?"

"Not a chance," he said.

"This, and I should never have told you." Chime was suddenly troubled, muttering to herself, and then she breathed in deeply, turning the knife in her hand. "Ah, but all is quiet in its way, and why not? Yes, Elliot, there was a traitor. Think of it. Who knew that you were communicating with the World? Only those on the RYA. Hence, one such must have reported you to the WSU. To stop you from getting the royals home."

Elliot's calm seemed to rattle like a window in an unexpected wind.

"No," he said. "It was someone in my town reported me to the WSU. I was always in the schoolyard sending messages to Madeleine. Someone must have seen."

"Well, perhaps," Chime allowed. "But, as you know, even though the WSU took *you* down, the others managed to rescue two royals anyway. But somebody reported this fact too, because *whoosh!* the WSU swept in again, blockading the other crackpoints."

Elliot placed the peeler on the counter, candy stick on its saucer.

"All right," he said. "Who? Who was the traitor?"

Chime shrugged. "I do not know. I *cannot* know. My clearance level is not so high. But I believe there was somebody there all along: That is the rumor among low-clearance Hostiles."

Elliot turned his thoughts over. He listened to Chime chopping potatoes. The rhythm was soothing. She was dropping the freshly sliced pieces into a pot of cold water, and each fall seemed like a perfect little *plash*, a playful dive.

So there was a traitor in the RYA? Well, the team had been disbanded now. It was the past.

It was the previous Elliot who'd been betrayed, so who cared?

He would put the information aside, he decided.

"I can't stay here much longer," he remarked, swiveling the candy stick again. "See, there's one thing that's in me, no matter who I am. Or two things. I need to run and I need to be outside. I'm a Farms boy, see, and what I do is, I run. Not just run. Ride my bike, drive the truck, toss around a deftball, and it's gotta be outside. Heck, even when I'm baking in the kitchen at home, the windows are open, the room is filled with light, and I head outdoors the second that I'm done."

It was strange how tranquil his voice sounded. Again these words had been elbowing around his head. He'd imagined speaking them in shouts with vicious edges, he'd been *made* of shouts and edges when he thought them. Now the edges were softened, rounded like bannisters.

"You've got the shoulders and the muscles," Chime observed, stepping back to study him. "I see it in your calves that you can run."

She swirled the point of the knife in the water. The potato pieces swayed and bumped.

"You've got the confidence too," she went on. "Even with all your different Elliots, you're a deep truth and your outline's clearly marked. This is why the girls will always like you, Elliot. I myself am drawn to boys with edges," she added, "so I cut myself on sharpness. Or I get too close to the edge and fall. But you, you're the boy with edges that are kind, and if a girl fell from your edges, you would catch her."

Elliot's calm made a neat, precise turn into sadness.

"You've got that wrong. I let them fall. I go after girls, win them over, then I see someone I like better and move on."

Chime smiled at him.

"That's not the same," she said. "You're allowed to fall for girls and change your mind and break hearts. It hurts but it's not cruelty, it's life when you are young. I'm your age, I think — I don't know for sure: In Nature Strip, we tend not to count years — and I think that at our age, we're allowed to move along."

The beautiful tranquility returned. Elliot matched her smile.

"Not sure I agree, but I'm liking your perspective."

After that there was a long silence, only broken once when Elliot announced: "I don't know what the sky looks like anymore."

Chime did not respond.

Elliot looked at the locked drawer. "You dropped the candy wrappers back in there," he remembered suddenly. "No wonder this place is such a mess."

Now she grinned at him. "What do you mean, such a mess?"

They stared at each other.

"I'm from the *Farms*," he insisted. "I'm a *Farms* boy."

Her smile deepened. "So you are."

Elliot fell asleep at once that night, and found himself smiling through dreams about rocking chairs, hammocks, steady-moving steam trains, and still, starry nights.

Abruptly, he woke and was himself again.

He sat up in the dark room, appalled.

There'd been a *traitor* on the Royal Youth Alliance? His heart thudded louder than his thoughts, and his thoughts scrambled away from him. He'd been *betrayed*? Someone had arranged to have him *killed* by the WSU? He pressed his fists to his forehead, trying to slow the rush, then realized he was breathing in gasps.

He was going to wake the room.

He lay back down, fixed his attention on the now-familiar sounds: creaks and mumbles from the beds, slow drip of another leak somewhere.

It wasn't true. He'd been in that schoolyard so often, brazen, sending messages to Madeleine. He'd asked two teachers about the science of cracks. It was probably someone from the school.

But creeping at him sideways came a memory: He'd told the RYA he'd figured out how to get through cracks. The Princess had told him to explain it later but, within hours, the choppers had arrived.

Chime was right. Someone in the RYA had betrayed him.

Who? he asked himself. Which one?

There'd only been the Princess and four others: Keira, Samuel, Sergio, and himself. *Keira.* She was the obvious choice. She'd grown up among Hostiles; her mother was a director. She'd only been on the RYA because the Princess was blackmailing her. She must be the spy.

She was gorgeous and sharp. Sometimes she'd seemed like the only sane one among that bunch. They'd danced in the Turquoise Rain. He had kissed her. He had —

His breathing had turned harsh again.

It couldn't be Keira. It was *not*. That hurt too much, long, thin lines of hurt, and then he recalled that it was Keira who'd helped bring him back from the World, arranged for him to stay here, and *wait* — the final line dissolved — he had spoken to Keira separately. He'd told *her* the method for getting through cracks. She must have let the others know, because the King and little Prince had been rescued.

It wasn't Keira. She was not the traitor.

So who was it?

It must be Samuel. Ha. He grinned. Hapless, hopeless, earnest Samuel, who, it seemed, had poisoned himself with Olde Quainte magic in an effort to help the Princess. It was surely a medical miracle that he was still alive right now. No way it was Samuel — but right as Elliot thought that, it occurred to him that Samuel had the perfect front. Nobody *would* suspect him. And he *was* from a Hostile town. A memory swiped at Elliot: the security agents holding Samuel's file. *You* live *in one of the most Hostile towns in the Kingdom! We're* appalled *by your presence here!*

Still, if it was Samuel, it could also be Sergio. He was from Maneesh. Maybe foreign Kingdoms were working with the Hostiles to bring down the royals? Sergio had been the Princess's best friend and stable boy for years, but wasn't that also a great front? The security agents had been just as incensed by his presence.

Well, what about those two security agents? They'd brandished those files on the RYA members, but where were the files on the two of them? Always in the background, pressed up against the walls like camouflage lizards.

Or was it Princess Ko herself? Why was she the only royal left behind anyway? Could be, she'd orchestrated the kidnapping of her family so she could take the throne herself. Maybe she'd only been *pretending* to want them back. How deep did the layers of deception go, where did the counterfeit end?

He felt clammy and feverish. His stomach was twisting.

He pressed his head into the pillow, breathed in and out.

Nothing was real. The only person he could trust was himself.

But *could* he trust himself? Hadn't he lost himself completely in the World?

Was it *me*? he thought. Did I do it in my sleep? Was I the traitor? He fell asleep.

Later that same night he woke again, his heart pounding with betrayal, his very self tangled in malice and deception — and then, weaving through the darkness, came the thread of light.

He lay perfectly still and watched, waiting for the light to take shape.

He saw it extending backward: It ran through the blur of his time in the World, back to *before* that, it was somewhere in the place after his dad had gone missing. It was getting clearer now. He could see it in the schoolyard in the night. There was the sculpture, and there it was, the light.

It was the Girl-in-the-World. It was Madeleine. He had no memory of her face, but the light was her essence. He saw that now. The nights they'd spent talking in notes. The scrawl of her handwriting. Her passionate ideas, her temper, her crazy sense of humor. He remembered the sound of her voice, speaking through chaos, pieces of her voice like a trail through the darkness. Her hands, the shape of her body pressed against his in the space between.

There was one true thing. Madeleine. The relief was beautiful. He fell asleep imagining her hands in his hands, holding one another in the darkness.

This time he slept until the morning.

7.

A few days later, Elliot woke to an empty room. The door was ajar, and the cold tap at the basin ran softly.

He got up and turned off the tap, tightening it against its drip. His face was paler than he'd ever seen it. Might be something to do with the lights here, he guessed, but seriously, you could mistake that guy in the mirror for a ghost.

Except that his hair was wild, and he had an idea that ghosts had tidy hair. What were you going to do in the afterlife if not look after your hair? His own had grown longer than usual, pieces of it stuck out in new and unexpected directions. Well, you had to give it points for imaginative effort.

He slapped his cheeks, trying to get some life back in there, and it came to him that the sound of slapping was the only sound there was.

He stopped.

Silence.

He looked around the room. The bunk beds were rumpled and unmade, and the wastepaper basket in the corner had been knocked over.

Silence poured on silence.

It was exactly half a second later that the noises of the compound resumed — an object fell, a voice swore, another laughed, the *beep-beep* of a door opening somewhere, a washing machine emptying itself — and he realized he must have just been caught in one of those random moments between noise.

It was enough, though. Inside that moment, he had seen them all, every person in that compound, rushing from the bunkroom, leaving him asleep. He'd seen Exit doors opening and closing, sealing shut behind them. He'd seen himself trapped.

He showered, dressed, and went to breakfast.

The Assistant was still at the table. He was leaning over a pile of documents, making notes. Chime was stacking plates.

"Where's everyone else?" Elliot asked.

The Assistant dropped his pen, picked up a mug, slurped coffee, then returned to his notes.

Chime continued stacking. "We were all called early for a meeting," she said. "There were visitors, arrived with news."

Elliot pulled out a chair and sat down. "The kind of news I can know?"

The Assistant glanced up at him, and smiled.

"*You*," he said, and shook his head, as if there was something profoundly admirable in what Elliot had just said. Elliot thought back over his own words. *The kind of news I can know?* Now where was the genius in that?

"It's in the newspapers, so sure," the Assistant went on. He scribbled something in the margin of his notes. "You already know, I assume, that the King has been in talks with the Jagged Edge Elite? About the restoration of the monarchy? And the release of Princess Ko?"

Elliot nodded. "Sure."

There were a couple of strips of bacon still on the platter, and a pile of cold toast. Elliot reached for the toast.

"It seems the talks have collapsed," the Assistant continued. "The King's gone into hiding someplace. Security on the Princess has tightened, and she's been sentenced to death. A Jagged Edge Elite court has found her guilty of high treason."

Elliot set down his toast. He set down the butter knife.

"To death," he repeated.

The Assistant studied him. He sorted through his pile of notes, pulled out a folded newspaper, and slid it across the table.

There, on the front page, was Princess Ko's face, beaming up from last year's official portrait. A smaller inset showed a more recent, hazy photograph: the shape of a princess behind a barred window.

Elliot turned the paper over and pushed it away.

"You've spent time with the Princess," the Assistant remarked. "I'd forgotten. At any rate, we'll stop the conversation here, before we stray into that murky zone again — between what everyone knows and what the Hostiles plan to do."

He returned to his notes.

"But isn't this what the Hostiles want?" Elliot said, voice verging on reckless. "For the royals to be dead? If the Elite are going to do it, why do the Hostiles *need* to make plans? Shouldn't they just sit back and cheer?"

The Assistant raised his eyebrows, but not his head. He continued working.

"Unless you think them killing a princess would make the Kingdom so mad they'd rise up in favor of the royals again."

Now the Assistant smiled broadly. "Elliot," he breathed. "Where did you *come* from? I guess I can say this. You're absolutely right. The execution of a princess is a risky move on the part of the Elite. We won't *rescue* her, but we will distance ourselves. Let the Elite take her down — and let them take the fall."

Chime was moving along Elliot's side of the table, collecting plates. She reached Elliot and stepped around him.

"I'm done with this one." He passed his plate to her.

"This, and you have not eaten yet." She pressed it back.

He returned it to the table with such force that the Assistant looked up.

"I need," Elliot said, "to go outside."

The Assistant took a piece of toast for himself, found the marmalade, and looked around for a knife. Then he laughed. "Want to rescue the Princess?"

"Just for half an hour," Elliot continued. "You can blindfold me while I go out, and when I come back, so I'll have no clue where this place is. Someone leads me away — to a field or something, I don't know — I take the blindfold off and get some sun. Some air."

Chime had set the plates and cutlery on a tray, and now she was wiping the table. Spraying it with something, then wiping. Both Elliot and the Assistant watched her hand scrubbing.

"I'm grateful for . . . I really appreciate what you've done, letting me hide here. I know I'd be dead if I was out on the streets. But see my face? It's like I'm dead anyway."

"Look, I hear you," the Assistant said. "I really do. And it's true, we might be able to conceal our location with that blindfold idea of yours. But even at a safe distance, you might figure out what province we are in. You can't know that. Not even that."

"Who cares if I know which province we're in?" Elliot argued. "There are Hostile compounds in every province in the Kingdom!"

"You know that for a fact?" The Assistant smiled.

Elliot held his gaze, then shrugged a little. Who really knew?

"Well, anyhow . . ." Elliot paused. He hadn't meant to say this. It was too risky.

Then a moth landed on the table right before him and, Ah, what the heck, he thought.

"Well, anyhow," he repeated. "I already know what province we're in."

The Assistant raised his eyebrows directly at Chime, but Elliot shook his head. "She didn't tell me. I figured it out for myself, some time back."

Now the Assistant steepled his fingers, and breathed so his nostrils narrowed. There was a long pause. "And?"

"I hear distant drumming in the night," Elliot said. "There's water leaking everywhere. The dirt here's darker than a mineshaft."

Another pause.

"Half the lettuce leaves are shredded like a miniature web snail's been at them. And that" — he tilted his head at the moth on the table — "is a red-spotted tree moth. Enough poison in it to kill a small cat."

Chime had stopped wiping.

"This is Nature Strip," Elliot said. "Any fool could tell you that."

The Assistant leaned back, weaving his hands behind his head. He was grinning. "All right," he said. "You win."

8.

So here he was with the blindfold tight around his head, the soft end of a rope in his hand, and Chime leading him through the Exit door.

He shuffled a few steps, thudded gently into Chime's back.

She didn't speak. He recalled that she'd asked him to be silent.

He could hear the Exit door slide closed behind him. The rope pulled taut. Chime was moving again. He faltered along into the darkness.

This was not outside. It was some kind of tunnel, he thought. Well, that was sort of disappointing, but fair enough. They could walk through a tunnel to get to the light. As long as they got there.

The ground was rock-hard beneath his feet. The air felt deep and thick with a clammy darkness that pressed right up against his blindfold.

He felt Chime hesitate, then start up again. He was trying to take sure steps — to trust her — but his body wanted to feel its way along, to shuffle and slide, to reach out with both hands.

Mostly, though, there was a singing inside him. In a moment, there'd be sunshine and wind, and he thought of how fast and how far he'd run, once they reached a field or whatever. In Nature Strip, they'd surely find one. He'd run laps, he'd run circles, hurdle fences. He'd run until he was just a shower of sweat, then he'd lie down, panting hard, close his eyes, feel the sun.

Then he'd figure out how to save Princess Ko.

He walked.

A sense of the familiar eased itself into the darkness around him. It was powerful, this sense. Embedded in the smells and in the closeness. He knew it absolutely, and it crouched just behind him, beside him, just ahead of him — but what?

There was a clicking sound: three rapid clicks, a pause, two short clicks. A rustling. Multiple, tiny, ripping sounds like fabric tearing. Apprehension shot through his chest and guts. A quick, sharp noise like *vip*, and of course, he knew. Certainty, even as he buckled against it, refused to believe it, and before he'd even sorted out that conflict, they were at him.

He dropped the rope and tore at the blindfold, but already the claws, the fangs, the lines of fire. He got the blindfold off, and it was real, here he was. In the cavern of a third-, maybe fourth-level Gray, and the Grays were awake and attacking from every direction. They were rearing at his jawbone, striking at his ribs, digging into the small of his back, tightening around his wrists and ankles.

Chime was shouting, but he was shouting louder, and a rake ran down his arm, a barrow crushed his shoulder. An outboard motor had come loose, the rotor of a chopper, the engine of a tractor, hurling at him, cutting deep and fast and hot into his flesh. Fishing wire whipped through the air and lashed his cheeks; fish hooks pierced his thighs and shins.

"Stop moving!"

Chisels, pliers, needles, an old electric kettle with a power surge, a spray of boiling water.

"Stay still!"

He was falling from a high tree branch and skidding down a gnarled and savage trunk. The trunk was decorated. It bristled with protruding broken glass and razor blades, every piece competing for attention.

Chime's voice was its own fire.

"Stay still," she was shrieking. "If you don't stay still, they'll kill you." Her voice scaled the air, reaching ugly: "Would you *quit — fighting — them — NOW!*"

A neat, swift slice. A sword cut him in two. One half fell one way, the other fell the other.

PART 3

1.

$\mathcal{K}$eira was sitting in her apartment in Tek, Jagged Edge, plugged into the media rundown.

The Kingdom was in a frenzy over the news that Princess Ko had duped them. Keira found that sort of funny. Like: *What?! Princess Ko's been running things?!* Uh, no. She hadn't been. Neither had the *King* run things, back before he got abducted. It was always the Jagged Edge Elite: her own province in charge. Only nobody ever admitted that.

The rundown moved on to the news that Princess Ko had been arrested, along with RYA members, Samuel and Sergio, on charges of treason and fraud. Police were now seeking the other member, Keira Platter.

Huh. That was less funny.

She'd only *been* on the RYA because Princess Ko had blackmailed her. She'd never even *liked* Princess Ko. Sergio and Samuel were okay if you were in a good mood, but they drove you nuts if you were tired, say. The only one of any value was Elliot. And now he was dead.

No way was she getting thrown in prison with that lot.

She left a note for the housekeeper, dyed her hair, changed her eye color, applied self-modification makeup, printed a set of false ID papers, packed her bike, and set off.

2.

$\mathcal{S}$he didn't know where to go. Probably another Kingdom or Empire would be best — maybe she'd get herself on a ship to the Southern Climes? But she made an insane decision. Before she skipped out on her Kingdom, she would visit Elliot Baranski's hometown of Bonfire, the Farms.

It would not be remotely fun, but it was the right thing to do. She owed it to Elliot to tell his mother the truth.

So, for the first time in her life, Keira rode her bike through the Farms.

All those wasted years! she thought. And: I'm finally living the tractor-and-bake-sale dream. You think I'm ever going home? Not a chance!

Etc., etc.

But she was just being funny.

The place was her idea of hell.

Even her bike was depressed. It kept breaking down. Keira was constantly pulling over by the side of a field so she could take out her tool kit. Each time she got the bike going again, the engine seemed to wake up with a wail of despair: *Oh, come on, we're still here?! In the Farms?! When will the nightmare end?*

Then the bike would settle into a moody rhythm, riding the empty highways a while, before once again fading into listlessness and shutting down.

After three days of riding — staying in roadside inns and eating at diners — she saw signs for Sugarloaf, the closest major town to Bonfire.

So she was almost there.

She slowed right down.

The roads seemed much the same as they had in the rest of the Farms, although locals would no doubt have plenty to say about that. They'd tell her that the soil was a *slightly* paler shade of black, you see now, and just put your nose up close and give it a big old sniff? You get the teeniest tang of spearmint crossed with the weird stink of that muscle-relaxant ointment? Well, *that* is the nutrient B-17, see, whereas farther up the road, you've got your B-226. Plus, see the teeny loreal flowers that cluster around fence posts? Well, the ones hereabouts have *five* petals, not four, see, which is just exactly why my granddaughter, Mary-Ellen, wanted *local* loreals in her wedding bouquet, which was a shame because turned out her betrothed had an allergy, so his throat closed up, and who needs *that* at a wedding, not Mary-Ellen, that's for sure! She's a perfectionist, see, and this was her big day.

And so on.

Or whatever.

They'd be wrong, though, Keira thought, if they tried to tell her that "hereabouts" was different. Hereabouts was exactly the same: too much here, and too much about. Too flat, too far, too horizontal.

The road signs for Sugarloaf multiplied. They got into a state. She was Five Minutes Away from the Hot Tubs and Water Beds of the Sugarloaf Luxury Inn! What was a visit to the Farms without a tour of the Sugarloaf Cherry Orchard?! A Lifetime of Shopping Dreams awaited her at the Biggest Shopping Mall in all of the southeast region of the Farms!!!

She passed the warning tower. Looked like they'd upgraded recently. She'd seen a lot of shiny new towers the last few days: Everyone trying to keep up with the Color storms.

She was on the main street of Sugarloaf.

She was leaving Sugarloaf.

Be sure to tell your friends and Come Again!

That was it. Sugarloaf. Done.

She caught a glimpse of the Sugarloaf Mall on the outskirts of town. It was about the size of her own local nail salon.

Bonfire was only twenty minutes away. She slowed so much her bike seemed bewildered. A pickup truck overtook her. The bike growled, mortified.

Bonfire billboards were appearing. They were mild and polite, as if trying to make up for the hysteria of their loudmouth neighbor, Sugarloaf.

The Watermelon Inn offered a delicious breakfast buffet. The Bonfire Hotel, on the other hand, had cheap rates and a swimming pool with slide. Le Petit Restaurant didn't really offer anything, it seemed, apart from its name and address: Town Square.

Welcome to Bonfire!

So she'd made it. She was here.

3.

*T*he first thing Keira noticed about Bonfire was that it must have fallen victim to a recent attack of Mauve.

Every tree bent so far sideways it either touched, or almost touched, the ground. Some formed arches, swooping gracefully, whereas others just leaned, like a person reaching for a dropped coin. Branches trailed into gutters. Closer to the town center, a few trees had been propped up and tied to stakes, and then, abruptly, they were standing tall on their own again. So that must be the point where the Mauve had faded.

It was a hot, dry day, and Keira had the sense that if she herself hadn't been moving, nothing would be. The few people around leaned in doorways, or sat on benches, and stared. She'd gotten used to the staring. Her bike was loud. Her clothes were Jagged-Edgian. She was a stranger.

A couple of kids sat in the branches of a tree. They also stared. She stared back, then blinked. The kids' mouths were blood-stained. Blood dripped from their chins, ran down their hands in fine lines. Her bike swerved. There were *vampires* this far south? Awake during the *day*? Then one of them plucked something, stuck it in his mouth, and chewed.

Huh. It was some kind of berry tree. That was berry juice.

She turned a corner, still riding slowly, following signs to the Town Square, and realized she was passing the high school.

She stopped, toes to the street, and peered in through the gate. Elliot Baranski had attended that school. Somewhere in those grounds was a crack through to the World. Elliot had found it.

Opposite the high school was a Sheriff's station. *Closed* said the sign that dangled from the doorknob.

You could do that? You could close a Sheriff's station in the middle of a Saturday?

Sure you could. You could do what you wanted in the Farms.

So long as you did it in a slow, easygoing, freewheeling way, and preferably with reference to your second cousin's pumpkin scones.

At the Town Square, she found a café with tables out front and ordered coffee.

She'd been wearing earphones, and now she dropped them on the table. The music played on in her head, then dwindled.

She looked around. There was a pub with a toadstool on its swinging sign. A Candy Shoppe. And that must be the restaurant from the billboard. *Le Petit Restaurant.* As she watched, a man stepped out of its front door. He was holding a big strip of cardboard. He ripped this in two and pressed both pieces into a trash can. Closer by was a grocery store. A woman approached it. She pulled a bunch of flowers from a bucket. Water droplets scattered. A girl sitting on the fountain's edge took an orange from her bag and peeled it.

One item at a time. Man rips cardboard. Woman gets flowers. Girl peels orange. It was like they were (badly) stage-directed. Or like people around here didn't know that things could happen all at once. They hadn't heard the word *simultaneous*.

"Here, I got you an ice pack."

Keira jumped.

The woman who'd just served her coffee was holding out a small blue pack.

"I can just tell you've got a headache," she explained. "The way your shoulders are? I was going to offer this right off when you ordered, but you were listening to your ear thingies, so I thought, I'll bet she gets those ear thingies out, then I'll bring her this, and that's just how it all played out, so here, see?" The woman pressed the ice pack against the back of Keira's neck.

Keira gasped.

"Good, eh? I know. This heat today! That's why you've got the headache, see? You just hold it there. Like so. You got it?"

Obediently, Keira held the ice pack to her neck. The shock of the cold had given her an instant headache, across her brow. She held the pack for a long, polite moment, then pulled it away.

"Thanks," she said.

The waitress smiled. "I take it you're just passing through?"

"Actually. I'm here to see someone. Can you tell me how I'd get to the Baranski farm?"

"Well, that's out on Acres Road. Don't tell me you know Petra Baranski? That poor woman. What she's been through! You know, the more I look at you, the more familiar you seem? I guess that can happen, faces being what they are, but have you maybe visited before?"

Keira spoke into her hand, elbow on the table, trying for nonchalant. "No," she said. "But this seems like a really sweet little town."

The waitress sighed, happy, gazing at the square. "Isn't it just?"

Across the way, an older woman sat sewing on the porch of a spearmint green house. She set down the sewing, picked up a jug, and poured herself a glass of lemonade.

There it was again. Pouring lemonade was a poem in three lines:

Set down sewing.

Lift up jug.

Pour.

In Jagged Edge, that would have happened in one slick smooth fast move. Not even time for commas.

Also, it would not have been lemonade.

"You said the Baranski farm is on Acres Road?"

"Exactly."

There was a beat.

"Well," Keira continued slowly. "I don't know where that is. I'm not from around here."

"Of course you're not!" the waitress agreed. "Here, let me draw you a map on the back of this napkin."

Out in the square, the clock in the tower struck twelve, each chime waiting patiently until the one in front had stopped.

4.

$\mathcal{T}$wenty minutes later, Keira stood in the driveway of the Baranski farmhouse and stared at the windows.

There was a party going on in there.

So, that was confusing.

One sad woman was what she'd expected. Instead, there was a crowd and it seemed not to have heard about the Farms rule of one thing at a time. There was chatting, shouting, laughing, music, passing of plates-glasses-trays, gesticulating, whistles, back slapping, and all of it crisscrossed and colliding.

Keira stood by her bike.

Maybe the loss had sent them crazy? Could this be Elliot's friends and family engaged in some kind of mob-hysterical grief?

Suddenly she realized what it was.

The wake.

Of *course* that's what it was. He'd been killed a couple of weeks ago, but then there'd been the efforts to retrieve his body from the ravine. Even once they'd realized no equipment could get down there, the authorities would have stayed in town, asking questions.

Things must have finally settled down enough for formal rituals. And *she* was here? Crashing the *wake*?

She had to get away, fast, before somebody saw her.

Right at that moment, somebody saw her.

A teenage girl with a broad face and braid glanced toward the window and pointed. Another girl joined the first. They both stared out at Keira.

Now Keira had no choice.

She approached the porch. The girls, she saw, were moving along the window, heading toward the front door.

They met her there.

The girl with the braid had tattoos on her neck. One was a skull and crossbones, the other a reindeer. These seemed inconsistent. For a moment, Keira's eyes were trapped by the inconsistency. She looked from one tattoo to the other until the girl tilted her chin making the reindeer disappear.

The other girl spoke. "Yeah?"

This second girl had short hair that was so blond-white it was worse than the sun. Keira sheltered her eyes with a hand. "I came to see Petra Baranski," she explained. "But that's okay. I'll come back later."

The first girl stared. "Why would you come back later? You're here now."

"Yeah. Makes no sense," the other girl agreed.

There was a long pause.

"Ahoy there, sailor," the tattooed girl remarked eventually.

Keira panicked. What did *sailors* have to do with anything? Then she remembered that her hand was at her forehead, like someone on the deck of a ship. She dropped it.

The two girls seemed to take that as a signal. They turned and headed back into the house.

"What are you waiting for?" the blonde asked, without looking back. There didn't seem any options. Keira followed.

She'd pretend to be somebody else, she decided. Some kind of salesperson. What would a Farmer want to buy? Well, something for the crops obviously, so what did *crops* need?

Here was the party. It was smaller than it had looked from outside.

Maybe eight or nine people altogether. They must have doubled themselves somehow, by being so *lively*.

Not so much now. They were all silent, staring at her. The only movement was from a few sets of jaws, chewing. A man in a Sheriff's uniform, a badge hanging crooked from his shirt, raised a pastry to his mouth and took a bite. So, now more jaws chewing.

Keira was trying to remember what exactly crops were. Well, she knew they grew in fields, and then people picked them or whatever, and eventually they turned into food. But what, in their essence, *were* they? Once she had a handle on that, she could figure out what crops might need.

And offer it at bargain-basement prices.

The two girls flanked her. They were smirking vaguely, like a pair of cats that have dragged in a mouse, knowing the owner won't want it in the living room, but pretending to be proud anyway.

"She was at the front door," the tattooed girl announced.

"Yeah," the other added. "This is —" She raised her eyebrows at Keira.

The room waited.

Crops grew in the earth, so they must be *plants*, Keira reasoned urgently. There was a plant in a pot in her apartment at home. What it had needed was water. That's why it was dead.

"Watering cans," she said aloud.

The jaws stopped chewing.

"That's quite a name," offered a man in a suit.

"I know who she is," said a voice. It was a mild voice; it had a young, harmless sound, which somehow made its words more chilling.

Take it easy, Keira told herself. There's no way he knows who I am. Wherever he is. Where was he?

"You're Keira," the voice added. "Keira Platter."

A boy about her own age stepped forward. He'd been hidden by another guy, who was stupidly tall. The one speaking was stupidly short. His hair looked like an electrical-wire disaster, and his face was wrong. It was sort of dusting away in chunks and flakes. A disease. That was something. Maybe the disease would kill him.

"You mean the girl from the Royal Youth Alliance?" someone else was saying. "Nah, this one's got a sort of longer face than her. And different hair."

"She's disguised."

Now everyone was peering at Keira, arguing among themselves, making observations about her nose, her shoulders, and the way she held her elbows at a sort of a crazy angle like someone about to swing a tennis racquet. (She dropped her arms, and the person speaking said, "Oh. Huh. Well, not so much now.") When the tattooed girl got down on her hands and knees to investigate Keira's ankles, muttering something about cows, Keira had had enough.

"Okay," she said. "You got me."

It took a while for everyone to be convinced. They'd been enjoying the argument, it seemed. Eventually someone pointed out that it would be strange to pretend to be Keira if you were not Keira, what with everyone being *after* Keira, and wanting to *arrest* her, and then the room was staring, silent, again.

"You were in the paper today," the blond girl told her. "You're missing."

"No she's not," said the other girl. "She's right here. Look."

Everyone laughed.

In Jagged Edge, there was a hologrammatic game kids played, where you had to maneuver out of a labyrinth before the monsters got you. Once, when she was very young, Keira had gotten trapped. She'd run the same loop for hours, swerving and ducking monsters, until she collapsed in a dehydrated fever. Afterward, her mother asked why she hadn't just switched off the game.

Well, here she was in a loop full of monsters again.

This time she'd beat the game. She'd deliver her "truth," get on her bike, and disappear.

She looked around at the faces, sorting them. There were the two girls from the front door, the short boy with the face falling to pieces, and the boy so tall he was more an object. One of those long, thin objects, like brooms or rakes. There was the Sheriff, another guy in uniform (deputy?), and two guys in suits. A middle-aged woman stood near the side table, holding a pair of tongs. So she was the only possibility.

That must be Elliot's mother.

"Are you Petra Baranski?" Keira asked.

The woman nodded once. Keira breathed out. She straightened her shoulders. She'd taken control of the game. Just follow this path, one step at a time.

"Could I speak with you for a moment," she asked, "in private?"

Now Petra used an edge of the tongs to scratch her own cheek. She pulled it away, leaving a red mark. "Well, what can we do for you, Keira?" she said, and Keira's chest tightened again. It was the tong-scratching thing really. Why not use your own fingernails?

Abruptly, Petra smiled. "Come on through," she said, stepping across the room, people parting before her. "We can talk a little. You want a cold lemonade and a slice of pie while we do?"

Keira shook her head. Petra led her into an adjoining room. She slid the doors closed, and sat down in an armchair.

The doors were frosted glass. Through them, Keira could see the outlines of the others. They were holding their positions like a shadow painting.

"What the heck's *that* about?" said the tattooed girl's voice, as clearly as if she'd been standing beside her. "Why's *she* here?" Several others hushed her. There were muffled giggles, then silence again.

They were going to hear every word.

Well, this was surreal, but she'd just have to go ahead. She shuffled her thoughts.

"First, I want to say how sorry I am about Elliot," she began. "He was a friend. I cared about him. I'm so sorry."

Elliot's mother blinked.

"Thank you," she said after a moment.

"But I came here to tell you something I told Elliot the day that he died. I think you deserve to know it too. It's about Elliot's dad."

"Elliot's *dad*?" Petra's voice was like a pounce. From behind the door, someone whispered, "What did she say?" and someone else responded, "She wants to talk about Abel," and then, "I know, but what did *Petra* say?" and "She didn't say anything, she just kind of exclaimed."

"This is difficult to talk about," Keira said, with a meaningful glance at the sliding doors, but Petra remained where she was and the chorus next door started up again: "She said it's difficult to talk about," "Well, why's she talking about it, then?" "Shut up, I can't hear what Petra said," "I don't think she's answered yet," and so on.

"What do you know about Abel?" Petra said.

"I know he's been missing for a long time," Keira said.

The room next door was utterly silent.

"I know his brother was killed the night he disappeared."

More silence.

"And I know . . . I'm sorry, but I know that Abel was also killed that night."

Petra's voice was as careful as bare feet negotiating broken glass. "How do you know this, Keira?"

Nothing was funny now.

"My mother is a Hostile. She's the person who killed them."

The silence through the door drew itself in like a mighty breath and burst forth in a muffled outcry.

Petra stayed quiet.

The sliding doors were thrown open. Faces pressed in on them.

"You should tell her." The tattooed girl was speaking. She narrowed her eyes at Keira.

"Cut it out, Shelby," several voices said in several different ways.

"No." Shelby shook her head hard. She threw a sneer at Keira. "I want her to know. She's on the run anyway, so who's she going to tell? Aside from other fugitives or whatever, and then who are *they* going to tell?"

Other voices spoke in a clamor. "You make no sense."

"Would you quit talking, Shelby?"

"She's a *Hostile*."

"No I'm not." Keira half stood. "My mother's a Hostile, but I'm me. She's in prison now." She turned back to Petra. "I'm so sorry. I'll get out of here."

She took a step away, but Petra reached up, touching her wrist.

"Wait a moment," she said in a voice that was sad, but that also held another, unexpected note. Was she *amused*? "I think that we should tell you."

"Ha!" shouted the tattooed girl, and again she was ordered to hush.

5.

*T*hey made a festival of "telling her."

Keira was unbelievably tired. Now that she'd done her own telling, all she wanted to do was get out of the Kingdom. Or lie down. It was midday too, which was the time each day when her adjustment to day dwelling faltered.

But they were all wanting promises of silence from her (sure, why not?), and explanations for what she planned to do next (none of their business?) and people kept bringing out more food from the kitchen, and eating it, as if "telling her" was hungry work.

At last, Petra spoke. Her voice was low and even.

"Elliot's alive," she said. "So is his dad."

Keira studied her. She gazed around the room, pausing on every face.

Oh, come *on*. She bit her lower lip hard, to stop herself from sighing. Now she had to deal with this? She got it, sure. Neither Elliot's nor Abel's bodies had ever been recovered, so denial was their go-to coping mechanism. But *all* of them? Couldn't some of them have turned to drugs or sex? Or obsessive viewing of old home movies of Elliot and Abel? Just to mix things up a little?

"They're in the World," Petra added.

Well, that was an inspired twist, anyway.

Now the others joined in, talking at once, telling Keira a story about how, when Elliot fell into the ravine, he actually fell through a *crack* into the World, and how Abel had fallen through the exact same crack way back, and now they were happy and safe in the World.

Ingenious.

"And you know this how?" Keira asked carefully, once they'd stopped talking and had settled down to eating again.

"A letter. You know there's a crack in the high-school grounds here?"

Keira nodded.

"A letter came through it."

"But the WSU would have sealed up that crack when they came for Elliot," Keira explained gently. She should probably take care not to shatter their delusions too fast.

"Someone show her the letter," the blond girl said. "It got through just in time," she told Keira. "A day later the WSU came through with detectors and sealed the crack."

A folded paper was handed to Keira.

The Sheriff spoke. "As a matter of fact, we're all here today figuring how to get our boys home. The crack being sealed and all, we'll need a detector, so as to *find* it, and then we'll have to figure how to *open* it. Might seem impossible, but we're not the quitting types."

"Not impossible." Keira unfolded the letter. "I can see cracks. I can unseal them."

Here was the silence again, but Keira was reading. The letter was straightforward. It said all the things they'd just told her. She frowned.

"This was written by Elliot's dad?" she said to Petra. "I mean, you recognize the handwriting?"

"You bet," Petra said, "but did you just say you can *see* cracks and *unseal* them? You're surely kidding us?"

Keira didn't answer. She was rereading the letter. Something weird was happening. Warmth in her shoulder blades. Her heartbeat so loud it felt visible. She grasped her left wrist with her right hand, then dug in her fingernails.

You don't cure people's delusions by buying into them.

But she was searing with hope. Elliot could be alive? Elliot's *father* too?

The others were arguing about whether it was possible to see cracks or not. Keira looked up.

"For most people it's not," she said. "But Night-Dwellers have great vision, right? So, mine was in the top percentile, then Princess Ko had me doing exercises to refine it. They worked. That's how we found the cracks and unsealed them to start getting the royals back."

There was an outburst from Petra. "But if you can do that, we can get through to Abel and Elliot! We can bring them home!"

Keira tried to lift her voice above the turmoil. "I can open the schoolyard crack for you," she agreed, "but you can only use it to send letters, not get them back across. It's too small for people. Still . . ." She was trying to think. "Still, we could get a message to them, to come to one of the people-moving cracks. If we could deal with the guards somehow, and figure out how to keep Elliot safe . . ."

The noise level in the room was almost Jagged-Edgian.

This was insane. It couldn't be true.

But she'd gotten herself deep inside the labyrinth now, and no way she was switching off the power. She had to play along: What if it were true?

That tall boy was moving close to her. He's like a thin tree without leaves, she decided. A Mauve attack would bend him to the ground. He'd need to be propped up with a stake.

She was finding herself funny again.

The tall boy was speaking. "You're a motocross champion," he said. "I read that somewhere." He pointed to the window and to Keira's motorbike outside. "That's why the bike."

They both looked out at her bike, and tree boy spoke again. "I'm thinking this news is cause for celebration." His voice was slow and reasonable. "And what I'm thinking is, the best way to do that celebrating is let me take a spin on that there bike."

Keira laughed. "Not a chance," she said. A Farms boy on her bike. Now that was funny.

6.

*M*uch later, after hours of talking and planning, they settled on the message they would send. It was straightforward: *This is a message for Madeleine Tully. Are Abel and Elliot Baranski there with you? If so, we want to bring them back to Cello. Meet us here Monday, midnight, to discuss. Keira.*

The Sheriff drove Keira to Bonfire High School. It was past midnight, and the air was warm and still. It took her a few minutes to find the crack, then another quarter hour to unravel it — it had been tightly knotted by the WSU. She posted the message.

The Sheriff remained silent beside her the whole time, only yawning now and then, and adjusting the angle of the flashlight when she asked him. Now he stared at the air where the notepaper had just disappeared. "Done?" he said. She nodded. Abruptly, he spun around and headed for his car. She walked behind him. Must be annoyed with her for taking so long, she guessed. Well, it was a high-risk thing, communicating with the World, especially for a Sheriff.

He got into the driver's seat, waited while she pulled her passenger door shut, then he broke into a low stream of curse words. So she was right. The cursing went on a while. She waited. Then he swung a giant smile her way and, "Holy *heck*," he said. "You could *see* that crack? You unraveled that crack? You sent a message to the *World*! To Abel and Elliot? You're better than a maple-candy chocolate cheesecake with a cherry-walnut strudel for dessert!" He turned the keys in the ignition. "Apologies for the language just now," he added, "but you being from Jagged Edge, I reckon you've heard plenty worse."

Keira thought about it. "True," she said.

A couple of days later, she went back to the schoolyard with the Sheriff, and had a conversation with Madeleine. The girl was infuriating. But they set up the transfer and, two days later, she helped to bring Abel and Elliot back home from the World.

7.

*K*eira took a deep breath of the night. It wound itself around her like a slinking cat.

It was past midnight, and the others were still partying in there. Someone had said mint should be added to a particular cocktail, and someone else had said, well, just scoot on out and get some, which Keira had found weird. Downtown was a twenty-minute drive from the farmhouse, not exactly a *scoot*, and what, the grocery store would still be open at this hour? In *this* province?

Turned out that mint could grow in gardens. Who knew? Well,

she must have known. In some part of her mind, she'd probably known, only she'd never had reason to visit that part.

She herself had offered to pick the mint. As soon as she'd stepped onto the porch, she'd remembered she had no clue how you "picked." Well, other than in the sense of choosing. She was fine with that. But what did mint look like in person? She'd only ever had it as a flavor, which was more like correspondence with mint. Ha-ha. So would it grow on a tree or bush or *vine*, or what? Then, if she did find it, how much did she take, like, all of it or what? Would she *damage* the *entire* farm somehow if she "picked" the mint in the wrong way? And so on with the questions.

She was thwarted.

So she stood on the porch and breathed in the night. Heck, that feels good, she thought, speaking Farms because, sure as hokey-pokey, did it ever. Feel good. The rich black curve of night, the wicked glow of moon and stars. The menace. She closed her eyes and heard darting rattles, distant snaps, a low buzz. It wasn't home, there was no music (no proper music anyway), no stadiums or dance arcades or traffic, but, in its soul, this was the night.

She'd been in Bonfire a week now, hiding out in the Baranski farmhouse. So she'd sorted out the people. That group she'd encountered her first day. They'd been getting together to "plan" all week, and tonight they were here to celebrate.

Five adults, four teenagers.

She ran through the adults.

The Sheriff. He did a lot of talking.

The Deputy. A younger guy, named Jimmy. He hardly spoke at all.

Two men in suits. They were a surprise. CI agents named Tovey and Kim. They'd sort of slipped out of their official posts: gone *renegade*, they liked to say. It made them chuckle. They were from Jagged Edge, so she felt drawn to them, and they often smiled her way as if they felt it too. A sort of Edgian secret connection. Agent Kim was always sketching in a notebook.

And finally, Elliot's mother. Petra. She seemed to spend her time out at the greenhouse or "heading out" in a truck, going who-knows-where. Something to do with "farming," no doubt. When Petra was at home, she was friendly with Keira, although mostly her friendliness took the form of asking Keira to help her "string beans."

Then there were the teenagers. They were trickier.

The girl with the braid and tattoos was Shelby. As far as Keira could tell, Shelby was all about muscle. And she had this unnerving habit of staring hard at Keira, suddenly throwing her a sneer like a high-speed dodgeball, then reverting to the long, blank stare.

The blonde was Nikki. She was strong too, but her features were finer. Her skin was perfect and, as far as Keira could tell, that was *real*. Like, no makeup. Unless she excelled at application.

Nikki didn't stare or sneer. She ignored Keira absolutely, as if she'd forgotten her existence.

The tall boy was Gabe. When you squinted way up into the distance you could see his face, and then you noticed that his ears stuck out and his nose was too long. So you looked back down.

The short boy with the mad curls was Cody. Turned out she'd been wrong about his facial disease. He was an "artist," apparently, and liked to work with various media. Plaster, gel, and glue were always stuck in clumps to his hair and skin. When he remembered to wash, his face was fine.

The two boys didn't take much notice of Keira, although they were polite. They offered her drinks and passed her cakes and pastries. It was more a theoretical polite.

That was it. Those were her "buddies" in Bonfire.

Except that now there was an extra.

Keira rested her elbows on the porch railings, opened her eyes, then closed them again, letting in more of the night.

The extra was Abel Baranski.

Elliot was in hiding with a Hostile branch, but Abel was here, in this very house. He was smaller and more bedraggled than she'd expected, but alive, and that felt so good she kept reaching for it, like reaching for a glass of liqueur. *Elliot's father is alive. My mother never killed him.* It rushed through her, intoxicating.

The glass would empty soon, she knew that. She'd grow indifferent to the fact. She'd remember that her mother had killed plenty of other people. Including Abel's own brother, actually. She'd remember that her mother was in prison, and that she herself was "wanted," friendless, no place to go.

But for now, those were some sweet sips of relief.

The front door opened. A figure moved right by her. She opened her eyes. It was the tall one. Gabe. He ran down the steps. She watched him bend, pluck at something, then stand again, his hands filled with green leaves. Unsettling. Tree boy gathers leaves. He paused in the darkness down there. "Abel wants everyone to come inside so we can talk about what to do next," he said.

He was looking right at her, glint of eyes.

"Okay."

Now he ran up the stairs — or stepped, it was just his leg span made it seem like a run — and into the house. The door swung closed. A scent spilled from behind him.

Ah, so that was mint.

8.

*T*hree days later, nine A.M., Keira walked through the gates of Bonfire High School.

She was dressed in Farms jeans and plaid shirt.

She had enrolled in the school for a term. Her name was Sophy Epstein. She was a cousin of the tall boy, Gabe. She was staying on his farm.

So all of *that* was unexpected.

The plan had been made at the party, after she came in from the porch. The gang would hide Keira in plain sight; in return, she'd make sure that Elliot stayed safe with her Hostile friends. There was talk about why she couldn't just hide with the Hostiles herself, but she said, "If I did, they'd expect me to do Hostile work for them."

Meantime, Abel and the other adults would figure out how both Keira and Elliot could live freely. The adults were hazy about this, but also wildly optimistic — which might have been the cocktails they were drinking. Or the mint. Hallucinogenic properties, Keira guessed, when used direct from the soil like that. It surely wasn't healthy.

Gabe had been chosen as Keira's "cousin" because his parents were away, and because everyone knew that, a generation back, a branch of his family had moved to Jagged Edge.

"People like to say they went to seed out there," Shelby had informed Keira. "So you'll confirm it for them. They'll like that. People like to be proved right."

Well, in Keira's view, the entire plan was flimsy as a hologram, and she still couldn't figure out how they'd persuaded her that this was better than finding herself a new Kingdom — but she wasn't keen on being proved right.

Now she walked beside Gabe into the school and felt small. That was his fault. Being so tall. She tried to straighten her back and walk on the tips of her toes. She knew he was just strolling, but those long legs of his, she had to run a few steps now and then to keep up.

She'd never been to a school in her life — they used home-based education modules and virtual classrooms in JE — but she'd seen schools in films. It was surreal how accurate those films had been. She'd always thought there must be an element of parody, but no, here were the kids, swarming through the gates, calling to one another, laughing, and shoving one another; some hunched alone, some hoisting musical instruments, a couple making out, a teacher snapping fingers at the couple so they drew apart and giggled. And so on.

A bell rang.

Keira froze, trying to sort out the code. But there wasn't one. It was just a long, shrill line. And it was coming from somewhere nearby, not from the warning towers.

"School bell," Gabe told her.

So those were real too. Unbelievable.

She shifted the backpack. Gabe had found this for her. It was a soft corduroy material, midnight blue. "That's my favorite color," Keira had said when he pulled it down. He'd glanced at her and away again. Then he'd run downstairs and packed the bag with a ring binder of paper, a zip-up case of pens, and a wrapped sandwich, which he'd cut into two triangles.

"The office is over there." Gabe pointed. "Tell them your name, and they'll give you your homeroom."

"My what?"

But he was turning away. Out of the crowd, a group was emerging and drifting toward them. Shelby, Nikki, and Cody.

"Hiya, Sophy," said Shelby.

"Hey, Soph. Hey, Gabe."

"Sophy. How's things? Got your schedule yet? You chosen your electives?"

Other kids passed, staring. "Who's *that*?" she heard someone ask, and then, "I think it's Gabe Epstein's cousin. She's Edgian, I heard." "Wild."

Shelby punched Keira's arm and wished her luck. Cody told her she should ask for a locker on the second floor 'cause they closed with a more satisfying click. He demonstrated the sound, tongue against his teeth. Nikki and Gabe pointed to the place where she should meet them at lunch. Then they were moving away.

"Catch ya later, Soph."

"See you, Soph."

"Bye, Soph. Good luck today." And so on.

By midday, Keira's wrist was aching, and she had to actually slap her own face to stay awake. It had stopped being funny again. *These people wrote things out by hand.* She'd thought the papers in the ring binder were meant for an origami class or something, and the pens for art, but no! Turned out that in every single class a teacher stood at the front of the room and said, "Write this down."

"Why?" she asked the first time it happened, and people snickered and twisted in their completely-ergonomically-unsound chairs to look at her.

The teacher pretended not to hear.

But seriously, why? Didn't they have this on data file somewhere?

She'd been about to pursue her line of questioning, when the teacher started talking. Then, as the talking continued, a terrible suspicion came over Keira. As far as school went, this was it.

A teacher talking.

That guy up there, all by himself? He was going to talk at them in that *deep, slow* voice, without even basic laser technology. No soundtrack. Not a single virtual representation.

How was anybody supposed to *see* what he was saying? Let alone stay awake? His words kept sitting on her eyelids.

As the day went on, it kept happening. The only variation was the method of monotony chosen by each teacher — high-pitched voice with regular upward sweeps in intonation; long, unendurable pauses midway through sentences; repetition of particular, inane phrases ("which is *why* . . ."; "as to which, see . . ."; "I'm *waiting*. . . ."). Some of the other kids yawned, she noticed, their heads sort of sprawled onto the desks, and a couple of times she saw people quietly napping. And they weren't even Night-Dwellers like her.

Mathematics seemed okay at first because they were allowed to solve problems themselves, from a book. But when she asked if she could borrow an algorithmic machine, people turned and stared. Some even winced, like her weirdness was hurting their faces.

They didn't *have* algorithmic machines. They used *paper* and *pens* and their *brains!* to solve these problems. The teacher seemed triumphant about this, which was truly mystifying. Not ashamed, but *proud.*

At lunchtime she sat in the school grounds with Gabe, Shelby, Nikki, and Cody. They all did their "Hey, Soph!" "Soph, how's the day going?" thing, which was already beginning to feel like a shell being constructed around her. She wanted to punch it open.

She tried to make things real by saying, "Is it just me or is this system inefficient? I mean, are the teachers seriously reciting the same facts, over and over, to different classes?"

The others widened their smiles and said, "You bet, Soph. Hey, want to come out to the dam at Sugarloaf later?" while their eyes slid toward one another, smirks around their mouths.

So she stopped talking and ate the sandwich Gabe had made for her. It was good. Fresh bread. Butter that tasted sort of bright. And some kind of fruit jam with little bits inside it that burst open and shot flavor.

The last class of the day was Computing Studies. It was held in a small, dark room that was labeled *Computing Machine Room*. That was funny to her. The idea that CMs needed their own room. Sort of like labeling a room *Electric Lightbulb Room* and then closeting all your electric lights inside it. Instead of hanging them up around the buildings where they might, I don't know, come in handy?

Shelby and Nikki were both in this class, and Keira was smiling at her thought when she saw them. "What?" they said, smiling back. "What, Sophy?" but she shook her head. They wouldn't get it. They were probably all in favor of locking away those three, boxy old Roxburgh Computing models that were lined up at the front of this classroom.

Everyone sat, and the teacher, an old guy wearing a loose tie, sat at one of the CMs. He half turned to the class, hands on the keyboard. So he was going to demonstrate, Keira guessed. Well, at least there'd be something to *look* at while he talked. Something other than facial tics and bad fashion choices.

The old guy was typing.

Keira watched the screen.

He typed a while, then stopped. He swiveled so he was facing the machine squarely. He typed again. He curled his hand into a fist and tapped his mouth, frowning. He switched off the machine, waited while it powered down, then started it up again. He frowned and pushed his chair along (with a shriek of floorboards) to the next machine. He went through the same process. Same with the third.

At last he turned to the class.

"People," he said, "I'm afraid we have a problem with the machines." He glanced toward the window at the back of the room. "Why not have us a breather? Looking mighty sunny out there."

There was a great slide of chairs moving backward and people standing.

"You're kidding, right?" Keira said. Her eyes ran down the lines of print on the three screens.

"Excuse me?"

"It's just the Straw-Hat virus."

"The what?" The teacher peered at her. "Not sure I know you. You sitting in today?"

"I'm Sophy. I'm new," she said. "You know that your machines have the Straw-Hat virus, right? It's common on the old Roxburgh models. You just need to use the Carlisle fix."

She felt the room still around her, and felt herself blushing. Maybe she was missing something here. Like this was a trick way he started every class, and there was some procedure they were supposed to follow next.

"Now, what language do you speak where you're from, Sophy?" the teacher joked. "The Carlisle fix, what?"

There were one or two obliging laughs, but otherwise the room stayed quiet.

Keira moved to the first computing machine. She put her fingers on the keyboard, and let them fly. A few seconds later, she sat back.

"There," she said. "Fixed."

She moved to the other machines and did the same.

"Well, what do you know!" the teacher exclaimed, studying each machine. "You went ahead and fixed them! Looks like we've got a class after all! Go ahead and sit down, guys!"

She felt a glow for just a moment — the beauty of computing machines, the pleasure of fixing a simple glitch, the old guy's smile — and then she turned and the glow snapped out. Every face was scowling.

She was an idiot. They'd *wanted* to go out in the sun. (Day-Dwellers. Of course they did.) She'd just killed a break for them.

Then the nice old guy spent an hour teaching them a programming language she'd known since she was two.

Gabe drove her back to his farm at the end of the school day.

He was silent. She watched through the window.

"Seriously," she said, "do you *need* this much space to grow food?"

Gabe blinked and adjusted his hands on the steering wheel.

"I guess I do eat," Keira admitted.

There was another silence, then Keira piped up again. "I mean, you could fit my entire city in that field, right? That's probably the reason for crop failures," she went on. "Too much space. We should suggest it to the Farms Provincial Council. Try *crowding* your crops."

She looked at Gabe again. His eyes were on the road. His jaw had a sort of set look.

"I guess you guys know what you're doing. Still. Could be the crops are just lonely and want some company?"

She was kidding. She was finding herself funny. Gabe wasn't. Unless he was laughing very deep within himself.

Ah, well. They passed a field of animals. Some kind of sheep, she thought, or goats. They were chewing and looking miserable and thin. Or did they always look like that? Maybe they'd just been *shorn*. She remembered the word "shorn" just as she reached it in the sentence. She thought about telling Gabe that, but changed her mind.

He turned into his driveway sharply, and they hit a rut. Her head bounced against the window. Ow, she thought.

That night, a Dark Gray thundered into town, and Keira huddled in bed while it pounded on the security shutters, shaking the windows in their frames. It swept around the farmhouse all night, so that sometimes the hammering dimmed and she drifted to sleep, but then she would wake with a start to find it back outside her room, pummeling so hard that her bed rattled. In the distance, she could hear glass shattering, animals shrieking, and once, the voice of a farmhand yelling abuse at the Gray from inside the barn. The Gray retaliated with a series of mighty thuds against the barn roof, and the farmhand's voice fell silent. In the morning, she and Gabe walked outside to survey the damage, which was not nearly so bad as she'd expected in the night.

*O*ver the next few weeks, Keira began to see how you dealt with school. You powered yourself down to a point of semiconsciousness. That's why the kids had half-closed eyes, she realized. You draped yourself over the furniture. You sketched humorous doodles in the margins of your notes and angled these toward your classmates, who rewarded you with crooked smiles. And when a teacher made a properly funny joke, or shared some anecdote about how their car broke down on the way to school that morning? You felt a jolt of pleasure. This sparked you up for a bit, then you dwindled again.

There was so much the movies didn't teach about school.

Still, it was okay sometimes. Brainstorming where everyone shouts turned out to be more fun and *strident* than virtual brainstorming. The History teacher, Mr. Guthrie, was good. She started to look forward to his classes. His voice played games with itself, slinking so low that it was almost out of sight, then leaping out with a boom, say. Also, it made stories out of facts. Keira found that if she closed her eyes, she could sometimes see pictures of his words inside her head.

Still, she was skeptical. It was all relative.

At lunchtimes, she sat with Gabe and his friends. They said "Soph!" a lot, and otherwise talked among themselves. She spent her time staring at the crack through to the World. There it was, a strand of light, hovering at waist-height in the middle of the schoolyard, and she was the only one who saw it. Kids would brush right past it, or through it even, without noticing. It would tremble or sway at their touch, then right itself again.

It was tightly knotted — she'd done that after they'd gotten the Baranskis back, so that the Girl-in-the-World wouldn't send something through and expose them. (You couldn't trust that Madeleine. She'd seemed weirdly *invested* in the whole thing. As if it had anything to do with her.) But any time she wanted, she, Keira, could unknot the crack and send words to the World. Staring at the tangled light each day was comforting.

She still hadn't figured out how you coped with a town like Bonfire. Its key problem, as far as she could see — well, its key problem was that it was in the Farms, and the best way to solve that would be to roll up the entire province and stow it in somebody's hall closet — but anyway, its *other* key problem was the people. There were too few of them. So the same people kept showing up everywhere. It was like a comedian had written three jokes and kept running through them on a loop.

She'd go to the Town Square with Gabe and the others and sit at a table at the Bakery Café, and she'd think: Why? Why are we here? There is *nothing new to see.*

Another thing she'd noticed was that all you had to do was agree with a stranger that yep, it sure was humid today, to become lifelong buddies. The girl who worked here at the Bakery Café was practically Keira's *soul mate* on account of that moment with the ice pack for the headache that Keira never actually had.

"Hey there, you! Why didn't you *tell* me you were Gabe's cousin?" the girl had pounced, seeing Keira on the street one day, early on. "Ah, I should've guessed anyhow. You and Gabe both have those great cheekbones! Sort of sharpish? Of course you're part of the family!"

That had not endeared her to Keira. Also, it underlined how poor the Farmers' eyesight was: Gabe's cheekbones were nothing like her own.

10.

$\mathcal{A}$fter weeks of summer, winter blew in one Saturday, and Keira woke to a window spangled with frost. Outside, rain fell steadily, and trees showered and drooped. Gabe was knocking on her bedroom door, calling her name. Before she'd replied, he threw the door open, tossed her coat onto the bed, and asked if she could give him a hand.

"You reckon you can drive a tractor?" he said once they were outside, huddled under coat hoods, rain hitting their faces and hands.

"Sure," she said, then shrugged. "I think."

Who knew, to be honest, but she hadn't ridden her bike since she got here — they'd locked it in a barn where it wouldn't attract attention — and the idea of turning an ignition, the roar of an engine, the shifting of gears, was blissful.

It turned out he wanted her to hook up a trailer to a tractor, and drive it across a field or something.

"Take this route," he said, pointing. "I'll meet you there," and he set off at a half run. Rain splattered behind him.

She hooked up the trailer. Her hands were purple with cold. She climbed up in the tractor, started it, and drove.

No problem. Easy. And, ah, it was good. Rumbling along. Sure, it was slow, but this was machinery and she was in control.

Gabe was in the distance, crouched down, close to a fence. She followed the route he'd suggested for a moment, then reconsidered. It made no sense to track along the outside like that. He must have been distracted by the rain and the rush.

She cut across the field instead, moving at a good, steady pace.

Halfway across, she was suddenly moving at no pace at all.

The wheels spun, mud splattered. There was a curious tipping sensation, and she realized that the right side of the tractor was slowly sinking. Everything tilted. She leaned against the tilt in a panic, but the tractor ignored her. A moment later, like it wanted to make its own decisions, it stopped sinking and held. She half stood and gazed around her. The tractor was wedged at a hilarious angle.

She looked across to where Gabe was, saw him stand, scratch the back of his neck, and look down the field toward where she should be. She saw him turning slowly. She saw him see her.

Even from this distance, she could see the amazement in his eyes. Then, there it was again: the habitual resignation, the firm set to his jaw.

It took them almost an hour to get the tractor out of the mud.

Gabe did not speak except to call instructions in his low, reasonable voice. Then he finished the work himself while she stood in the rain and watched. Back inside, they hung their coats, raindrops splattering. He handed her a towel and took one for himself. They went into the kitchen, towels still around their necks, and Gabe got out a frying pan. Keira made coffee.

The room crackled with their silence. It seemed to shout with every crack of egg into the pan.

But he kept right on frying eggs and bacon, slicing tomato and mushrooms, moving around her politely, not saying a word.

He was still wet from the rain. Drops of water slipped from his ears.

Those ears, Keira thought. Why would he wear his hair so short with ears like that?

In Jagged Edge, they'd have fixed them by now. An afternoon procedure.

Not that they'd been able to fix Keira's acne, of course. She'd had five procedures and tried seven different courses of drug treatment, but it kept right on breaking out. She touched it now. She hadn't had time to apply her concealer, and her fingers ran across the welts and bumps.

"Try merrylroot tea," Gabe said.

Keira's hands fell from her face.

"What?"

"Merrylroot. They grow it on Nikki's farm. Might clear up your skin." He shrugged. "Might not."

Her face burned and sizzled like bacon fat.

So that's how you're going to play it, she thought.

Later that day, Gabe drove her into town to meet the others in the Town Square.

"Soph!" they all agreed, as usual.

Then they settled down to their coffees and their Farms talk. Nikki was upset — something to do with a necklace her dad had given her for a birthday. She was sure she'd worn it when she took the harvester out that morning, but now it was gone. She kept feeling her neck for it. Keira asked what the necklace looked like, but Nikki ignored her. After a moment, she turned toward Keira and said, "I know, Soph! Right!" and then returned her attention to the others.

Everyone told Nikki it was sure to be in the harvester. Just check when you get home. Cody was excited because some fancy new oil paints had arrived. He said he'd paint Nikki's necklace back into being, that's how good these paints were. Shelby said she felt like blowing something up today, and she'd be happy to blow up the harvester for Nikki. The necklace will sail into the air, she said, above the other shrapnel, and then Shelby would fly her crop duster over the wreckage, and catch it. Elaborate, she admitted, but effective.

Keira looked at Gabe. He was silent.

She waited for him to tell about how she'd bogged the tractor and somehow connect that to Nikki's lost necklace, but Nikki herself changed the subject. "What do you think about the weather?" she said, addressing Gabe. At nearby tables, people heard the question and swung around, watching Gabe expectantly.

"Two more weeks of winter," Gabe told them all. "An afternoon of spring. Then I reckon on summer."

"Thanks," everyone said, and Gabe shrugged, "Could be wrong."

Nobody could predict the seasons in Cello. Meteorologists, sooth-sayers, psychics, magic weavers: Everyone tried, nobody succeeded. Of *course* Gabe would be wrong.

Keira gazed around the Town Square.

There they all were, the usual crowd. The only difference was they wore coats and scarves today, against the cold. The woman on the porch of the spearmint house, who sewed and drank lemonade, had a shawl around her shoulders. The waitress at Le Petit Restaurant was distributing menus to the outside tables with gloved hands.

The Sheriff and his Deputy were crossing the square. As usual, the Sheriff shot her a grin, and Jimmy, the Deputy, also smiled, but more moderately, his face resuming its melancholy expression at once.

"Why's he always so sad?" Keira asked.

The others looked toward Jimmy, then back at the table.

"Didn't used to be," Cody said eventually. "He's been like that since his girlfriend left. She was a teacher named Isabella Tamborlaine. She's the one who sold Elliot out. She told the WSU he was in contact with the World and then she took off. No one's seen her since."

"So he misses her," Keira said.

"He feels *betrayed* by her," Shelby admonished.

You can miss someone and feel betrayed by them at the same time, Keira thought, and she considered saying this, but then she felt Gabe pushing back his chair. She followed the line of his vision.

A woman and child were approaching from across the square.

New people! She'd never seen them before. The woman wore a big pouchy jacket and an orange woolen hat with a pom-pom. The child had a steady gaze and was grasping the legs of a doll that she had set onto her shoulders. The doll drooped against the girl's head.

Gabe walked away from the table, cutting the pair off in the middle of the square.

Keira watched them talk. Their voices carried. The woman was asking what Gabe thought about the weather, and Gabe was giving the same response.

At the table, the others were silent, returning to their coffee.

"Who are those two?" Keira asked.

The silence continued. Shelby ran a finger around her empty cup. Nobody looked at Keira.

"She may as well know," Shelby said, then she directed her gaze just above Keira's head. "That's Alanna Baranski and her daughter, Corrie-Lynn. Alanna runs the Watermelon Inn. Her husband was Jon Baranski. He's dead. As you know."

Keira swung her head back toward the little girl. The child had taken the doll from her shoulders and was holding it before her in the air, apparently addressing it sternly. It was a wooden puppet, Keira realized, not a doll.

That girl has no father. Keira's thoughts moved slowly and ponderously. *Because my mother betrayed him and had him killed.*

"You might not want to stare," Nikki pointed out.

Keira flinched and looked away, across the square again. *Stop thinking, stop thinking.*

She steadied herself by using her eyesight. She focused on the tiny pockmarks on the side of the fountain. A piece of paper drifting along the ground, scuffed with a muddy bootprint. *Bonfire Knitting Society Newsletter*, she read. Her eyes wandered again. There, still lying where she'd spotted it when she arrived today, was a silver necklace tangled with wet leaves.

"Does your necklace have a clasp like a T?" she asked Nikki.

"A what?"

"Is it silver? Does it have a bluey-green pendant shaped like a bean?"

"Yes," Nikki said irritably.

"It's over there," said Keira.

Everybody turned and followed the line of her pointing finger.

"Where?"

"With the leaves. See those leaves there?"

"What leaves?"

Keira sighed. Of course they couldn't see. Nobody could see what she could see.

She stood up, crossed the square the long way — following the edges — and felt the curious glances of Alanna and Corrie-Lynn Baranski, still chatting with Gabe as she walked.

"We need a Gold," the child's voice was saying. "It'll cure everything."

Gabe and the woman were laughing. "There's no such thing!"

Keira was careful not to look at them.

She picked up the necklace, carried it back, and placed it on the table beside Nikki.

"Tell Gabe I'm going for a walk," she said.

The others exclaimed about the necklace. Nikki held it cupped in both hands, grinning down at it.

They remembered themselves when she was a few steps away. "Okay, we will! Bye, Soph!" "See ya, Sophy!" "Catch ya, Soph!"

Late that night, Keira was almost asleep when she felt a twinge in her finger.

She slapped it. Insects biting.

The finger twinged again, and she sat up in bed and switched on the bedside lamp.

It was her communicator ring. Someone was trying to reach her. She touched the side of the ring.

Alongside her, a figure formed, curled strangely, folded almost, more horizontal than a figure should be.

Sergio.

Her mind was waking one step at a time.

That was Sergio. The stable boy. From the Royal Youth Alliance.

But wasn't he under house arrest somewhere? And why did he appear to be *lying in the air.*

"Keira?" he whispered. Static rushed at his word.

"Sergio," she said.

"It is beautiful," he murmured, "to see your face, but I plan to see it for a very short time so as not to endanger you."

"Thank you," Keira said vaguely. She was still trying to figure out the strange way he was holding his body. "Where *are* you?"

"I am being held captive, along with Princess Ko and Samuel, in the Cardamom Palace in Jagged Edge."

"I know," Keira said. "It's in the newspapers. Are you okay?"

Sergio shrugged. "It is late. I am sleepy. Otherwise, in fine health. I have just now flown up among the rafters. The Princess and Samuel are sleeping."

Of course. Sergio was an Occasional Pilot. He could fly when the urge hit him.

"Are the others okay?" she asked.

"They treat us well," Sergio whispered. "They are providing Samuel with medical attention, and he lives on so that everyone, they are amazed. The Princess wishes to achieve our release. She works at this like the mules of the Haighsay Desert in blanket season. But lately? I do not know. Her spirits are dimming. And you? Are you safe?"

"I'm fine," Keira agreed. "And tell the Princess it'll work out soon. The King is talking with the Elite. It's in all the papers. He'll get you guys released. The Elite have been running things behind the scenes for a long time — between them, they'll figure out a way to restore the status quo."

Sergio's eyes closed. He sighed deeply, opened his eyes, and smiled.

"Keira, this news, and you yourself, they are more beautiful than the wild white horses of the Upper Dksantians," he said. "And you would not believe their beauty. I will sleep now."

She saw him touch the side of his ring.

He was gone.

Keira stared into the space where he had been. She switched off the bedside lamp, lying back against her pillow. Something caught her eye at the window.

She got out of bed. At first, she thought it was snowing, and then she realized it was just a Silver flurry.

Silvers didn't do anything. They floated into towns, fell from the sky for a few minutes, then dissolved. But something made her hesitate by the window, press her fingertips against the glass, and stare into the night.

She thought of the outline of Sergio, suspended in the air. And what it was, to have a friend call her by name, look her in the eye, ask for her help, listen to her answer, trust her, call her beautiful. The Silver drifted like pale coins lit by moonlight, each piece falling and fading, turning, falling, fading. Without her noticing, her own tears began to fall too, as slow as the Silver, then faster. Her hand reached up and wiped each away as it passed her mouth or her chin. Eventually she caught the hand halfway to the chin and looked at it in surprise. She turned from the window, frowning, and went back to bed.

11.

A snowplow was growling at the night, maybe a block away, but this street billowed in white silence. Steam rose from the grates, and cold pressed the soles of her boots. Snowflakes, lost in thought, circled every streetlight.

Keira's backpack was heavy on her shoulder. She'd just been to the library, which stayed open until ten P.M. on Tuesdays, and, for the first time in her life, she'd "borrowed books" for an "assignment." The weight made her unexpectedly happy.

She stopped at the Bonfire High gates, which were busy collecting thin lines of snow, and peered into the schoolyard beyond. Glimpses of snow in there like secrets. She crossed the road.

The steps to the Sheriff's station were slick, so she paused on each.

Closed said the sign. Through the glass, darkness and a rectangle of light. She went in.

An open door glowed at the back of the dark station. A tap was running out there, and a sound like a teaspoon hitting metal. Must be the kitchen.

"It's like this," said a voice. "Here, take the milk. It's like, you can be lonely your entire life, without knowing it, and then you meet someone and you're not lonely anymore."

That was Jimmy speaking.

"Hello?" she called, but there was no reply. She waited, her night vision filling in the shapes: high counter, coatrack, desks, typewriters, chairs.

"No, let's use the bigger tray." The Sheriff's voice. "Okay, Jimmy, I hear you, but you're sending out another report? You reckon she's really missing and not plain up and gone?"

More clanks and shuffles from the kitchen.

Keira looked around again. The walls, she saw, were crowded: bulletin boards, framed photographs, maps of Cello. A bookcase stood alongside the kitchen door. It had an enthusiastic lean, she thought, as if it might topple forward any moment. Its top shelves were heavy with thick books, folders, stacked newspapers, and, unexpectedly, teacups.

Jimmy's voice was low now, so she almost couldn't hear it. "Don't you think it's possible someone *else* told the WSU about Elliot talking to the World? So it's just a coincidence Isabella disappeared that same day? What if she's in trouble someplace?"

Clink, clink, clink: Maybe they were lining up coffee mugs?

Keira rested against the wall between the framed photos, still sorting shadows. She saw a jar of coins; scissors and pens upright in a mug shaped like an elephant. A fax machine. A set of papers sat on this machine, maybe waiting to be sent. She tilted her head, and focused.

MISSING PERSONS REPORT, she read, and beneath that, the name: *ISABELLA TAMBORLAINE.*

"Seems to me . . ." said the Sheriff's voice. There was a pause, and when the Sheriff spoke again, his voice was muffled. "Here it is. What do you know about her, Jimmy? Truly? She came here from nowhere to teach Physics — just like that Mischka Tegan before her. Seems clear as day she was another Hostile. Maybe she hit it off with you, and that wasn't part of her plan? Or could be she thought romance with the local law couldn't hurt. You were taken in by her, just like Abel was taken in by Mischka. Don't go blaming yourself. She had a real compelling way. As did that Mischka."

There was a long quiet, then soft *pfft* sounds, plastic containers being opened. A creak that might have been an oven door.

That Mischka, Keira thought. Well, here's *that Mischka's* daughter.

She should have announced herself more loudly, not stood here eavesdropping. Now it was too late.

She studied the report in the fax machine again. There was a description of Isabella. *Tall. Dark hair. Eyes like fern fronds.*

Didn't sound much like law-enforcement language. Jimmy's voice came through again, a fine line of voice.

"You know what Isabella told me once? About this myth. Long ago, we were all two people. A man and a woman, or two men or two women, the point is, we were all joined up with someone else. Then we got torn in two, and now we're born looking for our lost other half."

"She told you that, did she? Hang on, don't slice it yet, we'll give it another moment to cool. And I'm guessing you and she were two halves of one of these original conjoined pairs? And you got lucky and found yourselves?"

"Hector, you don't have to use *that* tone," Jimmy admonished. "Don't you have any romance left in you? Weren't you and Simon like two lost halves, or like a person and his shadow, when you found each other? Didn't you feel like you'd been cut in two when he died?"

Keira tried to focus on the fax again.

Her posture is excellent, she read. *And her smile is slow and warm. She always wears a necklace with this heavy ornament like a big, shiny lozenge.*

"I'm sorry, Jimmy, you're right." The Sheriff seemed to be speaking through a mouthful. "I did feel that way when I lost Simon. Just, I'm so darn *mad* at that Isabella, for what she did to you and Elliot. I could just about strangle her. But friends always move on to angry a whole lot faster than the guy with the broken heart. That's the trouble. I gotta remind myself of that, and give you some time to catch up."

There was a brief, sad chuckle from Jimmy, and then, "How much you going to *eat* of that thing? There won't be any left for the others."

Hector sounded serious: "Ah, gotta make sure it's right. That's only fair. Here, you try it too, and as for that idea . . ."

"It's good," Jimmy mumbled. "Give us another slice. The others can eat cookies. If they ever get here? What time is this supposed to start anyway? Ho*ly*, it's more than fantastic, it's the best you ever made. . . . As for what idea?"

"That idea of us all being half a double person, in search of the lost half. That seems downright foolish to me. Like we're all snipped up like a jigsaw puzzle. How are you supposed to find your matching piece with millions of pieces blowing around out there? And no picture to study on the box. What if your match happened to get born in a different century? Or hit by a train before you ever met them? Or got sick and died when you'd both hardly stopped being kids? Jimmy, my Simon was great, and, sure, he was my other half, but I wouldn't mind meeting someone else sometime, maybe someone *better* than my other half."

Jimmy laughed. "Here, pour me a coffee, would you?"

"And it's the kinda talk lets people justify running off on their families: I *had* to do it, I met my *other half.* Pile of trash. Anyhow, if it was true, wouldn't most of us be walking around feeling lost and lonely?"

"Aren't we?"

Jimmy spoke in his reasonable voice, but Keira had to close her eyes against his words.

"Well, not me," Hector said.

Again, Jimmy laughed. "I guess I'll get over Isabella in time, as you say."

Keira's eyes opened again and flew back to the fax in the machine.

There is a scar on Isabella's ankle, she read. *It's like the letter P. A circle with a line affixed. Like a tadpole or a quarter note. Or maybe a balloon on a string.*

At that moment, the station door burst open and Gabe and his friends tumbled in, stamping snow from boots, shaking it from gloves and hats.

"Sophy!" they sang, catching sight of her, some of them shrieking it: "*Soph!*"

Then the adults arrived, and the meeting began. Abel called these regularly so everyone could share their progress. The two agents were trying to get an official pardon for Elliot so he wouldn't be shot by the

WSU when he came out of hiding. Abel himself was working under-cover with Loyalists to try to restore the monarchy and get Princess Ko released. The Sheriff and Deputy kept an eye on relevant Hostile activity. Keira tried to keep in touch with her contacts at the Hostile compound so she could let the others know how Elliot was doing — tricky to get a secure line, though, the Farms technology being what it was. And the teenagers kept an eye on any hints that Keira's cover might be loose.

As usual, the conversation circled, people ate baked goods, and nobody had a single item of value to report.

12.

$\mathcal{K}$eira sat at a table outside the Bakery Café.

It was a Friday evening, winter still, and the sky was whitish-gray, the square plump with crusty, old snow.

Across the square, she could see Abel and Petra Baranski at one of Le Petit Restaurant's outdoor tables. They came into town now and then, she'd noticed. Once, she'd seen them through the window of Abel's old electronics repair shop, Abel moving objects around, Petra sweeping. Abel must be planning to reopen his shop. Other times, they'd be dressed up, as they were now, Abel in collared shirt, Petra wearing lipstick, her hair in loose curls around her neck.

Romantic early dinner tonight, Keira guessed. She could see wine glasses on their table, and a tiny plate of olives.

Her own table was crowded with coffee, notes, and index cards. A breeze crossed the table and the cards trembled. Which was exactly how her stomach felt: trembly. She didn't even feel this way before motocross championships. She breathed in deeply to calm herself, but all that happened was she hit more nerves so the breath ended up in crumples.

She'd joined the school's history club the week before. Today was her turn to present. The meeting was at six P.M. That's half an hour still, she told herself. Crazy to waste thirty minutes of your life feeling scared.

"Who wants to join my new history club?" the teacher, Mr. Guthrie, had asked, and her arm had flung itself in the air. Unexpected. Afterward she told herself she'd done it because she still found that arm-raising thing hilarious. Seriously, what was with kids pointing at the ceiling when they wanted a teacher's attention? What did the ceiling have to do with anything? She'd taken ages to stop looking up to see what the issue was up there, like mold in the cornices or what?

She told Gabe and the others that she'd joined the club so she could seem like a genuine participant in the community. ("Soph! Good for you!")

But the real reason was she loved Mr. Guthrie's classes. It wasn't just that he made history into stories so vibrant she could've sworn he was piping pictures into her brain. It was also the way questions rose from his tales, and how he'd take these questions and turn them upside down. Tap on them gently to see what might fall out, or spin them sideways so they met other questions. It sort of reminded Keira of the music that played constantly at home — the soundtrack of her life — melodies rising in spirals from the drumbeat, twisting on themselves, diving back inside the song or melting like false starts.

So, she'd joined the club. And Mr. Guthrie had assigned her the first presentation.

The nerves were in her shoulder blades and temples. Sharp, little aches.

It's okay, she told herself, I've got index cards.

Gabe had suggested the index cards. He'd seen her practicing her speech at the kitchen table the night before, reading from a typed sheet of paper, and he'd opened a drawer and pulled out the stack of cards. "Check this out," he'd said, placing the cards in the palm of his hand, straightening his shoulders and staring ahead. "Blahdy, blahdy," he's said, solemn, and then, without looking down, he'd lifted up the top card and slid it to the bottom of the pile.

"Unbelievable," she'd breathed.

He had placed the cards on the table with the slightest smile. "Up to you."

But actually it was a good idea, so she'd come here after school today and transferred her speech to the cards.

It was about relations between Cello and its neighbor, the Kingdom of Aldhibah. At first, she'd thought she'd do one of the usual — the Battle of Faber-Regis, the Shadow Years, the Massacre in Olde Quainte, the Lamplight War — but then she'd decided to focus on small incidents instead.

Now she chose a random card to practice.

The Turnkey Crisis

This event followed a period of relative peace between the Kingdoms of Cello and Aldhibah. The doors in the great wall stood open, and citizens of both Kingdoms had been making their way easily back and forth. Then, after a perceived slight from the then Queen of Cello at a banquet, a decision was made in

Aldhibah. At precisely 3 p.m., there was a simultaneous turning of keys: All along the wall, the Aldhians closed and locked the doors. The gesture was meant as a snub: designed to symbolize an entire Kingdom turning its back on its neighbor. It is true that the doors were opened again in the following weeks, but to this day, an Aldhian need only mime the turn of a key in the air for a Cellian to feel the sting.

Keira replaced the card uncertainly. She chose another.
But her scarf was suffocating her. She pulled it off and draped it over the other chair. Her neck felt relieved.

The Sleight of Hand

This took place so long ago as to be almost the stuff of legend. The story goes that, in a time of great, mutual need, the two Kingdoms entered a bilateral treaty whereby they agreed to share their natural resources for a time. Specifically, they agreed that "all resources in all named provinces shall forthwith and for one score years be equally divided."

However, at the precise moment that the then Cellian King was signing this treaty, his council back home was officially "unnaming" one of Cello's provinces. All records of that province were erased, and reference thereto was strictly forbidden (so much so that the name itself has vanished from memory). The province, of course, has since become known as our Undisclosed Province, and the reason for this technical masterstroke — this sleight of hand — was that the region is the source of Cello's Wind. Of course, the Cello Wind is our most valuable resource, and the Aldhians were outraged to have been tricked out of their share in this way.

Incidentally, this episode raises many questions. What does a name mean? Can you truly be stripped of your identity in this way? And, once the province became known as the Undisclosed Province, did it then take on the characteristics of THAT name? These days the region is well known as a place of mystery, secrets, and shadows, and very few venture there. Was it always this way or did the dark curtain drawn across its existence so transform it?

It was a bit much, she saw suddenly. She was trying to draw out questions the way Mr. Guthrie did, but her points were totally obvious. Or totally obscure. Or forced? Mr. Guthrie would bite his lower lip with sympathetic amusement. The other kids would wince in their Farms way.

Now her *coat* was suffocating her. She pulled this off, along with her woolen hat.

Why was she so *hot*? Did she maybe have a fever? She should cancel her presentation! It would only be fair! What if she was contagious? What a shame! Oh, well. Never mind. But then she looked around and saw that, all across the square, people were shedding overcoats and gloves, and fanning themselves with menus. The temperature must have shot right up.

At Le Petit Restaurant, the manager was snuffing out the oil-burning heaters. Abel and Petra had stopped chatting to watch him do this. Now that neither was smiling, Keira thought they both seemed older and heavier somehow. Petra's lipstick was smudged, and there were shadows and sags beneath her eyes. A woman approached their table — it was the pharmacist who always wore violet nail polish — and Keira could hear her exclaiming, welcoming Abel back, and asking after his health. Both Abel and Petra beamed up, and then, as Abel engaged in chat, Petra's smile faded and she gazed into space, lines running down her cheeks.

Keira returned to her index cards. She took the final card.

These events may seem trivial but in a way, the small and the large, the micro and the macro, are one and the same. Words are altered on documents and a province disappears. An error is made by a Cellian pianist at an inter-Kingdom contest: An Aldhian singer, unnerved, misses out on a place. The Lamplight War begins a month later. A Cellian Prince disappears when he's about to be crowned King, and, years later, his mandolin turns up in an Aldhian junkyard. The Shadow Years commence. A Queen fails to recognize a Princess, and thus does not offer the appropriate greeting. Keys are turned in a wall. The Battle of Faber-Regis takes place just six months later. Are each of these minor events unrelated to the major that followed them? Are each isolated and insignificant? Or does each contain thousands of years' worth of bloodshed and mistrust? Does each stretch back as far as memory can take us, and canter forward into the unknowable future?

Again, Keira felt doubts circling. *Canter.* That was what *horses* did, not moments. She must have had Sergio-the-stable-boy on her mind. And what was she thinking, announcing that the micro and the macro were one and the same? No, they weren't. One was small. One was big. She reached for a pen to strike out *canter*, as well as the micro/macro line and as she did a splat of water hit the card.

Two or three others joined it quickly. The ink began to run.

She gathered the cards together, rain peppering her bare head. Around the square, umbrellas were popping open, people were running for cover, and vendors were hurrying to cover their stock.

This was *spring* rain, she realized suddenly. Winter was over. Spring had come to town.

That was when the clock tower began to strike.

She looked up, amazed.

It was six o'clock already! *Now* what had she done?

Her heart thudded madly as she threw her things into her backpack. She couldn't find the rubber band for the index cards, so she put them in her coat pocket instead. She pulled her hat onto her head as somewhere to put it. The clock was still chiming. It was only five minutes to the school if she ran — people would still be arriving and settling in at the history club. She'd be fine, she was not too late, she'd make it.

Then the chimes seemed to expand, rising above the clock tower, cloaking it, and she looked up, confused.

It was the warning bells.

The entire square paused, decoding the bells, and then someone laughed, and several people shouted, "Level 4 Blue!" or "It's just a Sky Blue!"

There was a rush for shops and pubs. Keira hesitated.

"You'd better come in here." Her friend, the waitress, was standing at the open café door, while other customers filed past, some annoyed, but most resigned and cheerful.

"I can't," Keira said. "I've got to get to the school." She swung her backpack onto her shoulder, draping her coat and scarf on the crook of the other arm.

The waitress's eyes widened. "Heck, school's finished for the day, isn't it? Sky Blues are pretty harmless, sure, but I wouldn't want to be caught outside in one!"

Keira pivoted on her heel. "I won't be," she called, "I've got time," and she started running.

The square was already empty of people, so her running feet

echoed like a drumbeat. Distantly, she heard the waitress's voice sing: "Get back here, you crazy!"

Streets were empty too. Cars had pulled over to curbs. It was almost dark, and the streetlights bowed in the rain. She turned onto Broad Street. People stared at her from behind shopwindows, and from inside houses. A teenage boy hurdled a fence, ran up a garden path and into a house. She could hear a mother's voice scolding. At another house, a woman hurried out, scooped up a dog, and ran back inside, slamming the door behind her.

Rain fell harder. Snow was melting, and puddles formed, expanding fast. She leapt over one, skidded, caught herself, and kept running. The air was gray with rain, but the Blue haze was approaching now. On a sunny day, it could be tricky to see a Sky Blue's approach, but today it was vibrant up there. Shouldering its way in, tearing through cloud, pressing its immense, vacant face into the sky.

She jogged steadily. She was almost at the school.

Up ahead, she saw a man darting out of the school gates. It was Jimmy, she realized. He'd been at the high school often lately: She kept seeing him disappear into the staff room or the office. Now he crossed the road at a sprint, ran up the stairs, and into the Sheriff's station. The door thudded behind him, rattling.

She was going to make it.

She was almost at the gate.

She was at the gate. She turned, and the Blue was everywhere.

Cylinders of Blue, some as small as trash cans, some as large as storm-water drains, rolled up and down the street and path at speed. The school grounds were awash with them. They tumbled and turned in there, high-spirited and hilarious. She sidled in through the gate, and right away a Blue knocked her back outside again.

She tried again, and a second Blue knocked her to the ground. She landed in a sprawl, water seeping cold into the seat of her jeans.

She stood up, ran at the gate once more, and this time found herself tripping back a few steps before she fell to her hands and knees. The Blues seemed to grin, waiting on her next move. Rain blurred her vision. She got back to her feet, three Blues hurtled toward her, so she ran.

They were chasing her along the middle of the street. For a moment she thought she could outrun them, but another swiped at her from her right. She darted to avoid it, and collided with a parked car. She was on the ground again. She was up and running. The Blues prodded her from behind. She was down again. Each time it was just a little push, gentle but firm: palms against your back, an elbow in your side.

Her backpack slid from her shoulder and splashed to the road. She tried to reach for it but was shoved away. She gave up and continued stumbling along.

She was passing houses. People pressed to the glass and stared out at her. She was falling, weaving, ducking, tripping, falling. Some of the people laughed, and she tried to smile back at them. It was pretty funny. Like a game. The Blues were winning, sure, but she could be a good sport.

Her scarf slithered from her arm and sank into a puddle.

Behind a window, the local vet beckoned her, mouthing, "Get in here! Come inside!"

She took a run at the shop, but the Blue was onto her, surrounding her so she felt herself lifted from the ground for a few steps before she fell. She tried again but the same thing happened, and quickly the shop receded as she was buffeted along the road.

The Blue was like a fast-moving river that was swelling out through the town. It scooted around trees and slid past buildings. She was caught in its rapids, bubbling along. She was breathless and exhausted. Her knees and elbows throbbed from hitting the ground.

She passed more shops, more staring faces, more smiles, some sympathetic, more people urging her to come inside. But each time she was swept from doorways in the giddy rush.

"Stop it!" she heard herself shouting.

It was like a crowd of kids, she thought, or puppies, who don't understand that the game is done. The more you press them away from you, the more they leap.

Each time she fell, it hurt a little more. Each time she got to her feet there was another flying shove.

"Stop it!"

A couple of them barged at her shoulder blades and she crashed into a snowbank, face-first. Her coat was wrenched from her arm and flung to the road, the index cards skidding from the pocket, and forming a trail. She grabbed at them, but the Blue urged her on, relentless.

It was night-dark now, so the Blue had an eerie glow.

She realized she was beyond the downtown area. No more houses edging the road, just fields and occasional mailboxes, hulking shapes of farm buildings in the distance.

There was a rhythm now to the Blue. It pummeled, waited, let her take three steps, and pummeled again. It was silent but she could almost hear it shriek with laughter at each push.

Fall, stagger, fall, stagger, fall, stagger, fall.

Her body ached. Dimly, she wondered where she was going.

She fell. Her palms were grazed.

She fell. Sharp pain in her knees.

She fell. Her shoulder was wrenched.

It was tireless, this Blue. Indefatigable.

She tried to admire its determined good cheer.

"Leave me alone!" she roared. Her woolen hat clung sodden to her head.

"Stop it!"

Crash.

"Stop it!"

Crash.

She gave up shouting, and the rhythm carried on until there was nothing much going on in the universe but falling and standing and falling. The tubes of Blue ran skittishly ahead, behind and around her, prodding and rollicking. A vision sprang up before her: the word *FUN!* lit up and flashing, rolling back and forth, another word, a tiny word, following.

Then it stopped.

As one, every cylinder lifted, and soared into the darkness.

She stood and watched the sky.

The Blue faded into the distance. She could hear her own breathing.

She kept walking. Shivers ran through her body.

With vague surprise, she realized that this was Foxall Road, and that the crossroad approaching was Carsons. She was almost at Gabe's farm.

The rain fell on, unperturbed, as if nothing had happened.

She reached the farm and turned up the driveway.

Gabe was opening the door of his pickup truck as she arrived. He wore his rain jacket, the hood casting a shadow over his face.

He looked at her curiously.

"I was just coming to fetch you," he said. "From the library. Wasn't that the plan? That I'd meet you there after your history thing?"

Keira stood in the rain. Wet hands seemed to be massaging her head through her woolen hat.

"Well, seeing you're here, can you help me out with something?" He closed the truck door with his knee and headed out across the yard, away from the house. As he walked, he drew a flashlight from his jacket pocket and switched it on. He swung the light back over his shoulder.

She followed.

The ground was slick and noisy with rivulets of melting snow. Each step was a squelch, and the water lapped over the sides of her boots. They crossed the first paddock, and the second, then he opened a gate into a smaller field.

Snow still iced this field although its edges ran with mud. Poking through the white were rows of tiny shoots, each no bigger than a hand. The rows stretched into the distance.

Gabe crunched toward the first row, and turned back to Keira, holding out the flashlight. "Hold this for me?"

She took a step, hit a slippery patch, and landed on her back in ice-mud-snow.

Gabe chuckled. "Watch your step there, Soph."

She screamed without making the decision to scream. She was lying on her back and she could feel it, the scream, in her chin and chest and down her spine. She was horrified but also strangely euphoric, and when it stopped, she took a breath and screamed again. Abruptly, Gabe was standing over her, his face anxious, his mouth moving, but she couldn't hear his words behind the scream. The scream was harsh like chain saws, and piercing like hot water pipes in panic. It was like music gone rogue, turned murderous, escaping.

She clambered onto her hands and knees, and turned the scream into words. "Would you *all* just stop with your *Soph! Soph!* like you want to bury me in *Soph! Soph!* You're all just one big monster made of *Soph!* and they never *look* at me, or *listen*, and it's *not* my fault my mother's a Hostile, and it's *not* my fault my mother killed people, and you didn't tell me *why* I had to take that route! How was I to *know* it was going to get bogged! And then you had to point out how *bad* my *skin* is when I didn't say a word about —"

She stopped. The rain fell. Gabe stared.

"About what?" he said eventually.

"About . . . your ears. How you should grow your hair long to cover . . ." Her words dwindled. "But you . . ." She started again. "I didn't *know* that would happen with the tractor!"

A frown crossed Gabe's face. He held out a hand as if to help her up, then withdrew it. He looked behind him, across the field.

"Can we just do this thing for now?" he said. Again, he offered his hand, and this time she let him pull her to her feet.

She stood beside him, feeling her own shrieks still falling from the air. The quiet floated back, then filled itself with smaller sounds: the agitated rush of melting snow, the quiet thoughts of an owl, all of it steeped in embarrassment and disapproval.

"What do you need me to do?" Keira asked.

"Just shine the light." He pressed the flashlight into her hand, frowning briefly again, then crouched down by the first of the shoots.

She stood above him. The circle of light hit the little plant, and she watched him take a gentle hold of it, examine it, then release it and stand up.

He moved to the next one, did the same thing, and then the next. Water trickled so reprovingly she had to speak to cover the sound.

"What is this? What are you growing here?" she asked.

He tore a leaf from a shoot, and shuffled to the next one without speaking. She followed.

"This is murlington," he said eventually. "It's a bit like corn."

"I know. I've tried it. It's good. You have to check this entire field?"

"Afraid so."

She looked across the endless rows.

He moved along the plants, and she shone the light at each. Now and then he pulled out a leaf or two, but mostly not.

"What are you looking for?" she asked.

Again, he was silent, concentrating.

"What are you looking for?" she repeated, and he glanced up.

"Sorry. Here. Come closer, and I'll show you. This tiny patch of white? It's a form of mold that can get these little guys after a rapid thaw like this. I need to get it off fast before it spreads."

Keira raised her eyes again. Her gaze ran along the rows. She focused.

"I can see it," she said.

"Yeah, you have to go right up close." He shifted to the next shoot, this time on his knees.

"No. There."

He glanced up. She was pointing about eight shoots along from where he kneeled.

"I have to check these first. Can't skip any."

She shook her head. "The next seven are fine. But that one there's got the white dots." She held his gaze. "Check all eight if you like."

He did. At the eighth, he tore away a single, tiny leaf.

"You were right." He straightened and studied her face. "See any more?"

She looked away from him, running the light along the shoots. "There," she said, pointing. "Five along."

Again he tested each one, and this time when he reached the fifth, he tore away the mold and stood up grinning.

"Where's the next?"

Keira switched off the flashlight.

"Seriously?" Gabe said to this.

"Better without it." She scanned the plants again. "My night vision kicks in. There."

Now he headed straight to her choice, plucked away the moldy parts, and stood again, waiting.

"No more in this row. Or the next. But the third row's got about five."

Row by row, she pointed out infected shoots. The rain fell softly, the wind drifted around them.

Once they'd reached the final shoot in the field, they both stood back while she scanned the field once more.

"We're done," she said.

He nodded.

They walked back to the house through the darkness. Inside, he switched on the light, hung up his raincoat, and turned to her.

"Thanks," he said. "That was . . ."

She was pulling off her hat. Water splattered the floor.

"Your lips are blue," he said. "You're freezing. Go take a shower and then we can talk."

"About what?"

"Well, about the stuff you were shouting out there."

"I thought you'd forgotten that."

He laughed.

When she came out to the kitchen, he was standing at the stove, his back to her.

Some kind of dark chocolate dessert sat in bowls on the table.

"How do you do that so fast?"

"The molten chocolate pudding? I don't know." He half shrugged, frowning. "It's a Farms thing. We learn to bake before we can walk, practically. Even Nikki and Shelby can do it if they have to. They're just not into it. Elliot's the best of us but Cody's a close second. You should try his cherry and chocolate profiteroles with orchid vanilla. Now *those* are a work of art."

He turned around, a mug of hot chocolate in each hand, and stopped.

Keira was wearing a T-shirt and trackpants. Her arms and neck were covered in red marks. Gabe's frown deepened in confusion at this. Then his eyes widened.

"Wait," he said. "Don't tell me you were *out* in that Blue?"

She bit her lower lip.

"For how long?"

"I don't know. The whole time."

"The whole time. *Keira.* That was the longest Sky Blue I've ever seen. Where were you? Downtown?"

"I don't know where I was. It sort of chased me halfway here. Then it stopped and I walked the rest of the way."

"Wait, you walked from downtown all the way here? You're pulling my leg. Nobody walks a distance like that. That's what wheels are for. I thought someone must have given you a ride! And you did that after you'd been out in a Blue?!"

He set the mugs on the table, pulled out a chair, and sat facing her, his frown almost a scowl.

"Who would have given me a ride?" she asked.

His eyes ran over her bruises again, and he shook his head slowly. "You're right. We're being too tough on you. I guess we don't like Edgians, for one thing. Or Hostiles. But it's more about Elliot — we sort of blame you for him. 'Cause it was your mother who betrayed his

Uncle Jon, so Jon ended up dead, and it was her that caused his dad to go missing all that time. So, you being a Hostile . . ."

"But I keep telling you. I'm not a Hostile. I'm not exactly a fan of the royals, but I swear I'm not a Hostile."

"Well." He sipped from his hot chocolate, his eyes on her face.

"And I helped *save* Elliot. I'm using my contacts to *hide* Elliot."

Gabe set his mug back on the table.

"They're Hostile contacts." He shrugged. "You can't win. Have some pudding."

She twirled the spoon in a circle on the table. They both watched it spin and then slow.

"It's true it's not your fault, what your mother did," Gabe said. "I'll talk to the others."

"Don't worry about it."

"No. I will. But you know, when they do their *Soph! Soph!* thing, they're just messing around. It's funny to them."

Keira picked up the spoon and used it to trace the scratches on the table. "When that Blue was chasing me, I saw the word *fun* rolling past my eyes. It was a sort of hallucination I guess. Another word came after it, only I couldn't tell what it was. Now I think I know. It was *malice*."

Gabe raised his eyebrows. "Ah, you're right, and that's a good way to put it. To be honest, I've never found it all that much of a hoot, the whole *Soph!* thing. Listen, though, y'know, it's also your face?"

She dropped the spoon and it clattered. Heat burst across her cheeks. She pressed her hands to them.

"Not your *skin*! You can't even *see* the breakouts most of the time, under all that makeup." He sounded annoyed. "I mean the *expressions* on your face. You know, your face never stops talking, even when you're silent? And it's got a heck of a lot to say about how much better you are than all of us. You think we're a bunch of hicks and you think our accents and our school and our clothes are all one big joke. I don't mind all that so much myself — this province is always getting trashed. For me, it's what your face does about *farming* itself — that's what really gets me."

Keira stared down at the surface of the pudding. It rose up in a perfect mound, two fine cracks running down the middle. Beneath those cracks she caught glimpses of a glossy chocolate liquid.

"I'm only joking when I go on about farming," she said. She tried to make her face not say a word.

"Sure, I get that." Gabe dug into his own pudding. "Please. Eat." He spoke through a mouthful. "It's kinda dumb, but the thing about me is, I'm all about the crops. It's like land and dirt and plants, well, they're part of me. You know how a plant can grow tall, but its roots'll likely go down even deeper than it's tall? On account of, it's looking for moisture and so forth?"

Keira tried to look as if she did know that.

"Well, they do. And it's sort of the same with me. I'm tall — yeah, don't act like that's news. Your eyes measure me against doorways and ceilings all the time. Your eyes are *always*, 'Good grief, the guy's a *tree*!' Whatever. That, I'm used to — but seems to me, I've got roots that stretch even deeper than my height. 'Cause I'm so tangled up with things that grow." He scooped out half the pudding, looked away, and spoke again. "So when you make fun, well, it hurts." He looked at her again, then leaned down to scrape his bowl.

Keira watched him. In her head, she argued for a while, back and forth, about farming and taking yourself too seriously. Then she dropped the argument. She let her face show that she felt bad.

Something occurred to her. "It's spring out there," she said. "We had two weeks of winter and now an afternoon of spring. Isn't that what you predicted?"

Gabe drained his mug of chocolate in one go, and set it down. "Ah, sometimes I get it right. Sometimes not. What'd I say would happen next? Summer? That'll probably turn out wrong. People like to ask me anyway." He shrugged. "Make a fortune, I could do it all the time. Come on, for crying out loud, would you try the pudding. I made it special to cheer you up."

Keira blinked. She thought people only made food "to cheer you up" in movies. Was he for real? She didn't know whether she should give him a withering look, or smile and say thanks. So she did neither; she obeyed him and tried the pudding. Right away, she had to close her eyes. It was like the opposite of her scream. It was a melody rushing through her face and chest and down her spine, the harmony rising all the time. It caught her somewhere deep in the stomach, deep in the center of her happiness. "Ho*ly*," she said, speaking Farms. "This is *amazing*."

"There's some ointment might help prevent bruising," Gabe said, "top right-hand corner of the bathroom cabinet." He pushed back his chair. "Or maybe the bottom shelf. You have a look. Thanks for outside. Now, *that* was some amazing. Saved me hours of work, which I sure appreciate, 'cause I am *beat*. Heading up to bed."

He was pale, she saw abruptly. His eyes were so close to being shut they were mostly lash.

"It'll be good when your parents get back," she said. "I know you're all tangled in farming and everything, but it's kind of crazy you running this whole place on your own, as well as going to school."

Gabe ran the water in the sink, rinsing his plate and mug.

He turned and looked at her. "You okay now?"

She nodded.

"Night, then."

He stepped toward the kitchen door and stopped. "Wait, why'd you keep running? When that Blue was after you, why not just curl up on the ground next to some building, say, and let them roll across you? Wouldn't have hurt near so much."

Keira laughed. "I guess because I'm an idiot? I didn't even think of doing that."

He regarded her through his half-closed eyes. "Not an idiot," he concluded. "Just not a quitter. Night." He left the room now, knocking on the wall once as he did, but a moment later he was back. "I wasn't pointing *out* your skin that day," he said. "You were touching it like you were sad about it. I was telling you how you might *fix* it." A slow smile formed. "Hide my ears by growing my hair. I don't see how *anyone* could grow enough hair to hide these guys," and, to Keira's amazement, he tapped his ears with something like affection.

13.

The next day was Saturday, and Keira woke late from a dream in which she was a glass bottle. She was rolling around on the deck of a ship that was caught in an electrical storm.

It took a few minutes for the room to stop rocking and lights to stop flashing.

Outside her bedroom window, the sky was blue, and the sun shone strongly on wet, sodden ground. Summer. So Gabe had been right.

She went downstairs in her pj's. The kitchen was empty, but there was a note on the table, alongside a folded newspaper.

Abel Baranski called. He wants us all to come to his place at noon. Don't try to walk. ☺ I'll meet u here and give you a ride. Hope u feel better. Look at this.

Beneath this was a wobbly arrow, pointing at the newspaper. Keira unfolded it and looked at the headline.

TALKS COLLAPSE — PRINCESS KO FACING EXECUTION

The kitchen counter leapt right at Keira, with outstretched, shoving hands. Or anyhow, that's how it seemed.

Keira and Gabe were the last to arrive at the Baranski farmhouse.

Petra led them into the living room, where the others were already seated, pie plates on knees.

"Hey, how's it going?" Nikki said carefully, and the others gazed at Keira. So Gabe must have talked to them already. She was so embarrassed she felt like taking a plate of pie and mashing it into her own face.

The adults smiled at her in their usual way, which somehow made it worse.

"Sit down," Abel said. "Sit!" His words teetered between hostly enthusiasm and impatience. He had a wild-eyed look, she thought, and those shadows under his eyes were droopy hammocks.

The moment Keira and Gabe found chairs, Abel sprang to his feet and began: "Thank you, everyone, for taking the time to come out here at such short notice. Today I want you to meet . . ."

"Well, now, that's no trouble," the Sheriff mused. "It being a Saturday and all, this town can *generally* take care of itself, although that is setting aside the hijinks we had at the Templetons' this morning. And you never can tell what'll happen with Color attacks these days. They're that much more frequent, and more get-up-and-go than a greyhound."

"That's true," Agent Kim volunteered, raising his pen from his sketchpad. "I've never seen a Sky Blue last as long as yesterday's." He returned to sketching.

Hector agreed. "They don't cause any real damage, those Blues, just like messing with people. Speaking of which, there's a rumor around that Sophy Epstein was out in it last night. I said, now that surely can't be so! But Jimmy heard it too, didn't you, Jimmy?"

Jimmy nodded. "People seemed convinced of it." He smiled.

Everyone turned to Keira, who shrugged, so they all spoke at once: variations on *"Why?!"* and a lot of talk about the bruises they could see now on her arms.

Abel's voice clambered up over the noise. "I don't want to waste too much of your time," he called stridently. "There's someone I want you to —"

There was a swooping sound. It was Agent Kim, ripping out a page of his sketchbook with a flourish.

"Here," he said, holding up the page. "Anybody know what this is?"

"Hang on," Abel began, but the others were leaning over one another to see. On the page was a simple black circle.

"It's a manhole cover," said Shelby.

"A picture of that round silver tray there." Petra pointed to the sideboard.

"It's a face," Nikki offered. "You forgot to add features."

"A basketball hoop," said Gabe, "without a net."

"Hole in the ground," said Cody. "Lid of a jam jar. Top of a drinking glass."

"Frisbee!" Petra shouted.

"Pancake!"

"Yo-yo!"

"Egg," said Shelby.

The others looked at her. "What sort of chickens you got?"

"A poached egg," she explained.

"Holy," muttered Abel. Petra chuckled.

Kim spun the paper back around again, and studied the circle himself.

Agent Tovey spoke up. "It might be nothing," he said, and Abel sighed. "But both Kim and I have caught glimpses of this image in our dealings with the WSU. Just a plain circle. Keira, what's with the ring?"

This last question came like a punch leaping up from his mild tone. Keira flinched.

"I'm just twisting it," she said.

"Why?"

Keira blinked. "A ring is a circle. The picture made me think of it."

"You should've shouted, then," Shelby advised. "Like this: *Ring!* It might have been the right answer. You might've won."

Tovey was still looking at Keira. The others waited, bemused.

"We don't know the answer," the agent said eventually, turning back to the group. "We don't know what the circle means."

"Well, anyhow," Abel said, "like I said, there's someone I want you to —"

The Sheriff interrupted. "But you think it *might* mean something?"

Tovey nodded. "Kim and I suspect it might be a symbol — a code of some kind — referring to a secret organization. It's becoming clear that there are links between the WSU and one or more of the Hostile branches. Maybe the circle indicates that union?"

Shelby frowned. "Then it'd be a *U*. For union."

"Or it indicates a new, more powerful Hostile group," Tovey said. "A supergroup: an alliance between several Hostile branches."

Abel cleared his throat, but Petra placed a hand on his arm.

"Speaking of Hostiles," she said. "Keira, is there any news from Elliot?"

Keira shook her head. "I haven't been able to get through to them the last couple of days."

Petra's smile grew, and tightened. "But he's okay, right?"

"I'm sure he is. They'd find a way to let me know if anything was wrong. I grew up with those people — they'll take care of him."

"I want to keep playing circle games," Shelby said.

"LAST NIGHT!" Abel shouted, like someone in a rock band announcing the next number. Everyone turned to him, impressed. His next words seemed spoken in the language of relief. "Last night, after that Blue was done, I traveled north. To an emergency meeting of the Loyalists. Now, you will have seen in the papers about Princess Ko facing execution? And the King having disappeared underground, once talks collapsed?"

There was a commotion of assurance that people *had* seen that, and wasn't it unbe*lievable*, and that's why you called this meeting, is what I've been assuming all along, and —

"Shush!" Abel shouted, then more moderately, but still stern: "*Hush*. The Loyalists have plans and I intend to play an active part. As I said before, we want to restore the monarchy. Bring back the remaining members of the royal family. For now, the King needs somewhere to lie low. And we want to help Princess Ko escape."

Again, the room erupted.

Too dangerous! The royals were fine in the World: Leave them there. Princess Ko would *never* be executed, there would be outrage! It was all just talk. Leave her be too.

"Well, I agree with Abel," Hector said. The others turned to him. "Pfft," he said. "Not that *he* should get involved. You stay put, Abel. We've only just got you home. I only mean I agree that Princess Ko needs rescuing, I don't trust that Elite bunch. They're looking to make some kind of statement: Let the public know that *they're* the ones in charge."

Agent Tovey gazed at Hector. "I think you're right," he said.

Keira was twisting her ring again. Sometimes it would catch, and she'd force it on around. She had a dilemma. Later today, she'd find somewhere quiet and think it through. Weigh up the factors. Make a decision — and then she found herself speaking: "I can get a message to Princess Ko."

So much for weighing factors. It was like with that scream last night: She was doing things without her own permission.

Now the room turned its skeptical gaze away from Hector and focused it, blazing, on Keira.

"This ring?" she told them. "It's a transponder. Ko has one too, and so do Sergio and Samuel, the others under arrest with her. So I can talk to them."

"The Elite would intercept transmissions," Agent Tovey said.

"Not this one. Before he vanished, Abel was working on technology using particles smaller than magic. You know that, right?"

Abel stared, but Tovey and Kim both nodded. "A listening device. We found it in his shop. We gave a sample to Elliot."

"Well, Elliot showed it to me. And I reconfigured the technology to make a transponder."

"You're not serious." Abel's voice was hoarse. "Elliot gave my work to a Hostile?"

"I'm not a Hostile," Keira said steadily. "My mother is a Hostile. Elliot didn't know that when he gave this to me, but you know what? I think he'd have given it to me anyway. *He* trusted me." Her voice was speaking without her again, running along two melodies, one strident, the other almost weeping. She reached for the strident. "I spent my childhood making listening devices for the Hostiles. I will never forgive my mother for using me like that, and I will never work for the Hostiles again. So. No, the Hostiles don't have this technology — not through me, anyway. But I'm giving it to you." She wrenched the ring from her finger and held it up to the room so it caught a triumphant flash of sunlight. Then she slid it back on. "Symbolically speaking, I mean. This actual ring, I'm keeping."

The room had fallen silent. People were glancing at one another, or keeping their eyes downcast. Then an awareness grew that someone was moving. It was Agent Tovey. He was jiggling his shoulders. It was so uncharacteristic that people switched their shock from Keira to him.

"I *knew* there was something special about that ring." He grinned. "Nice speech, Keira. Also, sorry for jumping on you earlier. It's just I *knew* there was something going on with that ring." He performed one more brief dance move, smoothed his trousers down, and resumed his usual expression of cool reserve.

"He misses intelligence work," Kim explained.

"But does *Elliot* have this ring?" Petra asked. "Can you contact *him* with this?"

Keira shook her head. "It's on his bedroom floor. I saw it there when I was staying here. Anyway, I wouldn't have wanted —"

There was a sharp burst of sound from across the room. The sliding doors sprang open. A figure emerged from the space between the doors.

"I couldn't wait any longer for Abel to introduce me," the figure said. "Pleased to meet you. I'm the King of Cello."

The figure seemed too slight to live up to those words. Then it stepped into the light, and they saw the zing of the man. It was something to do with the white of his teeth, the gleam in his eyes, the turn of his shoulders, and the general pulsating intensity of him.

Agent Kim stilled his pencil, murmured, "High drama," then resumed sketching.

"Oh, yeah," Shelby remembered. "Abel kept going on about wanting us to *meet* someone. Is this who you meant, Abel? Why'd you leave him sitting there in the dark all this time?"

Abel slumped. "The King is going to stay with Petra and me for a while. I thought I should sound you out before I brought him in. If y'all had given me a chance to get a *word* in . . ."

Everyone was looking at the King. His eyes brightened further as they ran around the room from face to face. "I've been listening to your conversation from behind those doors," he said. "And I heard words like *the royal family*. Listen to me now. Those are my wife, my sons, and my daughters. I'm getting them home, *all* of them, from the World, from prison, from anywhere they are, with or without your help, my friends. But which of you is it who just now claimed she could talk to Princess Ko using a ring?"

Keira raised her hand like a Farms schoolgirl.

"I know you!" said King Cetus. "You helped rescue *me* from the World! And now you can contact my daughter? *You* are my favorite person in this room."

Keira stared.

"Now," said the King. "I understand there's a crack in the high-school grounds here which leads to the World?"

"Yes."

"And somebody here can see it, open it, and send messages through it to a girl in the World?"

Keira raised her hand.

"You again! Who is this girl in the World?"

"Her name is Madeleine."

"Will you send her a note right now? Will you ask her to help us bring my family home?"

The Sheriff coughed. "Well, see now, it's best to deal with the crack late at night? When nobody's around."

"Why?" said the King. "It's Saturday. No school."

"I guess," Keira offered, "I could just send one note through now, asking Madeleine to meet us later tonight to talk."

"I'm crazy about you," the King said.

Keira tried to get her head around the idea that she, Keira, a girl raised by Hostiles in Jagged Edge, was sitting in a farmhouse in the province of the Farms, a plate of cherry pie on her knee, while the King of Cello gazed at her adoringly.

Nope. Her head couldn't do it. "Thanks," she said faintly instead.

PART 4

1.

Madeleine, are you there? It's Keira.

Yeah, I'm here. But just so you know, it's only luck that I am.
This parking meter is not exactly standing in my living room.
Even when I do come down this lane, I don't always look at it.
So you can't assume I'll get your note the same day that you
send it. How are Elliot and Abel?

You go by the parking meter without looking at it? Weird. Can
you check it regularly from now on? (Abel and Elliot got thru
fine. Abel's here; Elliot's in hiding with Hostiles.)

Madeleine stamped her foot so hard the muscle in her right
shoulder spasmed. She was standing in the midnight of a cold winter
night. Her pen slipped in her gloved hands. She wrote in a shivering
scrawl.

Weirder if I'd been looking at the meter. You locked up
the crack, remember? What's the story? Why do you need
my help?

*The King is here in Bonfire. He wants to get his family home &
he thinks he can use old contacts to get the guards away from
the crackpoints. Can you get URGENT word to the Queen,
Prince Chyba, and Princess Jupiter that they MUST get to
the crackpoints at the time and date we tell them? Emphasize
that timing is crucial and it's high risk — they should disguise
themselves as much as possible — things are in crisis here and
likely to get worse, so this could be their last chance.*

This note Madeleine read against the rhythm of her chattering
teeth. It seemed she had spent most of her life standing at this parking
meter either cold or outraged or both.

*Keira, before I run around commanding people to put their lives
at risk, can you guarantee they'll be safe? What do you mean
Cello is in crisis?*

A long silence and then Keira's reply.

*Not sure you need to know this but basically the Jagged Edge
Elite are in control, Hostiles gone silent, Colors intensifying, and
the WSU more powerful than ever. So, no, we can't guarantee
anything, but aren't you the one who went on about how we
shouldn't abandon the royals in the World? Now we're bringing
them home and you're still not happy?*

Madeleine was wearing her mother's coat under her own. This
seemed to be making her even colder. Each coat assumed the other
would do the work of warming her, so both just hung there thinly,
filling up with cold. She wrote a reply.

I'll get word to the royals, but I can't promise they'll go. They have amnesia, remember? I tried writing to them after Elliot left, and never heard back from the Queen or Prince Chyba. Princess Jupiter's been emailing me, but she still has no memories of Cello, and she said she'd never go back to that crackpoint — she almost lost her job waiting to be collected last time.

Why are you in contact with the royals now? We haven't asked you to do that.

A blast of ice-cold wind tried to tear this note from Madeleine's hand. She crumpled it tightly and wrote.

You know the crazy thing, Keira? I DON'T JUST DO THINGS BECAUSE CELLIANS TELL ME TO. I DON'T SPEND MY LIFE SITTING BESIDE A PARKING METER WAITING FOR YOUR SUMMONS. NOT THAT IT'S ANY OF YOUR BUSINESS, BUT I GOT IN CONTACT WITH THE ROYALS BECAUSE I KNEW YOU GUYS HAD ABANDONED THEM AND I <u>CARED</u>. I'M THE ONE WHO FOUND THEM ALL FOR YOU IN THE FIRST PLACE!!!

Keira's answer arrived quickly and scribbled.

Actually, it was me and Elliot and the others who found the royals. We fished at the Lake of Spells until we caught a Locator Spell, and we used that to get their current addresses. You just posted some letters for us. Thanks for that, but seriously? Anyhow, this is unproductive and it's too hot to keep arguing with you. Also, I have other things to do, *e.q., we need to rescue Princess Ko — she's scheduled to be executed same day we want to bring the others across.*

Madeleine wanted to reply with, *WHAT? Scheduled to be executed?!* or *How can I tell the other royals to go home if that's what happening to royals in your Kingdom?!* or *What do you MEAN "it's too hot" there?!* (She knew about the drifting seasons in Cello, but heat seemed conceptually impossible tonight.)

But she was suddenly exhausted. She wrote four words.

Tell me the details.

2.

Dear Princess Jupiter,

I haven't heard from you for a few days so I hope you're okay. I have news.

Your dad, the King, wants to bring you home. He's arranging a transfer. So, if you go to that same street corner at 10 a.m., Thursday next week, someone will collect you. Wear a disguise — I guess like a wig? I've couriered letters to the Queen and Prince Chyba (your mother and brother) too. So hopefully it'll be a family reunion.

Before you yell at me, I KNOW you said you'd never try that again. But they tell me this could be your last chance. And I think it'll be great. In Cello, you will probably bathe in your heated palace moat!

With mermaids! (Not sure. Nobody's ever told me if the moats are heated. Or if there are mermaids, but I don't see how they could justify having dragons and NOT mermaids. Inconsistent.) And you mentioned you have eczema? Well, in Cello, there'll be a Royal Surgeon (probably) who will treat you with the milk of the elderflower (not sure what that is) while silver fairies kiss your skin better (re fairies, see my comment about mermaids). So, that sounds better, right?

Anyway, if you do go to that street corner, promise me two things:

Don't wait for six hours again. If they don't come at 10 a.m., go home. You could give them ten minutes I guess, allowing for Cellian traffic jams, etc., but seriously. If nothing happens, just go home, email me, and I'll sort it out with Keira.

Once you do get back to Cello, be VERY careful. I don't mean to disrespect your Kingdom, but it sounds like a total disaster zone. I think you deserve to know: Your sister, Princess Ko, is "scheduled to be executed." They're planning to rescue her, so hopefully it'll be okay, and I'm sorry if this news is like a punch in the face. Maybe not, cause you don't remember her, or maybe it'll be the emotional jolt that brings your memory back. But I wish I could've told you more gently. Like poured the news into your ear very slowly, in the form of elderflower milk.

So, you're going home. I'll miss you.

Love,

Madeleine

3.

"Was it a vision, or a waking dream,
Fled is that music; do I wake, or sleep?"

They looked at Holly.

"It's Keats," she said defensively. "We're doing poetry."

Holly had brought them to the 2nd View Coffee Shop in Waterstones for their English class. Madeleine, Belle, and Jack had been chatting for the last ten minutes about Belle's plan to get an eyebrow piercing. Now they regarded Holly for a moment, then turned back to their conversation.

Holly chimed in again.

"I dream'd that as I wander'd by the way
Bare winter suddenly was changed to spring,"

"Did you?" Jack asked.

"No. Shelley did. The poet. That's Shelley."

"That'd be all right," Belle said. "*Whoosh.* There goes winter. Oh, look, it's spring — that was sudden."

They all turned to the window and watched the dark rush of rain.

"Poets often write about dreams," Holly said. "That's what I want to talk about today. Tell me: In what way is a poem like a dream?"

"Neither make sense," Jack said.

Madeleine held her coffee close to her cheek, warming her face. "Poems try to get under the surface of things," she said slowly. "They move close or circle from a distance. Dreams do that as well."

"That's excellent," Belle said. "That's like a poem right there. Holly, give Madeleine a sticker for class participation."

"I've been thinking about dreams a lot lately," Madeleine explained.

"Oh, well, you can stop now."

"Dreams are the darkness inside people," Jack said, "and so is poetry."

"No, poetry's about rainbows and butterflies and that," Belle argued. "You've got things upside down."

"Wait." Jack held up a hand as he reached for his backpack. He pulled out rain-soggy papers. The others waited.

"Shhh," he said.

"In what way," said Madeleine, "could we shhh any more than we already are?"

He peeled off a single sheet and held it up. "This is Byron."

"Of course it is," Belle said.

"It's dead unbelievable how relevant it is," Jack said. "Holly's going to give me *all* the stickers."

Holly looked concerned. "I haven't got any stickers."

"I'm going to read it out," Jack announced.

"You don't have to read the whole thing," Madeleine suggested.

"I had a dream." Jack stopped, and looked around triumphantly. They waited.

"That's a short poem," Belle said. "I like them short. They often go on too long, which is another thing the same about dreams."

Jack shook his head, weary with disappointment.

"Keep reading," Holly told him, and he did.

"I had a dream, which was not all a dream,
The bright sun was extinguish'd, and the stars
Did wander darkling in the eternal space,

Rayless and pathless, and the icy earth
Swung blind and blackening in the moonless air."

"You see?" Jack said. "That's dreams and darkness. In a poem."

"Depressing start," Belle said.

"Doesn't end well either," Jack agreed. "It's not like the mum comes in and goes, 'April fool's!' and switches on the light. It's more they eat each other and their dogs."

"I don't want to hear about people eating dogs," Belle said.

"Too late," Jack said. "You just heard."

"The Royal Society once cut open a living dog to see its beating heart," Madeleine said. "And they used a bellows to inflate its lungs."

"Bollocks," Belle said. "The royal family are nice. They'd never do that. They just eat sandwiches, mostly."

"Not the royal family. The Royal Society. They were scientists in the seventeenth century."

"Oh, well, that doesn't count. That's history."

Holly set down her coffee mug, leaned her chin into her hand, and looked at Jack. "You carry copies of Byron's poetry around all the time?"

"Why would anybody not?"

"Jack," Holly said, "what do you think it is about Byron that draws you to him so much?"

There was a sharp intake of breath from Madeleine. "You're being one of those wise teachers, Mum! The ones who ask the probing questions!"

Jack sighed contentedly.

"Well, I'm glad you asked that, Holly. Because there's a lot I could say about how Byron was dead sexy with curling eyelashes, which is me personified apart from the curling eyelashes. When he was in high school, his headmaster said he was a wild mountain colt with his mind in his eyes."

There was a pause.

"At this point," Jack said gently, "you don't all sit there like fish. You go, *Oh, I get it. Jack's a bit of a wild mountain colt himself. Just like Byron.*"

Holly waited for Belle and Madeleine to stop laughing, which took a while. She was still leaning forward, chin resting in hand.

"Here's what I want you to do, Jack," she said. "Find out all you can about Byron's life. The light *and* the dark."

"Your teaching's getting a bit ad hoc now," Madeleine declared.

"All that we see or seem, / Is but a dream within a dream," Holly announced. "That's Edgar Allan Poe."

"It's good the way you keep reeling us back in," Madeleine said. "That aspect of your teaching has improved. You're like a relentless, dream-poetry machine."

"How come you know so many poems about dreams?" Belle asked.

"I Googled them last night. Listen, why do you think poets are so drawn to dreams?"

"See? Reeling us back in. Nice, Mum."

"Madeleine."

"Okay, well, I've noticed that people can't say the word *dream* without their eyes going all soft and wistful," Madeleine said. "Which is a poetry thing. I mean, that's the effect poets want to achieve, so talking about dreams is like a shortcut."

"But actually the things our brains do at night should be called *sleep garbage*," Belle pointed out. "Not dreams."

"*Night* is relevant," Jack said. "It's like a poetic time of moons and stars, and the time when Madeleine used to climb out of windows and go dancing with strangers before she came here to Cambridge and reformed."

"Just keep in mind that that's my mother right here," Madeleine said.

Holly was leaning back, studying the cakes in the glass case behind her.

She looked back smiling. "What'd I miss?"

"I like your focus," Belle said.

"You know, that's something we discussed at our home-schooling teachers meeting the other day?" Holly stretched her arms above her head. "We're trying to figure out what to do now that we've lost two of our teachers. Belle, your mother seems determined not to teach. I thought I'd be able to change her mind. And with Denny gone too . . . well, it's disastrous. Darshana offered to take over the French teaching, but we pointed out she doesn't speak French. Another thing we discussed is how you all comment on our teaching. It's disconcerting and postmodern. We don't know how to deal with it."

"I like how open you are," Jack said. "Laying your teaching issues out for us."

"There," Holly said. "You're doing it again. It's like you're all *outside* the lesson, looking in. We think you need to be more present."

"Like you," Madeleine said. "When you do your sewing at the same time as teaching."

"Right," began Holly, and then, "Oh, ha-ha. That's different. That's multitasking." Holly glanced at her watch.

"Here's another one," she said. "These lines were written by a Chinese woman who was born in 1084. Li Qingzhao. You ready?

"This morning I dreamed I followed
Widely spaced bells, ringing in the wind."

There was quiet.

"I like that one," Jack said.

Holly spoke up again.

"Once a dream did weave a shade
O'er my angel-guarded bed."

"Oh, well, I think we've had enough dream poems now," Belle said politely. "Thanks, though."

Holly looked at her watch. "You're right," she said. "We're done."

"Shall we go get a falafel roll?" Jack suggested. "My horoscope today highly recommended Middle Eastern food, with extra points for crushed chickpeas."

"Has anybody moved into Abel's place?" Belle asked.

Jack looked at her. "Why do you keep asking about that flat?"

"Why do you lie about your horoscope?" she shot back.

Jack and Belle held each other's gaze. There was that jostling silence between them again. Even Holly noticed it. She raised her eyebrows at Madeleine.

"Anyway, before you all go, I need to give you an assignment," she said.

The tension folded and fell.

"Actually, the assignment's in your aura, Holly," Belle said. "It's sort of radiating out of your left ear? So you don't need to tell me. I can see it perfectly."

"You're making that up."

"I am," Belle agreed.

4.

Yo. Madz.

You crazy like a freakin school of plankton caught in one of them circles made of sound and bubbles that the humpback whales make to catch plankton!

Wait. What were we talking about?

I remember. You want me to try that street corner again. You crazy like a freakin school of plankton caught in one of them (etc.).

Nah. I'll do it. What've I got to lose? (Just my job, LOL.) (No. I'll only stay ten mins this time, like you say.)

Why do you say you'll miss me when I go back? Don't they have email in Cello? I was thinking, you can visit and we can hang in the dungeon (ha-ha, hang, I don't mean that the way it sounds, I promise never to schedule your execution, the way those douches have scheduled my sister's execution! What even? I mean it's not like killing someone's a dentist appointment! What's with the scheduling?) (But like you say, hopefully they'll rescue her.)

I also promise I won't go all, "I am princess, you are common scum, scrape the mud off my boots and put it on a sandwich and eat it!" on you.

Not to be stupid, but you're sorta my best friend here in Berlin. Seriously. And you're not even IN Berlin. Just, I mean, I haven't really met anyone I trust the way I trust you. Weird, I know, but true.

What'll it be like going back to Cello? I'm sorta excited but also sorta scared about (a) meeting the strangers who are supposed to be my royal family (e.g., Will they like me? And how am I supposed to talk? Once I've said "henceforward" I'm all out) and (b) how do I actually get there? Someone will collect me, right? And will they just sort of "magic" me there? Will it hurt? Or will they take me on a long, mad journey, so I should bring a magazine to read on the way?

Jupiter XXX

P.S. Are you still getting nosebleeds? Maybe stop picking your nose? LOL.

Dear Jupiter,

The most important thing that I have to say is this:

I DO NOT PICK MY NOSE.

The doctor says it's the cold air making the inside of my nose dry out, crack, and start bleeding. She gave me ointment that sometimes helps, and she said it could be "cauterized" if it keeps happening. It's still happening.

Actually, it might be the tension between Belle and Jack that's affecting my sinuses.

I'm very sorry but I don't think we will be able to keep emailing when you go back to Cello. It's a different dimension, see. I don't think they even HAVE the "World Wide Web," and if they do it'll be the Cello Wide Web. Cos, see, it's NOT in the World.

Also, it's illegal in Cello for people to communicate with the World. It's like a capital offence. (That's why Elliot got in so much trouble for writing to me.)

Yeah, it must be scary for you, going back. I hadn't thought of it like that — I was just thinking it was exciting, and I was sort of jealous because your dad wants to get you back, whereas mine ignores my letters. But if you don't remember who your dad IS, that's a whole other ball game.

I think you will remember everything as soon as you get thru, so then you'll be fine and you'll know how to speak Princess. Plus, I think people usually FIGHT with their family rather than worrying about whether they like them or not. So it'll all fall into place.

Finally, I don't know about your journey, sorry. They'll use a mirror and light to open the crack, and I think you'll just sort of instantly go through. The crack here is small, so Elliot and I only went to the space between. I'll be honest with you (I like how you said you trust me, but now I feel hyperaware that I have to be honest) — the space between DID hurt sometimes. It was loud and wild and I felt like I was having a fever fit. Another time, it was peaceful, but the total darkness terrified me. If Elliot hadn't been there, I would've freaked out.

It was beautiful, being there with Elliot. It was like there was nothing except him and me. I remember his palms, his chest, his chin, but it was like we were more than just our bodies. As if our essence was there in the darkness.

I guess this isn't very reassuring, but you'll probably just get through smooth and quick. I doubt you'll have time to read a magazine.

Bye,

Madeleine

x

Hey Madz,

Re this whole getting arrested if I talk to you thing, I'm the Princess, remember? So I'll just get my dad (the King) to change the law, and we can visit each other all the time. Not too often, so we don't get sick of each other (that happens with friends, no offence). But I'm not giving up on you.

You spooked me talking about the "space between," because what exactly is that?

Princess J xx

P.S. I've started trying to get people here to call me Princess J, instead of Ariel, as a sort of rehearsal for the Kingdom but they just stare & don't get me, as per the usual.

P.P.S. Only 2 more days to go until Thursday. Coolio. Won't have to work the Friday shift.

Dear Jupiter,

You're leaving tomorrow.

I should have started this email: Esteemed Your Royal Highness.

Oh, well. Too late.

Not sure you'll be able to change the laws — Princess Ko couldn't do it, and your dad is still trying to figure ways around it to get you home, so things might be trickier than you realise.

But you should totally give it a shot.

Sorry I spooked you about the space between. I don't actually know what it is. It's just, because Cello is another dimension, there is SOMETHING between our worlds. It's like a total emptiness and total darkness, but sometimes there are sounds or colours or lights.

I've been reading about alchemy lately, and two books I've read MIGHT be relevant.

The first one says there's "original material" from which everything was created. It's a sort of magical chaos, I think, which is still around, but out of reach. Alchemists used to try to find residue of it by spreading out burlap bags to collect the morning dew. The idea was, you untangle some original matter and then you sort of impress the "idea" of gold onto it. Anyway, it makes me wonder if the space between is where you'd find it?

The other book I read is by a guy named Jung. He thinks that whenever we look at darkness or chaos, we see the hidden parts of ourselves. So, for him I guess, the space between is like a mirror of the secrets we don't tell ourselves.

Jung thinks all the symbols in alchemy are a sort of universal language, like a web that links our psyches. Also, he talks a lot about people's dreams. He seems to meet people who have very short dreams, which never happens in real life, so maybe he made them up. My favourite is this: A man dreamed he was leaving a party and he accidentally took the wrong hat.

That's it. Dream done.

Jung thinks it means the man put on the wrong PERSONALITY, like he took someone else's character when he left the party. That's bollocks. The guy was just having one of those anxiety dreams where you do something stupid and embarrassing.

At the moment, you are wearing the wrong hat. Tomorrow, you will get your own hat back.

Well, that's enough for today. For good. Forever. Ha-ha.

It's almost midnight. I'm about to go have one more "conversation" with Keira about tomorrow's plans. So check email before you leave in the morning, in case anything else has changed?

And if anything goes wrong, email me right away.

Take care,

Have fun being a Princess,

Enjoy the cakes and bubble baths,

I don't know what else to say,

except

bye.

Love,

Madeleine

5.

$\mathcal{T}$he conversation with Keira that night lasted three minutes. Keira wrote first:

All good here. Anything new there?

Madeleine replied:

Nah, just freezing as usual.

Keira responded:

Not asking about the weather. Anything new from the royals?

Okay, Ms. too-cool-for-climate, nothing new from the royals. I still haven't heard from the Queen or Prince Chyba, but I guess there's still a little bit of time. Even if we don't hear, that doesn't mean they're not coming. Jupiter will be there.

Great. Thanks. Don't forget to tell them all to wear disguises.

I have. But they're sort of disguised already without knowing it if you see what I mean?

Not really. Gotta go.

Wait, is there any news about Princess Ko?

Not yet. We'll get her out tomorrow. I'll seal this crack again in next day or two. Thanks for yr help. Bye. K

Madeleine was turning to leave then — Keira's words could be the ones to go unanswered, for once — but she stopped and wrote a final note.

If anything happens to Princess Jupiter, I will personally blow open this crack, come through, and tear you to pieces.

She waited, shivering, for five minutes, but there was no reply.

6.

*E*arly the next morning, Madeleine received an email from someone named Sasha Wilczek.

That was Queen Lyra. Emailing from Taipei.

For the first time, the Queen of Cello was writing to her.

Madeleine: I do not know who you are or what you have to do with things, but I've had enough of the hiding & the running. I can't stand it anymore. I might as well be dead. The stress is making my rheumatoid arthritis so bad I'd quite like to be dead, to be honest. I'll be there. Do with me what you will — shoot me down on a street corner — but know that I have not breathed a word about any of them or their activities or the locations of their safe houses, etc., to a soul, so I deserve nothing but kindness. Sasha

Madeleine emailed back right away.

Hi Sasha, I'm not exactly sure what you mean, but I guess it has something to do with the alternate identity you've created for yourself. Nobody is planning to shoot you down on a street corner — they just want to take you home to your Kingdom so you can be the Queen again. (I can't actually guarantee your safety in Cello, as things seem a bit out of control there, so wear a disguise and be careful. But, nothing to worry about here in our World.) They'll be so happy to see you. M

Madeleine's mother was still sleeping, so Madeleine went out to buy bread and tangerines. When she returned, Holly was still not up. It was Thursday, one of their free days. Denny/Abel used to teach them today, but nobody had figured out how to replace him or Belle's mother yet. Temporarily, they'd labelled these as "study days" and, to celebrate, Holly often slept late.

Madeleine sat at the computer thinking it would be funny to do some actual "study."

"I've got a wicked headache," murmured Holly from across the room.

Madeleine swung around, knocking a pile of papers to the floor.

Holly chuckled sleepily. "That's the draft of my design essay. You'd better put it back in order." She yawned loudly. "Don't worry, this isn't *that* sort of headache. People without tumours get headaches too."

Madeleine bit her lip.

"Are you sure?" she said eventually.

"I am."

"Have you had any other symptoms? Have you been acting weird?"

Holly shook her head so it rustled the pillow. "I'm probably getting the flu. And you'd have noticed if I was behaving strangely again. Have I been?"

Madeleine continued to study Holly.

"It's hard to tell," she said. "You're always strange. You want some Nurofen?"

"I'll sleep it off." Holly turned over.

Madeleine wrote a new email to Jupiter.

Dear Jupiter,

If everything went to plan, you should be in Cello by now. If not, you will be mad at me and trust will be all blown to hell.

Well, I won't keep talking. I just heard from Queen Lyra — your mother — she's going to the crackpoint, so that's good news. You'll get to see your mum again. She sounds a bit confused but hopefully that'll get sorted once she comes thru & her memory returns.

I know you're scared, so I wanted to tell you this. A long time ago there was an alchemist called Paracelsus. He believed that the stars are made of the "quintessence" and that inside everybody, there's a hidden star.

So, there's a star hidden inside you. It's your quintessence.

You're probably long gone and listen to me, still talking.

M

P.S. It's the strangest thing to write to nobody.

P.P.S. Email me right away if you're still there.

P.P.P.S. My dad still hasn't answered my latest letter.

The room seemed to sway quietly to the rhythm of Holly's breathing.

Madeleine stared at the screen. There was no reply.

She began picking up her mother's essay. It was sprayed out on the floor, a series of half-hearted fans. She gathered pages slowly, stopping now and then to reach back up and refresh the screen in case Jupiter replied.

There was no reply.

Eventually, all the papers were piled on the table. She found the cover page.

Design Essay

Holly Tully, Student Number: 7891351 (C)

She smiled. Sometimes her mother seemed so young. She flicked through and realised there were no page numbers. Sometimes her mother seemed like an *idiot*.

How was she going to put it back in order? She'd have to read it.

She sighed, turned to a random page and read:

> After all is the rage of the inconsiderate. However, the twinning of elastic forms a car wreck. This, in itself, cannot justify the flourished redbrick nor the pipings of the muddle. Bathwater should always be sharp as a crisis of toadstools.

PART 5

1.

*E*lliot is tearing off the mask. It's taped to his hair. It rips away hair as he pulls. There they are, the Grays, crushing the bones in his face. Elliot is tearing off the mask. It's taped to his body. Strips of skin come away with the tape. There they are, the Grays, crowding in at him. He's tearing off the mask. It's taped to his eyes. Splinters of his eyes are ripped away. Elliot is tearing off his mask. There they are, the —

"You have to stay still," says the voice. "Or the poison will reach your heart and kill you."

Elliot tears off the mask. The Grays are there with rakes. He tears off the mask. The Grays shine a flashlight in his eyes, and the fine line of light turns to flame.

"You have to stay still," the voice repeats, matter-of-fact, someone at the Laundromat telling him he has to use the third machine along.

Elliot tears off the mask. The Grays are tossing balls of flame at him. It's a flame game. This, he can do. He's a deftball *champion*. He springs, stretches, catches the flame ball with both hands. His triumph cracks: His palms are alight! He shouts, incensed. "You're throwing *fire!*"

"You have to stay still," says the voice.

He tears off his mask. The Grays get him in a pincer grip.

"Stay still," the voice reminds him. "And tell me this. What color is the pain? How does it sound?"

Elliot tears off his mask. A thin arm snakes around his neck. It's the slender arm of a child. It's a very fine snake. The snake has bristles. The snake is tightening, the bristles are sharpening, the —

"You have to stay still," says the voice. "And tell me this. What shape is the pain?"

Elliot is tearing off his mask.

"You have to stay still," says the voice. "And tell me, how do you rate the pain? Out of ten, how do you rate it?"

Elliot is reaching up to tear off the mask, but he stops and snarls, "A *thousand*."

The voice goes still.

Elliot sleeps.

The days were full of underhanded mountains.

These mountainous days, he thought. Elliot slept, but they were always there, the mountains, waiting to rise beneath him. Each one prodded his back until he woke, then it tore open his flesh, shattered his spine and kept on rising.

"You have to stay still. What number is the pain? What does it look like?"

Once, he opened his eyes and caught a snapshot. Close walls. A man in a chair.

The mountain speared his spine again.

"You have to stay still."

He dreamed that Chime appeared and spoke: "For now, what you will do, and what you'll do is this. You will let yourself be sewn together. Your mouth will be sewn closed, your body will lie, perfect and still, while we fold you like a suit of clothes, your arms crossed at the front." Her voice turned low and mirthful. "Your legs, we will brush them down first, for they won't fold up without they'd break."

He screamed, and the voice of the man in the chair said, "You have to stay still."

Days veered between mountains.

He opened his eyes and a different man was standing above him, arms crossed, a muted smile. "What are we going to do with you?" It was the Assistant. His voice leaked irony. The irony turned acidic and splashed on Elliot's flesh.

"Tell me," said the man in the chair. "What shape is your pain? What is its color?"

Elliot roared.

The Assistant opened the door, and it closed behind him with a thud. The thud flung itself back across the room, belting Elliot with a gasp.

"You have to stay still."

The days subsided. Elliot found patches of sleep. He knew the pattern. Between patches, the Grays attacked. The man in the chair asked questions.

Once, he paused in a Gray attack and recognized the man.

It was Ming-Sun, from the bunk beneath Elliot's. He'd tried to befriend him before, and gotten nowhere. Now with all the questions?

"What shape is the pain?"

Elliot turned to shout at Ming-Sun for asking questions. "It's a stack," he screamed instead. "It's all piled up in a stack!"

Ming-Sun wound his fingers together, let the fingers flare, and closed them again.

Elliot stared at this, furious. He slept.

Chime was in the room.

The pain was there in long pale shreds, but he could see her through it.

"You took me into a Color cavern," he said, but he didn't recognize his own voice and it tore at his throat.

Chime nodded.

"Without protective clothing."

Her face folded a little, then she nodded again. "If we'd put you in protective gear," she said, "you might have guessed we were going into a Color cavern."

"But *you* wore protective gear?"

"Of course."

The pain took shape and color, embracing him from either side.

"You have to stay still," said Ming-Sun as usual. "What would you rate it now? What number is the pain, out of ten?"

"Five *thousand*."

Ming-Sun pressed his fingertips together and arched his hands so they appeared to rest on an invisible ball.

Chime watched.

The embrace loosened. There were cobwebs of pale sidling up to him again, but he could speak through those.

"You took me into a Color cavern *without protective clothing*," he repeated, hoarse and breathless.

"The Grays were asleep," Chime said. "All you had to do was be quiet."

"I *was* quiet. Why did they wake?"

Chime looked down at him, silent.

"Wait," said Elliot, but something struck him from the side and he lunged.

"You have to stay still."

He forced himself to stillness. "Wait. *That's* where Hostile compounds are. Hidden behind Color caverns. That's the secret. That's why no one ever finds them."

Chime tilted her head, shrugging one shoulder.

"You've been attacked by Colors before," she said. "You have the scars."

"Not like this."

"It was the year you were seeking your father in the caverns?"

"But he wasn't there!" Elliot shouted. "He was in a Hostile compound. But he wasn't *there* either. He was in the World!" He lost himself then, in stacks of truth, stacks of pain, layers of color searing his forehead.

"Stay still. Stay perfectly still."

When he woke again, Chime was gone.

3.

One night, he woke inside fierce clarity.

He was better.

It was deep night, but a small electric lamp burned beside him. Ming-Sun was asleep in the chair.

Elliot sat up. Nothing hurt. He was cured.

He swung his legs over the side of the bed. For the first time, he noticed that his arms and legs and torso were bound in bandages. He touched his face and felt bandaging there too.

He didn't need any of that anymore. He was better!

He went to peel a bandage back, then decided against it. There are more important things, he thought. He wondered what he meant.

Ming-Sun slept silently, chin sagging, doubling. Elliot crept past, opened the door, and found himself in a night-lit corridor.

Everything was quiet.

Important things, he reminded himself. He turned left. He passed closed doors with their signs. Briefing. Strategy. That one had a screw missing and tilted. The familiarity was so beautiful Elliot thought he might cry.

It was so *good* to be cured.

He found the kitchen, switched on the lights, and the warm surge and flicker nearly did him in. He *loved* this kitchen. And its lights!

The important thing, of course, was cleaning. He saw that now. A bucket of warm, soapy water; wipes, garbage bags, gloves (X-large, because his hands were thick with bandaging). He began to take items from the pantry and the fridge, stacking up canned beans, pasta, stock, unopened packets of corn flour, jars of dried rosemary and cloves. The garbage bags he filled with rotten potatoes, cream cheese turned blue, rancid butter, tea bags crawling with maggots. The sagging bulk of the garbage bags delighted him. Even better was sliding out the fridge shelves, blasting them with hot spray from the tap; reaching inside the pantry with a dripping cloth, wringing out the cloth, turning the water in the bucket an instant deep gray.

"This, and what can you be doing?"

He'd just lifted the bucket by its handle. Chime was standing in the doorway, dressed in the oversize T-shirt she always slept in.

"I'm emptying out this water," Elliot said. "It's turned black."

Chime watched as he tipped the water down the sink and refilled it. She came over to the deep freeze and drew out a stack of frozen meat.

"These are to defrost for the morning," she explained. "I had forgotten."

Elliot nodded.

"Your eyes are wild," Chime added.

He was back at the pantry, scrubbing again. Chime leaned against the bench, watching him.

"I believe as that you should be in bed," she said.

He ignored her.

"Elliot," she said, her voice the same low song. "You know that I meant to kill you when I took you to the cavern of the Grays?"

The cloth stopped swooping in circles. It concentrated on a single mark.

"This, and that was our plan all along," Chime continued. "You cannot bring the son of a Loyalist into a Hostile compound. Keira was a fool to ask us."

The cloth resumed its slow, circular movements.

"We needed you to be killed by Colors," Chime explained, "so that we could tell Keira it was an accident. Keira's mother still has much power, even behind bars, and we could not offend her daughter. Once in the cavern, I signaled the Grays."

Elliot turned. He wrung out the cloth into the bucket again.

"You woke the Grays?"

"Not just woke. Signaled. We have learned to use Grays and Purples as weapons. Some among us even *carry* them, in concentrated forms. Mischka set one against your uncle, for example."

Elliot waited for the noise to quiet. The garbage bags, boxes of food, dripping cloth, kitchen lights, all of it had begun shouting at him. It didn't quiet. He spoke over it.

"But you brought me back inside?" he said. "You saved me."

Chime shrugged. "I have failed," she said. "In the end, to watch them kill you, this and I could not do. I have failed."

"You might want to quit with the repetition of that phrase," Elliot suggested. He dropped the cloth into the water and looked at her. "Keira trusted you people."

"Some things," Chime said, "are bigger than trust."

Elliot remembered the Assistant's face looming above him — *What are we going to do with you?*

"But why are they keeping me alive now?" he asked.

Chime tilted her head.

"We're not," she said. "We expect you to die. None survive such an attack. Once you're gone, we tell Keira what happened. For now, while we wait, we keep the signals scrambled. Thus, she cannot get in touch until too late."

"But I'm better," Elliot whispered.

"We've given you Ming-Sun. He's a magic weaver. He cannot cure you, but he helps to ease your pain. I should have let you die at once, out in the cavern, but I failed. Hence you suffer a long, dark death. I am sorry. Does he help?"

"I'm better," Elliot insisted, and then he was tearing off his mask again, the Grays coming at him with their carving knives and scalpels, dropping from the ceiling and straddling his shoulders so they could run their nails across his face and wrench out chunks of hair.

Someone carried him back to his room. "Stay still," Ming-Sun intoned through the night. "And tell me, what tune does this pain play?"

This time he only answered with curses and shouts.

"You may feel well again," Ming-Sun told him the next morning when he was still curled up, groaning. "It's an illusion. Do not leave this room again. Do not clean the cupboards! It will only make your suffering worse. Now, tell me, how does the pain sound?"

"Tractor in a bathroom," Elliot breathed.

He watched Ming-Sun's hands flutter and felt the sharpness soften. He slept.

When he next woke up, the room was dark again. Two thoughts were vibrant in his mind: They expected him to die. He planned to live.

He breathed the second thought into the darkness a while: *I intend to live.*

But then what? If he did live, they'd stage another accidental death. Especially now he knew the secret of their compound location. (Dumbest hiding place ever: behind Color caverns. Also, ingenious.)

He thought about the Exit doors and the line that crossed his forehead. The answer was there in that line. The only way out was a different-colored line.

And the only way to get that was to become a Hostile.

He'd have to pretend.

The next day, he asked Ming-Sun to pass a message to Chime, asking her to visit him.

She came in the late afternoon, defiance in her eyes, but her head darting about like a dragonfly, and Elliot realized she was nervous.

"I just want to ask you a question."

Chime inclined her head.

"Why did you become a Hostile?"

"This, and I cannot tell you."

"Why not?"

Ming-Sun moved his seat so it squealed along the floor. Chime stood by the bed, staring at Elliot, her shoulders rising and falling.

"I see as what you are saying," she said eventually. "Very well. I came to be a Hostile through my father. He is a Color Bender, as I have told you. The Hostiles need Color Benders, and pay him well, for to monitor the Color caverns while they build their compounds, and to train and concentrate Colors."

Elliot nodded. That made sense.

"And then," Chime continued, "he fell to agreeing with their notions, as did I."

She folded her arms, and waited.

"So now," Elliot said, "will you tell me about these notions?"

She blinked. "Why?"

Elliot sorted through sentences, looking for something with enough truth to sound convincing. "It's like this," he said eventually. "Time is so darn strange. You have to live in it, then your mind shrink-wraps it, so when you look back, it's all compact. But you know what happens when I look at the year my father was missing? The year I was fighting and searching for him? It's not shrink-wrapped at all. It's one slow piece of memory after another."

She was frowning.

"It was Hostiles did that to me," Elliot explained. "They tricked my father and chased him to the World. They killed my uncle. I can't unhappen any of that, it's part of me now." He shrugged. "But it'd be good to know why it happened."

Chime glanced down at Ming-Sun. As usual, he sat straight-backed, eyes half-closed, hands on his thighs, silent.

She sat on the side of the bed. After a moment, she swung her legs up, stretched along beside him, stared at the ceiling, and began to speak.

"I'll start ten thousand years ago," she said.

Elliot laughed.

But she did. She took him through the history of royalty in Cello. King Sartor used to ride with bow and arrows, hunting peasants for sport; Queen Veneze first invaded Aldhibah, wanting their silkworm farms for her gowns. Various monarchs further undermined relations with their neighbor, through treachery and deceit — the famous unnaming of the Undisclosed Province; the breach by Prince Murving of the Twenty-Year Peace. Over the course of their consecutive reigns, each King Parashi (I, II, III, and IV) appropriated most of Cello's land and livestock, leaving their subjects to starve.

Chime told over twenty similar stories. Some Elliot had learned at school, but they'd always seemed like fairy tales to him.

"But the royals are not like that these days," he said, beginning to feel drowsy.

Chime said, "That is enough for now." She slipped from the room.

The next few days fell into a pattern. Afternoons, at three P.M., Chime would visit, lie down on Elliot's bed — she was so slight, it was like someone gently placing a coat alongside of him — and talk.

One day, she described a concept called democracy. He argued that regular people could never know how to run a kingdom or what was best for everyone, and Chime explained how the place could be divided into regions, people voting for their own representatives. That sort of made sense.

Another day, she told him how the royal marketing and PR people supervised the media, fostering a particular image of royalty.

"Did you know that King Cetus is quarter-Carthanian and a quarter Southern Climean?" Chime said. "And that the Queen has Mahlian blood?"

Elliot shrugged. "I guess. I don't know. Did I know that?"

"It's a matter of public record," Chime said, "but never discussed. The King's skin is quite dark, but his photographs are altered, to lighten him. The Princesses have dark skin also, and dark hair: They wear makeup to change this, and dye their hair golden-blond."

Elliot thought back to Princess Ko, and how some days her hair had seemed impossibly blond.

"Why would they do that?"

"The PR department insists Cellian royals maintain the traditional Cellian appearance. It helps to maintain the myth of superior royal blood."

"Well, that's just weird," Elliot said. "Anyhow, Cello's just about all mixed-race these days, so who'd care if the royals were too?"

He frowned, his thoughts circling. Then the circles thudded up against a truth.

"But you Hostiles kill people," he said. "It doesn't compare."

"Sometimes, this killing, it must be done," Chime said.

"Well," said Elliot, "you've lost me there."

Chime curled her legs beneath her, so the bed trembled. "Cello's Security Forces have slaughtered thousands of Hostiles, without trial. *All* of us here have lost friends and family in this way! They hunt us down and torture us! They lock us up for so much as *breathing* anti-Royalist ideas!"

"Okay," Elliot said. "But at least those guys are taking down people who threaten the Kingdom. You Hostiles blow up cars with babies in them. You shoot children on vacation with their families."

"There are many different branches of Hostiles, many styles of Wandering Hostile. Do you not think that the media might portray only the worst? And our mistakes? That they might be *making* us into monsters?"

"But you *are* monsters sometimes, right?"

She lay back down again.

"I'm a Nature Strip girl," she said. "We tear the bellies from living creatures and eat them to cure illness. We break apart the youngest Colors and use these to make protective clothing — to protect ourselves, to protect *you* from Color attacks."

"Not me so much," Elliot pointed out.

From his chair, Ming-Sun chuckled. They both turned to him, surprised. He rarely made a sound.

Ming-Sun's smile faded as he narrowed his eyes at Elliot.

"You'd better go," he told Chime. "He's about to have another attack."

"I will return," Chime said.

Elliot glanced at her, and a remote thought flared at him — today he'd forgotten to pretend — and then he was tearing off his mask again, this time shouting, "I've had *enough* now, make it *stop*, I've had *enough*," while Ming-Sun asked his regular questions and gave his regular admonitions to stay still.

4.

*T*he attacks came so regularly over the next thirty-six hours that Chime couldn't visit at all. Elliot was learning that the more precisely he answered Ming-Sun's questions, the better the magic worked. "It's like stains that I can't get out of my bloodstream," he said, "and my bones are rusting." "It's deep blue with edges of red." "My body is a forest, and they're splitting me up into kindling." "It sounds like an angry man laughing." "I'm a sheet of pastry, and they're cutting out circles with sharp-edged knives."

Each time he spoke, Ming-Sun's hands would braid the air. Each time, the pain would slow and subside.

By the end of those thirty-six hours, Elliot felt more battered and exhausted than ever in his life, but he also felt that something was different. The ceiling light seemed brighter. The air seemed calmer.

Ming-Sun dragged his chair close to the bed.

"Elliot," he said. "That is the attack that should have killed you. It did not. Against all odds, I believe you may be winning. The poison is leaving you. Attacks will recur, but in time, I believe they will stop altogether."

Now Ming-Sun fixed his eyes on the wall beyond Elliot's shoulder. "I will tell nobody this news but you," he said. "I will report that the attacks continue. I will change your bandages tomorrow and take out your stitches, but I will report that your wounds show signs of continued infection. I will tell them that you are in false recovery, that you can move about but that, in fact, you only have weeks left to live."

Elliot stared at the man's face. He could hear his own heart thudding like animals running on dirt.

"Meanwhile," Ming-Sun continued, now so close that Elliot could smell his breath, "you should continue your charade with Chime. It is a good plan. Yes, do not look startled, I see your plan. I believe you will convince her of your conversion. She feels remorse toward you, and affection. Thus, she wants to believe in you. In a few days, ask her to take you to the Cat Walk. She loves it. She will want to show you and redeem herself a little by sharing its joy. She will trust you not to run. In any case, she will reason, you are to die soon so what does it matter. Once at the Cat Walk, you can run. Now sleep."

This last he said in a sudden bark.

Elliot flinched.

"Sleep," Ming-Sun repeated more politely.

At once, Elliot closed his eyes. He felt himself fall toward profound rest. Then he opened his eyes and turned to Ming-Sun. "Why are you helping me?"

Ming-Sun shrugged. "I'm a deftball fan," he said.

5.

*E*verything happened as Ming-Sun had predicted.

Elliot felt better. He was well enough to get up for a few hours each day and to work in the kitchen, although he was not allowed to move around the compound otherwise. He always returned to his infirmary room, where Ming-Sun waited in his straight-back chair.

In the kitchen, Elliot and Chime continued their discussions. She taught him about political systems and inter-Kingdom relations. Sometimes he was weirdly elated to be *learning*, as if his brain had been crying out for it, but sometimes it got boring and he zoned out. Chime didn't seem to notice. She kept right on talking, chopping, frying, grating, talking.

The attacks stopped altogether. Ming-Sun said there could be one or two more, but that otherwise he was cured. He suggested Elliot shout and thrash about now and then in his room. The compound was accustomed to hearing this, Ming-Sun explained, so it would seem suspicious if it ceased. This was about the most humiliating thing Elliot had ever done, he thought. "Louder," Ming-Sun would whisper, and once Elliot whispered back, appalled, "Surely I didn't make as much noise as this?"

"More." Ming-Sun shrugged. "The pain is extraordinary. There is no shame in screaming when we hurt."

Still.

Strangely, Elliot began to feel a sort of wide sash against his chest, only this wasn't physical. It was emotional, he realized: a mix of anger and sadness. Sure, he had plenty to be sad and mad about: He was trapped, his life was in danger, his friend had betrayed him and taken him out to be slaughtered (she'd helped him in the end, but it still wasn't all that friendly a thing to do). But this "sash" feeling seemed bigger than all that. In fact, it seemed to have *swallowed* those facts and now it just sat there like a part of him. It was a new tone or atmosphere he carried around, that wasn't hinged to anything particular. He didn't like it.

"The first time we spoke of this," Chime said one day, "you said that the royals of the past are not those of today. You are right. But what truth can you know? With their marketing games? Shall I tell you some truths?"

"Sure," Elliot agreed.

"King Cetus is arrogant, lazy, and self-important. His preference would always be to party, rather than making difficult decisions. He achieves little, merely pretends to do so. The Queen also enjoys parties. She once expressed an interest in finances. Thus, with neither experience nor training, she began to oversee the Kingdom's economy.

The Commissioner of Finance can't take a step without her permission."

Elliot was slicing runner beans. He rolled these back and forth beneath his palms.

"The younger princess," Chime went on, "Princess Jupiter, inherited her father's wildness. His penchant for alcohol and drugs."

"Well, that I know," Elliot said. "Everyone knows that Princess Jupiter was out of control. But is that such a big deal?"

"Do you know that her escapades have cost the Kingdom thousands — tens of thousands — in cover-ups, in payments for the damage she has done? Her recklessness has cost lives. She once went to a Gangster party in the swamps of the Golden Coast; guards were compelled to follow. They were taken by a hovering Hideum. Do you know that Princess Ko, meanwhile, inherited her father's laziness? She spends her days lolling about in hammocks and horseback riding."

Elliot straightened. "Princess Ko," he said, "is a lot of things, but she's not lazy. I knew her. Remember?"

"She *was* lazy," Chime retorted, "before her family disappeared. And then what happened? She took control of the Kingdom like a child with a new toy. Recall how she treated you? We know little of what happened on the RYA, but we know this. She sent her best friend, Sergio, untrained, on a dangerous mission to the WSU. She bullied Samuel into using Olde Quainte magic, which was effectively a death sentence. She blackmailed Keira with the threat of her mother's execution, and she risked Keira's sight. She blackmailed *you* with threats to report you to the WSU for contact with the World. Then she forced you to continue that contact and, in the end, sacrificed you to the WSU anyway!"

"You know little of what happened?" Elliot said. "Sounds like you know everything."

"We had a spy among you, recall?"

Elliot had lost that memory somewhere behind the Color attack. It returned now, weighing down the sash across his chest. He resumed chopping, but slowly.

"Can you tell me who it was now?"

Chime shook her head. "This, I do not know. But consider how Princess Ko treated you. And consider how she treated her Kingdom! Why did she not inform us that her family had disappeared?"

"She thought it would cause chaos," Elliot said. "Seriously, she was trying to do the right thing. She thought Aldhibah would attack. She was tough but she was trying to save the Kingdom. She does *not* deserve to be executed." The knife sped up.

Chime placed her hand on his to stop the movement.

"Do you not think," she said, "that it was security's job to rescue her family, not a group of young people that Princess Ko chose on a whim? And that the Elite run things anyway, and so would have assumed control, as they have now? This, and should it not have occurred to Princess Ko that the Kingdom *runs itself* without her family at its helm?"

Elliot seemed to be frowning a lot today. "But if it does," he said, "if it runs itself, and the Elite are actually in control — who cares about the royals? Isn't it sort of ideal?"

"And so," said Chime, voice rising, "we have the corrupt and powerful of Jagged Edge, rubbing their hands like cartoon villains, making shady deals with Dark Quarters of Tek and Ganglords of GC, gathering treasure while the royals prance about as their puppets and oh yes, isn't *that* ideal?"

Elliot watched her. She was shaking, which he found oddly moving. He wanted to hold her and calm her.

"You got any more of that Vermillion candy?" he asked, remembering.

There were only two left.

"These last days," she admitted, "have been stressful . . . the sound of your screaming through the walls . . ."

Elliot sighed. His screaming again. It might not technically be shameful, but here he was, ashamed.

They sat down, feet up on the counters, and were silent for a while.

"What about the registration system?" Elliot said.

Chime sucked on the candy. Eventually she spoke, "What about it?"

They smiled at each other.

"Well, it's always made sense to me," Elliot said. "If a town doesn't like the royals, they register as Hostile, and then they're exempt from royal rule. That way, people who *like* royals get to keep the royal family, and people who don't, rule themselves. Why don't Wandering Hostiles just settle down in a registered town and stop blowing things up?"

There was another languid silence.

"When you say that Registered Hostiles can rule themselves," Chime said, "you forget that all who live in Cello are royal subjects. If you leave the borders of your town, you are subject to royal rule. Also, the royals control education, transport, foreign policy, the law. Every judge on every court was appointed by royalty. Every major decision affecting the Kingdom requires the Royal Stamp."

"Huh," said Elliot. He sighed, content, studying the candy stick.

"The royals have authority over everything, except the WSU," Chime continued. "And they do not like it when towns register. Discrimination begins. Major highways and railroads bypass those towns. Public funding ignores them, even in times of catastrophe. Not a single student from a Registered Hostile town has ever been awarded a King's Scholarship. This, and thus of late, towns declare themselves Randomly Hostile. They paint an *H* encircled with daggers. By this, they say they oppose both the royals *and* the registration system. But the crown simply treats them as registered, so it achieves no end, except that it says something of the mood of the Kingdom. Do you know of this new trend?"

Elliot said he'd heard something about it.

"You've always heard 'something about it,' Elliot," Chime said. "Only, you've never listened." They both laughed.

There was a longer silence. The calm filled it completely. The sash of anger and sadness slithered from Elliot's chest.

He saw that it was time. Over the last couple of days, he'd been calculating just how and when to ask, the right voice, the reasons he should offer, persuasive arguments, but now, with the calm, he simply asked.

"Can you take me to see the Cat Walk sometime?"

She narrowed her eyes, smiled, and said, "The Cat Walk? Of course. Let's go tonight."

6.

*T*hey did go that night.

Something was happening in the compound. Doors were closing, strangers arriving. Voices were rapid and raised. Footsteps hurried up and down the corridors.

Chime went to investigate. When she returned, Elliot was stirring soup.

"What's the story?" he asked.

Chime drew her thin shoulders up, but it seemed more a squirm of pleasure than a shrug. "The Director is free," she said.

"The Director? You mean Keira's mother? Mischka?"

"Keira's mother, yes. The Elite have assumed control over the penal system. She must have made a deal with them. They have set her free."

Elliot studied this news. It sat before him quietly. Mischka was free.

"Will she be coming here to this compound?" he asked.

This question stood, rather than sat, before him.

"Yes, she will return, but I cannot know when," Chime said. "Let us truly go to the Cat Walk tonight. They are all so distracted, it is perfect." She looked at the soup. "I will bring out the evening meal and then we can slip away. Will Ming-Sun wonder where you are?"

"I'll tell him I'm working late in the kitchen." Elliot kept his gaze steady.

She caught the gaze. "You will return with me from the Cat Walk?" she said lightly. "You know they will probably kill me if I let you escape?"

"I won't run," Elliot agreed.

This time, she found protective gear for both of them: helmets, jackets, pants. Elliot looked at these without comment, but he felt himself shaking as he dressed.

There was nobody around. The Exit door opened. They moved through the cavern of sleeping Grays, and Elliot focused on Chime ahead of him, ignoring the clusters and pods that hung from the ceiling and in mounds along the walls. He felt the Vermillion candy stepping up against his fear: surges of calm, a panic of calm.

Then they were outside.

It was night. There'd been plenty of darkness down in the compound, but this night darkness was so immense and generous it was almost humorous. He'd completely forgotten the stars and the moon, and now they seemed like part of the joke. The air was so light, he felt it couldn't hold him.

Chime was already running, flashlight swinging, and he followed, stumbling along. His legs seemed downright amazed to be moving in this way. It was typical Nature Strip terrain, rough and swampy, roots to trip them, thick forest either side of the track, mountains rearing up against a rich, dark sky. He ran and smiled at the space of it all, and the movement, and the cold against his face, and he felt a terror of happiness.

Ahead of him, Chime's shoulder blades moved in her shirt. He thought about stopping her, and holding her, all the fire and bones and energy of her, and he thought of the flats of her hands making music, and he watched the muscles moving in her arms.

It was only a ten-minute jog to the Cat Walk, and Elliot almost crumpled when they reached it. Chime caught him, and stood him up again.

"This, and I am forgetting you have been so ill," she said, then her eyes drifted away from him.

The Cat Walk ran between two high ridges, a rutted path as wide as a country road, pale and glowing in the moonlight. The Walk was empty now, the air cool and still. A few people were already sitting along the ridge, dark shadows wrapped in blankets. They glanced up at Elliot and Chime, eyes curious, then turned away. A small crowd had also gathered on the opposite ridge. Elliot watched as a man set up a camera and tripod. A couple of women held clipboards and binoculars.

It was quiet. The Tea-Wild Redbirds swooped and called, and the Curling Black Sombles chittered in trees. Chime led Elliot away from the other tourists and around a curve. She laid out a rug. "Here come the first ones already," she murmured. Elliot squinted.

"It's all right," Chime said softly. "They'll come right by us."

"Is it dangerous?" Elliot watched the distant blurs grow and sharpen.

"No." Chime reconsidered. "Unless they are disturbed by sudden noise."

The figures moved into a middle distance, more shapes appearing behind them.

"Why do they do it?" Elliot asked.

"None knows," she said. "Those women with their clipboards? There are always scientists, researchers, doctoral students. Some say this is a mating ritual, or a selection of leaders. Others argue the clay here has qualities that sharpen claws — but nothing is conclusive. Simply, there is a gathering of cats, from all over the Kingdom, every night at this time. Some cats come frequently, some rarely, but all come at least once. This, it has always been."

Elliot smoothed out a folded corner of the rug.

"This, it has always been," he repeated. There was nobody nearby. He lowered his voice. "What about Prince Chyba?" he said.

"Prince Chyba?"

"All the other royals, you've got something against — well, you haven't mentioned the little prince, but he's just a kid — but Prince Chyba, what's your issue with him?"

Chime tilted her head, so the moonlight formed a patch on her neck. "We have nothing against him. He seems a fine young man. He's intelligent. He likes music, animals, the idea of peace."

Elliot turned his body to face her in the darkness. "Well then," he whispered urgently. "Prince Chyba is heir. Sounds like he'd make a great king. Why not just wait for him?"

"Don't you see?" Chime had stopped whispering, but her voice stayed low. "That's the point. Even the best should not rule simply because he is heir. This is why *now* is the time to stop this, before Chyba becomes King. Support for the Hostiles will dwindle when he does, and then what? His firstborn is a tyrant? Or a hapless party guy like the current King, so everything is run by the Elite. This, and it must end now."

Elliot looked into the darkness. "I would never kill a person," he said.

"You wouldn't have to. Did we not send the royals to the World to start new lives? Is that ruthless killing? Elliot, inside your heart, you are strong and brave. You ask questions, and thus, you become your own person. Find your own person. He's not a killer, but neither does he allow his Kingdom to be ruled by darkness. Does he? But look."

She leaned forward and the triangle of moonlight vanished abruptly. "Here they are. Lions. Females. Behind them, panthers, more lions, male. And that's a score at least of leopards coming next."

Elliot heard himself gasp. Impossibly, cats of every size were striding past right below him. Immense tigers, sleek panthers, tumbling cubs, haughty little cats, some wild, some domestic, some slinking low as if to practice stalking.

Some cats played, leaping onto the backs of others, but most strode, silent, a stately swing to their shoulders. Panthers strolled together like shadows weaving.

Chime murmured the names: most he'd heard of, some were strange to him. There were cheetahs, snow leopards, clouded leopards, star-eyed bobcats, tawny jaguars. There were rabbit-eared sarcs, Golden Coast ocelots, coastal horned wildcats, and a single black-footed wolf-cat of Olde Quainte.

For a while, Elliot was mesmerized by paws — the vicious curve of claws against the big, vulnerable softness — and then he was taken by the moonlight on their whiskers, the variety of tails — some flicking or curling, some snaking, some standing straight like fur-lined flags — and then by their eyes — narrow, wide, round, golden, caramel, green. The smaller cats had fine and pretty features, the larger seemed grim, heavy-hearted, and impossibly wise.

Elliot was a Farms boy, so he was used to animals and he'd seen a cougar or two in his time, once even had to climb a haystack when a Sugarloaf lynx got into the barn looking angry. So he hadn't expected to think much about these wild cats. But wonder lay across his chest right where that sash had been. The more cats that passed, stately or sinuous, midnight blue or rich orange, the more he wanted. He wanted this to never end. Just keep right on walking by, you beautiful cats.

He could hear his breath speeding up. The wonder was piling on his chest, until it seemed like it might crack his ribs. It was forming its own steep ridge. It seemed like sobs of happiness were rising inside him too, and he trembled with this. There were tears in his eyes. Chime squeezed his hand.

That ridge across his chest grew higher. Its edges sharpened. Its weight was getting out of control. He turned away from the Cat Walk and looked toward the forest, to give himself a break. But the ridge kept right on sharpening, and there was something ferociously commonplace about it, and then he was tearing off his mask, he was tearing off his mask, and Chime's hands were over his mouth, and somewhere remote the sound of her hoarse urgency: "Stay quiet, stay still, stay quiet."

They were peeling his skin in smooth, swooping curves, and he was rocking in Chime's arms, pressing his teeth into his lip to hold on to screams. "Stay quiet," she pleaded, "stay quiet," and he saw himself running, hand in hand with the Girl-in-the-World, a memory of the shape of her, a twilight road, and it was gone.

The attack was fading. His eyes were still closed. He tasted blood.

"It's okay," Chime murmured. "It's okay, it's okay," in her low humming voice, and behind his closed eyes he saw his skin slip away, and himself clean, blinking paleness. He kept rocking but more slowly, and there were sudden twitches of his body, frightened of what had just happened, and little jumps of his breath like the residue of weeping.

"Open your eyes," Chime whispered, but he kept them closed and thought of the skin of the cats, how some were tight and sleek, some rumpled, but all the wild cats were right inside their skins. He thought of Chime and how she'd taken him into a cavern to kill him, she'd inflicted this pain on him, even though she was a friend, and that was because she was so much in her own skin. Her skin was her belief.

He thought of Mischka Tegan, or whatever her name was, and all that she'd done for her beliefs, how she'd tricked Elliot's dad and had his uncle killed, and how she'd almost been executed, but she was still on her way back to the Hostiles.

That much belief, and the sureness of Chime's eyes, and he wanted the same thing: the passion, the completeness. His life had been waking and sleeping, losing and fighting, and all the time he'd just been walking on the surface, never inside life, the way these wild cats were, the way Chime was. He'd never got under his own skin.

His father and his uncle had been wrong: He saw that now. The fact was, the royals twisted and poisoned the Kingdom, the same as the Grays had done to him. To live inside life was to go after the poison.

I got him, Elliot thought. *I got my Elliot Baranski.*

He opened his eyes. "I want to join the Hostiles," he said.

PART 6

1.

When the King came to live in Bonfire, things began to crackle and spark.

The King tapped two fingers against his own forehead. Or against the palm of his other hand. Or the shoulder of the person standing closest to him.

He spun on the spot and strode up and down the stairs like someone doing exercise. His head hunched in thought, then sprang up, eyes alight.

They held meetings in the Baranski farmhouse, and the King took control of every detail: how chairs should be arranged, when food should be served, what music played. He chose songs with electric guitar riffs, turning up the volume so everybody had to shout.

He handed out assignments to the agents, Tovey and Kim, to the Sheriff and Jimmy, to Abel and Petra Baranski.

"Get in touch with Carver Heywick, he owes me a favor — best way to do it is join his poker game. . . .

"Here's what you do. You find Sawhi Khai at the Vapors Head, and you play *three* games of snooker with her — it's got to be *three*, no more, no less — after that, you buy her a drink — whiskey sour . . .

"There's a guy I know will take care of those guards at the crackpoints — he's the best there is, no, wait, I'll tell you who's better . . ."

He'd stop, bow his head, tap faster, then look up and rattle off a phone number.

He asked Keira to send messages to Princess Ko via her ring, and to Madeleine in the World. He didn't ask anything of the other young people. "You've got homework and farms to run," he told them. "But keep coming to the meetings. You're good value."

The King was charming. He fixed people with his gaze, then looked away abruptly, so you wondered how to get the gaze back. He'd learned all their names almost instantly. He rigged up a basketball hoop outside the farmhouse and invited everyone out to shoot hoops. He'd stop halfway through shouting instructions, pick up a beer, and tip it back. They'd watch him swallow: glug-glug-glug. "You Farmers know how to *brew* as well as bake!" he'd shout, grabbing handfuls of bottles, tossing them around the room.

His spins of thought would turn themselves into dance moves. One night, he found Petra's guitar in the laundry closet. After that, he strummed through meetings: Setting the guitar down and picking it back up became part of his frenetic routine.

Also, he questioned everything. It reminded Keira of her history teacher, the way he'd get under the surface with his shoulder.

"Now, the court that signed my daughter's death warrant," he said one night, beating out a rhythm on his knees, "how does it have jurisdiction over the royal family? Why can we not *appeal* the decision to the Cellian High Court? Wasn't Ko's fraud on the Kingdom justified in the circumstances? Can't we issue some kind of urgent stay?"

The Sheriff and Jimmy said they'd follow up with lawyer friends.

"Why *does* the WSU have so much power, anyhow?" the King asked another night, with a violent strum of the guitar. He set the guitar down and looked around. "They can stop the *royal family* coming back from the World? I can't just pick up a phone and tell them to quit it? Am I not the freaking King of Cello?!"

Petra Baranski, who had expertise in World–Cello relations, spoke up in her calm voice. "It's like this. In the seventeenth century, when the plague came through from the World and spread outside our borders, we were under fire for letting it in. We were officially reprimanded by the United Assembly. The Aldhian foreign minister called for military strikes against us. He got a standing ovation. That kind of thing."

Petra was stacking cake plates as she spoke. "The cracks were sealed and the WSU established, but over the years, as the plague continued to rage, there were calls for us to take more action. There was chaos here in Cello at the time," she added. "The heir to the throne, a Prince Tobin, had vanished. People thought maybe Aldhibah had kidnapped him."

"The missing royal," Keira put in. "His mandolin turned up in an Aldhian junkyard years later."

Petra nodded. "Exactly. Anyhow, Cello agreed to make the WSU a separate arm of government, independent of royalty, with absolute power to seal ourselves off from the World. It can't be dissolved, except with the consent of Aldhibah."

The King plucked a tune on the guitar.

"In that case," he said, "get me the deed that established the WSU. Get me their Articles of Association. Let's see if we can't find a loophole."

"I'll look into it," Petra agreed.

"And who's the current Director?" The King turned to Tovey and Kim. "What have we got on him?"

Tovey and Kim grinned. They'd been talking to key figures in the WSU without luck. It hadn't occurred to them to go so high as the Director.

The King pointed to the ceiling. "Always start at the top," he said.

Within a couple of days, Tovey and Kim had traveled out of town, following up on the King's leads. Abel was making day trips to Loyalist enclaves. Keira was constructing her transponder rings for everyone. And, late at night, speaking to Sergio, who passed messages to Princess Ko. "We'll rescue the friends as well, of course," the King said. "Sergio and Samuel. Ask what medical provisions we need to arrange for Samuel. That's the sick one, right?"

The Sheriff and Jimmy were drawing up various legal documents at the King's request. "What in the heck is *this* one for?" the Sheriff would ask as he handed another over, and the King would laugh: "All part of the plan."

One night, Jimmy asked if they could turn down the music, as he had something to say.

Everyone was there: Abel just back from the north, and Tovey and Kim between inter-provincial meetings.

Jimmy cleared his throat.

"As you know," he said, "Isabella Tamborlaine disappeared the day the WSU came to town. I guess most folks believe she reported Elliot and then took off."

There was a careful quiet. People tried to keep their faces blank.

"I've kept right on believing in Isabella." Jimmy held on to his voice, but only just. "On account of, I loved her very much. I've been thinking her disappearance is unrelated to Elliot — just a coincidence of timing. I've been calling in and sending out missing persons reports. Speaking to teachers at the school. Following up on her past."

His shoulders sagged. He noticed this, seemed annoyed, and straightened.

"Teachers at school didn't offer much," he said, "except to confirm the worst. Seems Elliot had been asking Isabella how cracks worked. I still didn't see that as *proof* — so she knew he had an interest in the World? I said to myself — doesn't mean she *betrayed* him. But then, as I said, I looked into her past. And . . ."

He was speaking to the skirting boards now.

"Isabella doesn't exist," he said hoarsely. "She went to teacher's college, sure, and learned to be a physics teacher — *that's* all real. But before that? Not a single record. No family. No certificate of birth. The papers she used to apply for college were all forged."

He looked up, and his face, which had seemed fragile, was grim and gray as stone.

"Seems she *was* a Hostile all along, and I'm real sorry . . ." He raised his voice again, looking to Petra and Abel. "I'm real sorry that my girlfriend put your son in so much danger."

"Ah, you can't be apologizing for the things people close to you do," Petra murmured.

Jimmy sat back down and turned to the King. "Thanks for letting me interrupt," he said. "Carry on with your meeting."

The King slid the guitar to the floor and jumped to his feet. "You know what you need, Jimmy? A special drink I invented back in college. I'm going to make it for you right now. Guaranteed to disappear the past and make things brighter. Got any rum, Petra? And I'll need apple liqueur, GC teakwater, and what else? Well, a *whole* lot of other stuff." He reached out and mussed Jimmy's hair like a parent. Jimmy cracked a tiny smile.

2.

*T*he night before the Day of Mighty Rescue (as the King liked to call it), Keira stood out in front of Gabe's farmhouse.

She watched as the Sheriff's car bumped down the driveway and as it turned into the street and disappeared.

It was after midnight but still warm enough for a sundress.

Keira felt good.

The meeting earlier at the Baranskis' had been more festive than ever. The King had suggested they hold it outside, under the stars, so they could hose one another down while they talked. He'd personally lugged out the soundplayer and boxes, turning the music loud so that the jemima birds woke and broke into frantic shouting.

Everything was in place.

Tovey and Kim were waiting in Tek, Jagged Edge, where Princess Ko was being held. A team of Loyalists and former security agents were heading there now to assist in the rescue.

Meanwhile, the King had arranged for the WSU guards at all three crackpoints to be bribed or blackmailed. They would abandon their posts for ten minutes at prearranged times. Another agent had acquired a crack detector, and would use this to bring Princess Jupiter and the Queen across at the two locations in Ducale, Golden Coast. Next, a Royal Pilot would fly, by superspeed chopper, to McCabe Town in Nature Strip, where Prince Chyba would be collected. All rescued royals would be delivered to Bonfire.

Keira herself had just returned from speaking with the Girl-in-the-World. That was the only glitch, she thought, frowning. Madeleine still didn't have confirmation that either the Queen or Prince Chyba would actually come to the crackpoints.

Sometimes Keira wanted to reach through to the World and shake that Madeleine. Did the girl think one out of three was good enough? Why hadn't she just gone *over* to wherever the Queen and Chyba were ("Taipei" and "Boise," she remembered — they did look sort of far on the World maps, but that was the point of transport) — and convinced them?

Maybe Worldians were sort of slow, like Farmers. Actually, Keira had been noticing that Farmers often had flashes of smart inside their slowness. As if the slow was a framework for the fast. Whereas, Madeleine prattled in her scribble and threw her temper everywhere, but behind all that, her thoughts must drag like slugs.

Still, the King didn't seem troubled. Each time Keira mentioned her concern, he'd smile glintingly, as if he knew something she did not. "They'll be there," he'd say, and she believed him.

By this time tomorrow night, just about the whole royal family would be partying at the Baranski house. The only one missing would be little Prince Tippett, but he was safe in the Magical North with his nanny — actually, Keira wouldn't be surprised if the King had been secretly organizing to whisk the kid here too, just to complete the reunion.

Keira rubbed her eyes. She'd adjusted to Day-Dweller hours now, so she was tired.

She ran up the stairs to the farmhouse porch, turned her key in the front door, and stepped inside.

3.

*T*here were voices in the kitchen.

Her heart tumbled back down the stairs.

With all the chaos of the last weeks, she'd completely forgotten about Gabe's parents. She'd stopped worrying they might turn up one day.

She backed away, feeling for the door handle.

A light switched on. Gabe stood in the open kitchen door, looking at her.

He beckoned. She shook her head. He beckoned harder.

She walked down the hall. What had he told them about her? Had he pretended she was someone else? But everyone in town thought she was his cousin!

Gabe went back into the kitchen. The turn of his shoulders was angry. She followed him.

The room smelled of cigarettes and whiskey. A small figure was hunched in a chair. An empty tumbler and quarter-full bottle of whiskey sat on the table.

The figure looked up.

It was the King.

His eyes were bloodshot. His mouth sagged.

"Keira," he said, dragging the mouth into a smile that closed his eyes. He left the eyes closed, then opened them. "Did you know I spent a year in the World?"

"Sure." She looked toward Gabe, but he was making coffee, his back to her.

"While I was in the World, I talked my way into an executive position in an advertising agency," the King said. "Did you know that? It helped that I speak Jarmian — what they call French in the World — I lived in a city called Montreal and that was — where? Canada? Well, who cares. My Jarmian helped, but I had *zero* experience in advertising. Still got the job 'cause I knew how to talk myself up."

Keira sat down at the table.

"I gave myself a backstory as a rock star," the King continued, laughing. "I mean, my mind gave me that backstory. But that's how much I believed in myself. *Rock star!*" He strummed an invisible guitar, mimicked a crowd cheering, then rested his head on the table and closed his eyes.

Gabe brought coffee over.

What's happening? Keira mouthed at Gabe over the King's head.

The King straightened. "Absolutely nothing," he said, reaching for the whiskey bottle, "is happening."

There was a silence.

"He says there are no plans to rescue Princess Ko," Gabe told Keira. "He says nobody's on their way to help. The people who were going to do it have all backed out, or maybe weren't in in the first place. He's not clear which." Gabe paused to narrow his eyes at the King. "He also tells me nobody's bringing the royals from the World. Turns out, the agent who promised to get the crack detector never really promised. She just said she'd *think* about it. Now she's decided against it. Nobody has bribed or blackmailed any guards to abandon their posts. There was *talk* that people might, but they've all had second thoughts. Or maybe they were only joking. What else? Oh, yeah, there's no Royal Pilot with a superspeed chopper."

"I don't believe you," Keira said.

"Don't look at me," Gabe said. "This is *his* show."

Keira turned to the King. "None of this is true, is it? You're just being funny, right?"

The King winked. "I'm a very funny guy."

Keira looked back at Gabe. "Is this for real?"

"Seems to be."

"Where are Abel and Petra?"

"Asleep," the King said, closing his own eyes again. His hand tilted and so did the whiskey glass. Keira grabbed it, set it right, and slid it away from the King's reach.

"What are they doing, *sleeping*?"

"He says he was too embarrassed to wake them and tell them," Gabe said. "He came here. He wanted to see *you*. He thinks you can solve everything."

"Me? What does that even . . . ? But is he saying he was *lying* all along?"

The King stretched out to reach the whiskey glass, tipping it back and forth so it sloshed and splashed. "No," he said. "No. I never lie."

"He *thought* he could make it work," Gabe explained. "He says he thought if he kept talking and being his usual *charming* self, it'd all fall into place. That's what usually happens, apparently. Those were his words. His usual *charming* self."

Gabe's face was rigid with fury, but then the King pressed his palms to his eyes and cried out in a terrible voice, "Oh, my little girl, they're going to kill my little girl," and the fury fell right away.

4.

*O*n the night of the Cat Walk, Elliot and Chime returned to find the compound still in uproar. Nobody noticed their arrival.

Elliot slipped back to his room, where Ming-Sun waited in his usual chair.

"They're *still* in a state?" Elliot said. "It's that big a deal, the Director being out of prison?"

"It's a big thing," Ming-Sun said. "For certain people."

Elliot sat on the edge of his bed, thinking. "The Assistant," he said eventually. "He was angling for top position."

Ming-Sun's expression did not change. "You see much," he said, and then: "You went to the Cat Walk tonight?"

Elliot nodded.

"And yet, here you are, back again."

"I've decided to become a Hostile."

Ming-Sun studied Elliot then, unexpectedly, he yawned. It was a yawn that consumed his entire face. It concluded with a languorous hum.

"So you have," he said, and yawned again. "Well, let us see if the Assistant believes you. By the way, these yawns do not signify disrespect, nor boredom at your news. They signify fatigue."

"I'm beat myself," Elliot said, lying down.

"So. Let us sleep. Tomorrow will be another day of commotion, for tomorrow they execute the Princess Ko."

Elliot had already closed his eyes. He opened them again.

5.

$\mathcal{K}$eira and Gabe sat in silence at the kitchen table.

The King was passed out on the floor.

They had contacted Tovey and Kim, using the transponder rings, and the agents had been grave but unsurprised. "Suspected something like this," Tovey said. "None of the leads he gave us ever worked out."

"Only, he's so compelling," Kim put in, "so we believed *he* was getting somewhere even though we weren't," and Tovey's image nodded.

The agents promised they'd do what they could to rescue the Princess on their own. "But it's not likely," they added, their voices layering.

"Not just the Princess," Keira interrupted. "Sergio and Samuel as well."

"Who?"

Static ruffled the agents' faces and voices.

"Sergio and Samuel! You *have* to get them as well. *Not* just Princess Ko." She was almost shouting, and Gabe touched her shoulder blade.

"Of course," Tovey said once the static calmed. "If we can. Which, like we said, doesn't seem . . ."

The connection had broken.

Next, they'd phoned Abel and Petra and told them the news. Abel had been appalled, but Petra's voice had a sad resignation.

"They're all going to be lost," she'd whispered. "That entire family."

Abel had promised to try to find Loyalist connections who might help with the transfers from the World.

"But none of the names he gave me have been much help so far," he added. "So it doesn't seem very . . ."

"I know," Gabe had said. "It's not likely."

Now they sat and stared at each other across the kitchen table.

"Should we try to call Hector and Jimmy?" Keira asked. Gabe shrugged. "Don't know what they could do. Let them sleep. We should go to bed ourselves."

They both looked down at the King's form.

"What do we do? Just leave him here?"

"Absolutely," Gabe said.

Keira carried the coffee mugs to the sink. "Why'd he think *I* could help?" she complained. She was trying not to cry, or to care. The royals meant nothing. Who cared if they were trapped in the World? Who cared if they stood about on street corners waiting, and the Girl-in-the-World went wild about it? As for Princess Ko, she was a tyrant. Go ahead and execute her!

Keira felt a rush of dizziness.

Gabe was talking. "You helped bring the King across from the World. And Abel and Elliot. Maybe he thought you'd somehow bring the other royals too?"

They stepped out of the kitchen into the dark hallway.

"I'm too tired to remember where the light switch is," Gabe said. "I'll just sleep right on the floor."

"Here." Keira pulled him back to his feet. "Take my hand. I'll lead you."

Their fingers entwined. "Something weird's going on there," Gabe observed. "You're sort of twitching."

Keira withdrew her hand.

"It's my ring. Someone's contacting me." She flicked the light switch.

"Ah, now it's too bright." Gabe leaned against the wall, closing his eyes. "Tell them to wait until morning."

An image hovered at the foot of the stairs. A girl with long dark hair.

"It's me," said the image.

Keira stared.

"It's me. Princess Ko."

"No, it's not. Your hair's wrong."

"This is not currently relevant, but I haven't been able to *dye* my hair in prison. This is its real color. You know it's me, Keira."

Keira slapped her own cheeks trying to wake up. "Are you okay?" she whispered. "Is it safe for you to be calling me? What's that behind you?"

"I don't know. A bicycle, I think. We're in some kind of a shed. In the Farms. We escaped."

"She *what*?" Gabe's eyes flew open. He stepped close to Keira, watching the image.

"Yes, I had Sergio work on his flight without pause, and now he can do it at will. Rather than awaiting the mood. I had Samuel forgo his pain medication so we could accumulate a hidden stash. We used it to knock out the prison guards. Samuel has suffered, of course, and so has Sergio. But here we are."

"She brings out the best in people," Keira told Gabe drily.

"Sergio flew us here," Ko continued. "We're hiding. The boys are sleeping. They're exhausted. I'll wake them soon, though, so we can complete our journey before daylight. If we come to you, can you hide us?"

Keira and Gabe found themselves, unexpectedly, laughing. They were sinking to the floor with the laughter, falling against each other.

"Yeah, you can come here," Gabe told her eventually, breathless. "I'm Gabe," he added.

"That's Gabe," Keira confirmed, and she fell into another laughing fit. "You *escaped*. I can't believe that you *escaped*. You just went ahead and *escaped*."

"It's a whirlshine of relief," Ko agreed. "More so when we reach you. We have a map, so I think Sergio will be able to fly us to Bonfire, but where do we come once we get there?"

Gabe explained directions. "You took a huge risk," he said. "Escaping on your own. Why didn't you wait? You got the message that the King was organizing a rescue, right?"

In the image, Ko's head dipped. "I did," she said. "But you are referring to my father, and I know him."

6.

$\mathcal{E}$lliot woke early to slamming doors and voices raised and rushing.

"Come on," he said. "Still? How much can they have to *say* about the Director being free?"

Another door slammed, close by. Ming-Sun, in his usual chair, curled his mouth with irritation. "Wait," he said, and left the room.

A few minutes later, he returned, resuming his position.

"All across the Kingdom," he said, "prisoners are fleeing."

"What? Seriously?"

Ming-Sun shook his head. "No. I am jesting. The Director was released last night, as you know, and now it seems the Princess Ko has escaped. Quick!" He clicked his fingers before Elliot's eye. "How do you feel about this?"

Elliot swiped the clicking hand away. "What is that, some magic thing? Cut it out."

Ming-Sun chuckled. "No. I can just imagine the Assistant doing it. But seriously, what do you think? The Princess was your friend. She was to be executed today. Now she has escaped. And so?"

"What about the others? Are they out too?"

"Samuel and Sergio. Yes, them too. But I am asking how you feel about Princess Ko's escape."

Elliot frowned. The truth was, his first reaction was huge relief. But now he didn't know *how* he felt. He tried to get a hold of that sense he'd had last night, of being inside his own skin.

"Well, it's bad news," he tried.

Ming-Sun brayed. "This is not a job interview! And if it was, you would not get the job. You lie badly, Elliot. Tell me your truth. And its color! How does it smell? Describe its appearance! *Rate* your truth for me."

"Seriously?"

Ming-Sun drew out a handkerchief, blew his nose, then bellowed with laughter. "No," he said eventually. "I am joking."

"You sure are in a strange mood today, Ming-Sun."

Ming-Sun smiled. "I did not want you to die at the hands of the Assistant, nor did I want Chime punished for your escape. My secret hope was that you would be truly converted. It has happened. My relief makes me both joyful and extremely tired. Of course, we have yet to convince the Assistant of your conversion. Which brings me back to my question: How do you feel about Princess Ko's escape?"

Elliot tried again. He closed his eyes and visualized himself as a lion, but that only confused him. He looked stupid with a mane.

He thought of the Princess Ko that Chime had described, and then he thought of the Ko he had seen in conference rooms, in the tent by the Lake, in a boat at Olde Quainte — missing her sister, desperate for her family, demanding they get her little brother first, because he was alone and he didn't have his blankie — stamping her foot, holding brainstorming sessions, ruthless, callous, selfish as heck.

"I'm glad she's not going to be killed," he admitted in the end. "I don't want anyone killed, and she's young, and she did her best, and I *liked* her, even though she made me crazy. But I hate the idea of her and her family ever being back in charge. *That*'d be bad news."

Ming-Sun stretched and yawned. "Better," he said. "Now I will go back to sleep." He bowed his head to his chin and closed his eyes.

7.

$\mathcal{K}$eira and Gabe returned to the kitchen. The adrenaline and laughter had woken them. They looked at the King's sleeping form.

"Your daughter's okay!" they said to him.

He continued sleeping.

They looked at each other.

"You know," Keira said, "if Princess Ko can get herself out, couldn't we figure out —"

"I was thinking the same thing."

"I could open the cracks," Keira said, "but we'd need to get around the guards first."

"Drug them?"

"How?"

Gabe thought. "Barrington root. You grate it the right way, it'll knock you out just about instantly."

"Where'd we get that from?"

"Nikki grows it on her farm."

"Okay," Keira said. "But how do we get the guards to — what? Inhale it? Inject it?"

"Eat it. We'll bake it into something. Cody can do his profiteroles."

They smiled at each other, then Keira dropped her smile.

"But we need to get Princess Jupiter and the Queen from Golden Coast, and then Prince Chyba up in Nature Strip. We haven't got a high-speed chopper."

"We haven't," Gabe agreed.

They held each other's gaze, breathing fast.

After a moment, Keira said, "Doesn't Shelby fly a plane?"

They started making calls.

*　*　*

Two hours later, Shelby was flying her crop duster to Ducale, Golden Coast.

She was cranky at 5 A.M. She had half-closed eyes, a thermos of coffee, and a scowl. She wore track pants tucked into rubber boots and a faded T-shirt.

She didn't say a word for the first hour. Then she seemed to notice Keira beside her. At the same time, she became aware of the frayed edges of her own sleeves.

"You know anything about royals?" Shelby said into the mike attached to her earphones.

"Not a thing," Keira replied.

"You think I'm dressed okay?" Shelby frowned at the T-shirt sleeves again, and then at her rubber boots. "And what, are we supposed to bow and call them majesty or something?"

"No idea," Keira said. "I don't read royal magazines."

"Me neither." Shelby's frown deepened.

"We're rescuing them," Keira said. "What are they going to do, start complaining about fashion and protocol?"

Shelby flashed her a look that was maybe a twist of the lip or maybe a smile. Then she glanced around her plane. She'd taken out the hopper to make room for an extra fuel tank and for passengers.

"My favorite thing to do is fly a plane," she said.

Keira smiled.

Shelby didn't speak again until they landed in a field outside Ducale. "We're here," she said then.

There was a moment when this seemed a glitch in the plan, this field. Because where exactly were they?

But they walked across the grass to a highway, and a bus approached.

They flagged it down, and hitched a ride to the city. Again, there was a moment of doubt on a street corner.

But Keira asked a passerby how to reach the Harrington Hotel. The man was enthused to be asked. He described the route in detail, even advising them to take Third rather than Fourth Avenue, because the lights were out on Fourth, so crossing was a nightmare.

Shelby looked at Keira. "What's *crossing*?" she said. "Why's it a nightmare?"

Keira felt suddenly calm. Shelby, with her broad shoulders and studded armbands and tattoos, had never seen a real city. Keira took her hand as they crossed the first major road, and felt the warmth and the tension in Shelby, and felt even calmer.

At the Harrington Hotel, they walked right into the employee wing, borrowed a couple of uniforms and a cart, wheeled this into the elevator and up to the penthouse suite.

Two WSU guards were seated outside the suite. They didn't even blink when the girls offered them fresh profiteroles. They just went ahead, ate them, and sank down to the floor.

Shelby kept watch while Keira went inside the suite, found the crack, unsealed it, and held up a flashlight and hand mirror.

There was a kerfuffle of darkness, lights, sounds. A street corner. A girl wearing huge sunglasses, an overcoat, and a black wool hat.

"Are you here for me?" the girl said.

Keira took her hand. The kerfuffle repeated.

She was back in the penthouse suite. The girl stood beside her swaying. Her neck was scrawny. The overcoat was more frayed than Shelby's T-shirt.

"Are you okay?" Keira asked her.

The girl stared. She held out a hand, skinny wrist emerging from the sleeve. "I'm Princess Jupiter," she said. "Pleased to meet you."

They found their way to the Finance Department. Again, there seemed to be glitches. Walking through a city with a princess, for instance, even one disguised in sunglasses and a tattered coat. Also, getting up to the second level of the Finance Department.

Shelby solved the problems by sitting the Princess in a bus shelter, handing her a newspaper, and telling her to wait. Then she blew up a trash can on the street outside the Finance Department.

As alarms blared, everybody streamed out of the building, including the WSU guards. Keira and Shelby slipped inside. They found the office. Keira found the crack. She returned with a woman, also wearing sunglasses. A large floppy hat shaded her face.

"Your Majesty," Keira said politely.

The woman straightened. "Not a word."

"No problem," Keira agreed.

On the flight to Nature Strip, Keira and Shelby were elated. They'd bought doughnuts to celebrate their success. The Queen and Princess shared these, huddled in silence at the back of the plane.

"Blowing things up is my favorite thing to do," Shelby told Keira.

"I thought that was flying."

"No. Blowing things up. Flying's good, though."

Keira used her ring to contact Gabe and give him the news. Gabe reported back that Princess Ko had arrived safely, along with Sergio and Samuel. They were now eating pancakes, he said.

"Only one more royal to go," Keira said once Gabe had signed off.

They flew in silence for a while.

Shelby spoke suddenly. "When we all go to the Sugarloaf Dam, you never swim."

Keira raised her eyebrows. "No."

"We might have stopped calling you Sophy sooner," Shelby said, "if you'd swum. A lot of ways, it feels like you think you're better than us, and that's one. The way you sit up on the bank and just watch."

Keira adjusted the earphones. "I can't swim," she said.

"You're kidding me."

"Not much call for swimming in Jagged Edge."

Shelby laughed. "For crying out loud," she said.

In Nature Strip, they left the Queen and Princess in the plane and walked along the dirt roads of McCabe Town. It was dark now, and the streets were almost empty. They passed pubs and bars and heard music and voices, but nobody seemed to notice them. They practiced their Nature Strip accents as they walked. They both laughed.

At the Cast Iron Restaurant, three guards were smoking cigarettes on the front porch. Shelby told them she was opening a new eatery down the street and offering free pastries tonight. The guards ate the profiteroles and passed out.

Keira went into the restaurant. She found the crack in a corridor at the back of the dining room. The corridor ran past the counter, the kitchen, and the restrooms to a back door with a frosted-glass window.

She bumped her knee against a low table. A stack of folded cloth napkins, and a single menu: *CAST IRON RESTAURANT: Finest Eating Establishment in McCabe Town, Nature Strip.*

The restaurant must have been closed a while, but it still smelled of wood smoke, grilled salmon, and rain. Outside, wild beasts chittered.

She reached out and began to untangle. Her hands moved along the knotted light, taking one gnarl at a time. It was an easy one.

The back door of the restaurant swung open. Shelby's head appeared, along with a rush of sound.

"You nearly done?" she called. "Something's going on."

"What is that, a storm?" Keira called.

"Choppers. Sky's full of them."

"I'm almost done." Keira looked back at the crack and stopped.

It was knotted again.

She stared.

Who knew that could happen if you looked away?

"Two minutes!" she called to Shelby, and the door thudded closed again. She untangled as fast as she could. The knots were tighter than they'd been. Her neck was tensing.

She took a breath. She pulled on a thread. It slipped out of place and unwound. She smiled and carried on to the next. A rush of light caught her eye. She looked sideways. The tangles were back.

The door burst open again, and this time it sounded like a hurricane out there. Shelby's hair was blowing sideways.

"They're landing!" she shouted. "We've got to get out of here."

"Wait," Keira yelled back. "Give me a . . ."

She turned to the start of the crack, unthreaded the first knot, and then, as she watched, it reknotted itself and pulled tight.

Outside, the choppers roared. For a third time, the door opened. Shelby was shouting but Keira couldn't hear the words.

Her hands raced along the crack, untangling, unknotting, and just as quickly, the crack reknotted itself, lines of light circling and sliding into place.

A hand landed on Keira's arm. It was Shelby, beside her now, screaming in her ear.

"They're *right outside!*"

Keira looked at the crack. It was gnarled with tangles, more and more forming as she watched.

Shelby was dragging her. She gave up. They ran outside into a blast of spotlights and machinery. They swerved into the woods behind the restaurant. They ran at a crouch, splashing through mud and pushing through bushes. The Queen and Princess watched as they clambered aboard the plane, panting hugely.

Nobody spoke. Shelby switched on the magnetos, primed the fuel pump, and hit the starter. The plane took off.

They hadn't got Prince Chyba.

8.

*E*lliot was frying garlic.

Across the kitchen, Chime shaped ground beef, piling clumps onto a plate. They worked silently. It was late, and they were exhausted.

All day, the compound had thrummed with activity, and streams of newcomers had arrived, hungry.

The garlic hissed. Elliot added chopped onions. He was feeling reflective. News can zig and zag its mood through a place, he was thinking. This morning, there'd been a sort of confused amazement everywhere, about the escape of Princess Ko. Around lunchtime, gloom had crawled up and down the corridors. A source had reported that the Queen and Princess Jupiter were back from the World.

Almost immediately the gloom had been shot through with panic — they'll try to bring Prince Chyba back next! — and then a frenzy as everyone rushed to *stop* that happening.

So now the place was all about jubilation. The rescue of Prince Chyba, heir to the throne, had been thwarted. Only *just*, apparently, which made the party happier: better to win the game as the final seconds ticked away.

Elliot tipped a can of tomatoes into the pan, and as he watched them slide, it came back to him complete: a memory of another celebration.

It was at the Lake of Spells, in a tent. The RYA had spent three days fishing, day and night: Princess Ko, bossy and cranky; Keira, weird and sneering; Samuel, eager and hopeless; Sergio, a frolicsome lamb. Their personalities had clattered up against one another, but they'd stayed awake through an ice-cold night, fighting a monster, dragging on pondweed, and caught themselves a Locator Spell — nearly lost it when Samuel dropped it, and then Samuel nearly lost it with remorse.

Elliot closed his eyes, and there he was in the tent, the little spell on Ko's palm, the maps of the World spread around them.

Cellian, 17. Someone had scribbled that on a slip of paper. The spell had given them a street address in Boise, Idaho. *That's Prince Chyba done! That's Prince Chyba!* someone had shouted, probably Samuel, and Elliot recalled now how those words ran pleasure down his spine.

We've got Chyba!

Something was catching at Elliot now. He stirred the tomatoes. The kitchen door opened.

The Assistant leaned in, eyes bright.

"You," he said to Elliot. "Is it true?" He stepped in, letting the door slam behind him.

"Is what true?"

"You want to join the Hostiles."

The noise in the corridors carried on. Elliot looked across at Chime. She was filling a pot with water.

"Sure," he said.

"Look at me," the Assistant said, and he swung himself up onto a bench. At once, the Assistant's face turned pink and his hair damp in the heat.

Elliot picked up the plate of raw meatballs. He tumbled these into a pan. Then he looked at the Assistant.

But it bothered him, not to focus on the meatballs.

"Hostiles betrayed your father and killed your uncle." The Assistant enunciated each word. "Why would you join us?"

Elliot considered. He figured he should recite one of Chime's speeches about democracy. Or run through her list of tyrannical monarchs.

"Ah," he said, deciding on the truth instead. "That's it exactly. Hostiles did that to my family 'cause they believed so much in the Hostile cause. They believed because the cause is right. Which is the fault of the royal family. So, when you come down to it, it's the *royals* that betrayed my dad and killed my uncle, not the Hostiles."

The Assistant smiled. "Shake my hand," he said.

Elliot looked around for a cloth to wipe away the tomato sauce, but the Assistant grabbed his hand, then embraced him.

"Welcome," he said, studying Elliot with that admiring gaze. "I knew all along that you were special."

"And yet you tried to have me killed by Grays," Elliot said evenly.

The Assistant shook his head, as if Elliot had surpassed himself. "You," he said. "Now, listen." He ran his hands through his hair. A thin line of tomato sauce was transferred to his forehead. "We know where the royals are. Our source has got word to us. We know where the King has been hiding, where Princess Ko is now, and where the Queen and Princess Jupiter are currently heading. Do you want to hear where?"

"Sure," Elliot agreed.

"A little town in the province of the Farms."

Elliot waited.

"Bonfire, the Farms."

Elliot had picked up the spatula. It slipped. He caught it. "No chance."

"This is why I'm talking to you. Elliot, you are now the most important person in this compound. The royal family — minus Chyba! — are hiding in your town. Will you help us bring them down?"

Elliot stared.

"The royals. Bring down the *royals*, not your town. You could be vital: You have inside knowledge. Think about it overnight and let me know tomorrow."

"Nothing will happen to my town, or my family or friends?"

"Absolutely not."

"And we're not *hurting* the royal family?"

"Just ending their reign."

Elliot shrugged. "Then I don't need to think. Of course I'll help."

The Assistant looked up at the steam-filled air. He strode from the room, smiling.

PART 7

A person who can plan a lesson about poems and dreams is not a person with a tumour in her brain.

Madeleine was winding this sentence around her mind like a scarf. At the same time, she was half listening to Jack.

"He had fits of rage and melancholy," Jack said, "and a musical laugh."

"Did he?" Holly asked.

Madeleine looked at her mother.

"He did," Jack agreed.

There was a pause.

"Go on," Holly said.

It was Friday morning, and Jack was telling them about Byron.

"Remember?" he had said as he walked into Madeleine and Holly's flat. "You told me to figure out why I'm obsessed with him?"

Holly held her smile. Madeleine watched her mother. Did she remember?

"It was the day we did that lesson at Waterstones," Belle reminded her, following Jack into the flat and pausing between two armchairs. Belle could never choose where to sit. "The lesson about poetry and dreams?" She looked at Holly, and an expression crossed her face, as if she'd just been slapped. She blinked fast, and recovered. She chose a chair angled away from Holly.

That was when Madeleine had reached for a sentence — *A person who can plan a lesson about poems and dreams is not a person with a tumour in her brain* — and used it to muffle her thoughts.

"Which," Jack continued, "I think I also have. A musical laugh. Here's what, I'll laugh and you see if you can sing along with it."

"Why don't you tell us more about Byron first?" Holly smiled.

Madeleine dropped the sentence and grabbed at her mother's wry smile. A person who is *wry* is not a person with a tumour.

"He was also insane," Jack went on, "which is where Byron and I part company. On account of, I am sane."

"Are you?" Holly asked, still smiling.

It was not a wry smile. It was a neurological malfunction. Holly had not stopped smiling, Madeleine realised, since yesterday.

Yesterday, Madeleine had read her mother's design essay. Then she had checked through all Holly's papers and emails.

Some were garbled like the essay, some made sense. Each time she found the former, she stacked it into a pile. When she found the latter, she felt beautiful relief and stopped searching for a moment.

Eventually, she woke her mother and handed her the first set of papers.

That was when the smile had begun. As Holly read through her own notes, she had smirked. The smile had grown, turned upside down, broadened.

Eventually, Holly had let the papers fall.

"I see your point," she'd said. "Maybe we should call Dr. Mustafo."

Her mother remembered her specialist's name! She recognised that there was an issue! These seemed like excellent signs.

Maybe, Madeleine had thought, it was just that the tumour had left tiny traces behind, or echoes. But the echoes were fading. The more Holly wrote nonsense, the more she used up the fragments. Soon these would dwindle into nothing.

Dr. Mustafo had returned Holly's call within half an hour. An appointment had been set up for consultation and scans.

And now, here they were, listening to Jack discuss Byron.

"At school," Jack went on, "he sprinkled gunpowder on the floors, ripped down window gratings, and shot at the cook's hat. When he was older, he'd have parties where he made everyone drink from a skull filled with Burgundy. Once, he was on a ship and he sulked for days, then suddenly he got all this champagne, opened it, handed out pistols, and told everyone to shoot at the bottle tops."

A new idea was forming in Madeleine's mind. She looked at it with careful interest. Byron was mad. So was her own mother. It was healthy, occasional madness! Endearing, poetic madness! Nothing to do with a tumour.

She tried this as a new muffler — *it's just insanity!* — but it wasn't quite as soft or comforting.

"As you probably know," Jack continued, "Byron had sex appeal to burn. This is the bit where he and I get back on track as soul brothers. One of his girlfriends was named Caroline, and she said that she never forgot the first time he kissed her. This was in a carriage. He drew her to him *like a magnet*. That's a quote. Another time, he turned up at a hotel, thought the chambermaid was hot, and he *fell upon her like a thunderbolt*. That's another quote."

"That's disturbing," Belle reflected. "Falling on the chambermaid like a thunderbolt. It's not sexy, Jack, it's assault."

"Or maybe he tripped?" Holly put in.

"Well," Jack said, "I disagree." He consulted his notes again. "Turns out, if you go around falling on people like thunderbolts you end up having kids. And Byron had three. Or anyway three that we know about."

Madeleine focused.

"The first one was a boy," Jack said. "Nobody's clear, but they think Byron got a maid pregnant. He wrote a poem for the kid, and gave the maid some cash, but that's it."

"A poem by Byron," Belle remarked. "That's not to be sneezed at."

Jack looked doubtful. "If I ever have a son," he said. "I plan to do more than write a poem for him. At the very least, we'll kick a ball around."

"Good for you." Holly beamed. Madeleine's eyes flickered to her mother.

"The second child was a girl named Ada. We already know about her, on account of that project Belle did. She grew up to invent computer programming. Byron was married to Ada's mother, but he was a *demon* to her, so she left him, taking the kid, and he never had anything to do with her again."

Belle stared at the ceiling. "Who was the third child?"

"Okay, there's an eighteen-year-old girl named Claire — she happened to be the stepsister of Mary Shelley, who wrote *Frankenstein*, but that's another story. Anyhow, Claire and Byron had a thing, and Claire got pregnant. Byron went off chasing other people, and Claire had the baby on her own. She named her Alba, but Byron decided to change that to Allegra."

"Allegra's a nice name," Holly said.

"It doesn't explain why Madeleine hasn't baked muffins today," Belle said moodily. "I feel like one."

"It also doesn't explain," Madeleine said, "why Byron thinks he can change the baby's name when he's not even there."

"It doesn't," murmured Holly. All three turned to her. She was drifting. She snapped back into place. "What happened to Allegra, Jack?"

"Well, in those days, the dads got to name their kids," Jack said. "So that's why he changed it. Also, dads got to *raise* the kids, so Claire handed the little girl over. Byron stuck her in a convent when she was four. He had to, apparently, because . . ." Jack flipped through his notes. "Because she was *obstinate as a mule* and *ravenous as a vulture*. That's Byron's words. Anyhow, Claire hears that her little girl's in a convent and she's, like, you *wot*? She says, *Give her back to me, then!* But Byron says no. Meanwhile, the little girl's writing Byron letters asking him to visit. *My Dear Papa, it being faire time I should so much like a visit from my Papa,* she wrote. And *will you please your Allegra who loves you so.*"

"He'd better have visited," Belle said.

"He did not visit," Jack said. "He was busy."

"Busy doing what?"

"Sleeping late, then going to a field where he put silver coins into forked sticks and shot at them."

"It's like he never stopped shooting!" Holly said. The others hesitated.

"The cook's hat," Holly reminded them. "The bottle tops. And now the silver coins."

Madeleine felt exhilaration. Her mother had been listening! Her mother was *perfectly healthy*. Cook's hat, bottle tops, silver coins. This was a fur-lined Russian trooper hat with ear flaps! She pulled it down over her ears.

"What happened to Allegra in the end?" Belle asked.

"Claire kept asking for her back. She wrote letters saying, please let me have her. But Byron wouldn't even let her *visit* her daughter. Once she wrote this: *I can no longer resist the internal, inexplicable feeling which haunts me that I shall never see her anymore. I entreat you to destroy this feeling by allowing me to see her.* But he still wouldn't."

"This story's getting sad," Holly said. "I hope Claire got her daughter in the end."

"When Allegra was five, Byron heard from the convent that she was ill. Dangerously ill, they said. Then he heard that she was dead."

There was a deep silence.

"She did *not* die," Belle said angrily.

"When Byron heard about it, he went pale as a ghost and sank into a seat. The convent sent him Allegra's things: three coloured cotton frocks, a velvet frock, a muslin frock, a cap and gloves, a string of coral, and a silver spoon and fork."

"You can stop talking now," Madeleine complained.

"And they sent Claire a little picture of her daughter, along with a lock of her hair. Claire couldn't see scenery after that; she could only see *her lost darling.* That's another quote."

Outside, it had begun to rain. Madeleine looked at the window. It was crowded, not with raindrops, but with fine little dashes of rain, as if someone had scratched at the glass with tiny claws.

Everyone listened to the rain.

"Well, that explains your obsession with Byron anyway," Belle said. "It's because he was always abandoning his kids, and you have abandonment issues."

Jack looked at her steadily. "No," he said. "I have no issues."

"It's all about your parents," Belle persisted. "They abandoned you."

"They were killed in a car crash when I was two!"

Belle shrugged. Her mouth curled. "Same difference. You know nothing about them."

"What's that got to do with anything! And I know a lot about my mother! Her name was Teresa Lina Ballomabi, and she's my mum in *all* my past lives. I'll probably get to see her in the next life along!"

"Oh. Your next life along. Right."

Jack stood abruptly. A cushion slid to the floor. "I'm going," he said, kicking this aside and heading to the door.

Madeleine found her voice and her body rising both at once. "No, you are *not*!" she roared. "You are staying right where you are and you are *both* going to tell me what is *happening*! I've had *enough* of this *secret* fight that you two keep not *having*! As if it's not enough to have the Kingdom of Cello *sealed* away, and my dad *silent*, and *she's* got a tumour trapped inside her *brain*, and *nobody's talking about anything!*"

She stopped. There was a sharp, new silence. It flew in stares and glances, one to the other.

Jack was breathing hard. "Holly's not sick again? Are you?"

Holly held her palms out. "It's okay. It's just I've been writing some nonsense without realising it, which is maybe a sign. But I feel fine otherwise, so it's probably nothing."

"Ah, it's not nothing," Belle said. "It's in your aura, Holly, just like last time. I saw it when I walked in. You're in trouble."

Madeleine wrapped her arms around her head. Belle's words had taken out a central beam, and the ceiling was collapsing on her.

"But you got better last time," Belle continued, and Madeleine straightened. Belle's tone was so unfamiliar. "So you'll be all right. You'll get better again. Have you called the hospital?"

That's what the tone was. Kindness. She had never heard Belle sounding so kind before. The ceiling was falling again.

"Exactly," Holly said. "If I *am* sick again, they'll fix it. And yes, I've got an appointment, so everyone stop looking so pale and desperate. It'll be fine. Talk about something else. Like, what *is* going on between you two, Jack and Belle?"

Jack moved back into the room and sat down. "It's nothing," he said, sounding tired. "It's what always happens — Belle gets mad and starts attacking me, and I can never figure out what I've done wrong, and we end up fighting and then we make up. It's happened for years. I just don't feel like doing it again. I've had enough."

There was a long quiet. Belle was studying her fingernails.

"Ah," she said eventually. "It's — I don't know. I wanted to know if anybody had moved in downstairs."

The others widened eyes in confusion.

"It's not Jack's fault," Belle said, and then her voice lowered and almost disappeared as she hunched downwards and spoke to her own hands at high speed: "It's just I hate secrets too, like Madeleine, I can't stand *lies*, and I see them everywhere, all the sad, crappy auras, and people walking around pretending to be happy. And I can *see* that Jack's sad about his parents being dead, and I can *see* he's confused about it, but he just goes around pretending to be happy and going on about past lives and horoscopes and Byron, and it makes me so mad, cause all the time . . ." The others leaned towards her, struggling to hear. She was talking into her fists now. "Cause all the time, I've *got* parents, and my mother's the worst of the liars, cause she laughs all the time, like pretending things are funny when they're not. And she doesn't even *like* me — she got *bored* of teaching us, I mean, what kind of mother . . . and my dad doesn't *notice* me — it's just not . . ."

Her words turned into sounds, and the sounds became shredded sobs.

"Oh, Belle." The others reached for her.

After a moment, Belle shook her whole body and stilled herself. "I can't stand living with my parents anymore. I was thinking I could move into the flat downstairs if it's still empty."

She looked up, wiping her eyes fiercely. "This is so stupid compared to Holly's situation. Sorry, Holly."

Holly shook her head. "I'm going to be fine. And it's not stupid to be upset about your parents. Their behaviour is *unforgivable*."

"I think you *should* move out," Madeleine said.

Holly looked thoughtful. "I agree, but I don't see how you could afford the place downstairs on your own, Belle. As a student. You could move in here with us?"

They all looked around the tiny one-room flat.

"Nah," said Belle. "Thanks, though."

"Well, we'll figure it out," Holly said. "I'll ask Darshana and Federico for advice. Maybe you could even move in with Darshana for a bit? She's got more space, and she might love to have your help with her girls."

"You could probably get some kind of government money to pay board," Madeleine said. "And Darshana laughs a lot, but she means it."

Ever so faintly, Belle smiled. "That's true."

Jack looked at her. "Does this mean you're going to stop attacking me now?"

"I doubt it," Belle said, but she sounded cheerful. "You haven't admitted that your Byron obsession is all about your absent parents."

"Ah, Byron was a complicated mixture of dark and light who wrote beautiful poetry and loved people deeply and his crap parenting is nothing to do with why I spend my days thinking about him."

Holly stood. "Everyone needs a break." She steadied herself. "You should all go out for coffee. Come back later."

"I'll stay here," Madeleine said.

They listened as Belle and Jack walked out, arguing about Byron down the stairwell.

"You know," Madeleine said once the voices had faded, "I always thought Belle got mad at Jack because she fancies him."

Holly's face was childlike with exhaustion. "I think she does. More than fancies him. He's like her other half, and she can't stand loving someone as much as that. She's so fierce and independent. But he loves her right back, and she'll see that one day. And what she just said was also true. Things are always so complicated. It makes me want to lie down."

Madeleine took her mother's hand and led her to the bed. Holly smiled, but the smile fell immediately: a kite swept up by a sudden breeze and then dropped. Her head fell onto the pillow. Madeleine touched a fingertip to a tear on her mother's cheek.

"I didn't like Jack's story," Holly said. "I should never have told him to research Byron. And I hate how Belle's parents treat her. I hate it."

"Me too. Go to sleep."

Madeleine sat on the couch.

"I'll get better," her mother promised from the bed. "Just like last time."

Except that Madeleine did not have Butterfly beads this time.

This time, she did not have Cello. She was nobody. A girl sitting on a couch.

She thought about Byron's little girl in the convent, waiting for her father.

Byron himself had been abandoned by his father. *I want no more of him*, the man had said after a visit.

So had Leonardo da Vinci, she remembered. And Vivaldi had worked in an orphanage, teaching abandoned children the violin. Newton's father was dead before he was born, and his mother left him behind with his grandparents when he was three.

Each of her three hallucinations had been a story of abandoned children. In so many different ways, children got left behind.

They were a warning. She saw that now. Her own father had rejected her. And soon her mother would die.

She was going to be left alone.

Across the room, her mother was already sleeping. Her breath seemed shallow and uncertain.

Madeleine felt a strange rocking motion in her chest, as if a small ship were trapped in there. Impossible sobs rose in her mind. She was silent.

She stood suddenly.

If the hallucinations were a warning, there must be a solution! Something to stop this. She thought of the little boy Isaac in his garret room, alone with a reflection of himself. His alchemy. The idea of an elixir. Of course! She needed to return to that idea!

Alchemy had roots in Taoism, she remembered reading. The life force was the chi. Chi leaks away. You can accumulate life force and live for centuries. Chinese alchemists believed in drinking gold. Gold was the key to extending life. She needed gold!

All she had to do was read *more* of Newton, study his codes, figure out —

She stopped.

Newton had never made gold. He had never created the elixir. If he had, someone would know. He sought magic, but found science. Here, in the world, that was all there was, and science would not cure Holly. If the tumour was back, the doctors would use the same, grim words: inoperable, untreatable.

Magic was only in the Kingdom of Cello, and that had been sealed away from her.

A sudden shriek darted from Madeleine's throat, a sound like a chair leg scraping a tiled floor. She stopped herself. She would not cry. If she cried, she would turn into a howling freak.

She needed some residue from Cello. A fragment, an echo of Cello.

Maybe, she thought, with a flash of hope, Princess Jupiter was still here?

She sat at the computer, and opened her email account.

Nothing from Ariel Peters.

She hit refresh. Still nothing. She hit refresh again.

An email arrived.

It was junk. Someone named Gianni emailing her about "Monty Rickard." There was a paper clip meaning an attachment.

Monty Rickard. They used offbeat yet commonplace names, these junk-mail people. Names that sounded like people you knew.

She was angry. She opened the email to be angrier. Maybe she'd even open the *attachment*, she thought, and give her computer an inoperable, untreatable virus.

Dear Madeleine, she read, and the ship inside her tilted as if it might capsize.

Monty Rickard. She *did* know that name. It was the name Prince Chyba used.

This was Cello. Here was *Cello*.

She took a breath of jagged-edged hope, and read.

You don't know me, and I don't know you, but here we are.

My name is Gianni, and I'm a good friend of Monty Rickard's. I met him when he moved here to Boise, Idaho.

I want to tell you something that happened yesterday.

Yesterday, my buddy Monty called me up and he said, "Gianni, I want to do something dumb."

"What's new?" I said or something similar, but that was just talk, he was never dumb, or hardly ever.

"And I want you to come with me," he said next.

"You got it," I said.

Turned out he'd heard from the "Kingdom of Cello" again, and they were offering another chance to bring him home.

"This is going to sound insane," he said.

"Shoot," I told him.

"Ever since that last time, I've had this teeny-tiny piece of regret, like I should have waited a bit longer."

"Teeny-tiny?" I said.

"Right."

Anyway, long story short, we went to the "meeting place" he'd been given. Same intersection as last time. We were five minutes early. It was empty. Nobody around.

"Let's hit the road," I said. "Nothing doing. Tick that teeny regret off your list, 'cause what's life with regrets?" Something like that.

"No, let's wait," he said.

We crossed to the opposite side of the road. He wanted to do that. We stood and watched the corner, to see what would happen.

A woman rushed along the pavement like someone in a hurry, and stopped at the corner. Breathless. We could hear this from across the road.

Monty looked at her, and at me, and back at her.

The woman didn't look at us. She had a handbag over her shoulder. She stood on that corner, and unzipped it. Took out a pair of goggles, a bit like a welder might use. She put these on her head. Monty and I looked sideways at each other about that, and kept watching the woman.

Now she took out this little piece that we both thought was a gun for a moment. We had a sort of instinctive ducking motion, both of us. Then we realized at the same time that it was more like a drill.

The woman held the drill up. She didn't switch it on. There was no sound. And then, as we watched, she made a sideways swipe at the air with it. I mean, she ran it across the air like someone with a squee-gee washing a window. Only, no window.

Monty and I looked sideways at each other again.

The woman lowered the drill thing. Then she lifted it and did the swipe again. Around the same place in the air. Lowered it, lifted it, swiped again. This went on for a few minutes.

Finally, she stopped, and just stood there, staring at the air, her hands hanging by her side.

A car drove by. The woman looked at it and then, as it passed, she looked beyond and saw us. She stared at us. Mostly she was staring at Monty. She stared in this really hard way at him.

Monty gave her his grin. She sent it back as a scowl.

Then she went back to looking at the air.

"Let's go," Monty said.

We started walking back to my car. He wasn't saying much, which isn't like him. Monty, he knows how to talk. When he's not talking to people, he's talking to animals, and when he's not talking, he's making music. It's like he can't stop making noise.

Well, that's sort of funny what I just said.

I'm going to tell you what happened next.

We stopped in a 7-Eleven. He got a Slurpee. I took a picture of him with it on my phone.

Right after I took the picture, he handed me the Slurpee.

"No, thanks," I said.

But he shoved it into my hand. "Take it," he said, and that's when I looked at him. His face was a whole other color. The kind of color you know right away this is something else, this is another place, a call-for-help color.

"Sit down," I said, but he was already sitting, not sitting, more slumping, or falling. I don't know. Right in the middle of the sidewalk, he was falling, and that color on his face getting worse all the time.

I shouted at people. Someone called an ambulance. He died on the way to the hospital.

That's the story. That's what happened yesterday.

They said it was a massive coronary. Probably congenital heart disease, they said. He never knew he had it, or if he did, he never told me.

And the reason I'm telling you this is I don't know what else to do. Nothing like this has ever happened to me before. My grandpa died, but that was sort of awesome, I never liked him, and I got to take a week off school to go out to Sacramento for the funeral. The worst that has ever happened to me was my brother lost an arm in Iraq, and I was pretty sure nothing worse had ever happened to anyone or anything before.

But this is worse. Monty was my best friend. I know I haven't known him that long, but he was one of those people you know they're true all the way through. Not in an in-your-face way, he was always funny and he liked to chill, but he was true. And he made things happen. Got us building computer games. Started a band. Got his own dog-walking business going.

Which reminds me, who's supposed to walk the dogs tomorrow?

He was half-conscious in the ambulance, and he looked at me and his eyes had this sudden bright thing going and he said, "I know who I am."

"You bet," I said. "Just take it easy."

"It's all true," he said. "I am Prince Chyba. I am from the Kingdom of Cello."

He was finding this funny. He was laughing, and each time he laughed, it was like it hurt him a lot, so I was trying to shut him the hell up. The paramedics were trying to put oxygen masks or whatever over his face, and he kept pushing them off so he could laugh at me with his mad bright eyes. "Tell my family," he said, "that I said hey, and tell them, don't forget to feed the dragons in the Bay of Munting 'cause they go there when they've lost their hunting eyes."

That's exactly what he said. I thought it was the sickness.

I'm in his room right now, at his computer. At the hospital I looked at his phone to find numbers for family or old friends or even old modeling contacts — we never completely believed he was ever a model, but that was his story. But the only numbers were us — the friends he's met here. Now I've looked through his files and emails and everything in this room, and it's the same. Nothing but Boise, Idaho, and his life here.

I don't know how to contact his family. The only outside thing I have is you. Your letter to him, telling him to go to that corner, and giving your email address.

I'm pissed at you. I blame you. If we hadn't been there on that street, and passing that 7-Eleven, and getting that Slurpee, maybe it never would've happened.

Anyhow, those were his dying words — I am Prince Chyba. So I'm doing what he asked and passing them on, and maybe you can let his family know what's happened, so they can come and — I don't know, get his stuff.

I'm attaching the picture I took of him with the Slurpee. It's rasp-berry. Those were his favorite.

Sincerely,

Gianni

Madeleine sat back. There was noise in her head like birds shouting at dusk.

Prince Chyba hadn't been rescued. Prince Chyba was dead.

It was true she didn't know him, but somebody had lost a brother, someone had lost a son, a kingdom had lost its prince.

She stared at the email.

After a moment, she clicked on the attachment.

A photograph appeared on the screen.

She leaned forward. She looked at the face.

The face looked back at her.

Her mouth was open, she could hear a sound, long and thin, like a distant mechanical alarm, but the sound was growing and closing in on her, flooding the room, brutal and savage, high-pitched as a skyscraper, and still she didn't know that she was screaming.

PART 8

"You know, this is going to sound crazy and all, but I think there could be more?"

In Bonfire, the Farms, it was hot.

It was Friday morning.

In the living room of the Baranski farmhouse, a fan turned languidly. The curtains were drawn, trying to keep things cool.

There was silence. There was a dreamy awareness that someone had just spoken.

Petra and Abel were sharing a single armchair, Petra half on Abel's lap, leaning into him. They seemed to be melting together. Petra's eyes were bloodshot. Abel had his unshaven, unkempt look.

"Anyone want a cold drink?" Petra started to stand, then let herself fall back. "Ah, help yourself if you do. You know where the kitchen is."

Nobody had slept the night before. "I don't think I've ever been as tired as this," somebody said. "You know what we need? Watermelon."

People were too tired and too hot to figure out who had just spoken, or what the heck they meant about watermelon.

The King stood by the window, his hand at the curtain's edge, watching. The others watched him. He looked back at them sometimes, and his eyes seemed crowded. The King wore a T-shirt and jeans. You could see the tattoo on his neck, and the sweat forming under his arms.

Gabe was on the couch. So was Jimmy.

Princess Ko was here too. She was on the green corduroy armchair.

She'd arrived the day before, petals and twigs caught in her hair from flying, dust in her eyes, her nose red. She'd introduced her fellow escapees: Sergio, her best friend and stable boy, pale and drained from flying against mood, and Samuel, feverish and trembling. Both boys were now sleeping in the basement at Gabe's house.

"On account of, I've heard watermelon will wake you up when you're tired, and cool you down when you're hot."

It was the Sheriff. That's who was going on about watermelon.

Remotely, the warning bells sounded.

"What's *that* code supposed to be?" Princess Ko demanded.

"It's just a preliminary warning," the Sheriff told her. "Something's coming. They don't know what it is yet. It's a ways away."

Ko sniffed. "That's absurd."

There was another silence.

"Did anybody hear what I just said?" Jimmy wondered. "I said I think there could be more."

The heat had its fists on them. You could hear a cow in the distance. The cow seemed petulant. You could hear chickens. A lonely bird.

The King rubbed his eyes with his fists. He tapped on the window glass.

The telephone rang shrilly.

Petra got up and answered it. "Okay," she said. "Okay. No. Yes. Great."

She hung up.

"They've landed," she said. "They flew all night, and they had to stop twice to refuel. Shelby's gone to bed. She's given Keira her car, so Keira's on her way now with the Queen and Princess."

The warning bells sounded again.

"It's two different things," the Sheriff said, head tilted. "That's a Jangling Violet. And . . . Ha. That's a Mustard."

"How far away?" Gabe asked.

"A ways still. The shutters will dim both, but not altogether, the way Colors are these days."

"We should put the shutters down now," Abel said.

"But we'll need to let them in when they get here."

"There's still time. Leave them up. Those Colors are ten minutes away, at least."

There was another long pause. Princess Ko reached for a magazine from the stack on the coffee table. She fanned herself with it.

The Sheriff spoke up. "When's this summer going, Gabe?"

Gabe was silent.

"I'm not getting any sense," he said.

The room was silent again.

A distant engine sounded.

The King pressed his head up against the glass.

Princess Ko stood. She brushed down her clothes. She watched the curtained window.

The engine drew closer. It was coming up the driveway.

A car pulled up outside.

The sounds of doors opening and slamming.

Footsteps on the drive, and on the stairs, and on the porch.

Nobody moved.

Gabe looked around. He stood, walked to the front door, and opened it.

He came back. Keira was behind him.

She stepped into the room, leaving space for the people behind her.

"Here they are," she said.

A woman and girl entered. They both wore sunglasses.

The King stepped toward them. Princess Ko made a small sound.

The King's arms opened. His mouth opened.

He looked at Keira. "Who are these people?" he said.

"They're in disguise," Keira said.

"Who *are* these people?" he repeated.

"It's the Princess and Queen! Take off your sunglasses," Keira urged the girl and woman.

Princess Ko sat down again. "It's not them," she said.

The girl took off her sunglasses. "No," she agreed. "It's not us. I knew I couldn't get away with it. I mean, I *am* from Cello, and I *did* get taken to the World, and I *did* forget myself while I was there, but OMG, I'm pretty sure I never was a princess!"

Jimmy cleared his throat. "I told you there were more," he said.

PART 9

1.

*A*fter a scream of such magnitude comes silence like thunder.

The scream cuts like lightning, the silence is the sonic boom.

Madeleine found that she was standing. The desk chair was lying on its side. The silence pulsated. Fragments of her scream drifted around her.

Across the room her mother sat up in bed, staring. Horror flew back and forth between their eyes. Madeleine's nose began to bleed.

2.

*I*n the Bonfire farmhouse, the room kept perfect silence.

Everyone but the King was staring at the woman who was not Queen and at the girl who was not Princess. These two glanced at each other and then, helpless and apologetic, back at the room. The King crouched to the level of the windowsill and wrapped his arms around his head.

A cacophony sprang up outside. It was like thousands of bottles being poured into a great, sliding pile. It was an entire grade school shaking tambourines. The King's arms dropped from his head in shock, while everyone else took up his previous stance: arms around heads.

"What *is* that?" the King roared, furious, while the Sheriff shouted, "Someone get the shutters! It's the Jangling Violet!"

Both Abel and Petra tumble-fell-ran from their armchair. Security shutters slammed with their *clang, clang, clang.* The jangling dulled but carried on.

The King scowled at the curtains, now darkened by shutters. He turned his scowl onto the non-queen and non-princess. "Why are you *here*?"

They both flinched.

"She brought us here." The girl pointed to Keira.

Keira shrugged. This was true.

"I was in the World," the woman quavered. "Someone took me to the *World*."

"Me too," agreed the girl.

"It's not *my* fault," the woman complained. "I was *told* I was the Queen of Cello. I never *believed* it, I just wanted them to shut *up* about it."

"It seemed total *Quatsch*," the girl admitted. "But I was like, what the *Fichtenstein*, get a *geschenk* horse, don't look at its mouth, or whatever that thing goes. Where's the nearest train or whatever and I'll *auf wiedersehen* y'all."

"What is she *talking* about?" the King demanded. "And *you*!" He rounded on Keira. "Why did you bring me these strange people?"

Keira didn't even have a shrug to offer. That's how confused she was.

"Now, don't go shouting at *Keira*," the Sheriff scolded.

Outside, the clamor rose a notch.

Abel studied the shutters. "They're not working," he said.

"Colors have changed," Petra said. "They're stronger."

Princess Ko climbed onto her knees on her chair and spoke over the seat back.

"How old are you?" she said to the non-princess.

"Fourteen, I think."

"And you?"

The woman looked startled. "I don't know. Maybe forty-nine? Or forty-eight?"

"You're both from Cello?"

They nodded.

"And you've been living in Berlin, right? And you were in Taipei?"

Again, they nodded.

"Well, that explains it." Princess Ko sat again, her back to everybody. "The Locator Spell we used. We told it to find Cellians of those ages in those places. So it did."

3.

*M*adeleine stood with her head tipped forward. Blood dripped from her nose to the floorboards.

A man leaves a party, she thought, *and puts on the wrong hat.*

The blood hit the floor and formed a perfect circle, which instantly reshaped and spread. *The best kind of circles are the ones that are sort of squashed.* Jack had said that once. *The more squashed and oval a circle, the more eccentric it is.*

"Madeleine?"

The hat is a circle. It encircles the head. It encircles the dreamer.

The blood fell.

Splat, circle, break, splat, circle, break.

"Madeleine!" her mother said again.

A man leaves a party. He puts on the wrong hat. A man leaves a party. He puts on the wrong hat.

4.

*E*veryone was talking at once. The Jangling Violet was forgotten for brief periods, the way you forget overexcited children or animals prancing around your legs at a party, then notice again with intense exasperation.

"I *knew* there were more Cellians in the World," Jimmy was saying. "I was reading missing persons reports and I thought, *hang on. . . .*"

"Send these two back to the World," the King demanded darkly.

"They seem nice enough," Gabe said.

Petra begged, "Make the *noise* stop."

"See," Abel said. "Told you the shutters weren't working."

"The noise'll go when it's good and ready," the Sheriff declared.

"That's not helpful!" Petra yelled at both of them.

"Are you okay, Keira?" Gabe asked.

Keira leaned up against the wall, despondent.

"It was all for nothing," she explained.

"I'm not *nothing*," the non-princess exclaimed. "*ICH bin nicht nichts.* Ha-ha. Is that even a sentence? *MIR ist es nicht nichts!*"

Distractedly, Keira chewed her fingernails.

Jimmy raised his voice over the racket. "Whenever there's crossover between Cello and the World, it's a displacement of reality. Just a tiny one, so nobody much notices. Anyhow, I'm looking through these reports last night, just as a puzzle for myself really — mostly people who'd been living on the edges, street kids, drug addicts, say, and local law hadn't much followed up. I started seeing little references. Pictures switching place, tea leaves up and leaving their tea cup, and I knew — what is that *smell*?"

"That'll be the Mustard Green!" The Sheriff sounded cheerful. Every other face clutched itself into a wince.

"You got any disinfectant spray?" Gabe cupped his hands over his nose. "Scented candles maybe?"

"We all need to take it easy." Abel went to the sideboard and opened a cupboard. He turned back to the room as he did. "This is just a setback."

"A Mustard Green is not so much a *setback*," the Sheriff began, looking philosophical.

"Not the *Color*, I'm talking about the fact we've got the wrong people. So we start again. Find the *real* Queen and Princess."

"How exactly do we do that?" Princess Ko demanded, scrambling back onto her knees and glaring over the chair top.

"Easy." Abel shrugged. "We get in touch with Madeleine again. I want to check on her and Holly anyway. I think —"

"Well, of *course* you want to check on Madeleine and Holly," Petra burst out. She marched to the sideboard and slammed the door Abel had just opened. His hand jumped away just in time. "They're not kept in here anymore, they haven't been in *years*." She reached to a higher cabinet, drawing out a handful of candles.

"Not sure scented candles will do much against this stink," the Sheriff called.

Petra slammed the candles into holders. "You know, he was *very* close to that Holly while he was in the World? He felt *drawn* to Holly and Madeleine the moment he first saw them in a café? So he helped them find a flat right upstairs from him?" Her voice grew into a hoarse roar. "And I don't know where *Elliot* is! I never hear a word about *Elliot* anymore! How do I even know that he's okay?!"

"He's okay," Keira said. Uncertainty crossed her face.

"What?" pounced Petra. "What's that look?"

"What about my *son*?" the King bellowed. "Where's Chyba? I don't know if *he's* okay either! Not to mention my *wife* or my *daughter*." He threw another contemptuous look at the wrong wife and wrong daughter. They slunk back, ashamed.

"It was weird about Prince Chyba," Keira said. "I was opening the crack, but it kept closing. Who knows if Chyba was *there* anyway, but it was like someone was working against me on the other side."

"It probably wasn't even the real Chyba!" the King sneered. "That spell of yours probably found some Cellian *street kid* of the same age!"

Princess Ko reared up again. "How were we to know there were other Cellians in the World besides the royal family?!"

"I guess *Abel* was in the World at that time," the Sheriff mused.

"*We* didn't know that! And it worked for *you*!" Ko flung her arm toward the King. "*You* must have been the only Cellian of your age in Montreal! And Prince Tippett was the only one in Avoca Beach, Australia! We got you two back!"

"How did you know what city they were in?" Jimmy asked.

Keira spoke up. "I made a program," she said, "linking up Cello and the World. We told it the places they'd disappeared here, and it found the matching cities in the World. Then the Locator Spell gave us addresses in those cities."

"You probably made a mistake with the program," the King muttered.

Keira raised her eyebrows.

"She doesn't make technology mistakes," Gabe spoke up. He flinched. "Sorry. Got a strong sense of smell. This is doing me in."

The King glowered. "Well, *somebody* made a mistake!"

"You know, that could be so?" the Sheriff mused, and both Keira and Ko glared at him. He raised his hands, apologetic. "Seems to me, you ask a Locator Spell to find a Cellian of a specific age in a specific city, it would give you *all* the Cellians of that age. Not just choose a random one." He tipped his head to the woman and girl, now pressed together, like people in a crowded elevator. "So why didn't it give you these two *as well as* the real Queen and Princess? Assuming you put in the right cities."

"We did it right!" Princess Ko cried. "We put in exactly where they disappeared!"

Keira nodded and began to recite. "The King was at the Sandringham Convention Center. The Queen was in a second-level office in the Department of Finance. Chyba was at the Cast Iron Restaurant in McCabe Town, Nature Strip. Jupiter was in the penthouse suite of the Harrington Hotel. And Prince Tippett was home in the White Palace."

Now the King laughed. "Didn't I just *say* you had it wrong!" he crowed. "I don't know where Chyba and Tippett were, but that's not where the Queen or Princess Jupiter were that night! That's *not* how it was at all!"

5.

"*T*ell me, what it is? What's the matter?"

Holly was crouched beside Madeleine, holding out a towel. Madeleine ignored it. She was hunched over, watching the blood rain from her nose.

I can bake a dream, she thought, *I can bake a poem.*

She thought she should speak to Isaac Newton. He would make things clear. He was outside now, wandering the streets of Cambridge. He was buying gloves, stockings, a hatband, cherries. He was buying custard, herbs, beer, cake, milk.

Isaac Newton was watching a game of tennis. He considered how the ball spun and how it glanced. How it moved through the air, what the air was, why the ball moved and why it fell. He reflected on the curve and the trajectory.

Holly pressed the towel to Madeleine's face and held it there, and Madeleine closed her eyes.

She was running on a twilight road, Elliot beside her.

The answers are inside the hat, she thought. Isaac Newton bought himself a hatband. *A man left a party and picked up the wrong hat.*

6.

*E*veryone was looking at the King.

"Well, where *were* the Queen and Princess Jupiter that night?" Gabe asked at last. The Mustard Green throttled him suddenly. His face crumpled in despair.

Abel found matches inside a ceramic jug ("I still recall where the matches are," he shot at Petra), and lit the candles Petra had forgotten.

"Won't make a whiff of difference," the Sheriff said. "Ha-ha."

"Ah, shut your trap, Hector," Abel said, but mildly.

The King, meanwhile, was frowning. His triumph had slipped. He was thinking, head bent.

At last he looked up. "I see how it happened," he said cautiously. "We were in Ducale City: the Queen, Jupiter, and I." His voice became formal. "We were supposed to attend a charity gala at the Convention Center that evening. The Queen and I were getting dressed in our hotel room, when word came that Jupiter was at the railway station, buying a ticket to Tek, Jagged Edge." A touch of defiance crossed his face. "She did that sort of thing *all* the time." Nobody spoke. "At any rate, the Queen said we should skip the party and go and collect her. I felt we should leave her be, to learn her lesson. We quarreled. The Queen went to the station. I went to the party."

Outside, the noise started up again but with less enthusiasm.

The King continued, his voice even more regal. "Of course, I gave excuses for the absence of my wife and daughter. I said the Queen had gone to the Finance Department to deal with a minor emergency. This was accepted without comment. The Queen, as everybody knew, had recently assumed control of finances. I said that Princess Jupiter had taken ill and was sleeping in the penthouse suite."

Again, there was quiet across the room. The Jangling Violent had settled into intermittent clanks and dings.

"So what you're saying," Jimmy ventured, "is that the Queen and Princess were actually taken from the railway station?"

"Or maybe they were on their way back to the hotel," Petra put in. "Or to the Convention Center. Or they were *on* the train, someplace between Ducale and Tek? Maybe together, maybe apart."

The Sheriff grunted. "Hold your horses," he said to the King. "You said you *got word* that Princess Jupiter was buying a train ticket? So who gave word? Someone at the station recognized her? Security following her? So they must know what happened next?"

The King twitched. "Royal security, yes," he said. "They often kept an eye on Princess Jupiter for us. But that night, I told them to come back to the gala. And when I saw them, I told them . . . that Jupiter was back herself now, and was ill in the penthouse suite, and to leave her be."

"Now, why would you have done that?"

The King crinkled his nose. He spoke petulantly. "The Queen was on her way to get Jupiter! And who knew what scenes there might be at the station? She'd caused enough bad press already! I wanted the scenes to go unnoticed. Security talk, you know. They gossip."

"Well, now," Petra murmured into the new quiet.

7.

*I*t was easier now.

Madeleine was deep inside a darkness. It was soft, the darkness, and curved. It was a sinking hammock, and she sank with it.

She was far from her mother, and far from the room, and the email and the photograph and the scream.

Wake up. A voice smacked the side of her head. It was her own voice. She felt her lip tremble. She sank deeper.

Wake up, the voice commanded again. *Or you will die.*

You're being melodramatic, she responded tartly, and she disappeared inside herself again.

In disappearance, there was beautiful wilderness. Some important tearing away, some detachment. She floated into it. *This is the ether.*

You will die, the voice intoned. *So will your mother.*

The voice multiplied itself, adding clangs and jangles, until it was a voice made of clamour. *You're a girl in a tower. You watch and wait and hope. You wait for letters from your father. You wait for notes from Elliot. You close yourself inside half-waking visions. The lights fizz through your flesh. Wake up.*

She felt the first gust of uneasy.

To wake up now, she explained to her own voice, *would be to rip myself to shreds, to tear my flesh on the walls of this tunnel, to shatter my bones, and worse.*

Wake up anyway, the voice replied.

8.

"You know," Jimmy said at last. "I guess that fits?"

The King glanced at him irritably.

"Way back, I read the missing persons reports on the royal family," Jimmy explained. "With both the Queen and Princess Jupiter, none of the witnesses had actually *seen* them. The Queen was supposedly in an office in a building that had closed for the day. Witnesses were cleaners. The Princess was apparently inside the suite. So I guess maybe they *weren't* there, behind those closed doors."

"They weren't," the King said sharply. "I just explained that."

"Well, now," the Sheriff said. "We're only just catching up to you, King Cetus. Give us a moment."

"Still," Jimmy mused. "Why was there a tremor in reality in both those cases? That's why I figured they were taken to the World. Cleaners and chambermaids told stories of strange little things. There must have been *some* kind of crossover right around that time." He looked at the non-queen and non-princess.

"Is that where you two were taken?" he said doubtfully. "From the Department of Finance, and the Harrington Hotel?"

"I don't know *where* I was," the woman whispered. "I'd left my husband. He's a Ganglord of Golden Coast, but I will *not* and I have *not* told you his name nor his gang nor anything that could be construed as . . . Anyhow, yes, I was sleeping in an alcove outside a building. It had big sandstone bricks — I grazed my knuckle on them — so it might have been a government establishment of some kind! I don't know!"

"Big sandstone bricks," the King said grimly. "Could be the Department of Finance. When was this?"

"I don't know! Two years ago? Three? I don't know. Leave me be!"

"I was in the kitchen of the Harrington Hotel," the girl said. "I just remembered. That's helpful of me, at least?"

"When was this?"

"It was Elina's birthday, so that's what, April?"

"We don't know this Elina, nor her birthday," the King said grimly.

"Last April?" the Sheriff asked.

"Nah, the April before that, I think."

"That's not when the royals disappeared," Jimmy said.

"So I was with Elina and my friends," the girl continued. "We sort of broke in as a joke? And the food. So, we were busting our guts laughing, and I do not know *how* we thought we'd get away with it, it's sorta kickin' funny that we did. But we didn't. I mean, we didn't get away with it. 'Cause some guy in a suit takes my arm and says, 'Come this way,' and I was like, they got me, but I was trashed so I didn't care, and then I was *whoa, WHAT?!* 'Cause I'm suddenly standing outside in a whole other city. I remember that now. And then . . ." She lit up. "I'm living in Berlin and I think my name is Ariel Peters and I keep getting *ink*! And eczema. Then someone tells me I'm Princess Jupiter of Cello, and I'm like, *Blitzkrieg!!* Or whatever."

"That's more or less how it happened with me," the woman spoke up. "Except nothing like it." She chuckled. "But some parts. I was sleeping, as I said, and a man in a suit told me to move along, and suddenly I was in Taipei. I thought I was from New Zealand." Her chuckle was upgraded to a chortle.

"What's New Zealand?" Gabe asked.

"It's a country in the World. I was living with these humorless kids, teaching dancing, and *aching* all the time with arthritis, and *I* started getting letters about the Kingdom of Cello, telling me that I was a queen."

"I don't even *look* like Princess Jupiter," the girl said. "Why'd you bring me here?"

Keira sighed. "I had no real clue what Jupiter looked like except she's skinny and she's trouble, and you look like both to me. No offense. Besides, you guys were supposed to be disguised, so Shelby and I thought you were, you know . . . disguised."

"Well, *I* look a *lot* like the Queen," the non-queen put in. "So don't blame yourself!" Then she laughed hysterically.

9.

$\mathcal{T}$he door swung open, and Belle and Jack followed it inside.

They were tripping over each other's words, holding takeaway coffee cups. They stopped.

Blood was pouring in a line down Madeleine's chin, staining her shirt and jeans. Spots on her shoelaces. The floor was blood-splattered. Holly crouched, a blood-soaked towel over her arm.

"You need to make that stop," Jack said.

"Ya *think*?" Belle said, withering.

Exhaustion poured through Madeleine's body to her feet. From her feet came a surge of energy. This shot up and out of her head.

"I think I'm in shock," she said. Her voice surprised her. It was husky. Another wave fell, another rose.

"You've had plenty of bleeding noses before, Madz," Belle said. "What's the big shock?"

Jack had disappeared into the bathroom. He came out with more towels.

"I don't know what's wrong with her," Holly said.

Madeleine pointed to the computer monitor.

"See that boy?" she said, and again her voice sounded strange. It was the scream, she realised. She'd damaged her vocal cords.

"That boy is my brother. Chyba. And he's dead."

Holly kept her head turned away from the screen. "Madeleine's lost her mind," she smiled.

"Wait." Jack pressed the clean towel to Madeleine's face. "You mean Prince Chyba of Cello? You think you're related to him?"

"We're from the Kingdom of Cello." Madeleine pushed Jack away so the blood flowed again. "And we need to get back."

Belle was tching like a squirrel. She looked from Holly to Madeleine and back again.

"You know," she said slowly. "That would make sense."

"It doesn't make sense," Madeleine said. "It's all wrong. We're wrong. This is wrong. That's why we're sick. And if we don't get back to Cello now, I think we're going to die."

Holly laughed into the quiet of the room. "I'm the one with the brain tumour," she said.

Madeleine's eyes closed with the next descent of fatigue. She was going to fall with it. The strength pushed up again but clumsily.

She half opened her eyes.

"You could squeeze lemon juice onto the inside of your elbow," Jack suggested. "Cause isn't that the sign of a Cellian?"

"I don't need to," Madeleine said. She fell sideways onto the couch. "I remember everything. All I need to do is get to Cello."

"But how?" Belle raised an eyebrow. "You need to go to one of the cracks and do the light and mirror thing, right? You should go to Berlin. Isn't that where Abel and Elliot went through?" She was frowning in concentration. "But you need someone on the other side to *open* the crack, right? Cause it's sealed? I should've paid more attention when you talked about Cello."

"Now you've all gone mad." Holly's voice turned paper thin and high. "I'm going to get angry!" She tried to laugh.

Madeleine let her head fall forward. The blood poured from her nose to the couch now. Everybody watched.

"There's not enough time," she said to Belle. "We need to stumble."

"You need to stop your nosebleed," Jack said. She kept dodging him. "Hold still, Mads, seriously."

"What do you mean, 'stumble'?" Belle asked.

"People sometimes stumble between Cello and the World," Madeleine explained. "It happens by accident. When there's absence and emotion." She stood and stepped towards her mother. Everything was sapphire. The falls were coming faster and heavier; the surges lost interest at her ankles.

"I need to stumble on purpose," she said.

She took her mother's hand and clutched it hard.

"You're hurting me," her mother said.

"I am going to stumble to Cello," she said.

Jack had his phone out.

"Yeah, you go ahead," he said. "I'm calling an ambulance."

"If it just takes absence and emotion," Belle said, "you've got both."

"I know." Madeleine looked at the picture of her dead brother on the screen. Her mother stood beside her, dying.

She closed her eyes and tried to focus. She thought she should start small.

Absence. A chair missing a leg. A mug without a handle.

Emotion. A child threading a blankie through his fingers. A father clenching his fists and swinging them down through the air.

"No, I mean you've got both right there," Belle said, "in your aura." She pointed with her finger. "Try to see them, Madeleine."

Absence. A mirror.

Emotion. Piercing light.

Can you focus and stumble? She lost her grip on everything a moment.

"They're both right *there*," Belle said again. "You freakin' tosser. Absence and emotion. Right *there* in front of your *face*."

Madeleine opened her eyes and there they were, etched in the air, squares of space, one empty, one full.

She grasped at them with her free hand. They misted sideways. She lunged. They slipped right through her fingers. Her heart seemed to tumble in its beating. They disappeared.

She took a deep breath, narrowed her eyes, and there they were again. The empty space, the full space, marked out before her eyes. Now her hand moved slowly, more slowly, edging closer to the empty space and full. Closer, then closer. Her fingers trembled, her arm jerked a little, and she stilled it. Closer still and then with a flick and a twist of her wrist her hand closed on them both. A searing pain shot through her body like the crack of a whip.

She tightened her grip on her mother. They stumbled into Cello.

PART 10

1.

*O*utside, snow fell. There appeared to be about thirty horses galloping across a field. The figure standing on the roof of the barn, waving his arms and shouting, was Gabe. Five or six farmhands were pelting toward the horses from the opposite direction. Snow began to mix with Spitting Fuchsia, and the farmhands stopped to slap their own cheeks.

Keira was watching this through the kitchen window. She looked toward Gabe on the roof of the barn. He was still gesticulating about the horses. Fuchsia was showering on him, but he seemed oblivious.

It was funny, Keira reflected, how she'd found the Farms too quiet when she first got here.

* * *

Two days before, Keira had rescued the royal family.

Only, she hadn't.

Now and then she got a snapshot memory of herself, driving toward the Baranski farmhouse, a queen and a princess in the back. She'd been trying not to smile. Sure, she'd missed out on Prince Chyba, but two out of three was good! And what were the chances of the daughter of a Hostile, a girl from Jagged Edge, bringing two royals back home?!

Zero, it turned out. She'd been bringing random strangers.

She was so embarrassed by the snapshot memory she wanted to cringe inside out.

Anyhow, the chaos at the Baranskis' had calmed, and the Jangling Violet and Mustard had faded. Hector had offered to drive non-queen and non-princess to the station so they could make their way home. Not that they had homes, everyone realized uncomfortably. Well, to their *neighborhoods*. Their people. Petra had packed bags of pastries for their journey. The King had given them envelopes of cash. They seemed cheerful about both this and the pastries. He'd asked them not to tell anybody what they'd seen here, and they'd said they were too confused to know what he even *meant* by that. They'd left with the Sheriff.

After that, the room had been moody and depressed. They'd decided to reconvene the next afternoon.

The next day — yesterday — everyone had returned to the Baranski farmhouse. Once again, there'd been dejection.

Then the mad thing had happened.

A woman and a girl had turned up.

The right ones.

The missing Queen and Princess.

They'd gotten *themselves* back from the World.

Which sure changed the mood! Everything bleak and then ding-dong! (or "knock, knock," actually — they hadn't rung a doorbell) — the solution! It was like having a huge assignment for school and not even knowing how to *start* the research, then someone hands you the final product: printed, ring-bound, and with a fancy heading on the title page.

Ha. She'd spent too much time in the Farms. School assignments in her previous life were *never* printed and bound; you just messaged them in.

Anyhow, there they were, Queen and Princess, two complete assignments on the porch. A bit battered, though, as if the printer had mangled some of the pages.

Petra had opened the front door, recognized them right away, and hustled them into the Baranski living room. The reunion went like this: The Queen and Princess stood on one side of the room, while the King and other Princess stood on the other side. There was a long, gaping silence. Their eyes began to gleam sort of *insanely*, then slow tears fell from *all* their eyes. *Then* they rushed together and turned themselves into a giant, swaying tree.

Keira had actually found it quite moving.

"Where were you? How'd you get here? What happened?" the King gasped and stuttered.

The Queen said they'd been together, in Cambridge, England, the World, the whole time. The Princess said they'd "stumbled" themselves home (Petra seemed to know what that meant; everyone else just flickered their eyes at one another, like, *"huh?"* and then flickered back with, *"oh well, go on"*).

They'd arrived in a town called Ruleton, they said, in the south of the Farms, and walked here through the night. The Sheriff was saying, "Well, now, how in the heck did you know to walk *here*, of all places?" when the next surprising thing happened.

Abel Baranski walked into the room, wanting to know what all the commotion was about — he'd been upstairs making a phone call — so, of course, everyone wanted to show him the Queen and Princess. The tree broke apart, obligingly, but instead of saying, "Well, how about that! It's their majesties!" or whatever, he shouted: "Holly! Madeleine!"

Madeleine, the girl from the World and her mother, had been the Princess and the Queen all along.

That startled Keira into quiet. She stepped back and whispered to Gabe: "I wasn't very *respectful* to Madeleine in my notes to her. I mean, I didn't treat her like a princess at *all*," and Gabe said, "Well, you don't seem altogether the respectful type, Keira. So I wouldn't worry." This was true. She'd never been remotely courteous to Princess *Ko*, for example. So she cheered up and turned back to the commotion.

Only, it had stopped. The Queen and Princess were revealing the final twist. Prince Chyba was dead. He had died in the World, of heart failure.

Keira's first thought was that this was quite good.

It meant everything was squared off. No loose ends in the World. The entire royal family accounted for.

But then she remembered that Chyba was a person, maybe even a nice person? She looked across at the royals and felt guilty. The four had separated. Their faces, which they were trying to hide behind their hands, were ugly.

Keira walked out of the room, out of the house, through a gate, and across a field. She kept walking until she reached a greenhouse, and then she stood outside this, kicking at the dirt for a while. Eventually, she turned around and went back to the house.

The others were now sitting in a close circle, talking softly.

The King was strumming on the guitar, now and then pausing mid-strum to breathe a short laugh at something someone said. People were sharing stories about Chyba — it was mainly the Sheriff, Jimmy, Petra, and Hector doing the sharing, which was odd, as they'd never met Prince Chyba. Their stories came from newspapers they'd read over the years. But the royals seemed to like hearing them.

Chyba had found an injured lion cub on the side of a street when he was six, apparently, and he'd hidden it in his coat, and taken it home to raise. There'd been trouble when it was discovered, almost fully grown, in the pantry of the White Palace. At twelve, Chyba had decided to single-handedly broker a peace deal with the Kingdom of Aldhibah by sending them his deftball card collection.

The stories went on. People laughed. Sometimes the Queen said gently that she suspected that story wasn't true.

"He never stopped talking," one of the two princesses said, and the other one said, "I *know*," but none of the royals offered an anecdote.

Each time the King paused in strumming, the Sheriff would suggest another song that he knew to be a Prince Chyba favorite. (The Sheriff owned souvenir albums on all the royals, he explained.)

"Oh," Princess Jupiter said suddenly, "just before he died, he said to tell his family *hey*, and that we have to remember to feed the dragons at the Bay of Munting because that's where they go when they've lost their hunting eyes."

Everyone went very quiet. Keira noticed shoulders shuddering.

Keira was about to leave again when somebody asked whether Chyba had had a heart condition.

"Well, that I don't know," the Sheriff admitted.

"He didn't," the Queen said, and there was a long pause.

Petra said. "I keep wondering if maybe there's something about the World that makes people from Cello get sick?"

The King set down his guitar, frowning.

"I did a lot of World Studies," Petra explained, "and I remember reading a theory that Cellians lose themselves *completely* in the World: not just their memories but, eventually, their health as well? Eventually, they die. It was only a theory, though, and nobody seemed to credit it much."

"I had migraines when I was in the World," the King said, "and haven't had them since I got back."

"I had asthma." Abel raised his eyebrows. "Thought it was allergies, but maybe . . ."

Gabe pointed out that the non-princess had mentioned eczema, and the non-queen, rheumatoid arthritis. The real princess said she'd had a lot of bleeding noses, then she turned uncertainly to the Queen.

"I was pretty sick too," the Queen said carefully. "I guess I should see a doctor sometime to — find out if I'm better?"

"It was the World that killed Chyba?" the Sheriff asked slowly.

Nobody said anything, and Keira felt an immense weight in the room. She thought about the crack in the air of the corridor, and how she'd untangled it, and it had tangled, and she'd untangled, and it had tangled, and she imagined, for a moment, the young prince standing on the other side, alive, hopeful, waiting to come through.

From there, the conversation drifted into talk about life in the World, and they all compared false memories, and laughed at one another's inventions. The Queen and Princess talked about friends they'd made there, including teenagers called Belle and Jack. Abel had plenty to say about "Belle and Jack" too, and then he said, wasn't it the darndest thing, how he'd been living downstairs from the Queen and Princess of Cello all that time? Never even knowing he himself was from Cello, or even remembering what Cello *was*?

Hector exclaimed. "Well, no wonder you were drawn to Holly and Madeleine!" he said. "They were the Queen and Princess! A part of you probably *knew* that, or at least knew they were from Cello!"

Abel laughed and looked at his wife. Petra's face said she was reserving judgment. But she changed her position in her chair, to one that seemed a little more relaxed.

The King leaned over to the Queen, stroked her hair, and said, "I'll never lose you again."

It had been getting darker and chillier for the last half hour, and now seemed like exactly the right sad and beautiful moment for the evening to end and everyone to get some sleep.

The Sheriff pushed back his chair. "Well," he began.

But that was when things began to shift out of alignment.

The Queen said she wanted to call Prince Tippett in the Magical North. There was an argument. It was a mild argument, with everyone still using their gentle, loving voices, but basically the other adults said it was too dangerous. Hostiles would be monitoring phone calls to the Palace, they said. The Queen insisted. Eventually, they persuaded her to wait, but her shoulders were high and her face was closed.

Next, the Queen and Princess asked everyone to please call them Holly and Madeleine from now on. They'd discussed this on their walk here, they said. They'd become more like "themselves" in the World, and wanted to hold on to that.

Once again, there was a mild, loving argument. The King was opposed. He wanted his *real* family back, he said, not distorted and artificial constructs created by the subconscious. That seemed an impressive sentence, and everyone looked to the Queen for her reaction.

She pointed out that "Holly" was her actual middle name, which must be where her subconscious had found it, so nothing *distorted* about that, and anyway, her real name had been *Claire* before the Royal PR Department made her change it to Lyra when she married the King.

So *Queen Lyra*, she said, was the artificial construct all along.

"Well, Jupiter's been Jupiter all her life," Princess Ko put in, and the Queen said yes, but the PR Department had named all their children, and she'd always found the names a bit ridiculous, and actually preferred Madeleine.

"You always found my name ridiculous?" Princess Ko said coolly. "What name would you find preferable, then?"

Her sister told a story about how she'd been emailing the non-princess in Berlin, which was funny, she said, because it was like she'd been emailing *herself*, but the point was, now she thought of *that* girl as Jupiter, which made *her* even more Madeleine, so there was that.

Most people were bewildered by this, partly because they were trying to keep up with the loop in logic, and partly because they didn't know what *emailing* was.

The King interrupted the bewilderment by kissing the Queen's head again — this time it was more of a bump of his mouth followed by a delicate removal of one of the Queen's hairs from his lips — and saying: "I'm just happy to have them back, whatever their names. Our family will spend a night together, under one roof, for the first time in over a year. Assuming the Baranskis have room for us all?"

"Of course," Abel and Petra said together.

"I'm not staying here," Princess Ko asserted. "I need to be with Sergio and Samuel. I'll go back to — whatsit?" She looked over at Gabe, biting her lip.

"Gabe," he said.

"Gabe's house," she said firmly.

"I'd like to be with Ko," the other princess said, and she also looked at Gabe. "Can I stay too?"

Gabe scratched his head. "I guess, if you don't mind the attic?"

Unexpectedly, the girl laughed at this.

"Well, I want to be with my daughters," the Queen declared.

"In that case . . ." The King stood. "I'll come to Gabe's house too."

"There won't be enough room," the Queen told him. "You'd better stay here."

"Well, I guess we could find . . ." Gabe began.

"There won't be enough room," the Queen repeated firmly.

So now it was early the next morning.

The King was still at the Baranskis'.

The Queen and Princess — or Holly and Madeleine, if that was so important to them — were sleeping upstairs in the attic. Princess Ko was in Gabe's parents' room. Sergio and Samuel were downstairs in the basement.

She, Keira, was already awake. A Night-Dweller on Farms time. Crazy. But it made her sort of proud. She was washing up her breakfast things, which was ridiculous. They should have a machine to do this! Still. It made you feel good, soapsuds washing whiteness right across a plate.

Gabe was outside on the roof of the barn, horses were stampeding, and a Spitting Fuchsia was falling. The Color had probably spooked the horses, she realized, but what must those horses' feet be doing to the crops?

Hooves, she realized.

That's what you called horses' feet.

Then she remembered Sergio's obsession with horses.

"Sergio!" she called in the direction of the basement.

After a moment, Sergio shot up the stairs, smiling his familiar Sergio smile, and moving with his Sergio deerlike spring.

"It is as beautiful as ever to behold you, Keira," he cried. "I find that I cannot believe it is truly you."

"Thanks, but you see those horses?"

Ten minutes later, Sergio was outside in the snow, still in his pajamas, surrounded by trembling horses. He was stroking and talking to each in turn, and then he was leading them slowly down the drive.

The farmhands stood watching in amazement. The Spitting Fuchsia faded.

From the roof of the barn, Gabe looked across at the house, caught sight of Keira at the kitchen window, and raised a hand to her.

2.

O ver the next few weeks, winter settled in, and Bonfire was thrashed by a Color storm.

The warning bells rang almost continually. Rare Colors — Colors that people had forgotten existed — hurtled through the town: Corals, Jades, and Saffrons. They were accompanied by more common, vicious Colors, like Grays and Purples, and by sly Colors, brazen Colors, and Colors that ricocheted and clashed.

School was canceled. The town was in lockdown. In the splinters between Colors, people rushed out to gather food and water, and to repair or reinforce security shutters.

Gabe and his farmhands dragged tarpaulins over crops, and harvested what they could, sprinting for cover when the bells started up again. Sometimes Gabe didn't have time to get back to the house, and he'd spend the night in the barn or in the farmhands' quarters.

In the farmhouse, Keira became boss. She knew where the bath towels were and how you worked the tricky hot-water tap. She could handle the coffee machine, and she'd watched Gabe often enough to take over the cooking.

The others in the house respected her authority. She liked this. There was very little else that she liked about the others.

The Queen almost never left the attic, except for meals. When she came downstairs, she smiled remotely. She offered to help in the kitchen, but then she'd pick up a knife and her hand would tremble, and she'd put it back down, smile her teary smile, and try again. It took an hour for her to chop an onion.

Madeleine was as silent as her mother but in a grim, angry way. This was unexpected. It was true that the Girl-in-the-World used to write furious notes, but Keira had always regarded the fury as flimsy and papery. Something you could blow away with a puff of air. Of course, that might have been because the fury was written on paper. Anyway, it surprised Keira to pass Madeleine on the staircase and feel as if she was passing a girl-shaped brick of rage. Or to sense some fierce energy in the corner of the living room and realize it was Madeleine, curled up in an armchair, staring into space. She was *always* curled up in that armchair. Sometimes she spent the night there. But when she did come into the kitchen, it took Madeleine about three seconds to chop an onion.

Princess Ko would disappear for hours, then turn up and say she'd been there all along. When she was there, she was also angry, but noisily. She slammed doors and shouted. She was angry with Samuel for being sick, and angry with Sergio for not being able to help him — apparently, Samuel only had enough medication to last another month, and Ko wanted Sergio to fly across the Kingdom and find more, which Sergio would have done but the sky was full of Colors — and angry with the Colors for filling the sky, trapping her in this house, and angry with the warning bells for being so *jangly*. She'd *never* liked jangling of *any* kind, she said. She was angry with her brother, for dying. She was also angry with her mother and sister for having been in the World, and for having forgotten her existence, and for being back from the World now, and, most of all, it seemed, for drinking so much *tea*. She was *sure* they never *used* to drink tea.

"It's from living in England," they explained.

"I don't even know what England *is*," Ko roared. "Stop using stupid words like *England*!"

With Keira, Princess Ko was formal, and she refused to make eye contact. This made sense because they'd always despised each other, but if their eyes had met they might have realized that they also respected each other, and that they both felt proud of what they'd achieved on the RYA, and both felt battered by the way the Kingdom had turned on them, and both felt terrified by how sick Samuel was. So, it would be a mistake, to let their eyes meet. At least, that's what Keira assumed was going on.

Sergio was okay, but he spent most of his time spoon-feeding Samuel medicine and water. When Keira went down to the basement to do laundry, she would look across at Samuel, lying in the camp bed with his rasping breath, and his flaking skin and strange welts, and she'd feel like either slapping him or bursting into tears. Stupid boy poisoning himself with Olde Quainte magic. He couldn't even speak! And he used to have so much to say! It used to drive Keira insane, the way Samuel spoke, and now his silence made her want to throttle him.

It really undermined the experience of doing laundry. Pulling soft, warm linen from the drying machine might have been pleasant if it hadn't been for the silent, dying boy.

The other annoying thing was that the King kept turning up at the door. "Cut it *out*," Keira said to him each time he arrived. "You're going to get yourself *killed* out there!" He would raise his chin and say, "It is worth the risk to see my wife and daughters," as if he was doing something grandly courageous. But his wife and daughters kept sending him away. Keira became brazen in her irritation.

"It's not *brave* — it's *stupid*," she told him. "If you *die* out there, your family will get even *more* morose and insufferable than they already are!"

The King would smile gently, as if she was kidding. But she wasn't.

One day, during a rare afternoon free from Color, the King turned up in a car, with Abel driving, and announced that they were taking the Queen to Sugarloaf Hospital to see a specialist. The King had brought disguises along for both himself and the Queen, which Keira found sort of amusing.

But they were terribly solemn, straightening their wigs and wiping away smudges of lipstick.

When they came back later, they were full of celebration, because, they announced, the Queen did *not* have a brain tumor.

"Well, great, I guess," Keira said. "Neither do I."

Nobody seemed to find her funny, but seriously, who knew there'd ever been a chance that the Queen *had* a brain tumor? Not Keira. So it was hard to get excited that she didn't.

Madeleine cried about the news for over an hour, curled up next to her mother on the couch. Keira began to feel guilty and unpleasant about her own lack of reaction. She also wondered if maybe Madeleine's tears would melt that brick of rage.

But the next day Madeleine was concrete again, and soon the moodiness settled back over the household.

3.

*I*t was a few days after the news about the nonexistent brain tumor, that Keira and Madeleine were sitting side by side at the kitchen table. Gabe had brought in several buckets filled with bruised plums, and the girls were making these into jam.

That was the idea anyway. Neither of them had a clue how to make jam. They were following instructions in an old book they'd found in the kitchen drawer, but these seemed to assume a lot of knowledge. What was *pectin*, for example? And what was a *slotted spoon*?

"I like the name anyway," Madeleine said. "Slotted spoon."

"Me too," Keira agreed. Actually, she was pretty neutral about the name, but for Madeleine to say that she *liked* something seemed like a shot of melody in a song that was otherwise relentless thrash.

They'd pulled all sorts of bowls, pots, empty jars, crockery, and cutlery out of the cupboards, and these were scattered over the table. Then Keira opened the third drawer down and pulled out a big spoon with slits in it.

She held it up. "Slotted spoon," she whispered.

Madeleine raised an eyebrow. A dimple flickered in her cheek.

"Now what do we do with it?" Keira asked the recipe. The recipe was silent.

Madeleine said she remembered reading somewhere that you could peel fruit more easily if you dunked it in a pot of boiling water for half a minute, then ladled it into a pot of ice.

"You could use a slotted spoon," she said, "to *ladle*."

So they did this, and now they were peeling plums.

"This is working," Keira said.

Madeleine nodded.

"It feels good, doesn't it? When they just slip out of their skins like this?"

This time Madeleine tilted her head, noncommittal.

But it did feel good. There was no question, Keira thought. Commit, Madeleine! She was a bit annoyed for a moment. Then she calmed down.

"I guess it feels good to be back in Cello? Back with your family?" she tried.

Small talk was not something Keira had ever done in her life. She didn't believe in it. Probably, she thought, she was doing such a bad job now because of lack of practice. But she had a faintly urgent sense that this might be her only chance to break through to Madeleine.

Madeleine had stopped peeling the plums, and was looking at the recipe again. She didn't answer.

"I think we're supposed to squeeze some lemon juice on the ones we've done," she said. "To stop them going brown."

"Oh, well," Keira said. "Haven't got any lemons. Who cares if they're brown?"

"Does Gabe have lemon trees?"

Keira shrugged.

After a moment, Madeleine returned to peeling plums. They were silent.

Then Madeleine spoke in a low voice. "You know," she said, "when I was in the World, I didn't even remember I *had* brothers and a sister? My mind translated them into friends. I thought they were a bunch of kids we hung out with on vacations. Which makes sense because I never used to see them except on vacations."

"Huh," Keira said. She tried to think of something to counter that. "Well, your sister really wanted to find you," she said. "You know she formed this group called the Royal Youth Alliance, right? And we all had to basically give up our lives to track you down and bring you home? She was a total tyrant."

Madeleine nodded. "Elliot told me about the RYA. I was helping, remember? Only, I didn't know it had anything to do with me. In my head, my sister, Ko, was a friend named Tinsels. I emailed her and she pretended not to know me."

"She probably *didn't* know you, whoever she was. And your actual sister wasn't some friend who ignored you — she was always Ko and she was trying to get you back," Keira said. "Same with your dad. He didn't get far, but he's been working like mad to get you home from the World."

A figure appeared in the kitchen doorway. It was the King himself, looking small. He'd just been upstairs talking to Holly again.

"You realize the warning bells just rang?" Keira scolded. "So if you're thinking of leaving right now you will literally get *shredded*."

The King shrugged. He was looking at Madeleine.

"It's true," he said. "I was determined to bring you home."

Madeleine had opened a sack of sugar. She dug a spoon into it, drew it out, then tipped the sugar onto the tabletop.

"Huh," said Keira, watching this.

"When you were in the World," Madeleine said, now making patterns in the sugar with her fingertips, "you thought you were a former rock star, right?"

The King nodded.

"And you knew you'd had a fight with your wife and kids?"

"Right."

Madeleine concentrated on the sugar. "In all the time you were in the World, did you ever try to get in touch with them? Like, try to make it up with your family? Did you ever try to track them down?"

The King was silent.

"I missed you all *so* much," he said after a moment. "And when I heard your mother's voice singing on the recording that Ko sent me, I *remembered*, and then —"

"But did you ever try to track us down?"

"I missed you so much," he whispered.

"Because *I* tried to contact you, you know. Twice. I wrote you two letters. You never answered."

The King came over and put his arm around Madeleine's shoulder. She shrugged him away.

"It's fine," she said. "I know you didn't get them. But you never tried to contact us, did you? You hated me. You were always mad at me. I don't blame you. I was selfish and spoiled. I was always making trouble. It's my fault that Mum came after me that night, and it's *my* fault, all of it, that the entire *Kingdom* hates me."

She pushed her chair back, so the King half stumbled to get out of her way. "And there are knotted Charcoals *everywhere* around here!" she shouted, and ran from the room.

Keira and the King looked at each other. "Knotted what?"

The King sighed and walked toward the back door.

"I swear," Keira said, "if you go out there, you will be torn to *pieces*."

He chuckled sadly, and opened the back door.

"I'm not *making a joke*!" Keira shouted after him.

A few minutes later, the Queen ducked her head through the kitchen door, looked around furtively, confirmed that the King had gone, and came into the room. She was wearing jeans and an old sweater with torn sleeves. She must have found these in the attic. Her hair was loosely braided. She looked like anybody's mother.

"Please call me Holly," she murmured as usual.

Keira was never sure what to say to that. *Okay, then. Hi there, Holly?* It seemed weird.

The Queen — *Holly* — sat at the table and began to read the recipe.

As usual, she was quiet, with a faded sort of smile, but then, unexpectedly, she started speaking.

"You know, I never knew my son very well," she said. "The other day, when we were all sharing stories about Chyba? Did you notice that his family didn't contribute?"

"Oh?" But of course she'd noticed.

"I never knew any of my children well," Holly continued. "I got to know Madeleine this last year, but before that, life was always just . . . I don't know, a *party*."

Keira nodded.

"A party, and the Kingdom's finances. I got so interested in those."
She laughed oddly. "Nobody believes this, but I was actually quite
good at them."

She began pushing around the sugar that Madeleine had left on
the tabletop, making it into a tiny mountain range.

"You can peel plums if you like," Keira suggested, but Holly didn't
seem to hear.

"I have this memory of Chyba, though," she said. "I wish I'd shared
it the other day. It was when he was about nine. We were at some
opening or something, and they had six tiny planes doing an acrobatic
display. They were all bright red, these little planes, flying in formation. Curling upward, zipping past, looping around, leaving their
trails of smoke." She used her hands to demonstrate the flight paths.
"I was standing beside Chyba, and I remember I looked down at him
and I said, 'I wish they'd just *land*!' Right away I thought, wow, that
was a dumb thing to say to a nine-year-old boy. He won't get it at all.
He'll want them to keep flying. But do you know what he said?"

Keira waited.

"He looked up at me, and he said, 'I know. It reminds me of a
clown I saw in a show one time, when I was about five' — I remember
thinking how cute it was, how he talked about being *five* in that
grown-up way, when he was still only nine at the time — anyway, he
said the clown had climbed up on some kind of board on rollers, so
the board was sliding around, and the clown balanced up there, juggling, and it kept looking as if the clown would fall, and when he
finally jumped down from the board, everybody had cheered, and
Chyba said he'd felt like they were cheering because the clown had
stopped. Not for what the clown had done, but because the clown was
safe. Like the applause of relief."

Holly closed her eyes.

"I remember thinking: This kid is amazing!" she said. "So much empathy! So wise!" She opened her eyes and looked at Keira. "Anyhow, last night, I was thinking about how I grew up wanting to be a fashion designer — not a *queen*, not a *finance minister*, but a fashion designer — and I started a course in that when I was in the World. So I was thinking about that, and I suddenly remembered the conversation about the planes and the clowns, and I found myself wanting to call Chyba, right away, and *tell* him that I want to be a fashion designer. I stayed awake the entire night playing our conversation in my head. I would say to Chyba, 'Guess what I started when I was in the World?' and he'd say, 'What?' and I'd say, 'A fashion design course!' and it went from there. He was really nice about it, in my imaginary conversations. He was supportive and enthusiastic. He had suggestions for what I should do next. He told me I should keep it up here. His voice was so gentle and thoughtful. I had that conversation with Chyba, inside my head, maybe ten thousand times last night. I never fell asleep. Now and then I'd change what I said, and each time, he'd reply with exactly the right words."

Keira looked at Holly.

If you get caught in a shower of Bright Orange, small discs hit your skin, burn like candle wax, and harden. You have to scrape them loose. Keira felt as if Holly's words were Bright Orange.

Holly stood.

"I saw a lemon tree from the attic window," she said. "I'll go pick some, and we can squeeze it on this fruit."

"You can't go out there now," Keira said. "The bells have been ringing."

Holly took a jacket from the hook. "I'll be quick."

"Seriously, you can't go out. There are Purples and Grays on their way."

The back door slammed. Keira gave up. These people were impossible.

And *holy heck*, as the Farmers said, talk about your dysfunctional family.

4.

*L*ater that night, Keira and Gabe were drinking hot chocolate in the kitchen, enjoying the silence of the sleeping house, when a sharp rapping sounded at the back door.

It was Jimmy. He came in showering pieces of snow and breathing steam.

"Cold like you wouldn't believe out there," he said, dragging off his coat and gloves. "Won't keep you. Just doing the rounds after that Purple-Gray storm this afternoon. Checking everybody's okay. *Holy.*" He shuddered. "That wind is blowing direct from the Magical North."

He pulled up a chair at the table, warming his hands on the mug of chocolate that Gabe set down before him.

"You and Hector must be busy with these Color storms," Keira commented.

"Never been so busy in all my life," Jimmy confirmed, and he gave them a rundown on the damage to the town and farms, the families that had packed up and fled to cities, the animals lost or left to starve, the folks who'd gotten themselves killed or injured, some directly from Color attacks, and some doing darn fool things like climbing up on the roof during an ice storm to clear traces of Bronze from a chimney.

"Madness," Gabe said. "Bronze won't do anything but alter the smell of the wood smoke. Leave it until after the storm."

"Exactly. Tell that to Shayna Tilnouth, laid up with a collarbone broke in five different places."

"Five!"

"Well, now, I may be exaggerating. Still."

"Talking about darn fool things that people do," Keira said. "If you're going out to the Baranskis' at some point, will you tell King Cetus to stop coming over here in the middle of Color storms?"

"He's not!" Jimmy said.

"He is," Keira and Gabe told him at once.

Jimmy leaned back in the chair, and breathed deeply. The warmth of the kitchen and hot chocolate seemed to be soothing out his rumples. "They're right through the Kingdom, you know. Not just here in Bonfire. At least it's stopped the nonsense with the Hostiles and the Elite and so forth." Jimmy set down his mug. "Well, if you're sure you're all good here," he said. "I should get on my way." He looked around the kitchen, not moving.

"You need anything else?" Gabe asked.

Jimmy looked over at him. "No, no, I'm all good." But still he didn't move. "Can I tell you kids something?" he said eventually.

They nodded, and waited.

Jimmy pulled on his lower lip. There was a long pause.

"You bet," Gabe prompted him.

The pause continued.

"Fire away," Keira suggested.

"Well, it's just . . ." Jimmy shook himself. "Haven't told anybody this, not even Hector. It's this call I got, right before the Color storms started bringing phone lines down and up like yo-yos."

He massaged his forehead with his fingertips, as if he was trying to move the call around inside his mind. Then he looked up at them both.

"The call was from Isabella," he said, adding formally to Keira: "She was my girlfriend. The one they say betrayed Elliot to the WSU."

Keira nodded. "I know about her."

"She was nice," Gabe told Keira. "She was a great physics teacher too. I had her last year."

"Thank you," Jimmy said.

"You take physics?" Keira said, surprised.

"If you'd paid any attention to my schedule," Gabe said, "you'd know that."

"Why should I pay attention to your schedule? I've got my own. I'm just sort of surprised that you take physics."

"You think there couldn't be a Farms kid smart enough?"

"Well, it's not *that* so much —"

"You don't think *I'm* smart enough. You think —"

"You want to hear about Isabella's call or not?" Jimmy half yelped.

Keira and Gabe turned back to him, contrite.

Jimmy waited a moment, to be sure of their attention, and then began, "She said she was real sorry about disappearing," he said. "She said she's not a Hostile, and she never called the WSU on Elliot. And well, now, I know I'm biased and all, but the way she spoke, about how she really liked Elliot and she'd never have done a thing like that, and she was almost crying, and so forth — I guess I just believed her." Jimmy gave them a hopeful look.

Keira and Gabe returned his gaze. Eventually, they both nodded.

"Like I said," Gabe offered. "She was always nice."

Jimmy seemed pleased enough to carry on. "Anyhow, the next thing she said took me by surprise like a bear in the pantry. She told me she was from . . . well, she said she was from the World."

There was a long pause.

"And that the WSU is after her," Jimmy tumbled onward. "So that's why she had to run. And she said that's why she'd had a false name — and she studied physics so she could try to find out about cracks — and she came to Bonfire in the first place because she'd heard that there were people here secretly working to create cracks."

The silence hummed on.

"Holy," Gabe said eventually.

Keira considered her fingernails. "Did you believe her?" she asked.

"Well, it's just about the craziest thing I ever heard," Jimmy explained. "So I didn't see a reason *not* to believe her, if you get what I'm saying. I mean, why would she suggest such a thing. That she was from the World!"

Gabe and Keira glanced at each other, then down at the table.

"I guess, so you'd stop thinking she's a Hostile who sold out Elliot," Keira hazarded.

Jimmy's face fell.

"Still." Keira wanted to prop his face back up. "Maybe she *was* from the World? Did she seem weird or anything?"

Jimmy smiled. "Sure. A little. But in a good way."

"I think there's not much difference between Worldians and Cellians," Gabe offered. "Madeleine, Holly, and Abel talk about the people they met there as if they were just regular."

Jimmy was nodding urgently. "Exactly. I mean, I don't intend to hold it against Isabella! It's not her fault she's from the World!"

"Can't be," Gabe agreed.

"Makes her even more special!" Jimmy added. "Plus, she keeps apologizing for not telling me sooner. She thought it might endanger me to know."

They regarded one another thoughtfully.

"Remember how we realized that Cellians who go to the World get sick and maybe even die — like Prince Chyba?" Keira said. "Do you think that happens in reverse too? I mean, do people from the World get sick when they come here?"

"Or maybe it's the opposite," Gabe suggested. "Maybe they *never* get sick. Maybe they're sort of shiny with health?"

"Well, I don't know about that," Jimmy said. "Isabella had plenty of your regular colds. And I remember once she tore off a fingernail by accident, right down to the quick, and she got an infection under the skin. It was all puffed up and pink. Her index finger, it was."

He held up his own index finger, and all three gazed at this.

"*Keeps* apologizing?" Keira said.

"Excuse me?"

"You said that Isabella *keeps* apologizing. Not that she *kept* apologizing in her call."

"Slip of the tongue, I guess," Jimmy said, and then he spoke fast, into his fist: "Or maybe, when she called, she was asking if she could come see me, and I said yes, and she's hiding out in my place right now." He looked up, pretending he hadn't said anything just now. "Slip of the tongue," he repeated.

The telephone rang.

"That'll be Isabella," Keira joked. "Asking you to pick up some milk on the way home."

Jimmy cleared his throat.

"Phone lines working again," Gabe said. "Been a while. I'll take it in the living room." He ducked out of the room. The ringing stopped.

They could hear Gabe's voice, its tone of low surprise, a long pause, Gabe's voice again.

In the kitchen, Jimmy pushed back his chair.

"Well, I guess I won't be keeping you," he said.

Keira stood too. She thought about saying something, decided against it, then said it anyway. "You really believe she's telling the truth?"

Jimmy half shrugged, then nodded firmly. "I believe every word," he said. "I never stopped believing in Isabella."

"She's from the *World*," Keira said eventually.

"Love her anyway," Jimmy smiled.

"But don't they have the plague over there?"

"Not all of them." He smiled again. "And sometimes I think that whole plague thing is what you might call a scare tactic."

Keira raised her eyebrows. "Well, the royal family seems fine," she said. "And Abel. After all that time in the World. So you might be right."

Jimmy chuckled, and nodded.

"I'm glad your girlfriend's not a traitor," Keira said. "We won't tell anyone she's in town. But if she didn't tell the WSU about Elliot, who did?"

"That's the question," Jimmy agreed.

They heard Gabe speaking clearly: "Okay," he said. "Okay, I'll let them know. You look after yourself now, buddy."

A receiver clicked back into place, and Gabe returned to the kitchen.

He paused in the doorway. He was holding a torn envelope, and his face was the same shade of white.

"That was Elliot," he said.

"Elliot?" Jimmy and Keira exclaimed. They stared through the door, as if Elliot might walk up behind Gabe.

Gabe nodded. "He's run away from the Hostiles and found the secret Loyalist army. He says the army can protect the royal family. He wants them to meet him at this place, so he can lead them to the secret location." Gabe held up the envelope. An address was scrawled across it.

Jimmy shook his head. "The royals aren't going anywhere," he said firmly. "That phone call could have been the Hostiles."

"It wasn't," Gabe said. "It was Elliot."

"No, I mean, they could be making him do it. It could be a trap."

Gabe curled the envelope in his palm. "Elliot says the Hostiles know the royals are hiding out in Bonfire. He says they're on their way here to get them. He was calling me instead of his parents because he thinks the Hostiles listen in on his parents' phone calls."

Jimmy shook his head again. "Don't even tell the royal family about this," he said.

"Too late," said a voice, and Madeleine was standing at the kitchen door, right beside Gabe. She was wearing pajamas. Her hair was tousled, but her eyes were bright.

"Where did *you* come from?" Gabe demanded.

"I was in the armchair," Madeleine said. "I woke up when the phone rang. I heard the whole conversation."

"Madeleine, you know your family can't go to Elliot, right?" Keira said. "What Jimmy said is true. This is exactly what the Hostiles would do. They'd use Elliot to lure you all there. It's not Elliot's fault. They've probably threatened his family or something."

Gabe frowned. "He didn't sound exactly like himself," he said. "And he says he's in the Magical North. That's Wandering Hostile territory."

"I trust Elliot," Madeleine said simply. "I don't care what my family does. I don't care what any of you say. I'm going to meet Elliot, and nobody's going to stop me." She swiped the torn envelope from Gabe's hand.

It was the first time Keira had seen Madeleine smile since she arrived.

PART 11

1.

It was dark in the kitchen.

Madeleine tried to slide rather than walk. Her backpack waited on a chair. She opened the fridge and took out a couple of apples, half a cherry pie, and a chunk of cheese. In the bread bin, she found a loaf of rye. She pressed all this into the top of the backpack. There wasn't enough space. She returned an apple.

On the wall, an illuminated clock said 4:15 A.M.

Who knew what time Farmers got up? Any minute, probably. She needed to move faster. It felt dreamlike, was the trouble.

Every moment since she got here had felt dreamlike. The light was strange. Objects seemed to slant toward her, smirking. She wasn't sure if this was a Farms thing, or being back in Cello after so long, or remembering herself. Or the unexpected smallness of her father. Or knowing that her brother was dead.

So many possibilities.

She found a bar of chocolate in a cupboard, and it slid neatly into her backpack.

There was the issue of money. In Cello, she'd always had plenty. In the World, she never had a penny. She stopped. Who was she again? What *currency* did they use in Cello? The kitchen tilted and grinned at her.

Well, she'd figure out money as she went along. Running away was her thing. She was an expert.

She looked around for paper, took a gas bill from behind a magnet, and turned it over. There was a pen in the second drawer, she remembered. She wrote a note to her mother and sister. She added a P.S. saying thanks to Gabe and apologizing for taking food and blankets, and another P.S. to Keira, asking her to please look after her family. What about those boys in the basement? Well, she hadn't even *met* the sick one, only heard about him. Sergio, though, she'd known for a long time. He was the stable boy and her sister's best friend. *Hey, Sergio,* she wrote, and then stopped. This was ridiculous. Why did she talk so much on paper?

She put the note in the center of the table.

Her coat was on its hook, gloves and scarf in the sleeves. She put all these on, sat down, and pulled on her boots.

She stood again, reaching for the back door.

"Call yourself my apologies," someone whispered, and she jumped as if struck in the ribs.

2.

$\mathcal{A}$ boy was standing behind her.

Moonlight, bright from the snow outside, spilled through the back-door window and touched the boy's face.

The face was swollen. His eyes were slits. Strange patterns and welts ran down both cheeks, and a purple line struck across his nose.

It was the sick boy from the basement, she realized.

"As to a circus train in tree stumps," the boy hissed. "I have startled you. Call yourself my further apologies, and greetings. Your fine and beauteous Highness, I am Samuel of Olde Quainte."

Olde Quainte. Of course. Madeleine had almost forgotten how they spoke. It was sort of fun hearing it again, like going back to an old fairground.

Although, at this point, surreal.

"Nice to meet you," she whispered back. "I'm Madeleine, and I'm really sorry but I have to go now. Talk another time? Bye."

She wrapped her gloved hand around the door handle.

The boy touched her shoulder.

"I needs must trouble you further," he murmured. "I am Samuel, as perchance you heard me just now say. I was chosen by your sister, the good Princess Ko, as a member of the Royal Youth Alliance. While such a member, I was poisoned by Olde Quainte magic."

"Okay," Madeleine agreed. "Um, yeah, I heard about that. Sorry about it. I hope you . . . get better."

She looked behind him into the darkness of the kitchen. Was someone moving around upstairs?

"You are kind as to a paintbrush in the cartwheel," Samuel

whispered. "I believe you are now setting off on a journey to the Magical North? Call yourself my greatest wish is to accompany you."

Madeleine blinked. "I'm not — no, no, I'm just —"

"From the basement I hear much," Samuel explained, his voice switching between low murmur and breathy whisper, back and forth. "I heard that Elliot telephoned, asking the royal family to meet him in the Magical North. I heard others oppose this with heat. I heard you, Princess Jupiter — call yourself my pardon, you wish to be Madeleine — I heard your determination. I perceive now that you are slipping away betwixt the fall of the sun and its splendid rise upon the dawn, that is to say, in the *night* — ah, I see in your eyes that you are frustrated by the wanderings of my speech. Your sister was much the same. Ha! As to a — no, I will be short. My greatest wish, I say afresh, is to accompany you."

Madeleine pressed her gloved fingers to her forehead.

"I'm sorry, Samuel," she said, "but I need to go alone. And I don't — I don't see how you can *travel* anywhere being so sick. I think you should go back downstairs to bed, and maybe when you're better . . ."

Samuel shook his head firmly.

"I must needs go to the Magical North so I can visit the Lake of Spells," he told her. "I am not *going* to get better, Your Royal Highness. I will soon die. My only hope is to catch a Curing Spell at the Lake. I have bethought me this as I lay in the basement these last days. And call yourself my forgiveness, but I am now quite well enough to travel. I have, this moment, taken my medicine a dozen times over, and that will give me strength enough to journey for some days."

Upstairs, a door creaked.

"I have to leave," Madeleine told Samuel. "I'm really sorry but I need to — a *dozen* times over? Do you mean you've taken twelve times the dose? Is that safe?"

"In addition, I have prepared a schedule of transport to reach the Magical North most efficiently, as to a rosebush in the drainpipe. Have you such a schedule, Your Highness? There is also this, that I have money enough for us both for the journey. It has long been secreted in the ruffles of my clothing. Have you money enough, Your Highness?"

Madeleine blinked.

"It is also this, and call me foolhardy as to a jackhammer in mid-yawn, but by taking twelve times the dosage, I have depleted my supply of medicine into — well, into nothing. If I spend the next week *here*, it will prove a fine and energetic week, and then I will die in splendid suffering. If, perchance, I spend the next week traveling with *you*, I will reach the Lake of Spells and *perhaps* I will find me a solution."

A toilet flushed upstairs. There was the sound of a shower starting.

"I have this rucksack borrowed," Samuel continued, his voice becoming almost conversational now. She saw, for the first time, that a large bag stood behind him. "Plentiful supplies were, perchance, stored in the basement! I have protective gear although I hear they are not much use against these stronger Colors, but if we take the transport I have chosen, it will have security shutters, so there is that, and I've a tent, a solid one, of fine canvas, or perhaps the material is —"

"All right!" Madeleine cried. "Let's go!"

She threw open the door.

"How do you plan to reach the railway station?" Samuel chatted into the cold blast of air. "That is first on my schedule. Train to

Carmine, Jagged Edge. My only glitch, however, was how to reach the station."

They stepped into deep snow and blasting wind.

"I'll borrow one of the cars here. We can leave it at the station."

"Ah, yes. They have plentiful vehicles, as to zucchinis in a hat made out of hydrogen, but Madeleine, I cannot *drive*, can you?"

Madeleine pressed the door closed behind her and squinted into the wind.

"I was a bad girl for years," she told him. "Of course I know how to drive."

3.

S amuel's itinerary collapsed almost immediately.

At the station, it turned out that the train line to Carmine, Jagged Edge, had melted in a second-level Maroon, so they had to take a train to the border of Olde Quainte instead. From there, a stagecoach would carry them to High Wrexham.

They slept for the train journey and arrived to discover that they had only five minutes to reach the stagecoach landing. Madeleine took off at a sprint. The wind was on her face, the sun was on her neck, this was what she did! She ran! It felt great. Then she heard a whimpering and turned back. Samuel was leaning forward, his hands on his thighs. He looked up. "Please, may we not *stroll* rather than run?"

For the first time, she regretted bringing him along. Earlier, when he'd paid for their train tickets, the decision had seemed brilliant.

It took twenty minutes to get across town, but the stagecoach had been delayed, so it didn't matter. They even had time for Samuel to buy them both spiced hot ciders, and Madeleine found that she was fond of her decision again.

Now, as the coach swayed along dirt and cobblestone roads, and Samuel smiled around at the soft leather seats — they were the only passengers — it made perfect sense that he was there. She had the odd feeling that she'd half known him a long time: as if he was the kid who always played in the yard next door, without her ever having taken much notice of him.

She watched through the window. Colors had battered this part of the Kingdom. Trees leaned up against one another. Thatched cottages tilted precariously, or knelt crumbling. Roofs were either punched with holes or missing altogether. Outside the houses, men and women stared grimly at the passing coach, then resumed work with their shovels or brooms. Often, the coach had to veer around litter: an overturned stroller, two painted wooden doors lying side by side.

They rode through a village called Llanfair Nod.

"They've had a fifth-level Scarlet through here," the driver called back to them.

"Indeed!" Samuel called.

The residue was everywhere: running down walls and drainways, splattering trees, and etched in vibrant patterns on the faces and bare arms of every villager.

"That will take days to wash out," Samuel observed.

Madeleine nodded.

"I suppose I look a little that way myself," he added after a pause.

She turned to him. He looked worse. There were patches that could have been Scarlet residue, but there were also fine purple lines, raised and ugly bumps, swellings, distortions, and mottled rashes.

"Does it hurt?" she asked.

"As to a flitting song in dishrags," he smiled.

Madeleine tried to figure that out, but he kept on smiling, so she unstrapped her backpack instead and took out the bread and cheese. The stagecoach stopped suddenly, and the cheese slipped to the floor.

"Children crossing!" the driver called to them.

"He's informative." Samuel peered through the window. "And quite correct. Those children appear young to go about the roads unsupervised."

Madeleine retrieved the cheese. She tore some bread, and passed both to Samuel.

"Did you know my little brother, Tippett, spent a year in the World all alone?"

"I have heard this."

Madeleine rested her head against the window. "My mother's been phoning him, you know — when the line's working. Even though she was forbidden. And Ko's been secretly slipping away in Color storms for some reason."

"The females in your family have spirit! It is splendid, as to a —"

He was thrown forward as the carriage stopped abruptly.

"More children!" the driver shouted. "I nearly hit that one!"

"As to a rolling pin in turtle shell!" Samuel called in sympathy.

The carriage started up again.

"I saw a kid run onto a road once," Madeleine remembered. "This was in Cambridge — where I lived in the World. I was sitting in a café, and outside the window I could see a mother with a little kid.

The mother was talking to someone. Suddenly, the kid just sort of darted right across the road."

"Dangerous!"

"Right. But it was fine because there was no traffic. The kid ran straight back, and the mother was still talking and hadn't even noticed. And then, about two seconds later? A truck went by."

Samuel breathed in sharply. "And so, had the child taken flight just moments *after* he or she did — forgive me, I cannot recall if you have specified the child's gender — there would have been calamity!"

"Exactly."

"But as it was, all was well." Samuel shook his head slowly. "What and ho, such a thing."

"What and ho," Madeleine agreed. She looked at Samuel. His reactions were great. It was good to talk to an enthusiastic listener. She'd been so silent these last few days.

"I remember it made me think that terrible things are always on the verge of happening," she said. "They're always being *just* avoided. And it's the same with wonderful things. It's only when — I don't know, the stars are aligned — that something great happens. And you have to catch the moment or you miss it." She frowned at the window. "What *is* that? A Slate Gray or something?"

"Someone has spilled a sack of flour!" boomed the driver's voice. "Do you see?"

"Yes!" Madeleine and Samuel chorused.

"And the rain has fallen so now it is glug and glue!" The driver chortled. "As to a scissor-snake in radishes!"

"As to a netted branch of clover!" Samuel retorted, and there was even heartier laughter from outside.

So that was another good thing about Samuel. He was Olde-Quaintian, and a lot of this journey would be through that province.

She wouldn't even have known the driver was making a joke, let alone how to respond.

They sat forward, listening out in case the driver wanted to chat on, but he was silent, so they settled back.

"Go on," Samuel said. "You were describing your pursuit of moments."

Madeleine laughed. "I don't think it was anything so intense as that. It's just, I'm always looking around corners. Like, I never stop watching for something special. Which can get sort of tedious, 'cause mostly it's not there."

Samuel's right eyelid was swollen. He touched it lightly, then nodded. "Yet somehow you found your way home to Cello. Splendid as to a knitting needle in a deck chair!"

Madeleine studied him. She pictured a knitting needle sitting on a deck chair. It didn't seem all that splendid.

"It's like this," she said. "Imagine you run away from home, and you don't really like where you end up. It feels wrong. Then you find out about this other place: this magical place, and you think that everything would be okay — everything would be *wonderful* — if you could just get to that place. And you want to be with people from that place, and talk to people from that place, and you kind of *long* for that place, and then, suddenly, you're *there*. . . ."

Samuel spoke under his breath. "You've come full circle."

"What?"

"Nothing. Go on, Madeleine. Continue."

"No, you're right. I've come full circle. That's it exactly. I'm back where I started, and it's like a freakin' lesson from a fable or something. We had a governess once who used to make *everything* into a fable. It made Ko insane. *Just give us the facts!* she used to say. But the governess would love this one. 'Cause it's like the truth was right there all along. Or you can't run away from your*self*, or whatever. I can't stand it. I wanted magic so badly, and now it's like there's no such thing. I mean, I know we've *got* magic here in Cello, but it's just, like, whatever. There are Occasional Pilots who can fly, and a Lake of Spells, and the Wind blows away disease, and magic mists around the Magical North, but so what. Do you see what I mean? I mean, what's magic? It's not even relevant. It's just another thing."

Samuel was looking at her oddly.

Dark lines of magic were running in his veins, scabbing his hands, swelling his fingers, blackening his nails.

"That was really stupid, what I just said," Madeleine stated. "I apologize."

4.

O ver the next few days, they had to change plans constantly.

The Maroon had destroyed several other train lines, and a thundering Taupe had blown up a swag of trains. At the same time, Wandering Hostiles had been taking out bridges. Scuffles were erupting between Loyalists and Hostiles. The Elite had sent out special forces to quell the violence, but mostly they only increased it. Several towns were in total lockdown, gates chained shut.

They found their way to bus terminals, where they waited for hours before somebody shouted that no bus was coming. They took paddleboats, or hitched rides in the backs of trailers, and found themselves backtracking or lost.

For the first two nights, they slept in fields, in the tent Samuel had taken from Gabe's basement. But on the third night, as they were setting up camp, a fierce wind sprang up, so the tent turned inside out, the canvas punching their faces.

In the end, they ran across the field toward distant lights.

It was an amusement park, closed for the night but with one or two lanterns still shining. A giant wooden face, complete with open mouth and teeth, served as its entry gate.

They stopped and looked around. For a moment Madeleine thought that some kind of animal was scraping across gravel toward them, then she realized it was the sound of Samuel's breathing. She looked at him. He was hunched and shivering in the wind.

She looked at the wooden teeth. Each was hollow. "Get in there," she said, pointing to one. "Don't start *talking* again, just get in."

They each climbed into a tooth, side by side, and crouched deep inside.

"Ingenious!" Samuel's voice rose up from his tooth. "We are safe inside cavities!"

They were silent for a while, listening to the wind. It quieted briefly and Samuel's voice sounded again. "Your Highness?"

"You seriously have to call me Madeleine."

"Very well. Your Highness, I have been thinking of what you said the other day? In the stagecoach? Recollect?"

"It was stupid," Madeleine called to him. "I'm really sorry."

"As to a woolen scarf in sunshine! No. I do not mean your reference to magic being nothing. That amused me merely. I mean your words about how you are always searching around corners for something marvelous. It has come to me that this is a sign of a magic weaver! Are you, perchance, a magic weaver?"

Madeleine laughed. Her laughter echoed strangely.

"I'm not a magic weaver," she called.

"How can you know this?"

"Well, for a start, I've spent a lot of time in the Magical North, and there's magic everywhere there. I never saw any of it. Isn't that what magic weavers do? See magic?"

There was silence from the tooth. The wind set up a louder hum, and Madeleine pressed herself deeper.

"Well!" Samuel's voice piped again. "Do you ever have visions? Or waking dreams? That would be another sign."

Inside the wooden tooth, Madeleine laughed again and then instantly wanted to cry. She wasn't inside a tooth; she was inside a memory. She was fierce with the memory of Auntie's Tea Shop and telling Jack and Belle about her hallucinations.

She closed her eyes and ran through the three hallucinations. It hadn't happened since she'd been back in Cello, she realized, and her bleeding noses had stopped. The boy running through the market-place, the office with the —

"Samuel," she said.

"Yes?"

"Can you stand up again?"

He stood, shivering, the wind pasting his hair to his head, moon-light shadowing his cheek. She studied him.

"Okay, get back down."

They both crouched again.

"You're the boy from my hallucination," she said quietly.

The wind sighed, long and languorous.

"I am what?" Samuel called.

"I saw you, before I ever met you. You were running through a marketplace, and then standing in an office building."

Samuel was silent.

"Are you there?"

"How splendid," Samuel's voice rose up uncertainly. "You dreamed me! As to an — as to a what? Well, it will come to me."

"Weird, right? The last few days I've been feeling like I've known you a long time, and now I see why. I guess I didn't connect you with that vision or whatever at first, because . . ."

"Because I am so tainted by black magic."

Madeleine pushed her backpack around behind her so it was like a cushion. She put her feet up against the opposite wall of the tooth and leaned back. Above, she could see stars. "You know, the marketplace I saw could easily have been in Olde Quainte. You were being chased by a bunch of boys — has that ever happened to you?"

There was a low chuckle from Samuel. "Call yourself the truth of that statement. Indeed, and I have been so pursued often betimes!"

Madeleine remembered the man at the desk in the vision. "But I guess you've never met Leonardo da Vinci," she joked.

"Call yourself my pardon, never met whom?"

"Leonardo da Vinci. That's what happens next. You're in an office building and Leonardo da Vinci — he was a famous painter — he's sitting at the desk."

"Leonardo!" Samuel's voice was warm. "I greatly admire his work!"

"You what? No, he's from the World. You must be thinking of somebody else."

"Indeed, and I am not." She could hear him moving about in the tooth. "Leonardo visited our Kingdom often, Madeleine. I am a student of World history — hence, your sister chose me for her Youth Alliance — and I have read much about Leo. That's how we knew him, as Leo."

Madeleine was on her feet again, gasping in the wind. "Are you serious!" she shouted. "But that's what I *said*! I said to Belle, I bet Leonardo came to Cello! Through a cave!"

"Sit down," Samuel called to her. "You will blow away. Yes, I recall a tale of his finding his way through as a boy. His favorite provinces were Jagged Edge, where he studied the technologies, and the Undisclosed Province. Also, I think he was much taken with the Cat Walk in Nature Strip."

Madeleine sank down again, her cheeks aching from her grin. "Maybe that's why I saw you! I was a Cellian girl in the World, and you're a Cellian boy who knows about the World!"

"There are four hundred and twenty-six of Leo's paintings in the World-Cello archives," Samuel said. "He was prolific. I enjoy them immensely. Especially his Mona Lisa series."

"You're not serious."

"There was a woman of the Undisclosed Province named Lisa. You know that they speak there with their eyes? Leo was intrigued by this phenomenon. He painted at least twenty portraits of this Lisa, trying to capture her eyes."

Madeleine was giggling.

"What is it amuses you?"

"Don't worry," she said, and her words caught in a yawn. It was a happy yawn. "Do you think you can sleep in that tooth?"

There was shuffling. "As to a sword fight in a moonbeam," Samuel mumbled. "Well, I will do what I can. Call yourself a good night, Madeleine."

Madeleine tilted her head so she could fill her eyes with stars. She thought of the haze over Leonardo's life, and then of his sfumato effect: the smokiness, the dusk and shadows, he liked to use in paintings. She laughed again. "You may paint your picture at the end of the day when there are clouds or mist," Leonardo had advised, "and this atmosphere is perfect." No wonder he liked the Undisclosed Province: Twilight was relentless there, the light always dim.

She imagined herself at Cambridge, Federico warming his hands by the gas fire, his hat on the desk, Belle and Jack insisting that Madeleine *shut it*, while she ignored them and exclaimed: "He loved the Cat Walk! No wonder he covered pages with sketches of cats!"

She was happier than she'd been in months. She was on her way to see Elliot. She would tell him this story about Leonardo. She would hand it to him in long, decorated paragraphs: the vision, Belle's presentation, Samuel's accent and locutions, the fairground, the wooden teeth, the cold wind, the Mona Lisa, the coincidence, how much she missed Jack and Belle — all of it. She would give all this to Elliot, and he would take it in exactly the right way.

5.

*T*he next day, they caught a train that was so crowded they had to stand in the vestibule. Several other travelers stood or sat on luggage.

Outside, warning bells rang constantly, and the train security shutters clattered open and closed.

"Why don't they just leave them closed all the time?" Madeleine wondered.

The train line was skirting the Inland Sea, so the view, when the shutters were open, was of waves clutching at sunlight, ships in mist, and fishing villages.

"The prettiest scenery in all the Kingdom," Samuel smiled, leaning up against a pole.

They were sharing the chocolate bar from Gabe's kitchen.

"I only have two days before I'm supposed to meet Elliot," Madeleine said. "You think we'll make it?"

"As to an earplug in a catapult."

"That's never helpful," Madeleine said.

Samuel smiled to himself and held out his hand for more chocolate.

They passed a village coated in Ice Blue. The streets were empty, but on the outskirts, a child had frozen mid-leap in a meadow and a man had been caught climbing a stile.

"They'll thaw," Samuel said.

"Will they crash to the ground when they do?" Madeleine asked.

"As to a double chin in lacework."

"Again, not helpful, and actually pretty annoying."

A moment later, the train began to slow and then stopped. There were mutterings, and then someone called, "Indeed, and there's a Pale Gray. Call yourselves a look now."

Everyone crowded the windows. The fields here ran down to a village nestled in a valley. It was shrouded in a mist of Gray.

"Is it not merely a mist?" someone asked.

"No. You see the ragged edges? That's certain of a Pale."

The others agreed.

"The poor good people as live in there," an elderly woman observed, addressing her husband. "They'll be sensing that something is ever so wrong and not knowing why. They'll be cranky and sharp-tongued as I am with you when you return from market without eggs."

"Indeed," the husband agreed complacently.

A conductor was leaning through an open window with a megaphone.

"Your village is coated in Pale Gray! Pale Gray alert! Pale Gray!"

"They're too far away," someone murmured.

A moment later, the train crackled with an announcement. Unexpectedly, the driver had a Farms accent. "Apologies for the delay, folks. As you may have noticed, that little village just to the east of us — Sederidge, I'm told — looks to be under a Pale Gray. There'll be kids being expelled from school, marriages breaking up, friendships torn to shreds, and who knows what the heck else. And if it doesn't shift soon, the moodiness might settle there for good. Now, our train is equipped with handheld fans, and anybody wants to might join us in helping out these folks? We'll stop here half an hour or so and see what we can't do."

"Unorthodox," somebody said.

"These are troubled times," the elderly woman countered.

The doors trundled open, and groups of people spilled from each carriage. Others settled onto empty seats to wait. Train conductors handed out little fans, and everyone set off across the field.

The sky was blue, the sun warm, and the atmosphere robust and upbeat.

"I keep thinking about how Leonardo da Vinci was here in Cello," Madeleine told Samuel as they walked.

"Indeed," Samuel agreed.

"And it makes me wonder if the other famous people from my visions might have come here too. Would you know? Because you know so much World history?"

"I cannot know," Samuel said promptly. He kicked some brambles aside.

"Oh."

"I cannot know," he repeated, "unless and until you *tell* me who was in your dreams."

Madeleine gave him a look, but he was walking at a sturdy, steady pace and didn't notice.

"A scientist called Isaac Newton," she said, "and a musician named Vivaldi."

"Vivaldi!" Samuel exclaimed. "I have read of him! Yes. He came much and often too. I believe he was drawn to the Farms. Especially its fiddle playing."

"Ha!" Madeleine said. "Wait. You're joking, right?"

"Do you not know me yet? Rare and betwixt do I joke."

"But Vivaldi was a genius! People said his music was like nothing ever written before. He composed twenty-seven cello concertos, among the first ever written, and when he played violin solos himself, the audience was gobsmacked! Are you saying he was influenced by fiddlers in the Farms?"

Samuel shrugged. "Why not? Farmers are fine musicians if you care to listen. I believe Vivaldi studied with some. Perhaps he heard the Cello Wind? If so, twenty-seven cello concertos are no surprise. As for the other name — Isaac Newton — I have seen that name before. He was, at one time, a president of the Worldian group that called themselves the Royal Society?"

Madeleine nodded. "They were scientists."

"Some of its members used to visit Cello frequently. And I recall . . . an article, or perhaps a letter. Allow me pause to breathe." Samuel stopped. Other passengers passed them, some glancing at Samuel's mottled face with interest. "I have it. It was an 'Account of a Journey into an Adjoining World.' It was submitted to the Royal Society when Newton was its chair. It was amusing, I recall, for it speculated that Cello was affixed to your World by magnetism, and proposed an expedition, with botanist and surgeon, to explore our Kingdom thoroughly."

By now, Samuel had sat down on the grass. Madeleine sat beside him.

"And what did Newton say?" she asked.

"Oh, he rejected the whole idea as fancy."

"Strange," Madeleine said. "They were obsessed with the idea of other worlds back then. Worlds on the moon; inside the center of the Earth. And the Royal Society gave everything a chance. Like, they sat around a table, once, and watched to see if a spider could escape from a circle of powdered unicorn horns. They didn't actually *have* a unicorn horn, of course, they probably had the tusk of a narwhal. I guess Cello just didn't fit into any of Newton's theories of the universe. Poets didn't like him, you know: They said he'd killed off magic. Keats said he'd *unweaved the rainbow*."

"I am somewhat at sea here," Samuel said, "but I perceive that you read much when in the World. As to a wicker chair in artichoke." He clambered to his feet. "I am ready to carry forth. Others have already reached the edges of the Pale Gray."

Madeleine peered into the distance. Tiny pieces of the Gray were stirring in the fan-created breeze.

"But tell me, Madeleine," Samuel said as they set off, "those episodes you experienced. Would you say that they were dreams or visions?"

Madeleine laughed. "That's the question."

"Quite," Samuel frowned. "That was my question."

6.

On the evening before the scheduled meeting with Elliot, they arrived at the riverside village of Shy-Marlow.

They had traveled in the back of a hay wagon that day, and now they stood in the village square, brushing hay from each other's hair. Samuel pointed to a map that was painted on the cobblestones.

"Your meeting with Elliot is twelve thirty tomorrow?" he said. "On the southern edge of Lake Swithburne, Magical North?"

Madeleine agreed.

"It seems to me that it is no more than a four-hour hike from here to that lake." Samuel pointed. "As to a hockey stick in scented caterpillar."

"We should start walking now, then," Madeleine said. "It's only five o'clock, and it's summer, so it'll stay light. We can camp at the lake tonight."

Samuel knelt by the map, and ran his fingers across it. "It seems a tiny lake," he murmured. "Far smaller than the Lake of Spells, which is another several hours' journey to the north." He glanced back up at her. "Indeed, and I suggest we set off on the morrow. Our journey is almost complete. Let us celebrate by staying in an inn tonight. We shall arise early and depart well fed and rested."

"But what if we get lost on the way?" Madeleine argued, "I think —" and then, as Samuel held her gaze, she faltered. "Are you okay?"

"Call yourself my apologies," Samuel said with great formality. "I am not unwell."

Then he curled himself onto the ground and closed his eyes.

*   *   *

Half an hour later, Madeleine had helped Samuel to the Woodsman's Tavern on Shy-Marlow's High Street.

Their room was small, almost filled by the two large beds, each draped with a feather-down quilt. Samuel lay on one of these, breathing with a slow, scraping sound. His face seemed a spider's web of raised crimson veins.

"I suppose the medication is fading," Samuel whispered. "It has not lasted quite as I assumed. As to a . . ."

"I'll go and find a doctor." Madeleine stepped toward the door.

"No. No. There is naught a doctor can do. I needs must rest, that is all. Please, stay with me and we shall converse."

There was a jug of lemon water on the sideboard, and a bowl of wild berries. "You can see the river from here," Madeleine said at the window, and then warning bells clanged importantly, and the inn's shutters rushed the room to darkness.

"These Colors are getting to be too much." Madeleine lit the lanterns.

From the dim light of the bed, Samuel took another rasping breath. "Yes," he agreed. "It is tiresome."

Madeleine poured him water, and waited while he drank.

"It wouldn't be so bad," she said, "if it wasn't for the Knotted Charcoals everywhere."

"Knotted what?"

"Charcoals. The Knotted Charcoals."

Samuel handed back the glass and leaned against the pillow, breathing more quietly. "I have heard tell of Charcoal Blacks," he said, "but never a *Knotted* Charcoal."

"Well, me neither," Madeleine admitted. "And actually that's just the name I've given them. I mean those little patches of Charcoal that are flying around everywhere? They're all knotted up."

Samuel studied her. He scratched his ear. "You are suggesting," he said, "that you see patches of tangled darkness in the air?"

"Not *suggesting*," Madeleine said. "I do. Look. There are some. They're all over Cello. Ever since I got back from the World, they've been driving me crazy. That farmhouse of Gabe's was full of them, especially when people were around. That's why I spent so much time in the empty living room. I mean, they don't hurt you or anything, they're just *there*."

"Can you see them now?"

"I can't believe you're asking me that. There are about five of them circling you."

Madeleine sat on the edge of his bed, and held out the bowl of wild berries. Samuel waved these away.

"Madeleine," he said. "You are a magic weaver."

"Oh, cut it out with the magic weaver stuff." She felt irritable. Samuel looked terrible, and she didn't know how to help.

"Those patches of black you see are moments of pain, anger, illness, wrongdoing, sadness, and fear," Samuel said. "Magic weavers can see these, although most need to focus to do so. Hence, they ask people to describe their pain — its appearance, color, sound, ranking, and so forth — anything to make it vivid. It then comes into focus and the magic weaver can see the knots and untangle them. You must be quite a magic weaver, for it seems you can see the darkness without even concentrating."

"I'm not a magic weaver," Madeleine said. "You're sick, and it's making you delusional. I told you before, I lived in Cello all my life — except for that time in the World — and I never saw magic once. These are just Charcoals."

Samuel smiled kindly. "I read much about magic," he said, "when I was on the RYA. Magic weavers must be active of body and fierce of mind. Perhaps you used your time in the World to develop your powers of mind? Of concentration and introspection? Call yourself my apologies, Madeleine, but your reputation as a princess was not particularly *academic*. Yet, it appears you read often in the World?"

"I did," she said. "But you're talking bollocks."

"As to a teaspoon," Samuel muttered. "This bollocks? Another thing I read was that magic weavers need to know themselves. One cannot focus upon the *outer* unless one has confronted one*self*. Now, by going to the World — perhaps even by going to the space *between* — perchance you have done this? Have you ever disappeared deep inside yourself?"

Outside, the warning bells signaled the all clear. The shutters flew up, and Madeleine blinked against the sunlight.

"You're talking rubbish," she said.

Samuel was still smiling to himself. He sat up and crossed his legs. "How did you and your mother get back from the World?" he asked. "I believe I heard that you stumbled?"

"I made us stumble," Madeleine said.

"Nobody can make themselves stumble."

"Well, I did."

Samuel shook his head. "It has never happened."

She considered tipping the jug of water over his head. "I knew you needed absence and emotion to stumble," she explained patiently. "I saw them in the air, and I sort of grabbed hold of them and held my mother's hand and we stumbled."

Now Samuel scrambled onto his knees. "Ho ho! You *saw* absence and emotion! Madeleine, it is definite! Naught but a magic weaver could see such!"

"Belle saw them. She's the one who pointed them out to me."

"Belle. Who is this Belle?"

"I told you about Jack and Belle! They were my best friends in the World. Jack can read the stars, and Belle can read auras. I think that's why she could see them."

Samuel paused. "Interesting. At any rate, Madeleine, I assure you that none has ever stumbled by choice before. It happens when emotion and absence are so powerful they crack open reality. Whereas you took hold of their concentrated forms! It must have been agony! With the tangled darkness you can see here, it is not a matter of taking hold: These must needs be untangled."

"Those are Knotted Charcoals," Madeleine persisted.

"There is no such thing." Samuel lay back down again. "I will rest a day or two while you go to meet Elliot. I would only hold you up. Is that to your liking?"

"I'm not leaving you here."

"You needs must," Samuel said. "Elliot will be waiting. Eventually, I'll make my way to the Lake of Spells. Meantime, once you arrive in the Magical North, you will see pure magic everywhere. This, one day, you will learn to weave into spells."

Madeleine frowned. "Hang on," she said. "Do you seriously believe I could do magic weaving? I mean, you think I could make a spell that could heal you?"

"Theoretically, yes. More simply, however, the patches you see around me are the black magic I suffer. You could untangle them. That would ease my pain."

"Seriously?"

"You persist in doubting me. Madeleine, if I have been one thing it is earnest. Anxious too, in the past. This poisoning, at least, has made me see that anxiety is as to a buttercup in sand dunes."

Madeleine moved closer, studying the knots that hovered by Samuel's shoulders and chest.

"You think I can just unknot these?"

Samuel sighed and closed his eyes. "Call yourself my foolishness. I have not been clear. *Theoretically*, you could. But even the greatest magic weavers practice for years. You must learn to loosen threads precisely or you yourself will suffer. Nor yet can any living magic weaver conjure a spell to cure Olde Quainte magic. Your sister summoned the greatest to my hospital bed. She beckoned, too, the noblest physicians and apothecaries. This was all before we were placed under house arrest, of course. I needs must tell you of the ointments, salves, poultices, bone marrow transplants, veritable *battery* of magic and non-magic that your sister insisted they try. None worked. All that was left was the medicine that helped to ease the pain and prolong life. That, now, as you know, is gone." He turned his head to the side, tucking his arm under the pillow.

Madeleine reached toward the closest knot. It appeared to be soft and filmy. She touched it and sprang away. "It stung me!"

Samuel opened his eyes.

"Do not try. It will only harm you. The truly marvelous thing is that you can see — most magic weavers need tools to focus, as I said. Perhaps your World friends helped you find your focus? Jack taught you to see the distant magic — the stars — and Belle to see the magic close to you? Or perhaps it is your own imagination."

"I don't know." Madeleine watched the knots through narrowed eyes. "I'd like all the credit for myself. But I miss Belle and Jack. A lot. They were awesome. I never got to say good-bye to them," she added.

"They are part of you now and always will be." Samuel's voice had slipped into a murmur. He was falling asleep. "How grand that they filled you with awe. Good night, Madeleine, I will see you on the morrow. We will breakfast, and then I will fare you well."

Madeleine looked down at him. His breathing was like boots on gravel.

She reached out slowly for the knot once more, then swore and sucked on her stinging hand.

She waited, glared, and reached for it again.

Two hours later, Madeleine had finished unknotting the smallest of the darknesses. Her fingers and palms were studded with blisters. She was drenched in sweat. Samuel's breathing was softer. His face looked calmer. The swelling around his eyes had gone down.

"I'll untangle the rest through the night," she told him. "And when I get to the Magical North, I'll weave a spell that cures you."

Samuel slept on.

"Well, anyway, I'll try," she conceded. "Who knows how you weave a spell. And I can't believe how much this unknotting hurts."

She turned to the window. Outside, the light was turning mild and blue with dusk.

Tomorrow she was going to see Elliot. She and Elliot would lead the Loyalist army. They would save the Kingdom; they would cure it of Colors.

She imagined Elliot's face. She imagined how their smiles would grow as they approached each other. She imagined saying, "Hey, Elliot." Telling Elliot: "Turns out, I'm a magic weaver." She imagined his eyebrows lifting at that. She imagined reaching out to touch his face around his smile.

PART 12

1.

*T*he car turned into an empty parking lot. Gravel was bright with sunlight. The tires made a friendly crunchy noise. A bicycle wheel was hooked onto a tree, and it spun in the breeze. *LAKE SWITHBURNE* said a wooden sign, but they couldn't see the lake from here: It was blocked by a stand of snow-draped pines.

Elliot looked around the car. There was the box of tissues on the dashboard. The plastic bag full of trash, its handles wound around the gear stick. The stack of music files.

Beside him, the driver pulled on the handbrake and switched off the ignition. The engine blinked into silence.

"It's noon," said the driver. "We're half an hour early."

The driver was Mischka Tegan.

2.

$\mathcal{M}$ischka had arrived in the Hostile compound two days after the Assistant accepted Elliot as a Hostile.

Her arrival altered the tone of the place. Voices and footsteps seemed both calm and brisk now. Five of the permanent residents, including Chime, were sent to other compounds. A new chef arrived, reorganized, and cleaned the kitchen. Food standards rose dramatically.

Elliot was told to do nothing but rest and exercise. His bandages were removed.

He didn't meet Mischka until five days after her arrival. Early one morning, while he was still asleep, she came into his room. She asked Ming-Sun to leave them. Then she sat on Ming-Sun's chair and studied Elliot's face as he awoke.

Elliot sat up.

For the next ten minutes, neither of them said a word.

At first, Elliot was trying to figure how to stop himself getting up and hurling this woman from the room. But she just sat there staring. He started noticing things about her. Her elegant posture. Her chewed nails. Her thin sweater, sleeves pushed up to her elbows. The uneven dusting of makeup. Her cheekbones, sharp like her daughter's. He looked at the line of her nose, and at her eyebrows. She seemed to break into separate parts. His anger also fragmented. The noise of it quieted.

Right at that point, Mischka pushed her hair behind her ears.

"You recognize me," she said. "I taught at your school. I hung out with your dad. You knew me as Mischka Tegan."

Elliot blinked.

"I believe you also know that I am Keira Platter's mother."

He didn't nod, but stared.

"I've been a Hostile for years," she continued. "I went to Bonfire to work with your father and uncle. We knew they were Loyalists, and very bright inventors. A Hostile alliance had been formed, and we had in mind a scheme: Figure out how to cut through to the World, and send the royal family across."

Her voice was clear, low, and authoritative. Like a teacher setting out the background to an experiment.

"But your dad and uncle found out who I was. I called in help. It was a bad night. Your uncle ended up dead. Your dad ended up over the ravine."

She stopped speaking. Again, they stared at each other. Her face colored. "I'm so sorry," she said. She pushed her chair back and walked out of the room.

A few days later, Elliot woke again to see Mischka seated by the bed. He had to disentangle himself from his dream.

"It's time to make the call," she said.

"What call?"

"The Assistant tells me you'll help us by using your contacts in Bonfire."

He was still trying to break out of his sleep.

"Most of the royal family is staying at the farmhouse of a friend of yours named Gabe," Mishka continued. "The King is with your parents."

"How do you know all this?" Elliot asked.

She shrugged. "We know. You should call Gabe rather than your parents. They'd be more likely to pick up on any hesitation in your voice. Tell him to have the royal family meet you at Lake Swithburne in the Magical North a week from today. Say you've hooked up with the Loyalist army."

She waited.

"*Is* there a Loyalist army?" Elliot said. "I mean, I know there was a King's army, and Security Forces, and, I don't know, Central Intelligence. What's happened to them all?"

"They're scattered," Mischka told him. "Many are with the Elite, some have joined us. A handful *have* gone underground and are working with Loyalists like your parents to reinstate the royals. They have no hope. If they attempt an uprising, they'll be brutally crushed. Once we take the royals out of the equation, we save these people's lives. We also take the first step toward democracy."

Elliot hesitated.

"All we're doing is sending them back to the World," she said. "All of them this time. They'll forget who they were. They'll make new lives. We'll give them passports and money. They're a deeply flawed family, and they're going to be fine. Once they're gone, your parents will be safe. And we can get to the real work of taking down the JE Elite, and establishing a democratic Kingdom. A Kingdom without poison."

He made the call.

A few days later, Mischka was back again, this time telling Elliot to pack for a road trip. "We need you to come along. Princess Ko knows you. She'll see you on the lakeshore. She'll bring the family right to you. I step out and take them to the World. Simple."

"But how do we know they're coming?" Elliot asked. "Shouldn't I call Gabe again and find out?"

Mischka shrugged. "We don't know. Most probably, they won't. No doubt they're suspicious of your call. But calling again would be a mistake. It would confirm any suspicions they might have. So. We go.

We check. I've got people to see on the way, so it's no sweat. It'll be a road trip. Let's get moving."

Half an hour later, and for the third time since his arrival, Elliot was walking through the Exit door, and into the cavern of Grays.

3.

$\mathcal{M}$ischka's car was the latest model Marsdon Tianna. It was fitted with transparent shutters, and a sleek stereo. They stopped right away for gas, and Mischka bought bottles of soda and bags of candy.

Like she said, it was a road trip.

Mischka was very keen on pink mallows. She only ate the kind they made in GC, she said. Everything else was just sugar. She drove fast and well. If somebody cut in front of her, she seemed intrigued rather than annoyed. She tilted her head and braked. Mostly, she was silent, listening to the kind of JE electronica that Elliot had never much liked. There wasn't any point to it, so far as he could tell. Now and then, she would switch off the music and chat.

"You might be wondering how we're going to send the royals across once we get there," she said their first afternoon on the road.

Not so much. He'd been assuming there was a crack someplace near this lake.

"No. No. Well, who knows? But we have the technology to open and seal cracks now. Sleek little device it is. It's in the trunk. I'll use that to take them over."

Elliot was watching Nature Strip scenery through the window. The Moving Mountains were on the horizon. He was trying to catch them shift.

He turned back and looked at her.

"You're kidding," he said. "You just switch this thing on, and it opens up a people-moving crack?"

All that time he and Madeleine had tried to figure out how to do that, and the "device" was right there in the trunk.

"It was luck. The Hostile alliance had people all over Cello working with inventors, scientists, and so on," Mischka said. "But nobody was getting anywhere. We thought your dad and uncle might have made a breakthrough: That's why we had people in your town, trying to find out."

"Olivia Hattoway," Elliot recalled. "The Twicklehams."

"Right. Anyhow, then we got an unexpected break. Turned out there was an organization we'd never known about. Not Hostile, not Elite, not Gangster. More powerful than all three. They know everything! They have control over the WSU and the press! They got in touch, and told us they had the technology we needed. See, they wanted to work with us to get the royals to the World. Their only condition, they said, was that we had to leave Princess Ko."

Elliot watched a passing truck. Department of Illumination, it said on the side. It looked beat-up and dirty. So did its driver.

Mischka laughed. "We agreed because we thought Princess Ko was an idiot."

"She's not."

"Anyhow, the night they took the royals across," Mischka continued, "I hear that was a fiasco. They got the two princes over, fine, but there was a mix-up with the others. They were all supposed to be at a Convention Center. Easy. Next thing, word came through that the Queen was at the Finance Department and Jupiter was sick at the hotel. Our people came through from the World in those places, ready to grab them. But no luck. Now they're in a panic. Time's running out. Next thing, we hear they're getting on a train, so we came through *there*. We had people stationed all over the World that night, ready, and we had keys you could use to coordinate World and Cello locations."

"Keira made a computer program that could do that," Elliot said.

Mischka tapped on the steering wheel. "She did?"

"And you know she can see cracks and unseal them herself?"

"Impossible."

"She trained her eyes. I mean, Princess Ko made her train her eyes and her vision got so refined she can do it now."

"How about that?" Mischka reached to turn the music on again. "My clever girl."

4.

The next time Mischka pulled over was at the Green Spot Diner in a mountain town called Ralk. It had a fish tank in the window. The fish seemed listless.

Mischka said she was meeting a contact in the kitchen.

"Here?"

She smiled. "Order what you like."

Elliot sat in the booth and ordered coffee and a stack of pancakes with bacon. He recalled vitamins, and added a side of fruit. The *Cellian Herald* was folded on the seat beside him.

There was that T. I. Candle again — the guidebook author — writing another column. Elliot read it while he ate.

Look, there's not much to say, is there?

Or perhaps too much.

The Kingdom of Cello is in crisis. In all my days — and my days have been plentiful — I have never known such disarray. The Colors blaze and thunder. The death and wounded tolls climb steadily. Colors tear through shutters and savage towns.

People are leaving Cello! "What?!" you cry, and I nod vigorously. Yes! I know! The horror! People don't leave our Kingdom, they FLOCK TO OUR SHORES!

Only, they do not. Not anymore! Tours, tickets, flights are being canceled. Cruise ships no longer stop at Cellian ports. Sales of my Guidebook are diving like the herons of the GC Swamp when they spy a Spotted Wing-Gnat. Every Kingdom and Empire has issued travel advisory warnings, ranking Cello (Cello!) as high-alert danger!

Bulldozers run day and night as shelters are constructed beneath towns. Bells ring so frequently that I feel that our Kingdom is a giant mechanical toy, marbles loose in its works!

The Color industry itself is in overdrive: There are persistent calls for volunteers at the warning towers. Conferences and training seminars are scrambling to tackle the issues. New Color monitors are being rushed through training. The market is flooded with shoddy shutters. Color Benders are working such long shifts that they are endangering themselves with exhaustion. Meanwhile, all over the Kingdom, scientists have turned their attention to the problem of the Colors! Some provinces have declared martial law; all are in a State of Emergency.

I could go on!

Do you know, I will!

I was traveling through the province of Golden Coast the other day, with a dear friend (Ruby). We saw Color shelters, makeshift homes, tent cities! Fires blazed in the distance! Power lines sagged under the weight of Colors. In supermarkets, children ran about, wild-eyed, while parents stockpiled water, flashlights, batteries. Riverways, pipes, and drains had been infected or blocked by Color. Animals had shouldered their way from the Color-burdened swamps and were wandering streets, or turning up in cellars! Colors were eroding, rusting, and excoriating public buildings! Babies couldn't sleep! I couldn't sleep! (And that's unheard of!)

To say that nerves were strung would be an understatement. I saw a woman shriek at the sight of sunlight on a slick of oil. A child's toy wagon sped by, and a group of men in suits clambered up a drainpipe, one by one. A sheet of cellophane caused a five-car collision. Leaves flutter — a flock of dewbirds pass — petals on the breeze — anything that hints at Color brings on hysteria!

In certain towns, desperation has given rise to preposterous defenses against Colors: People chant, link arms, dig moats, and fill these with bubbling teakwater. (Teenagers scoop it out at night and get into mischief.) They try to scare Colors away by playing the bagpipes. They sprinkle themselves with herbs, spices, and vinegars. They pay vast sums of money to tricksters and charlatans who offer bottled syrups or pills that they claim will grant immunity.

We arrived at the pleasure town of Bubbles yesterday, only to find fear and unease creeping down the streets ahead of us. Not just creeping, but sweeping and lashing and beating! People wept at windows. There came the awful howling of a grown man who, we were told, had seen his entire family slaughtered. Dogs were silent and watchful. Buildings had collapsed under the weight of heavy Colors. I saw numbers of people dead on the side of the road: Others swayed, lost, on the verge of crumpling.

It was by no means pleasant.

And as if all the Colors were not enough, it seems violence is breaking out all over the Kingdom between Hostiles, Loyalists, and the ruling Elite. Indeed, if people weren't constantly distracted by rampaging Colors, civil war might possibly erupt!

As an aside, the Cello Wind has not been heard for months.

And speaking of the Cello Wind, our neighbor, the Kingdom of Aldhibah, watches Cello's decline with silent interest. It has reinforced its borders — Colors have never been known to stray beyond Cello, but with these new strengthened Colors, none can be sure. It has also reinforced its military ranks. Indeed, if Aldhibah wished to invade and annex our Undisclosed Province — thus taking control of the Wind — now, I suspect the Aldhians are thinking, now would be just the time. . . .

Elliot closed the paper with his usual feeling that, if T. I. Candle walked in the door right now, he'd sock him in the nose.

5.

*A*s the road trip continued, as they stopped in fancy hotels and sat by fireplaces stacked with wood, reading menus with items like Pear and Gorgonzola Salad with Candied Walnut, and listening to murmured conversations about whether honey was good for your skin, Elliot felt that sash across his chest settle in again.

It wasn't a sash anymore actually; it was a sweater.

Everything annoyed him. Once, Mischka stopped at a deftball stadium for a meeting. Two big guys in suits approached. They handed her a glass of wine. She asked about the game.

"The second half was better," said one.

"Oh, damn," said the other. "I shouldn't have run away. I missed it."

"The first half was just . . . setting the scene."

"Making a statement of intent," Mischka suggested, and the two men nodded.

Now, in the past, Elliot would have been ecstatic to be here, listening to talk about professional deftball, in a private box at the Henry Lawde Stadium, one of the best in the Kingdoms.

But watching them, it came to him that they were speaking in code. Their handshakes, their phrases, the glass of wine, it was all part of the process and the game. They were getting off on it, he thought. They were the shadow figures, the key players behind the scenes. They were so tangled up in their words and their games, but did they even know what they were talking about?

Elliot watched as the three sat down. One man set his spectacles on the table, and they sat there on their haunches. The other man touched his ear. There was a tiny circle on the earlobe, Elliot noticed.

It was insane, but that circle made Elliot want to punch a wall.

He wondered if everybody felt this way, and he'd just not noticed it before. This cranky, weary feeling. Things like brushing his teeth turned into an insurmountable chore. He accidentally slammed his hotel room door that night, and realized that he was cursing in the back of his mind. It was like a stranger was in there muttering furious words just beneath his own thoughts. An angry stranger, keeping pace with him, snarling right along with every movement that he made.

The morning of the meeting day was bright and blue.

They set off early but smoke tendriled up out of the engine, and a red flashing light appeared on the dashboard.

"That doesn't look right," Mischka said.

She pulled over to the side of the highway. There were picnic tables and a water fountain. It was a good spot to break down.

Mischka opened the hood, frowned down, looked at Elliot, and shrugged. Cute gesture.

Elliot studied the engine too, but it was nothing like Farms machinery.

"I'll make a call," Mischka said.

While they waited, she and Elliot sat at a picnic table. Mischka seemed lost in thought, then she suddenly smiled.

"All that work that the Hostiles did taking the royals to the World," she said, "and next thing you RYA kids were bringing them back. Even with a traitor among you!"

Elliot tried to smile, but truth was, he didn't much feel like it.

"Of course, I heard all this from prison," she said. "How the royals kept returning like an ant infestation."

A mechanic's truck approached down the highway.

"I went to the World and stopped Chyba coming back, though. It was my first shot at using that crack technology, right out of prison. Someone on the other side was opening the crack, and I just kept right on closing it. I saw him, you know. Prince Chyba? Across the road."

She curled a loose hair around her finger. She liked to do that, Elliot had noticed. Then she'd look down in surprise at the ringlet that formed.

Now she stood up, smiling at the motor mechanic.

"This time, we'll make sure the royals stay away for good. Assuming they come today. And don't blame yourself." She turned to Elliot suddenly. "Don't blame yourself if they don't."

Elliot was way back in the conversation. "Who was it?" he said. "Who was the traitor on the RYA?"

Mischka looked at him vaguely.

"Was it the security guards? Were they working for the Hostiles?"

"Well," Mischka said. "I know it wasn't the security guards. They're Elite, not Hostile. It was someone on the RYA."

She stepped toward the open hood of the car. It took twenty minutes for the mechanic to fix, and they continued on their way.

6.

They walked beyond the trees and down the path to the lake.

It was crisp and brisk, and the sky was very high. Bright snow ran beside them, curving up and over bumps.

They turned a corner and there it was, Lake Swithburne. Frozen silver and blue, blinking in the sun.

It was almost silent. Across the lake, a couple of people were skating. An ice-fishing tent stood in the center. Sounds carried strangely; the skates seemed to cut right by them.

Mischka smiled. A pair of binoculars hung from a strap around her neck. Under her arm was a tan leather satchel with buckles. That must contain the crack technology, Elliot guessed.

"See that?" Mischka pointed to a tree, just around the curve. As far as Elliot could tell, someone had hung a whole bunch of closed black umbrellas on every branch.

"Wouldn't want to be here after dark." Mischka widened her eyes at him.

He looked again. "Those are vampire bats?"

"You've never seen them?"

He shook his head.

She laughed. "Don't worry. Safe by day. Come. I'll buy you a coffee. We still have time."

There was a small kiosk in the opposite direction of the vampire bats.

They got their coffees to go, and stood under the blue sky, watching the skaters. The ice-fishing tent flapped in the breeze.

A swooping filled the air. A flock of dragons crossed by high, wheeling and rising, scales catching the light.

They disappeared.

"Beautiful," Elliot said. Mischka nodded.

Way across the lake, the figure of a girl appeared. She was wearing a backpack, and carrying skates over her shoulder. The girl held a hand to her forehead, then lifted an arm and waved across at them.

Mischka raised her binoculars.

"That's Princess Jupiter," she said. She moved the binoculars around. "Nobody else." She grinned at Elliot. "But you got one. You got us a royal. Well done, Elliot, you got one."

Mischka stepped away from Elliot.

"I'll wait by the kiosk," she said. "She's expecting a teenage boy. You won't be threatening to her. Just say hey. I'll do the rest."

Elliot scratched the back of his neck.

There was a silence.

The other skaters were heading off the lake. They crossed paths with the girl who'd just waved. He heard them chatting briefly. The others took off their skates. The girl sat down. Elliot watched her pull off her boots and pull on the skates. He watched her lean forward, presumably to lace them.

He looked across at Mischka. She was still sipping from her coffee cup. She looked happy. She took the satchel out from underneath her arm and opened the straps.

He looked back at the girl. She seemed small.

"Hang on," he called to Mischka. "You're going to send Princess Jupiter across to the World all on her own?"

Mischka smiled at him.

"I don't think we should do it," Elliot called. "Okay to send a whole family together, but just one girl? That doesn't seem fair."

The girl had her skates on now. She was stepping onto the ice. She was slipping a little, holding out both hands.

Mischka was watching her.

She'd found her skating feet now. She'd straightened up. She was skating slow and graceful toward them.

Mischka tipped the last of her coffee onto the snow. She stood smiling. The sun caught her sunglasses. It glanced off the buckle of the satchel.

It came to Elliot right then.

A flock of truths.

They'd already tried sending the royals to the World. *They keep coming back like an ant infestation.* It hadn't worked. Why try again?

He looked back at Mischka.

She was opening her satchel.

We have learned to use Grays and Purples as weapons, Chime had said. *Some among us even carry them, in concentrated forms.*

Elliot turned back to the girl on the lake.

She was wearing a woolen hat and a blue scarf. Her coat flew behind her.

He took a step.

That flock of truths was all on his shoulders now, digging with claws.

He had to warn Princess Jupiter.

If he warned her, he knew exactly what would happen. He looked at Mischka again, and she smiled at him. She would turn that satchel onto him.

Grays or Purples, whatever she had there. They would attack him.

He stood silent.

I can't do it again, he whispered to himself. *I can't do it.* The tearing off of the mask, the knives, the razor blades.

"I can't," he said aloud. He was muttering to himself. He sounded mad, he knew. But he said it again. "I can't. Don't make me do it again."

The girl, Princess Jupiter, skated closer.

"Run," he said.

Mischka glanced his way.

"Run!" he shouted.

He ran toward the lake, falling forward at each step in the deep snow, his boots dragging. He could feel his shoulders cringing already.

"Turn around!" he howled.

On the lake, the girl kept skating.

"Elliot!" she called. *"Elliot, it's me!"*

That voice, he knew the voice, and now he knew the shape of her, the sense of her, and that wasn't Princess Jupiter at all.

That was *Madeleine*.

His Madeleine, the Girl-in-the-World.

He turned back to Mischka and shouted urgently: "It's not Princess Jupiter! It's Madeleine! She's from the World! It's a mistake!"

Mischka stared back with a look that was part exasperation, part amusement. "That," she said, "is Princess Jupiter."

For a moment, Elliot felt happy. This was just a nightmare — it must be! The Girl-in-the-World was here in the Magical North, which made no sense! And Mischka seemed to think that Madeleine was Princess Jupiter, which again made no sense!

But the hope was inside truth. This was real. It was happening right now.

He was on the ice now. He bellowed: "Turn around! Run!"

Mischka's voice spoke. "Oh, Elliot."

Madeleine was slowing. She was frowning at Elliot. He saw her gaze shift toward Mischka and then back to him.

He slipped, skidded, and stumbled on the ice toward her. He fell to his knees and scrambled up again. *Click-click-click*, a pause and another two slow clicks. They were already coming, it was third-level Grays again, he knew their shadows, their approach, he could smell them, taste them, they were coming right for him and for Madeleine in front of him. They were going to kill them both.

"Get away!" he screamed at Madeleine.

But she was skating even faster now, directly toward him. She was speed-skating, her coat forming a straight flag behind her. Her hat blew off her head. Her eyes narrowed to lines.

She closed in on him with her arm outstretched. She grabbed both his hands in hers, and then she was swinging him in a circle, swinging him behind her so fast that he crashed onto the ice, and slid away.

He tried to scramble to his feet, shouting at her to get down. The air was dark with Grays. She had turned from him and was facing them. Her hands were waving in the air. She was trying to keep her balance. There was a moment when his heart broke at that: They would hurl her to the ice and tear her to pieces, and there she was, trying to keep her balance.

Then her hand waving became precise. Her fingers were fluttering. She was playing an invisible flute. Now she was skating in a tight circle around Elliot, her hands moving so fast he almost couldn't see them.

The Grays flew toward her and then, an arm's length from her face, they stopped so abruptly he imagined a thud. They curved around and swooped again. Again, they stopped short, now reeling back and slicing toward her at a different angle.

She spun on the ice, her hands climbing the air.

The Grays gathered into a column, high above them. Madeleine and Elliot looked up. The Grays climbed higher, crowding the air. There was a long pause.

Elliot had time to notice that Mischka Tegan was standing on the lakeshore watching, slowly shaking her head, disapproval, or maybe disappointment, in her expression. The kiosk across the way shone silver in its security shutters. The skaters on the other side of the lake had disappeared.

When he looked up again, the Grays were so high they looked like a great metallic dragon. Then they were diving. The dive was magnificent, a mighty burst of speed. Elliot closed his eyes, covered his head with his hands, buried himself face-first in the ice. He waited for the claws.

He waited.

There was a long silence.

He realized that it wasn't just silence; it was a breeze, the clinking of distant shutters, a bird's hesitant call, footsteps on dirt, the cutting of skates on the ice.

He looked up.

The Grays had gone.

At the shore, Mischka Tegan was striding away, satchel high beneath her arm.

Madeleine was still spinning on the ice, her hands still sorting through the air.

PART 13

1.

$\mathcal{I}$t seemed to be a dash, and then the dash grew long, it was a line.

The line stopped. A second line appeared beside it.

So it was parallel lines, Keira thought.

A road. A river.

The points joined. A rectangle. A tablecloth.

Keira felt herself nodding. Tablecloth. Now that made sense. She slipped down to the ground. It was gluggy with melted snow.

A thaw had come in the night. The sun was out.

The tablecloth flung itself upward, down and away, and something new began at once.

A circle. A series of dots surrounding the circle. A dash *beside* the circle.

Exquisite, thought Keira. Now I see.

It was the first Color-free day in a week. Not a single warning bell all morning. Yet here was a Lime Green drawing pictures in the air. It must have slipped by the towers unseen.

Clever, she thought. You're very smart, Green.

It was slithering now, rising up and down.

That's a snake, Keira decided. You mean there is a snake in our midst.

The curves grew taller.

Those are mountains, not a snake. So I should climb a mountain? We should all climb mountains?

Gabe was beside her. He was also cross-legged in the mud. Green shapes were patterning before him too.

They'd been walking somewhere, she recalled, she and Gabe.

They'd set out from the farmhouse.

The Green changed again. A series of *w*'s. Those were upside-down birds. Birds signaled flight. She glanced up at the blue. She should fly? The shapes erased themselves. She leaned forward.

Where had she and Gabe been going?

She had no idea.

The Green formed itself into a series of numbers. 7 11 2 7 00 222. She added up the numbers. They circled and switched places. She added the new sequence.

Probably, they'd just wanted to get out of the farmhouse.

The 7 in the series tipped to its side, forming a partial triangle now. Several others joined it so it seemed to scream along, a row of pointed edges.

This last week in the farmhouse had been edges and angles. A week ago they'd woken to find Madeleine was gone. She'd left a note saying she was going to meet Elliot.

Next they'd discovered that Samuel had also disappeared. He hadn't left a note.

The house had lost its mind.

Seriously, Keira told the Green. It lost its — well, okay, she conceded. Houses don't have minds.

The Green seemed satisfied. It erased itself and began to form a musical staff. A treble clef appeared. Eighth notes, quarter notes, and whole notes.

The Queen and Princess Ko had both shrieked that they had to go after Madeleine. The others had ignored them. There'd been a snow blizzard and a Color *hurricane* outside that day. Both had continued until last night.

"I will *not* lose another child," Holly had howled.

Princess Ko had slammed doors so hard pieces of wood had splintered.

A couple of days later, the King arrived, crawling through the Colors on his hands and knees.

No one had been happy to see him.

"This is what she does," he'd said grimly when he heard the news. "She runs away."

That had not been helpful. Holly had almost thrown him down a staircase.

"Perhaps it will be all right," Sergio had said. "Perhaps she will reach the meeting point, and Elliot will take her to a secret Loyalist army. And so. The Kingdom will be saved. Beautiful."

Nobody had paid any attention to him.

He had returned, gloomy, to the empty basement.

Today, Keira thought, is the day of Madeleine's meeting with Elliot.

She wondered if Madeleine had reached the lake, and if Elliot had been trying to lure the royals there on behalf of the Hostiles. It didn't sound like Elliot, but it sounded like the Hostiles. She wondered if Madeleine was alive.

The Green lined up more numbers. Keira began to see their pattern.

A vertical row of letters appeared. She saw that she should make these into a word. Somehow the numbers and the letters would add up, and *that* would answer her questions.

What about Samuel? she thought. Will you tell me where *he's* gone?

But she was asking this more out of duty than because she wanted to know. Sergio was morose about Samuel — he'd stopped hopping around like a kid on a sugar high — but everyone else seemed to find Samuel irrelevant. He'd probably gone to a doctor or something, people said vaguely.

"Maybe Madeleine and Samuel are together?" Gabe suggested.

The others thought it was just a coincidence, their vanishing same day.

Actually, it was a relief that Samuel was gone, Keira admitted now. He'd become un*bearable* with the welts and swellings! Dying away in the basement.

It was polite of him to leave.

The Green spread itself wide, forming a starburst. Keira smiled. It spiraled and became a line of trees. Each tree blossomed. Flowers fell.

I see what you mean, she said to it.

You want me to dance. No. Everything is — wait, she'd had it a moment.

Show me again.

The Green formed itself into the shape of a balloon.

"Close your *eyes*!" shouted a voice. A small hand grabbed Keira's shoulder, little fingers digging in. "Both of you! You idiots! Close your *eyes*!"

Keira brushed the hand away.

The Green was the shape of a bird. The bird's wings opened and closed. It wheeled. Its beak dwindled. Its wings grew. Antennae appeared. It was going to be — what? I see just what you're saying!

"Oh, for *crying out loud*." Two hands shoved Keira sideways so she fell into the mud.

2.

$\mathcal{K}$eira frowned into the sunlight.

She looked across at Gabe, also sprawled in the mud.

His eyes ran left and right, like someone trying to catch up with his thoughts.

"Don't you dare turn around."

The child who'd just tackled her stood and glowered down at them.

"*Don't* you turn around!" she repeated.

What are you going to do when a kid tells you not to turn around? Keira swiveled back toward the Green.

"STOP that! You *look* at me! I *told* you!" The girl's fists were pounding Keira's shoulders.

Reluctantly, she turned back.

"Keep your eyes on me. Both of you. Okay. Wait. Wait. It's gone now."

Keira and Gabe spun.

There was nothing there.

"It goes if it doesn't get attention," the child explained. "You realize that was a Lime Green? You know people die from that, right? They get so drawn in, they can't stop watching. Their minds get all tangled trying to figure what it means. Thinking it has some sort of message."

Beside Keira, Gabe sighed deeply.

"Corrie-Lynn," he said. "You just saved us. I know exactly what a Lime Green does, and there I was, stuck in it anyhow."

"I know too," Keira said. "I remember hearing about them and thinking they'd never get me. But I was totally *transfixed*. What time is it? We must've been here for hours. Thanks," she said to the girl. "Seriously. Thanks."

She was trying to figure out how she knew the girl's face. Also, the name. Corrie-Lynn.

"You're both as muddy as my bike," Corrie-Lynn observed.

A child's bike was lying on its side in the grass.

"You rode out here all on your own?" Gabe said. "You ever met my cousin, Sophy? Soph, this is Corrie-Lynn. She's Elliot's cousin."

Corrie-Lynn Baranski. The girl whose father had died.

But the girl, unexpectedly, was rolling her eyes.

"That's not your cousin named Sophy, if you even *have* a cousin named Sophy," she said to Gabe. "That's Keira Platter. She was on the RYA with Elliot. She's done something weird to her face, changed the way she looks, and her hair's wrong, but I can still tell it's her." She reached for Keira's hand and shook it. "Pleased to meet you, Keira."

Keira felt as if a traffic signal box had gotten rammed inside her throat.

"Anyhow, I can't stay 'cause my mother thinks I'm in my room," Corrie-Lynn continued. "I only came to show you this."

She took a book from her bicycle basket and held it up.

The Kingdom of Cello: An Illustrated Travel Guide.

"It's got an appendix." Corrie-Lynn was flipping pages. "Like a glossary of Colors? And there's a way to fix Cello in here."

Keira and Gabe glanced at each other. They straightened their faces again as Corrie-Lynn looked up.

She regarded them sternly. "I mean it," she said. "I'm not being cute. I'm referring to a particular Color."

"Okay," Gabe and Keira said, contrite.

"It's a Gold."

"No such thing," Gabe said at once.

"They're just a myth," Keira agreed.

"Yeah," said Corrie-Lynn philosophically. "That's what everyone says. But listen to this. I'll read it out to you:

"**Gold**. *Many claim this Color does not exist, and I myself have undertaken futile expeditions to locate it, once fracturing my arm in the attempt. (That is another story — and an amusing one.) Legend says that the Gold, unlike all other Colors, can be made. One requires only a magic weaver, a truth seer, and the Philosopher's Stone. Legend further holds that, once made, Gold is the Elixir that can cure an ailing Kingdom.*"

Corrie-Lynn looked up.

"See?" she said. "It can save the Kingdom. If Elliot was here, I'd tell him to go make a Gold — like, find a magic weaver and a truth seer and that stone thing. But since he's not, you could do it, Keira. On account of, you were on the RYA. And you can help her if you like, Gabe," she added generously.

"Thanks," Gabe smiled.

"Can I read it myself?" Keira asked.

She would read it to humor the girl, she thought, but everybody knew that Gold did not exist.

She looked at the page. "What's this?" she said.

"It's the Guidebook." Corrie-Lynn was patient. "I told you. It tells all about Cello, and the appendix has —"

"No. There's something *behind* the words." Keira held up the book.

"Don't know what you're talking about," Corrie-Lynn said promptly.

"She's got super eyesight," Gabe told Corrie-Lynn. "She can see things other people can't."

"There's some kind of a code behind the words," Keira said. She was turning pages, back and forth. "It's everywhere! Numbers and letters. Circles all around the edges."

Gabe frowned, uneasy. "Could it be residue from the Green maybe? You sure it's there?"

Keira kept flicking.

She turned to the front cover. "T. I. Candle wrote this? He's been writing columns for the *Herald*, hasn't he? I don't like him."

"Neither does Elliot," Corrie-Lynn reflected.

The sound of a car approached. All three looked toward the road.

Corrie-Lynn grabbed the Guidebook, tore out the page, and handed it to Keira.

"Go make a Gold and save the Kingdom," she said, reaching for her bike.

"I'll give you a ride back to town," Gabe offered.

"Nope." She was pedaling already. "Need some air."

They watched as she sped down the driveway, pursued by muddy spray. When she reached the road, her feet dropped to the ground. The car turned in. A window was lowered. Corrie-Lynn spoke to the driver, then hopped back on her bike and rode away.

"Looks like Jimmy," Gabe said. "It sure is all happening today."

Keira folded the torn page into her pocket. "He's got people in the car. Can't tell who they are."

The car bumped toward them and stopped. They waited in the sun.

Three doors opened, sunlight dashing against metal and glass.

Jimmy stepped out. A boy and girl followed. The boy was grinning, the girl blinking rapidly.

"Hello there," Jimmy said, his voice unusually formal.

"Hello there back," Keira and Gabe replied.

"These two" — Jimmy indicated the strangers — "have just turned up at the Sheriff's station. Seems they're from the World. Let me introduce you. This is Jack and this is Belle."

"Hiya," the boy said.

The girl tilted her head. "All right?" she said.

$\mathcal{K}$eira and Gabe stared.

After a moment, Keira spoke. "You're proper Worldians?"

"Proper," agreed the boy, Jack, his grin widening.

"They're friends of Madeleine's," Jimmy said. "They're looking for her. She inside?"

"She's gone. She left a week ago. To meet Elliot."

"We know Elliot," the girl put in. She had a soft baby face, Keira thought, so you expected her to be docile, but her eyes and her voice were unnerving.

"You surely didn't let her go?" Jimmy demanded.

"We didn't let her. She just went. In the middle of the night."

Gabe was still staring at the newcomers. "How'd you get through to Cello?" he asked them.

"We'd seen Madeleine and Holly stumble," Jack explained. "I thought, hang about, does that mean they sort of created a crack? And we could use it?"

"No, you never," Belle said. "I thought it. Only without the *hang about* part. I would never think those words to myself: *Hang about.* What sort of a tosser would think that? Would you?"

She looked at Keira, challenge in her eyes.

Keira took a step back. "No," she hazarded.

These two had the wildest accents — maybe a cross between OQ and NS but with some JE edges thrown in? But also none of the above — and who knew *what* they were talking about.

Also, had anybody checked them for plague?

"All right," Jack said to Belle, "keep your trousers on. Anyhow, we did the candle and light thing right where Mads and Holly disappeared, and it worked. We got through. Easy. Then we just asked around for Bonfire, the Farms."

"People have been friendly," Belle added, shooting another defiant look at Keira.

What? Keira thought.

"They keep telling us we're lucky we got here this morning instead of any day last week. There's been a Color blizzard or something? Wicked."

"You haven't been telling people you're from the World?" Gabe asked.

"Nah. We just say we're from out of town. Just Jimmy here, we told. We remembered Madeleine talking about a Sheriff and Deputy who were friends with Elliot. We had to find Madeleine, see? 'Cause Federico put a letter in his hat."

"Federico's his grandfather," Belle explained. "He lives with his grandfather. I've just moved in with a friend named Darshana Charan. So, see, you don't have to live with your parents." Sure. That made things much clearer.

"He's been sending us messages in his hat all along," Jack smiled. "Like, his assignments have been *coaxing* us towards the truth."

"Unless Jack's mother's a lunatic," Belle added. "And Federico's gone along with it."

Gabe and Keira glanced quickly at each other, then back to the strangers. Jimmy was scratching his eyebrow, trying to look polite.

"The other day," Jack said, "my grandfather put a letter from my mother in his hat."

"As you do," Belle put in.

"Well, as Federico does. We just got through that," Jack said patiently.

"I know. I was just having a larf."

Keira accidentally sighed.

"Sorry," Jack said. "We're going on a bit. Anyhow, you want to see the letter? I always thought my parents were killed in a car accident, but looks like they weren't. Well, she doesn't mention my dad, but she says she's my mum."

He took a folded worn paper from his pocket and handed it over. Keira and Gabe read together.

My dearest Giacomo,

"That's my name," Jack put in, pointing at the paper. "My proper name, I mean. But you can call me Jack. Either one, to be honest. Up to you."

"Thank you," Gabe said politely. He and Keira looked back at the letter. Their arms touched. This was comforting, in the madness.

My dearest Giacomo,

I am your mother, and I love you. I am about to take a journey, and am writing this in case I don't return.

I hope to return. I intend to.

But there's a chance that I won't and, if not, Federico will give this to you when he thinks right.

I will begin with my story.

My name is Teresa.

I was born in Venice, Italy, in 1700. I do not know who my mother was, except that she was most likely young and poor, for she left me and my twin sister at the Ospedale della Pietà as infants. This was a kind of musical orphanage. Each foundling was given a number, and branded with the letter "P." We were divided into groups. The figlie di coro studied music – voice, violin, flute, oboe, cello, bassoon – and performed for the public, hidden from view by a lattice of ironwork. The figlie di commun were those without musical talent. They were given a regular education, and taught to be seamstresses, lace makers, sailmakers, pharmacists, and cooks.

My twin sister was musical; I was not.

One day, a friend dared me to creep into the room of the violin master, Don Antonio Vivaldi.

Unexpectedly, he returned. Hearing his approach, I hid in the corner.

As I watched, he took a candle, lit it at the fire, lifted a mirror from the wall. He raised both candle and mirror – and disappeared.

You can imagine my confusion.

I stood, uncertain. But I was a willful child. After a moment, I simply did the same – lit a candle, raised the mirror he had dropped – and I found myself somewhere other. That is the only way I can describe it: somewhere other.

You may find this difficult to believe – for I have asked Federico to raise you as a regular child of the World if I do not return – but there is a place called the Kingdom of Cello that adjoins this world. It is a place of magic and marvels.

I will not linger on details of this Kingdom. I will only say that, over the next several years, I found every opportunity I could to slip into Don Antonio Vivaldi's room, and through to the Kingdom of Cello.

I told nobody of my discovery – not even my sister, although I loved her and did not resent her talent (she was a beautiful cellist) – I kept it as my secret comfort. I was a commoner, awkward and shy, but I knew a fairyland!

As I grew older, I made friends in Cello, and traveled its provinces. I spent less and less time in the World — I stayed on at the Pietà as a teacher; my twin married a gentleman who had seen her play. She moved away and had children.

In Cello, they know of the World but contact, or the use of cracks, is forbidden. A "World Severance Unit" (WSU) enforces these laws.

If anybody had known I was of the World, I would have been arrested. I told nobody.

Eventually, I settled in a province called Jagged Edge. For some years, I did not return home.

This was when I discovered something remarkable.

If you can do basic arithmetic, you may have already guessed at this. At the very least you've been perplexed by my casual reference to having been born over three hundred years ago? I hope so. You seem very bright to me now, but you never know how children will turn out.

Here is the remarkable thing.

If a Worldian stays in Cello, he or she ceases to grow older. For Worldians, Cello is the key to immortality.

For years, I remained the same age, and I was happy. I made more friends. I moved about to avoid suspicion. Sometimes, I met OTHER visitors from the World.

One such visitor became my lover. I had a child with him.

This child, dear Giacomo, was you.

You were born in 1815.

I suppose this is shocking to you.

Don't be shocked! You'll get used to it. I did.

And perhaps you have always felt that you were an "old soul"? Perhaps you even have memories of some of your many, many years as a very young child?

After you were born, I spent a couple of years traveling back and forth between the World and Cello. My Worldian friends showed me other secret cracks, in other parts of Cello. I found my way to different parts of the World through these. Those were wild and wonderful times! You were adorable! You still are, as I write, although I am a little weary of your temper tantrums.

What happened next was that the WSU found out about me. I avoided arrest, but they sealed all the cracks that I knew. I was trapped in Cello.

You were two years old.

You still are two, now, all these years later. You may appreciate why I am weary of your temper tantrums?

Much as I loved Cello myself, I could not keep you there, always a very young child. You needed to live your life, to grow and change. I needed that too. I searched for the answer to how to cross over to the World again— for the secret to opening the cracks. The difficulty, of course, was that the WSU knew of our existence. I had to change my name and move about a great deal.

Eventually, I discovered a secret organization. These were Worldians who had been in Cello for hundreds of years. They called themselves "The Circle." I joined the organization. I was elated! It seemed they had a machine that opens cracks! Certain of their members crossed to the World at regular intervals, bringing back news and scientific discoveries, etc. I applied for a position as one of these "messengers."

There was rigorous training before I would be granted use of one of the machines. I completed this with flying colors. As soon as I was appointed messenger, I intended to take you to the World and never return.

Only, the day that I received my appointment, I learned a terrible truth about this organization. Do not concern yourself with the secret. Suffice to say that I felt deeply ashamed of my fellow Worldians, and I knew that the Kingdom of Cello must be informed. The organization had to be disbanded.

So. I pretended all was well. I took possession of the crack-making machine. I used it to come to the World. I traced the descendants of my twin sister's family and discovered Federico, living here – where I now write – at Trinity College, Cambridge.

(So Federico is not your grandfather. He is your great-great-great-great (etc)-nephew (I'm uncertain of the greats). (You should respect him anyway.))

I told him my story. He seemed delighted. He said that he would keep it in his hat.

But now I must return briefly to Cello. I am going directly to the offices of the Cellian Herald, to tell them the truth about this organization.

Then, at once, I shall return.

I hope that you will never read this letter.

With much love,

your adoring mother,

Teresa Zina Ballomabi

Keira and Gabe reached the end of the letter at the same moment. They looked up, blinking in the sun glare.

"What's the terrible secret?" Keira asked, at the same time as Gabe said: "What's this secret organization?"

Jack shrugged. "My grandfather told me that I shouldn't try to go to Cello, 'cause if my mother hadn't come back, it meant there was trouble."

Keira looked back at the letter.

"Only, he's not your grandfather," she said, "and you're about two hundred years old."

"Not wise, though," Belle assured her. "He didn't even *realize* he had two hundred years of memories, he just thought he had past lives." Apparently, she found this hilarious.

"Anyhow." Jack ignored the hilarity. "Our friend Madeleine actually had a hallucination about a big part of this story, so we came to Cello to find her and see if she can help me find my mum."

"She went on about it," Belle said thoughtfully, "and we never listened. Should've, I guess. Might've saved us a trip." The laughter started again.

"You know your friend Madeleine is actually Princess Jupiter?" Gabe asked.

"Oh, yeah, she told us right before she left," Jack said. "We didn't believe her."

"I believed her," Belle said, "you tosser."

Jimmy stepped forward again. "Well, if we go on inside, these two can at least meet Madeleine's mother and sister?"

"Holly's here?" Jack said. "Brilliant. We know her. She's wicked."

There was another moment of bewilderment.

"Well, you go on in," Gabe said eventually. "Keira and I were just on our way someplace. We'll catch you later."

"Farmwork?" Jimmy asked.

"More or less," Gabe said.

He and Keira glanced at each other.

4.

*T*hey watched until the farmhouse door closed.

"How about those two?" Keira said eventually.

"I liked them."

She looked up. Gabe was still tall. He was always tall. His face up there against the blue, smiling.

"But you can't distract me," he said. "We've been interrupted by a Green, a small girl, the Guidebook to Cello, a Deputy Sheriff, and a couple of kids from the World. I'm starting to think you've arranged all this on account of you suddenly regret agreeing, and you're thinking I'll forget. I won't."

That morning, Keira had been up early, before Gabe even, and was at the table eating breakfast when he walked in.

"The Colors have stopped, the thaw's come, and the sky's blue," she'd told him.

Gabe had studied her a moment.

"I'm thinking this news is cause for celebration," he'd said, voice slow and reasonable. "And what I'm thinking is, the best way for you to do that celebrating, is let me take a spin on that bike of yours."

Keira had laughed a sudden burst of laughter.

"Sure," she'd said, and he'd switched direction mid-stride, so that instead of heading to the coffeepot, he was approaching the back door. He'd opened it, turned, and looked at her.

She'd shrugged and joined him outside.

Then the interruptions had begun.

"Come on," Keira said now, and started heading to the barn, where her motorbike was locked. He walked beside her, silent.

They reached the barn door. Her hand touched the handle.

Something hit her shoulder with a soft thud.

"For crying out loud," Gabe said.

They both turned to look.

It seemed that tiny apples were falling from the sky. Bright little balls of color.

"That's a Crimson," Keira said. "Those are rare."

They pressed back under the doorframe for shelter.

"Never seen one before," Gabe said.

"Me neither."

"It won't last long," he continued.

They looked at each other.

"What's the story with it?" Gabe said after a moment. "If you catch one, everything turns sharper for a moment?"

"I think you see things you already knew," Keira explained. "But they come together and start to make sense."

"Ah, well," Gabe said. "If it just tells us what we already know, we oughta ignore it, and go on in for your bike." But he stayed where he was.

"Might not ever see one of these again," Keira said.

Gabe sighed. "Well," he said. "I guess it'll only take a moment."

They glanced at each other, then both reached out a hand and caught a Crimson.

A zigzag flew through Keira's mind. She closed her eyes to watch it. It shot backward, forward, up and down. At the same time, there was the sensation of something being wrenched and pulled upward: some heavy, complicated object, an engine maybe. She panicked at that, but the lifting continued, and then there was a sweet sense of weightlessness. She felt herself smiling. The zigzag flew faster in the fresh new space.

It was over.

She opened her eyes.

She was sitting on the step, leaning up against the barn door. Gabe was beside her.

"What did you see?" he said.

She turned to him.

"You," she said, surprised. "I saw your face every time someone asks you about farming. Or about the seasons. They ask you all the time."

Gabe chuckled. "They do."

"And I saw your face every time I talk about your parents, and how it'll be good when they come back."

A quiet formed beside her.

"They're not coming back, are they?" she said. "I'm an idiot. How did I not notice? It's like you turn into a shadow every time I mention it. And you're tired of having to do everything on your own, and you want to help people when they ask you about farming and the seasons, but it feels like you're carrying the farm *and* the town."

Gabe stretched his long legs out, and swung his big sneakers from side to side.

"Well, yeah," he said. "They're not coming back. I guess nobody likes to admit that. My dad was attacked by a second-level Purple years back now, and he lost most of the movement in his right side. He goes away for rehab a lot. This last time it's been over a year."

"What about your mother?"

"She's a tough one. She's from north of the Farms — that's your industrial region. She always thought we were too soft for her. She went back north and got a job running a factory couple of years back. She sends money now and then, calls me every month or two. But no. I'm thinking, why would she come back?"

A tractor engine started somewhere. Birds made a racket in the trees, excited by the sunshine. From the farmhouse came the distant sound of the Worldians laughing.

"You haven't asked what I saw."

"Okay," Keira said. "What did you see?"

"I saw you. In particular, your face that day when I told you I'm tangled up in farming. And I saw how keen you are on motocross, and computing machines, and how you got into that history club. I figure, you've got all this passion and you want to get tangled up in it, the way I am in farming, only you can't. And then I saw your face every time someone mentions your mother, and that explained why you can't. You're all tangled up with *her*. Every time you *un*tangle, she tangles you back up. You say she has nothing to do with you, but you don't actually believe it. Not in *here*." He touched her neck, just beneath her chin, and ran two fingers lightly down her throat.

She thought about joking, *Not in my esophagus?* but didn't.

"You know that exercise where you imagine something lifting you up from the top of your head?" she said instead.

"Can't say I do. But go on."

"It's an exercise to stretch out your spine. But I feel the opposite, I feel like there's something pushing down on the top of my head. It makes me want to creep out of my life. When I think about my mother and the people she's hurt, I feel like I'm being dragged along a road behind a speeding car."

Gabe nodded.

"I used to think," Keira continued, "that it was good to feel this bad. It's the Jagged Edge ethos, see? Feeling the extreme. But I don't know. Maybe it's not good."

"It's not," Gabe confirmed. "And your mother will never be a patch on what you are. You're better and brighter than you know."

"I never told anybody that before," Keira said. "About how bad I feel."

Gabe reached for both her hands, one at a time.

"The other thing I saw," he said, "was your little fingers." He tilted her hands in his. "They've both been broken."

"They have."

"'Cause you're a motocross champion. They always get broken little fingers, champions, 'cause little fingers catch on things when you ride fast."

Keira took her hands back, but Gabe kept his gaze on them and something crossed his face as he did. Something ran right down his features, as if her crooked little fingers had suddenly caught him off guard.

"You still letting me take your bike for a spin?" he said abruptly.

"From what I hear," Keira said, "you usually ride a motor scooter, and those don't even have gears. They're like lawn mowers. You're not taking my bike for a spin: What I meant was, I'd take *you* for a spin."

"Well." He thought about that. "I guess there was always going to be a catch. Least this way you'll get to see what *real* motocross is." He was unfolding a sleeve of his shirt as he spoke, stretching it down over his hand. Now he leaned around Keira, turned on a tap, and ran the cold water over his sleeve edge.

"You got a little mud here," he said, pressing the damp, cold cloth onto her cheek.

"One thing we should get clear," Keira said, "is that riding across fields is not *real* motocross. Real is what we do in stadiums. Jumps, backflips, and acrobatics. Style, difficulty of trick, best use of a course, and crowd reaction. That's real motocross."

Gabe was still rubbing at her cheek with his shirt. He swiped it down around her chin, and started up on the opposite cheek.

"Sounds like you're reading from a rule book," he said. "You know that motocross actually started right here in the Farms, right? The word *motocross* comes from a combination of *moto*, which is the Jarmian for motorbike, and *cross*, which refers to cross-country. I mean real country. Rugged terrain and so forth."

"Just because it started in the country doesn't mean it has to stop there!" Keira said. "You keep evolving, and you end up in a Jagged Edge stadium. The short straights, the tight turns, the intensity. That's the real test of skill."

"Busting a tire on a broken bottle or a sharp rock or a nail. Hitting a tree stump. A dead cow in the grass. Creeks, log crossings, the smell of mud and dirt. Now *that's* where you see talent. Wind on your face. Power of your bike."

"Power?" she said, withering. "A scooter?"

"That's what's real," Gabe continued. "The surprise. Not the control."

Keira blinked suddenly. "Why are you still cleaning my face? There can't be *that* much mud."

Gabe sat back, letting his damp sleeve fall.

"Wasn't any mud at all," he said. "I just wanted to clean off that makeup of yours — the modification makeup. All of it. It was just — I liked seeing the real of you when you were talking just now. That fragment of you that you gave me — and I wanted to see more —"

"You took off my makeup? You can see what I look like? You can see my bad skin?"

"Ah," he said. "You're beautiful. Cut it out."

His shoulders moved, and he was kissing her. That big hand of his was on the back of her neck. There was so much gentle and warmth in the kiss, and a lot of words, and that expression on his face when he looked at her broken fingers, and his expressions like *cut it out*, and how he thought she was better and brighter than she knew, and how he wanted her to be untangled and happy, and how he liked it when she joined the history club, all of that was there in his kiss.

He stopped.

"You're still taking me for a spin, right? Even though I did that?" A frown ran across his face, all the way to his ears.

She laughed. She reached for his hand and squeezed it, to reassure him, and then she thought: I'm going to kiss him myself. So she did. She put her own words and her thoughts about him, and how much she liked his height and his ears, and how much she liked the way he made her a chocolate pudding when she was sad, and how generous he was when people asked about farming and the seasons, and how overwhelmed he felt sometimes, here on his own, and how proud she was of him, for doing this on his own, she put all that into the kiss. She thought: I've never done that in my life. Kissed somebody in that way, with all of that behind it.

It made the kiss run right through her body and his body, and all the way out and up to the sky, across the Kingdom, and back into the place where their mouths met.

They sat back, leaning up against the doorway again, facing forward, holding hands, sun on their faces.

Way across the field, the door of the farmhouse opened.

Jimmy stood in the doorway.

"Guess he's heading back to town," Gabe said. "We've got a couple more houseguests now, you think?"

"Just what you need." Keira smiled.

"Well, least they know how to laugh," he pointed out.

Keira watched Jimmy stride toward his car.

"I wonder how he feels about having a girlfriend from another century," she said. "I mean, he seemed okay with her being from the World, but this is a lot to get your head around."

Gabe was quiet, he was moving his thumb about on Keira's palm. He stirred suddenly.

"What, you think Isabella might be that old too?" he said. "As old as that boy's mother? I didn't even think of that, but you're right. If Isabella's from the World, and Worldians live forever here, well, Isabella could be even older! She could be a thousand years old!"

"No," Keira said. "Isabella *is* Jack's mother."

Gabe laughed. "How do you figure that?"

"I saw that as well," Keira said. "With the Crimson. Isabella had a scar on her ankle that was shaped like a letter *P* — that was in a missing persons report about her. In the letter, it says that they branded everyone who went to that orphanage with the letter *P*. And Isabella told Jimmy she'd been studying the cracks, trying to get back to the World. That's why she did physics, and why she came to Bonfire."

"Well," began Gabe. "I'm not sure that's enough."

"The woman who wrote the letter said she had to change her name," Keira continued. "The letter was signed Teresa Lina Ballomabi. Switch those letters around."

"I can't."

"Well, if you did, you'd get Isabella Tamborlaine."

"Not a chance," Gabe said.

He picked up a stick and wrote the names in the mud, one after the other. Ran the stick between both a few moments, then whistled through his teeth like a Farms boy.

"You're right," he said. "And she's right here in town, hiding at Jimmy's. That boy is ten minutes from his mother."

"That Crimson was something else," Keira said, speaking like a Farms girl herself.

"Well," Gabe said. "It was. But I've got to admit, I noticed your crooked fingers a while back. They always break my heart a little, every time I see them."

They leaned together and kissed again.

PART 14

1.

S omeone was spilling drops of hot wax onto her hands and arms.

Madeleine woke.

She was lying beneath a pile of blankets. Her face felt chilled. She was in a tent. Pale light fell through the canvas.

Her hands and arms were covered in blisters. Her body ached with exhaustion. From outside came the hush of wind and low voices.

Elliot's voice, she recognized.

Now a second voice cried, "Call yourself my humble suggestion that we build a fire! Or that we did so, had we the *means* of building a fire."

That was Samuel.

She pushed the blankets aside and crawled out of the tent into deep snow.

The frozen lake shone under dusk light. Elliot and Samuel turned toward her, dark shadows.

"You have awoken!" Samuel said. "I myself felt so refreshed upon awaking late this morning that I set off to find you here, and lo! I found you! Still here! Elliot procured this tent from the kiosk over yonder and placed your sleeping form within."

Elliot was still. His face was shadowed, but she could see his eyes staring hard at her. "You saved me," he said, his voice distant. "The Grays were attacking, and you saved us both."

Madeleine looked beyond him, across the lake. It was silvery pink now.

"I don't know how I did it," she said. "I saw this mist, and I started braiding it together, like a barrier."

"Your Highness!" Samuel cried. "It is as I said! You are a talented magic weaver! It is *intuitive* for you, and that is rare!"

Madeleine looked at her palms. They swarmed with blisters. "I guess I need practice," she said. "And stop calling me 'Your Highness.'"

Elliot remained where he was. Why did he not move closer?

"You're Princess Jupiter," he said, still remote. "But you're also Madeleine."

"I'm just Madeleine." The lake and its shores were empty. "So where's the Loyalist army?"

The tent fluttered in the breeze.

"I didn't know you were Princess Jupiter."

"Well, me neither." Madeleine tried to read his expression through the fading light. "Are they far from here?"

"I have no idea. I don't even know if there *is* a Loyalist army. I was working with the Hostiles. I didn't know the plan was to kill you. I thought we were sending you back to the World."

The words sailed through Madeleine, taking her with them. Now she was a vast distance from herself. "You were going to let the Hostiles send me back to the World?" she said from this distance. "Alone?"

"I told the whole royal family to come," Elliot pointed out.

Madeleine's voice dropped away, out of her reach. She stared at the outline of Elliot's face.

"I didn't know you were Princess Jupiter," he said again. "She's trouble."

Samuel spoke softly: "Oh."

"But I told you *I* was trouble," Madeleine said. "I told you all about me, at the parking meter. I'm the exact same person." Her voice was growing. "And you were going to let them send me back to the World?"

"The royal family," he said. "I was going to send the royal family back. I thought you were Madeleine."

There was a long pause.

The ice of the lake raced up Madeleine's spine and into her voice. "I thought you were Elliot," she said.

Elliot did not move. Samuel's head bowed. The three stood in the falling light.

"Well," Madeleine said eventually, still ice. "I guess we just sleep here tonight, and figure out what to do in the morning." She ran her eyes around the lake again — the closed kiosk, the snow-laden trees — and stopped. She stared. It must be her imagination. She squinted. "Those are *vampire bats*!"

Samuel gave a cry.

"Oh," said Elliot, sounding confused. "I forgot."

"You *forgot*?" It felt good, this surge. "You *knew* there were vampire bats there, and you *forgot*!"

"Well, they're on the other side of the lake," he said defensively.

"Who *are* you?" Madeleine stamped her foot so it disappeared deep into the snow. She dragged it back out so she could stamp again. "You think vampires stay on their own side of a lake?" She was wrenching the tent poles out of the snow. "We have to get out of here. The sun's about to set." She scrambled under the falling canvas, dragging out blankets, and tossing them at Elliot and Samuel.

"I'm sorry," Elliot said. "I have no experience with vampires."

"But don't you learn about them in school?"

"Okay. It was stupid of me. I wasn't thinking. I'm kinda distracted."

"If we go fast," Madeleine began, but there was a rush of air above them.

They looked up. Dark shapes soared steadily toward them through the sky, growing larger.

"Call yourselves my fear we are too late," Samuel whispered.

$\mathcal{T}$he shapes landed before them in a ripple of thuds. Madeleine screamed.

"Cut that out at once," said a voice, sharp and alarmed, and it was Madeleine's sister, Princess Ko.

She embraced Madeleine. "You're *alive*," she said, "which is a flash of sunlit dew, but you won't be for much longer if you wake those vampires up. Don't you see them across the lake there? Why would you *camp* so close to vampires?" The Princess turned her disapproval onto the boys standing by Madeleine. "Elliot. Samuel. It is fine to see you both — surprising to see Samuel, of course, but also fine — yet again I must ask why would —"

"Where did you *come* from?" Madeleine breathed.

The other shapes moved closer, resolving themselves into Sergio and Keira.

"From the sky. Sergio flew us here," Ko explained. "Occasional Pilots are useful on occasion, ha-ha. We have come to the Magical North on a mission, and also to ensure that you are safe, Madeleine. We knew this was the date and location of your meeting with Elliot." She turned to him now. "I doubted you, Elliot, but I see that I was wrong. I apologize."

"No need," Elliot said, his voice layered with meaning.

Sergio was exclaiming. "It is Samuel! How can it be? I thought I should never see you once again, for you were gone in the night, *pfft*, but now? Back once again! And here is Elliot and also Madeleine, and there is so much to say, we will be talking and talking all the night!"

Keira had been facing away from the others. Now she spoke up mildly. "Yeah, we should probably hold the talking and talking. One of those vampires just woke up."

For the next hour, they stumbled through darkening woods, not speaking except to argue in low voices about the best way to reach a road, or to swear when they slipped or ran into a tree branch. Now and then, Samuel gasped loudly, and the others hissed, *"What?"* and Samuel whispered, "Call yourselves my apologies. I thought I heard a vampire in pursuit," until Princess Ko commanded him to cease and desist with the gasping.

"Perhaps," Samuel murmured, "Sergio could fly us all to safety?"

Keira looked up. "Vampires like the sky," she said. "We're safer on the ground."

"Not to mention, Sergio just flew all the way from the Farms," Princess Ko scolded. "He will be too fatigued for flight."

"This has some truth," Sergio admitted.

Elliot said, "I think I hear a river."

"In what way is that helpful?" Madeleine demanded so scornfully that the others were surprised into silence again.

Eventually, the sounds of a rushing river filled the air. There was no room for any other thoughts. Lights flashed in the distance.

"Headlights passing," Keira called over the river rush. "There's a road ahead."

"Must be the Sir Laurence Highway," Princess Ko shouted. "It runs parallel to the River Elegant. There'll be sled stops along it! We're safe!"

They began to run.

Almost immediately they came to a highway sled stop. They crowded into the empty wooden shelter, its walls dimming the roar of the river.

"Now," said Princess Ko. "Before I explain our mission, I want to know what's going on here. Something is up. You and Elliot are both behaving strangely, Madeleine. So is Samuel, but he's always strange, so I'll allow that. Madeleine?"

But Elliot spoke. "I joined the Hostiles."

A whistle of silence shot through the group.

"You were forced to pretend," Ko said after a moment. "That is disappointing, but understandable. Do not blame yourself."

"No. I believed in their cause. I wanted to help take down the royals. I didn't mean for anyone to get hurt, and I didn't know that Madeleine was a princess. But I did believe in them."

There was another, shriller silence.

"You're a Hostile now?" Keira asked.

Elliot blinked. "I don't know," he said eventually. "Today was terrible. I made a terrible mistake." He outlined what had happened, Samuel interrupting now and then to enthuse about Madeleine's magic weaving. "She saved our lives," Elliot concluded. "She was great. And I'm furious with Mischka and the Hostiles for tricking me. But I don't know if I'm still a Hostile now, or not." He glanced at their faces and away again, his gaze on a steady distant point, hands in his pockets.

Princess Ko stepped close to her sister. Her mouth forming various shapes. When she did speak her voice was twisted to a higher pitch.

"A part of me is not surprised that my sister is a magic weaver. I have always known she was special. As for you, Elliot, let us talk later. For now, I shall explain our mission. We wish to find the author of the Cellian Guidebook. We believe he may know something about an organization called the Circle."

She told of the arrival of Belle and Jack — "Belle and Jack are in *Cello*," Madeleine interrupted. "*My* Belle and Jack?"

"Yes," Ko replied. "They're in Bonfire right now. They are profoundly curious individuals, Madeleine, but it is clear that they care deeply about you. At any rate, Jack had a letter —"

But Madeleine had covered her face with her gloved hands, and she was crying silently. Elliot watched her. His expression faltered and fell.

"Jack had a letter," Ko repeated, and she outlined the letter from Jack's mother, and its references to the Circle.

"The agents, Tovey and Kim, suspect the existence of a supergroup called the Circle," Keira put in.

"Exactly," Ko continued. "So the letter interested me. But then it seemed Keira had also found some kind of code in the pages of the Guidebook, with circle references! This, of course, may have been nothing but a coincidental printing error that has led us on a wild-goose chase."

Keira shrugged. "Ah, well."

"Ah, well, indeed," said the Princess. "At any rate, nobody else seems to be saving the Kingdom, so I thought I would give it a shot. As a first step, I wish to speak with the guidebook author, one T. I. Candle — I recall him attending royal functions in my childhood. I have verified that he lives in Lanternville, which I believe" — Ko paused to consult the map and timetable printed on the wall of the shelter — "I believe to be approximately one hour due east of here."

Samuel, who had been swaying while Ko spoke, as if dancing to some distant, gentle music, spoke up. "We go on the morrow!" he pronounced. "A good night's sleep for one and all now, and I believe I see the lights of an inn just a stone's throw away!"

"We go now," Princess Ko declared. "Not tomorrow. Rumors abound that something important is happening tomorrow, so we need to follow up on this *tonight*. A sled will be along shortly."

"Well, then! As you wish, my good Highness!" Samuel staggered slightly. "Perhaps if I *myself* might remain at the inn. My health, after fleeing through the woods, is somewhat failing. . . ."

It was agreed that Samuel would take a room at the nearby Jongleur Inn, that Sergio would remain watching over him, and that the others would ride, by husky sled, to Lanternville. While these arrangements were being made, neither Elliot nor Madeleine spoke a word.

3.

The husky sled hissed through the mountains at a hush, trailing creases in the snow. Elliot and Keira rode backward, Elliot's head turned to the side so he was always watching the night. Madeleine, opposite him and alongside her sister, also turned her head. At first, she did this so she wouldn't have to look at Elliot, but she found herself studying the landscape. The Magical North had become two places, she realized. It was the province she knew from her childhood — dark woods, blue-white snow, and clusters of distant spilled lights that grew into the golden-orange glow of villages; steeples, sculptures of wolves, wooden walkways; dark, cold smells of old ice and moss, richer smells of spruce, rowan, and pine, and crowded fragrances of wine, beer, wool, and spicy sausages — but now also it was a province of rivers, streams, and skating ponds, each shrouded in the finest, strangest twists of silvery fog. She wanted to reach for it, untangle it, weave it, see what it could do.

I see magic everywhere, she almost said. *How did I miss this before?* But she caught Elliot's eye, and said nothing.

They reached Lanternville as the town clock struck ten P.M.

"Do you know where T. I. Candle lives?" Princess Ko asked the husky driver, and as the sled moved away, the man's voice came, muffled by his scarf: "Hereabouts!"

Once the sled had disappeared, they stood by the town well, looking in vague directions. Elliot slid across the icy cobblestones, and stopped at a clustered signpost.

"Look at this," he called after a moment.

The Tavern, said one of the signboards, an arrow pointing left. *The Square,* said another. *The Well. Maybelline's Hosiery. The Sparkleshine Hattery. The Dwelling of T. I. Candle.*

"He's got his own sign," Keira said.

"Convenient," Princess Ko said.

"Self-important," Keira corrected.

The arrow pointed toward the main street. This was steeply angled and dimly lit by lanterns and moon. They passed shops, cafés, a pub, and reached a row of attached houses, each painted a different, bright color. The consistency, Madeleine thought, is in the peaks of their roofs, the rise and fall of those peaks. Also in the white of the snow: white above, white below. She watched her feet in the scuffed, polished, ruffled snow, looked up at the snow-draped chimneys, railings, and ledges, and her eyes fell on a tiny board: *THE DWELLING AND OFFICE OF T. I. CANDLE, Esq.* A wooden owl dangled on chains from this board.

The four of them stopped. The house was dark and silent.

"I guess he's asleep," Elliot said.

"Then we will wake him," Ko declared, reaching over and clattering the knocker.

The sound echoed up and down the street. It faded. Nothing happened.

Keira was peering through the window in the door. "The back-door latch is open," she said, and raised an eyebrow at Ko, who nodded. Keira disappeared down a side laneway.

"I like her more all the time," Ko said, smiling.

Elliot and Madeleine glanced toward each other, realized they were doing this, and glanced away again.

The front door opened. Keira stood in the doorframe.

"Come on, then," Ko said.

Again, Elliot and Madeleine caught each other's eye, then both walked inside.

At the end of a narrow hallway, a door opened onto a study. Ko shone a flashlight over a dark fireplace, a stack of wood, a desk, book-cases, a sudden curl of black against crimson. The flashlight jumped at this, then held. It was a cat, sleeping on a cushion.

A candelabra stood on the mantelpiece. Keira moved across to this, and there was the flash of a match being lit, then the candles flickering one by one. The room seemed to wake up, drowsily. Now they saw framed certificates and maps on the walls, a half-empty glass of wine, ink pot, loose papers, and books.

"We'll look for clues," Ko whispered.

Madeleine ran her hands over the papers on the desk. *A Treatise on the Colors of Cello*, she read, and *The Shifting Seasons of our Kingdom: A Proposition*. There were printed papers, hand-scribbled notes, sketches, and rows of figures. *The Cat Walk and Cosmology: Certain Philosophical Questions*, she read, and then: *The Moving Mountains: A Very Pleasing Divertissement*. There was a list headed *Philosophical Equipment*, another, *Mathematical Equipment*, and a third, *Items Purchased*. *Cherries*, she read, *marmalade, milk, cheese, butter.*

The others moved around the room, pulling books and papers from shelves. The cat stared at each of them in turn, speechless.

"Everything I'm reading is what you'd expect in a guidebook writer's office," Elliot said.

"Same, I guess." Madeleine turned over a bound journal.

Annalen der Physik, she read. Clipped to the front was a note: *As requested, the Einstein pieces — special relativity is in 1905 vol, his gravitational work, 1916.*

The margins of the journal crawled with tiny scribbled notes, diagrams, question marks, and exclamation points.

A note was pinned to another stack of pages: *Here's the latest on the death of wave/particle duality & of Schrödinger's cat (ha!) etc, & on new idea that multiple, jostling invisible universes (each operating according to Newtonian law (!)) is true explanation for quantum weirdness.*

Madeleine flicked through more loose papers, catching names: John Dalton, Henri Becquerel, Max Planck, Marie Curie, Ada Lovelace, Hugh Everett, Howard Wiseman.

This is all *Worldian*, she realized, then said it aloud: "There's a lot of stuff here from the World."

"Indeed there is!" agreed a voice, and there was a crash as Keira dropped a book and swore.

A man stood in the doorway. He wore striped pajamas and a heavy crimson robe. His hair was white, swept back from a high, pale forehead, and falling majestically to his shoulders. His nose was proud, and he raised this now toward the ceiling.

"Had you forgotten we have electricity in the province?" He reached for a switch, and an overhead light buzzed. The cat sniffed, irritated, stood, and turned a circle. The man, however, seemed cheerful. "It is not often I have visitors this late at night! Certainly, it is rare to find four young people bustling about in my study while I sleep."

"We have questions," Princess Ko declared.

"And you believe the answers to be in my study?" He leaned against the doorframe.

"Why does your Guidebook have secret messages behind the print?"

The man startled. He wiped his hand across his mouth. He resumed his lethargic stance.

"It does?" he tried.

Keira drew the torn page from her pocket, unfolded it, and handed it to the man. "Here," she said, pointing. "Also here, and here. It was on a lot of other pages too, but I've only got this one."

"You can *see* the code there? With your *eyes?*"

Keira shrugged. "I've got good vision."

"But this *is* extraordinary! I've never known such eyesight, even among the greatest Night-Dwellers of Jagged Edge! I'd very much like to conduct a number of experiments on you!"

"Yeah, that's okay, thanks," Keira told him.

"Well, we shall get to that. In the meantime, perhaps I should introduce myself. Traveler. Guidebook author. Owner of the house in which you have been making yourselves so marvelously at home. To put it more briefly, I am T. I. Candle."

"No, you're not," said Madeleine. She blinked once. "You're Isaac Newton."

4.

*T*he man's face changed. A rush of color, something lifting and falling both at once. His smile became a complicated grimace.

"It is long since I have heard that name," he said, and then the smile returned. "*Sir* Isaac Newton, is what you intended, I assume."

"Sure," said Madeleine, staring.

"Who's Isaac Newton?" Keira asked, while Ko demanded: "In that case, where is T. I. Candle?"

"It is I," said the man, "and here he is."

"Whatever is he going on about?" the Princess complained.

"T. I. Candle *is* Isaac Newton," Madeleine said. "He's from the World."

"Perhaps you should come into the drawing room," Newton said, "and I shall tell my tale."

They followed him through to a room decorated exclusively in bright crimson. Each of them reeled at this a little. Newton didn't notice: He was regarding the fireplace.

"Perhaps one of you might get that fire lit," he suggested before sitting in one of the armchairs and staring at a signet ring on his finger.

After a while, he looked up. "Sit!" he said impatiently. "Are you building up the fire there? Good, yes, that's the way. I would curl some pages of the newspaper like so, if I were you. It works a treat." He twisted his hands to indicate. Elliot, stacking wood and kindling into place, ignored him.

"As a boy," Newton said, "I was sent to a town called Grantham, to board with an apothecary named —"

"Clarke," Madeleine said.

"Quite. He had a wife and three children, named —"

"Arthur, Edward, and Catherine."

Newton looked up sharply. "I cannot abide interruptions," he said.

"You shouldn't blame her." Elliot spoke from the fireplace. "She knows a lot about you. I just remembered. She used to tell me all about you."

"And she is a magic weaver," Ko said. "So you should respect her."

Newton twitched. "You're a magic weaver?"

"Go on," she told him. "I won't interrupt."

"Very well. I was very much alone." Newton settled back into his story, comfortably. "Despite the three children. They were not my friends: quite the reverse. Arthur, in particular, used to bully me. In any case, one day, I was carving pictures into the walls of my room. I picked up my candle to hold it closer and — a boy appeared beside me. Extraordinary. Even now, centuries later, I can feel the shock of that moment. He was not there — and then he was. He was from the Kingdom of Cello, you see. There must have been a crack in my room, and he'd been holding a mirror. Thus, the crack had opened. But we understood that some time later. The boy's name —"

The man shot a warning glance at Madeleine, but she was silent, so he continued.

"His name was Tobin. He was a Prince of Cello, and exactly my age. He was so bright, such a lively mind. We became great friends. Hidden in my room, we talked about everything: his world, mine, the secrets of the cosmos. We explored the fields around Grantham, made kites, lanterns, wooden clocks. He took me to Cello, and we ventured far and wide, to the Lake of Spells, to Nature Strip. Once, he and I saw a Crimson; it is a Color that falls like apples. If you catch one, you see truths you'd always known. Years later, I saw another, and my thoughts collided, and I knew precisely how matter is drawn to other matter, how planets interact. . . . But that first childhood encounter with Tobin was the most precious. He and I continued partial to the color crimson ever since." He paused, smiling vaguely.

"I like it too," Keira said. "But what you've done to this room is known as overkill."

"Excuse me?"

"Never mind. Go on with your story."

Newton crossed his legs. "By odd coincidence, Tobin and I were very similar of appearance. Almost, we could have been twins."

"Mirror images!" Madeleine cried. "I saw you both in a vision! You were leaning over a patch of sun and . . . Okay, yeah, I know. Keep going."

"Almost," he repeated sternly, "we could have been twins. We tried an experiment. We traded places: He became me, and I him. It was a great success, and after that, we exchanged positions regularly, playing each other's parts, delighted by our game. It did cause some confusion: Tobin was more sociable than I. Our handwriting changed. Over time, we became more adept at swapping. We realized that Tobin lost his memory if he spent more than a few days in the World, so we were careful not to stay too long."

Newton again studied his signet ring.

"I fell in love with this Kingdom," he said. "The Colors so fascinated me. They inspired my color theory, you know. Tobin, also, loved my World. And we loved each other — we exchanged rings." He looked up and drew his robe closer. "We also had disagreements. I felt that Cello should remain a secret from the rest of the World; Tobin wanted to communicate it. He thought the World should establish a World-Cello Harmonization Society such as existed here. He even informed members of the Royal Society about Cello! I kept stamping out fires he had set. I knew that the World could not cope with Cello:

The World relies on truth, you see, and to introduce the magic of Cello would be an utter implosion of reality. It requires the highest sensibilities, the most refined intellect, to comprehend both truth and its implosion. We quarreled often, Tobin and I, around this time, about numerous things, small and large, and our greatest quarrel took place in the 1660s. It left us both furious. Sulking, I came here and played the role of Prince Tobin, while he went to the World, and played me — and, before we could cool down, before we were reconciled, the plague found its way through to Cello. You probably know, from school, that this was catastrophic for Cello. The cracks to the World were immediately sealed. The Harmonization Society was disbanded, and the World Severance Unit established. I was trapped here; Tobin, in the World."

Sadness enveloped the room. Newton shook it from his shoulders and carried on.

"I continued to be Prince Tobin, and as the years passed, I realized something remarkable. I was not growing any older. Cello had made me immortal. I saw that I should disappear before they crowned me King — that caused another scandal: my disappearance — but I simply set off to explore the various Kingdoms and Empires. And that has been my life ever since. Each generation, I return to Cello and reinvent myself, always settling in the Magical North, and befriending the royal family. I am so fond of royals. And I am fond of my new self. You see, once Tobin was gone, I could *transform* myself into him. Rather than an awkward recluse, I could be urbane, affable, and sociable. As a tribute to him and our partnership, I call myself T. I. Candle."

"*T* for Tobin," Madeleine guessed. "And *I* for Isaac."

"Precisely. Tobin and I were reflections of each other. The Candle is for light, of course. Mirror and light. And that," Newton concluded, looking around the room at their faces, "is my story." He swiveled toward the fireplace, which crackled with high flames. "You've done quite a good job there," he remarked. "A fine and blazing fire."

"Well, you haven't," Princess Ko asserted. "You haven't said a word about the Circle."

"I haven't?" Newton settled himself back into the chair. "Imagine that."

5.

"The Circle," he began affably, "has lodges in every province; an elaborate system of signs, grips, and tokens; influence in every major institution and media outlet; and an ingenious means of communication. That is to say, a new edition of the Guidebook is printed every year, and distributed throughout Kingdoms and Empires, and only Circle members know how to see the code behind its print. At least, only Circle members *could* see it, until this very night, when this young person revealed her talent!" Newton turned a fierce, admiring gaze onto Keira.

"Get to the point," Keira snapped. "What does the Circle do?"

Newton bit the edge of his thumbnail. "Let us take a few steps back," he suggested. "Not long after I settled in Cello, I was approached by a group of Worldians. They'd been here in Cello for centuries, which made them quite smug. They called themselves the Shining Ones. You see, not *all* Worldians lived forever here at that time.

Others would *seem* to have the hang of eternal youth and then, boom! They would age and die. Nobody knew why. So, as well as being smug, this group were uneasy. At any moment, they feared, that could happen to them too. They wanted me to solve the conundrum." He paused, closed his eyes as if to relish a memory, then opened them again. "In the end, it was perfectly simple. It's a question of balance, you see. For each Cellian who goes to the World and remains, one Worldian gains a lifetime — a segment, if you will — of immortality. The inconsistency resulted from ad hoc movement back and forth, you see. It was all the open cracks. The solution was simple. *Keep the cracks sealed*. The plague was a wonderful opportunity. All we had to do was maintain the fury of the other Kingdoms and Empires and let them do the work of ensuring that the WSU would *itself* be immortal. Irrevocable. All-powerful. Next, I constructed a device which could open and close cracks."

"You what?" said Elliot.

"He's pretty smart." Madeleine watched Newton's face, not looking at Elliot. "I told you that. At the parking meter. He built a small reflective telescope once. If he has a problem, he invents something to solve it."

"Quite. So. I constructed this device and this circle of new friends — we began to call ourselves *the Circle* at this time — began to use it to take Cellians to the World. It grew into a system. Cellians are taken to the World at regular intervals, and deposited, thus maintaining the Circle's immortality."

"I don't get it," Keira said.

"It's simple," Newton insisted. "It's a question of balance. You see —"

"No. I get that part. I don't get how you can just *take* Cellians to the World."

"We take the riffraff, of course — the homeless, the wandering, the criminal underclass — those who only harm Cello, and surely benefit from a new start in life. They suffer memory loss, of course, and I believe there may also be some minor health consequences, but that is a necessary by-product of the system."

"You have got to be joking," Princess Ko said.

"Where is the humor?" Newton asked stiffly.

Madeleine was frowning. "Cellians in the World don't just suffer *minor health consequences*. They eventually get sick and die. My mother was dying of a brain tumor. My brother died of heart failure. Not to mention that losing your own identity is a kind of death in itself."

Newton's face mirrored her frown. "What are you saying, child? Your mother? Your brother?" and Elliot was staring: "Your brother is *dead*? Prince Chyba died?"

"He tried to come home to Cello, but somebody stopped him and then it was too late," Madeleine said, and then she swung back toward Newton. "Don't you recognize us? I'm Princess Jupiter. But I call myself Madeleine now. That's Princess Ko."

There was a long pause. Newton narrowed his eyes, looking from one to the other. "Of *course!*" He leapt to his feet, his dressing gown flying open to reveal his striped pajamas. He pulled it closed and tightened the cord. "Your Highnesses, what an honor to have you in my home! I've met you at royal functions, you know, but you were much younger then, and you both look so different with dark hair. Of course, I've heard all about you finding your way back to Cello from the World. It was amusing to me. After all the work that was put into sending you across!"

Madeleine heard herself sounding like a small child. "But why would you want to send my family to the World?"

"Perhaps you know the theory of royal blood?" Newton sat down again, pulling on his lower lip thoughtfully. "I have read and written on it, and once theorized that the life of a royal Cellian would be worth, say, fifty regular Cellian lives. It seemed to me that we could guarantee several generations of immortality if the royal family was transferred to the World. I shared this theory with key members of the Circle, and they found it enchanting. Not long ago, they learned that some branches of Hostiles had formed an alliance and were endeavoring to open cracks themselves, so as to abduct the royal family and exile them to the World — for political purposes, of course. It struck us that we could work with the Hostiles to test my theory. Not telling them our reasoning, of course — the idea of royal superiority is contrary to everything the Hostiles believe. Ironic. That is to say, we provided them with the crack-opening devices. They used these to send the royals away. Of course, we stipulated that one princess, you, Princess Ko, be left behind."

"Why?" Princess Ko demanded.

"To continue the royal line, of course. If the theory was correct, we'd want more royals produced, to send to the World."

Unexpectedly, Princess Ko giggled. "How did you know I'd have children?"

"Good point. I didn't. But surely that is your plan?"

"No, actually. It's not."

Keira interrupted. "How can you believe that royal blood is superior? No offense to Ko and Madeleine, but they seem like your average people to me. Besides, royals marry *commoners*, so their blood would have gotten diluted over time."

"Intermarriage may *strengthen* royal blood." Newton sounded almost dreamy now. "Perhaps different races add *power* to the recipe."

"I'm not a recipe," Madeleine said.

"I beg to differ. We all are."

The cat slipped into the room. They watched it study each of them in turn. Elliot offered a hand, and the cat curled against him.

"Ah, here is Patricia." Newton pushed himself to a standing position. "A signal for my royal guests and their friends to leave, and for I myself to retire again to bed."

The room seemed to close in for a moment.

"Just a second," Princess Ko said. "Aren't we missing something?"

6.

*I*f you are referring to my seeing you out," Newton smiled, "recall that you let yourselves in. I suggest you do the same in reverse."

"I mean," Ko said, "you just told us all about the Circle. Don't you have to kill us now?"

"Don't trouble yourself," Keira put in, "if it's a bother."

Newton raised his eyebrows. "You are powerless against the Circle," he said. "A handful of young folk? Nothing but drone flies buzzing. For your own safety, I shouldn't mention any of what I have just explained, for if you *do*, they'll swat you with barely a twitch. Indeed, my sources inform me that the Jagged Edge Elite will declare themselves the rulers of Cello tomorrow, five P.M., during the Provincial Council meeting in Tek. It is to be broadcast throughout the Kingdom. The King is to be formally deposed."

"Treason," Keira said, impressed.

"Quite," said Newton, "but the Circle supports the Elite's proposal, so the Elite will succeed. You will cease to be relevant, young princesses and friends. And so, as I said, to bed." He stepped toward his staircase.

"I have a question," Madeleine said.

"No more questions."

"Why do you call it the Circle?"

Newton stopped. "Consider this. You spin a stone on a string. It whirls around your head. It is drawn to the center — that's centripetal force — and also drawn away — centrifugal force. A circle is formed because the two forces hold each other in perfect balance. That is to say, opposites — reflections — form perfection."

The four stood, watching Newton's hand describe a circle in the air.

"I always thought circles were better tangled up, or stretched or squashed," Madeleine said softly. "Twisted to form a figure eight. Curving and flowing like dancers . . . skaters." Her voice drifted.

Elliot watched Madeleine's face as she spoke. Abruptly, he turned to Newton.

"If you invented a machine to open cracks to the World," he said, "why didn't you go and get your friend Prince Tobin? You said you were both trapped. You could've got him."

"Yes. I suppose I could have."

"He was a royal. Did his royal blood give you fifty lifetimes of immortality, or whatever? Is that why you left him there?"

"I didn't have the data at the time, to confirm or disprove my theory."

"What if he wanted to come home?" Madeleine asked softly.

"Well," Newton said, "I have learned since that he lived out his life as me admirably, becoming warden and then master of the mint, serving as president of the Royal Society, being knighted, publishing the thoughts that he and I had once shared on the nature of light and color, of reflection and refraction, the origins of whiteness, prisms, and rainbows! No doubt, he entirely forgot his own identity, his Kingdom, and me. No doubt, he was happy."

"Until he died an agonizing death from kidney stones," Madeleine said.

Newton turned toward the stairs.

"I'll tell you what I think," Elliot said, his voice clear and courteous. "I think this perfect balance idea of yours is a load of trash. Seems to me, you might have been somebody special once — somebody Madeleine admired — somebody who knew how to love the sort of light that your Tobin offered. But then, when he was trapped in the World, you thought you might as well just steal it. You left him in the World so you could take his life. And now that Circle of yours is doing the same. Over and over, stealing people's lives to keep on living."

Newton scratched a spot on the bannister.

"And I'll tell you something else." Elliot's face was grayish-white under the light. "I'm not well acquainted with you, Isaac Newton, but I've read some of your Guidebook. And you know what? I always said you were a tosser."

"And so to bed," Newton said again. Slowly, he walked up the stairs.

PART 15

1.

*B*y the time they returned to the Jongleur Inn, it was past midnight.

Samuel and Sergio were waiting up for them. Camp beds were arranged for everyone, so there was almost no floor visible: You had to climb over beds to get around.

Everyone was drinking cider and talking, except Elliot.

Elliot sat on his camp bed. He leaned against the wall, legs stretched out. He stared at his jeans and their frayed edges, studied the squares of color patterning the quilt. The sound of the river chattering outside blended with the chat around him.

In Elliot's mind, he saw glimpses. A girl skating across a lake, her coat soaring behind her. A woman raising binoculars.

He saw Ming-Sun on a low chair, hands fluttering.

He saw Chime sitting on the kitchen counter, heels thudding, tomato sauce.

He saw himself, long ago, in an empty high-school ground, stamping against cold, waiting for the Girl-in-the-World.

Across the room, somebody asked what a jongleur was. Samuel was prattling an answer, but Elliot could not make the sounds form words. Now the kid was gathering objects — a clock, a balled-up sock, a cider mug — and he was tossing these into the air. "In Olde Quainte, we all must learn to juggle! But I was the best in my class!"

The others were laughing and shouting at him. Sergio whistled. There was a pounding on the wall and a shout: "Enough noise!"

Samuel murmured, "As to a sausage in a windmill."

Elliot found himself smiling. His forehead felt heavy over the smile, but there were Samuel's weird phrases, and Sergio's dance-bouncing, Princess Ko's blazing eyes, and Keira's sardonic eyebrow lift. This was the Royal Youth Alliance, together again, and in its own, strange way it had been good. Even if Madeleine, his Girl-in-the-World — she was sitting cross-legged on the floor, watching the others, silent now, like Elliot — even if she had turned out to be a lie, well, at least the RYA had been real and true, at least —

The ridge across Elliot's chest lit up suddenly. The heat burned his throat. Because the RYA had also been a lie. He kept letting that truth slip, but there it was. There'd been a traitor.

He felt his bed bounce as Sergio landed on it. "I am on my way to the bathroom!"

"Okay," Elliot said, and then, "Wait."

Sergio stopped midstride.

"Do you think someone on the RYA was a traitor?" Elliot asked.

Sergio nodded slowly. "It must have been so." He raised two fingers and stepped these through the air. "Somebody was always a step ahead of us."

"That doesn't . . . bother you?"

"Of course! We were betrayed! You, in particular, were thrown to the wolves."

"Who do you think it was?"

Sergio considered. "I know it was not this person." He pointed to himself. "Neither was it Princess Ko. So?"

They both glanced across at Samuel, now juggling a fountain pen, a cake of soap, a sneaker, then looked back at each other, smiling.

"Perhaps those two security agents?" Sergio ventured.

Elliot shrugged. "Maybe. But I've been told it wasn't them."

"The only other is Keira," said Sergio, lowering his voice. "There is the issue of her mother. It could be that Keira tries to unravel herself from her past, but sometimes gets caught again?"

Elliot nodded slowly. He thought about Mischka Tegan, her hands on the steering wheel, the soft insistence of her voice, the way she wound pieces of her hair around her fingers. He thought how easily he himself had fallen for her spell. Imagine if she were your mother?

"I also think," Sergio went on, "that she has perhaps finally set herself free now. . . ."

Across the room, Keira was speaking animatedly, her eyes bright.

"She does look different. You're right. So, you think we should let her alone? Not call her on it, I mean?"

"You were the person most betrayed," Sergio said. "So that is not for me to say. But my father used to tell me, we forgive our friends their darkness and focus on their light. Assuming the light returns. If it doesn't, well, the friend must want to sleep, so shut the door and leave them to it. He also used to say that we allow our friends to continue on their paths to the bathroom. Well, no, he did not ever say that, but do you mind?"

Elliot half chuckled, or not quite half, more a quarter, and the bed lurched as Sergio sprang from it to the floor.

The bathroom door closed. Elliot sat back again. He closed his eyes. The others continued their loud conversation.

He heard the toilet flushing, the bathroom door opening. He felt the bed shift as Sergio climbed over him again, back to the others. The noise of laughter and talk blurred, becoming static.

He fell asleep.

2.

*H*e woke again.

Nothing had changed.

The room was still bright. The others still babbled. He was still on the camp bed.

But now he was turning. His body was turning. He was rising to his knees, the bed shaking beneath him.

"It's you," he said. "You're the traitor."

Nobody heard him.

His voice sounded a low, escalating roar like a theme park ride setting off up a slope. "It was *you*, Samuel. You're the traitor."

There was a tumble of soft thuds as Samuel's juggling objects fell.

"The Locator Spell," Elliot said. "You dropped it. Why would you have done that if you were the best juggler in your class?"

The room, which had paused, broke into murmurs.

"Ah, but now . . ." Sergio began.

"As to a . . ." Samuel breathed.

"Elliot," Princess Ko said.

"You achieved nothing on the RYA," Elliot continued. "Sure, you

409

got all the archives for us, but you wrote them out so we wouldn't see the vital parts."

"The vital bits were blocked!" Samuel protested.

"Who blocked them? I think it was you. I think you gave them to us figuring we'd never see through it."

"As to a . . ." Samuel repeated.

"You're from one of the most Hostile towns in all of Olde Quaint," Elliot went on. "You pretend to be helpless, and pretend to regret your mistakes, but all the time you're passing information to the Hostiles."

He turned to Princess Ko. "Who was the first royal you guys got across after I was gone?"

"My little brother. Tippett."

"And what did Samuel do when that happened? Did he leave the room? Go warn somebody maybe?"

Sergio frowned. "I think he did leave the room, Elliot. But this was because he was *ill*. The Olde Quaint magic, you see."

"He's making it up. He hasn't got poisoning at all. Nobody suspects him because we think he poisoned himself for the cause, but he's faking it. He must be. He's still alive. After all this time, why is he still alive?"

"Indeed," Samuel said softly, and Madeleine rose up with a face like a snarl.

"He was nervous," she hissed at Elliot. "Samuel dropped the spell and made mistakes because he was nervous. He *told* me he used to be anxious. He's calmer now because he's almost *dead*. Not *everyone* is born smooth and gorgeous like you, Elliot. Not everyone can be the local hero who's never dropped a ball in his life. And not *everyone's* a traitor like you are."

Elliot let her words pound him. It felt good.

He felt himself pounding right back. "*Me*, a traitor? Who are *you*? You pretend to be a girl in the World. You *pretend* to be my friend. Night after night I'm standing in the high school telling you my secrets. I baked you freaking *cookies*, I held on to the *sound of your voice*, I thought you were the *point* to *everything*, and turns out you're just a selfish, spoiled princess and the *opposite* of everything good!"

The thumping on the wall started up again. Madeleine shrieked right through it. "I *trusted* you! I traveled across the *Kingdom* because you told me you'd *save* my family, but you were going to let them *kill* me!"

"You're part of the royal family!" Elliot bawled. "You've betrayed the entire *Kingdom*! Your family is *destroying* this Kingdom! The King is a drunk! Princess Ko is a *tyrant*. And as for you, Princess Jupiter, do you know how much harm you did, *always* running away? People *died* because you wanted to have *fun*."

"It is perhaps a place to stop there," Sergio murmured.

Madeleine wrapped her arms around her head. Her shoulders moved strangely.

Elliot looked down at himself. He was kneeling on the bed. His knuckles were clenched and crimson. He was perfectly still, but everything inside him seemed to be wrenching itself into pieces.

"Neither of you meant to betray the other," Samuel said calmly. "Elliot thought he was saving the Kingdom. He believed the royal family would be sent safely to the World. Madeleine didn't know she was Princess Jupiter." His voice withered into silence, and Madeleine looked up at him.

Samuel's voice resumed. "When Elliot realized what the Hostile plan was, he tried to warn you, Madeleine. He must have known the Grays would be unleashed on him too, but he shouted anyway. That was courage as to a lion in a glass of fresh mint tea."

"There is nothing to suggest," Princess Ko interrupted with unexpected heat, "that a lion would be any *more* or *less* courageous, if placed into a glass of fresh mint tea."

Samuel turned to Elliot. "Have you seen Madeleine's hands? She suffered much to save you both. She has courage also — she is brave as to . . ."

"A lion in mint tea," Sergio prompted.

Samuel sighed. "You both believed in the other," he said, "and you were right to believe. As for me . . ." Samuel's voice grew wry. "Well, I'm afraid I *did* drop that spell on purpose. Elliot's quite right about me."

3.

*E*veryone was ready for a joke, so they took Samuel's declaration with quiet smiles, while they reflected on his wisdom about Elliot and Madeleine.

"My pardon," Samuel said after a moment, "but that was not an effort to be witty."

Madeleine glanced at him. "You're not a Hostile."

"Indeed, and I am not," he agreed, and he bowed his head, pushed back his hair, and turned down the top of his earlobe.

Nobody took any notice. They continued roaming their own thoughts.

Samuel straightened, exasperated. "Can nobody *see* what I am showing you?" He pressed down his earlobe once more.

A tiny circle was etched onto Samuel's ear.

"Huh," Elliot said politely. "You have a . . . wait. You are *not* suggesting you're part of the Circle!"

"Indeed, and I am. Why do you think I did not come along to see Sir Isaac Newton? Long and I have known him. He'd have greeted me as an old friend."

Half smiles froze around the room. Uneasy glances darted.

"I was born in Durham, England, in 1496," Samuel pronounced. "A fine year to be born, other than the Black Death and so forth."

The uneasy quiet was transforming itself into a stunned silence.

"Shall I tell my tale?" Samuel inquired. "Very well. I grew up cheerful but awkward, and there were those who liked to taunt me. I lost my parents to a drowning accident when I was eleven. Not long after this tragedy, there came a day when three bigger boys chased me through the market. They threatened to toss me in the river, weighed with stones, to join my parents. The loss of my parents was still big in my heart, fear of these boys was like gunpowder . . ." Samuel smiled. "Madeleine dreamed these events, you know. Anyway, such absence and emotion can prompt a stumble to the Kingdom of Cello, and this, they did. I found myself in an office tower in Jagged Edge. Leonardo da Vinci was there. He befriended me. He introduced me to the Shining Ones — as they then were — and I joined them. I did not age beyond twelve. Leonardo, incidentally, was opposed to immortality and returned often to the World to avoid it. Ironic, as he now has a strong dose of immortality himself — in the more theoretical sense of the word."

Nobody spoke.

Samuel propped a pillow behind him. "I remember going to the Lake of Spells with you all, and being so afeared the magic would exclude me! The jig would be up! One must be under sixteen to enter, recall? However, in my heart, I suppose I am still twelve."

Elliot frowned. "Just to be clear," he said. "This is all a yarn you're spinning?"

"A what I'm whatting?"

"You're making this up. The way people tell ghost stories at summer camp. To be funny. Only you're still working toward your punch line."

"I am many things," Samuel said patiently. "But as to a butterfly wrapped in sticky destiny, I am *rarely* funny! Call yourself my deepest apologies, Elliot — Ko, Keira, Sergio — but I was the traitor in the RYA. You see, I have lived long in Cello, under the care of the Circle. Not long after my arrival, I settled in Olde Quaint and learned the language. I drifted between villages, always the newcomer. The Circle is my only true family. Now and then, they ask me to perform a favor for them, and the latest was to join the Royal Youth Alliance — using my World knowledge — and ensure that the royal family would never be rescued."

The room was perfectly still.

"I cannot believe you," Sergio whispered.

"Indeed, and I can scarcely believe it myself," Samuel sighed. "In my defense, I believed nobody would be harmed. I thought the royals safe in the World. True, I tried to undermine your every effort, Princess Ko, every moment of every day, at the same time as *appearing* to help. I dropped the Locator Spell. I suggested we enter the word *Cello* into the spell, hoping we'd only snare cello players. And so forth. And yes, I transcribed the accounts so you'd miss the vital parts, and when Ko demanded the originals, I reinforced the black-outs, little knowing you would use a *spell* to remove them. And yes . . ." Samuel paused. He reached for his cider mug, found it empty, ran a thumb around its edge, and turned to Elliot. "Yes, when you told us you had solved the cracks, I got word to my friends at the Circle at once."

A pale sadness washed across Elliot's face.

"They promised me you would not be hurt," Samuel whispered. He spoke slowly. "But it is clear that they contacted the WSU, assuming that this would take you out of the equation, and stop the royals from being rescued. And thus, you, Elliot, were placed in great danger. Call yourself my deepest regret." Now he roused himself. "Most recently, I kept the Circle informed from Bonfire while we were there, again believing — as I had been assured — they would only have the royals sent back to the World. Not hurt them." He turned to Madeleine. "It seems the Hostiles had their own plan, Madeleine, and I owe you my apologies as to a pumpkin —"

"You might want to skip that bit," Keira suggested.

"It reinforces the apology!"

"No, it sort of undercuts it."

Samuel considered. "Perhaps you are right. I will not last this night, I fear, but I wish to tell you, Princess Ko, that you have always had my heart. Thus, my heart broke each time that I betrayed you. Perhaps it will help, a little, knowing that?"

"Not in the least," Ko said promptly.

Sergio looked from Samuel to Ko and back again. "Still," he said. "Ko has always been drawn to bad boys (and bad girls), and in a beautiful twist, Samuel now turns out to be far more wicked than the wild and wicked stallions of Innismore Plains!"

"Thank you," Samuel said, closing his eyes onto a smile. "I've always been so very *good*, you see."

4.

"I have a question," Keira said.

Samuel opened his eyes and gave a single, slow nod.

"Look, you might've been around for centuries, but you're also just some kid who's been selling us out, so maybe quit with that wise guru nodding thing."

"Very well, but where is your question?" Samuel said. "I will not last the night."

"So you said. But if you're immortal, you'll last *all* the nights. And I *thought* you were sick because you used the OQ magic to help us. If you were actually working against us, why would you have used the OQ magic? Or anyway, why are you sick?"

Samuel raised himself a little higher. "I will not last the night," he began.

"Oh, he's a broken record," Princess Ko complained.

Madeleine squinted at Samuel. "I can see more black patches, so you are getting bad again. But I'll just unknot them and you'll last the night."

"You would do that? Despite my treachery? Your kindness! It is as to a termite in a pot of cold spaghetti!"

"No, it's not," Ko said firmly. "The two are unrelated."

Samuel propped himself higher. "Despite Madeleine's kindness — and setting aside its relationship to termites which, Ko, I believe you have not altogether — anyhow, despite all that, I do not believe I will last the . . . I see you have all tired of this phrase. Call yourselves this. There are things I wish to say. Will you hear me?"

"It depends how loud you speak," Sergio declared.

"And whether there's any ambient noise," Keira reflected.

"Quite," Samuel agreed vaguely. "At any rate, yes, I may be technically immortal, but OQ magic is the one thing that trumps that. And yes, I did use OQ magic — with no success — for that, I hoped to find some potion that might save both the Circle *and* the royal family."

"So you're not a total badass," Keira pointed out. "What is that *sound*?"

It was a soft trill: the telephone that stood on the table by Samuel's bed. "Complaints about the noise," he guessed, reaching to answer it.

A moment later, he replaced the receiver. "Not complaints," he said, mildly surprised. "It seems there is a gentleman downstairs, who wishes to see Madeleine and Elliot."

"What gentleman?" Ko asked.

Samuel opened his palms in a shrug.

Madeleine and Elliot looked at Samuel. They looked from him to the telephone, to the door, and then to the others in the room.

"Eventually, you'll have to look at each other," Keira said.

But they only glanced at each other's shadows as they walked down the stairs to the lobby.

5.

Wooden skis had been affixed to the wall, crossed to form a large X. A vending machine glowed. A man in a hooded parka sat in an armchair, sipping from a thermos. As they approached, he stood, drawing back the hood to reveal white locks. It was Isaac Newton.

"Ah, good, you are here," he said, turning his back on them at once, so that his parka rustled noisily. He moved into the wine bar that adjoined the lobby. It was empty, the bar itself in almost-total darkness, but Newton set his thermos on a tall table anyway. He pulled out one, two, three bar stools, and gestured for Madeleine and Elliot to sit.

Their eyes swerved to catch one another as they did.

"I asked after you at the husky sled stop," Newton explained, "and was directed here."

"Okay," Elliot said after a beat.

Newton drew a crushed sheet of paper from his parka pocket and pushed it across the table. They peered down, trying to read in the dim light.

"It's the page from my Guidebook," Newton said impatiently, pulling it back. "The one your friend Keira handed over? After you left, I was looking at it, contemplating the girl's remarkable vision, and then the printed words themselves leapt out at me. Here. I'll read them to you." In sweeping tones, he read: "*Gold: Many claim this Color does not exist, and I myself have undertaken futile expeditions —*" He glanced up, frowning. "Yes, yes, I'll skip that bit. Here we are: *Legend says that the Gold, unlike all other Colors, can be made. One requires only a magic weaver, a truth seer, and the Philosopher's Stone. Legend further holds that, once made, Gold is the Elixir that can cure an ailing Kingdom.*" He stopped reading and rolled the paper up with a triumphant flourish.

"But that's just a story, isn't it?" Elliot said. "There's no such thing as Gold."

"Quite." Newton rested his elbows on the table, affable. "I quite agree. And yet perhaps not? Recall that I mentioned a great quarrel between Tobin and myself, just before the cracks were sealed? It was over this very question. You see, Tobin had found an ancient scroll containing the words I just read. He wanted us to try it. He thought he could be the magic weaver, and I could be the truth seer. I thought it was nonsense, the idea of making gold — creating an elixir."

"No, you didn't," Madeleine said. "You studied alchemy all your life."

Newton gave a breath of laughter. "Both Tobin and I studied alchemy obsessively. We joined alchemical societies. We were fascinated by it. But for different reasons. Tobin believed in its magic; I wanted to comprehend the science behind it. When Tobin found these words on the ancient scroll, he took them at face value." Newton uncurled the paper. "I believed they were mere codes: signifying a formula, a set of elements. We fought. We separated. The cracks were closed." He unscrewed the lid of his thermos and raised it to his mouth, eyes darting around the room. "Reading this today, it occurred to me that the Kingdom is certainly ailing. Colors out of control, crops failing, the Hostiles, the Loyalists, the Jagged Edge Elite, all at one another's throats, the Circle — my Circle — tightening its stronghold around all. What if a Gold *could* save us? What if Tobin was right about this? A magic weaver and a truth seer would be required and, I understand, Madeleine, that you're a magic weaver?"

"I think so."

"She is," Elliot confirmed.

"And you." Newton turned to Elliot, his eyes bright. "You are a truth seer."

Elliot raised an eyebrow. "First I've heard of it."

"You don't know it yet? That can happen. A truth seer may have to grow into his vision. But I believe it is what you are, Elliot. I saw it suddenly — being something of a truth seer myself — once you had gone. Come. Think. Have you not noticed a tendency to see through nonsense to the truth? Or for truth to leap at you fully formed?"

Elliot shook his head firmly. His eyes slid toward Madeleine. "I just told Samuel he was a traitor who was faking OQ poisoning. I know nothing."

"But Samuel *was* the traitor," Madeleine argued. "You were right about that."

"Ah." Elliot was dismissive.

Madeleine was studying Elliot in profile, thinking fast. "When your dad went missing," she said slowly, "you knew he hadn't just run off with the teacher, like everybody thought. You saw *that* truth."

"I thought he'd been taken by a Purple," Elliot objected. "I didn't see that he'd gone to the World!"

"Well, now, truth seers can't see *all* the truth," Newton interjected. "Nobody can, not all at once. It would kill you, or anyway blind you. Truth seers catch sight of *pieces* of truth."

"So does everyone," Elliot said.

"On your last day in the World . . ." Madeleine was thinking aloud. "My nose was bleeding and you told me something serious was going on there. You were right about that too. Although, maybe" — she smiled quickly — "you were just flirting with me."

Elliot's eyes flew toward her and away. "Not sure I'd flirt about a nosebleed," he said, smiling faintly, and in that moment, she caught something, the spark of him, the Elliot of him. It was gone again now: He was back under his shadow.

"Anyway," Elliot said. "I don't remember my time in the World."

Newton was standing, zipping up his parka. "Perhaps I'm wrong," he said. "But you saw the truth about me, Elliot. The words you spoke tonight? About me and about my Tobin? You saw through to my essence." He tightened the lid of the thermos, shuddering slightly. "I did not enjoy it in the slightest."

After a pause, Newton spoke again, rapidly now, his eyes on the table. "Not the whole truth, of course. What you didn't know — what you could not have known — was that after the cracks were sealed — when I believed I had lost Tobin forever — I tried to make Gold on my own. The idea possessed me that *this* was how I could find my way back to Tobin. Of course, it was foolish. There was only *me*. I was lost, broken, desperate, stupid. I fractured my arm. The story of how that happened is not an amusing one at all. My heart, my soul, the very essence of me was fractured by my loss, and I don't believe I ever healed right. Once I had calmed down enough, I created a crack-opening machine, but by then it was too late. I had hardened myself against Tobin and love. I had met the other immortals. I had new, ruthless, selfish goals. And, as you pointed out, Elliot: I wanted to steal Tobin's light."

He looked up, bowed slightly, pulled his hood over his head, and walked toward the doors of the Inn. These slid open. Newton paused and stepped back, watching the doors falter and close again.

He turned and hurried back to them.

"Almost forgot," he said. "You need a magic weaver, a truth seer, and the *Philosopher's Stone*, don't you?"

"That's what it says," Madeleine agreed.

"Do you know the original name for the Undisclosed Province? Its real name?"

They both shook their heads.

"It was Philosopher's Stone," Newton said. "That could be relevant."

"Could be," Elliot agreed.

Newton turned again, and this time he headed directly into the night.

6.

$\mathcal{B}$ ack in the room, the others were waiting expectantly.

"It was Isaac Newton," Elliot told them.

"Isaac Newton," Samuel repeated musingly. He was lying on his bed now, staring at the ceiling. He shuffled himself into a sitting position. "As to a wicker outdoor dining set in winter, I believe that Isaac Newton is *wrong*."

"No kidding," Keira said.

"He is wrong to help the Circle take Cellians to the World, yes, I see that now. But I believe there is a greater wrong at the heart of his philosophy. He sees Cello as magic and the World as reality, and he believes that the two should be kept separate. However, it has become clear to me that we need both. Magic and reality are reflections, shadows of each other. By sealing the cracks — by running a line between Cello and the World — we stop them interweaving. Thus, there is nowhere for sadness to go."

Madeleine blinked at him. "Sadness doesn't *go* anywhere. It just is."

"I beg to differ. I believe our two dimensions were once aligned so that sadness could move between dimensions, always transforming into beauty. Here is my theory: Despair from the *World* should flow to Cello, transmuted into the Cello Wind. *Cello's* melancholy, meanwhile, becomes color and light in the World. Tell me, how often do we hear the Cello Wind these days?"

"Almost never," Sergio said.

"Exactly. And is there color and light in the World?"

"Sure," Madeleine said. "When I was there, I saw both."

"Your eyes adjusted," Samuel said placidly. "When you *first* arrived, did it seem colorless?"

"I guess. Yeah."

"No doubt, older Worldians reminisce about brighter days, when apples shone a brilliant red or green. Each generation, the Wind gets quieter here, the colors grow duller in the World. And *meanwhile!*"

This last word he punched, startling the room.

"*Meanwhile*, the sadness remains trapped. It loops back on itself. In Cello, Colors have accumulated to breaking point. The World, and Cello both, are heavy with captive sorrow." Samuel's voice grew distant. "Consider screams of pain and grief, the anguish of unanswered pleas. Those who sit alone and whisper, *Help me*. Those who stand on street corners, shouting those same words, while crowds pass by, unheeding. Those who breathe, *I love you*, into window mist, addressing one who does not hear, or does not care, or does not even exist. Tears that fall unseen in cars with windows closed. Dreams that ache. Letters unread, messages unanswered. Tell me, have you never been alone, howling in your bed at darkest night, and thought: *This agony? What can it be for?*"

The room was quiet.

"The agony is meant to be translated. It is meant to travel to another dimension — to Cello or the World — where it becomes beauty and right. Energy never disappears, you know. It changes form. That's basic physics."

Samuel touched his face. Lumps seemed to grow beneath his fingertips. A purple vein snaked from his right temple to his chin.

Madeleine moved close to his bed. "I'll start untangling for you."

"Leave it. It will not change my path. But call yourselves my pardon, I have interrupted your tale. What did Isaac Newton want with you?"

"He wanted us to make Gold," Elliot said, and he and Madeleine explained.

"If it is so," Samuel said eventually, his voice rasping now. "If you are magic weaver and truth seer. If you can go to the Undisclosed Province and make Gold. If the Gold can indeed heal our ailing Kingdom — then the way it should do that is by opening the cracks." His voice fell to a whisper. "Once the cracks are open, we will have it again, the constant, seamless flow. The Wind will blow here again. The Colors will flow out."

He fell back against the pillow, eyes closing. Madeleine's hands began to twist the air around him.

The others watched her in silence. Eventually, one by one, they curled up and fell asleep.

Elliot stayed awake the longest. The ridge in his chest was a chasm now. Cold air blew right through him. When he did sleep, he woke often, and each time, he saw Madeleine, a dark silhouette, hands twirling, flinching, pausing, and then starting up again.

Once, Elliot woke from a dream in which he was a kid taking a bubble bath. He realized that the sound he'd been hearing was not crackling bubbles, but Samuel's breath. Another time, he thought termites were quietly chewing the frame of his bed and again he realized it was Samuel making those small, strange, scritching sounds.

In the morning when Elliot woke, Madeleine was sitting perfectly still on the edge of Samuel's bed, and Samuel had stopped breathing altogether.

$\mathcal{I}$n the breakfast room of the Jongleur Inn, there was the urgent roar of the river outside, the quiet clanging of cutlery, and whispers about the boy who had died in the night.

"That's his friends at that table over there," somebody hissed.

"Not saying much, are they?"

"I heard it was the worst case of Olde Quainte poisoning the doctor had ever seen."

"In shock, I expect. Or possibly just not feeling chatty?"

An ambulance had taken Samuel's body away. The doctor had raised mocking eyebrows toward Madeleine: "You tried to save him with magic weaving! *That* was never going to work!" Then her gaze had fallen on Madeleine's blistered hands, and she'd reached for a salve and bandages, saying firmly, "But you'll certainly have eased his final suffering."

Now Madeleine was looking at her white bandaged hands and at the mushrooms, tomatoes, and scrambled eggs on her plate. These kept disappearing into blackness, then reappearing in all their gaudy colors. It was fascinating. She couldn't figure it out, and then she could. It was her eyelids: They kept closing, wanting sleep.

"It seems *ridiculous*," Keira said suddenly, "that someone who talked as much as Samuel did could be dead."

"It is always so," Sergio agreed, "when the people with much character die. That is when death is at its most impossible."

Princess Ko's eyes were red. "We'll have a memorial service for him tomorrow," she announced. "Meanwhile, today we save the Kingdom."

The others turned blank faces on her.

"Recall that the Jagged Edge Elite will declare themselves the rulers of Cello today?"

"They do that," Elliot said, "and the Hostiles will attack. They'll use their Color weapons."

"And if the Hostiles attack," Ko continued, "the Loyalists will rise up against them."

"Civil war," Keira said.

Ko nodded. "We must prevent this. After breakfast, Sergio will kindly fly Keira and myself back to Bonfire, where we will collect my father, the King, and proceed to Jagged Edge to reclaim power. Meanwhile, Madeleine and Elliot will do as Isaac Newton suggested and go and make Gold."

Madeleine had just taken a drowsy sip of orange juice. It spluttered everywhere.

"By five P.M.," Ko remembered. "Try to make Gold by five P.M."

Madeleine, awake now, said, "This is where Samuel would say, *as to a turkey in black tie*, meaning, *what* the . . . ? No offense, Ko, but you'll *reclaim power* and Elliot and I will *make Gold*?"

Ko jiggled her shoulders as if Madeleine was being frivolous. "Didn't Isaac Newton tell you Gold making was possible?"

"Only with a truth seer," Elliot said. "And I don't believe that I'm one for a second. I nearly got Madeleine killed yesterday because I didn't see what Mischka was up to. That's a pretty significant truth I missed right there."

"Well, my mother excels at concealing truth," Keira told him. "Best truth seers in the Kingdom have been bamboozled by her. You not seeing what she was up to isn't relevant."

Princess Ko spoke in such abruptly ringing tones that people at nearby tables turned. "Elliot, you *saw* that our Kingdom needed saving!"

"Not relevant either," Keira put in. "A blind armadillo could've seen that."

Ko ignored her. "You *saw* that the royal family is deeply flawed. You were right! What was it you said about me? That I am a tyrant? Certainly, *there* is a truth."

"Well, again —" Keira began, but the Princess threw her napkin at Keira's face, which surprised her into silence.

"Elliot was *right* that the Kingdom would be better off without me," Ko continued. "I let *all* of you risk your lives. Now Samuel is dead. I risked Keira's eyesight. I caused Sergio *agony*, forcing him to learn how to fly at will."

There was a long pause.

"You could put a positive spin on that," Keira said thoughtfully, "and say that in a lot of ways, you're just a kick-ass personal trainer."

Sergio cleared his throat. "I want to say this, as Ko is my best friend, and it is this. She is ruthless, yes, but she does what she thinks right to save her Kingdom and her family. Keep in mind, also, that she was raised by a PR department. *Princesses have blond hair*, they used to say, *princesses have fair skin*. They made her dye her hair and wear makeup. She could never be herself. *Princesses follow the rules. Princesses never cry*, they said, and so she became *angry* whenever she felt hurt."

"Or maybe I've just got a bad temper," Ko reflected. "But thanks, Sergio. That was nice of you. I always secretly wished I'd been more like Jupiter — Madeleine, I mean — though. She threw the makeup away and she dyed her hair every color except blond. She got in so much trouble."

"This, to me, also was beautiful," Sergio said. "And Elliot, it is true that Princess Jupiter ran away often, and there was a terrible incident when royal guards pursued her into the Swamp of the Golden Coast and were killed. But she did not mean to put their lives at risk. And can you blame her for running? She ran from an alcoholic father, and the myth of royal blood. She knew something was wrong, but she didn't know how to fix it, so she ran, they brought her back, she ran again."

Elliot's face had rumpled. His head tipped slowly forward, and he placed his elbows on the table and held his fingers to his forehead, propping himself up.

"You know what," Keira said. "You seem different, Elliot. It's like you're seeing truth, sure, but only the bad truths. When I knew you on the RYA, I remember I felt like you saw all of me — good *and* bad — in a way nobody else ever had. So it makes sense to me that you're a truth seer. But now, like I said, something's wrong."

Elliot spoke to the surface of the table so nobody could hear him. "There's a tear right across my chest," he whispered.

"And another thing," Keira said. "You've got these tiny specks of Color on the surface of your skin. What's *that* about?"

Elliot straightened and spoke in his regular voice. "I've got what?"

"I guess nobody else can see those 'cause they're so small, but it's like you're sweating Color. It's on your face and your neck."

Everybody stared at Elliot's face, trying to see specks of Color.

"He looks color*less* to me," Princess Ko said. "Paler than white."

"Right there?" Keira pressed a fingernail into Elliot's cheek.

"Nothing."

Madeleine turned to Keira. "Is it one Color or a mix?"

"A mix."

"Then maybe it's one of those lethal Color combinations? I remember seeing a documentary about them years ago. If you're exposed to certain combinations, they get into your system and — I don't know — mess with your psyche. Have you been out in a Color storm lately, Elliot?"

"Just the Gray attack."

Sergio was bouncing on his chair. "Gray, Vermillion, and Green," he said. "That is one of the lethal combinations. I also saw this documentary. Have you been exposed to Vermillion and Green, Elliot?"

"Not Green. But I've done a lot of Vermillion candy lately."

"Ah!" Sergio smiled. "The Vermillion candy, it is good, no? We used to enjoy it in the stables long ago, Ko and I. Remember, Ko? But you are sure there was no Green?"

"Nope. I'd know if I . . ." Elliot stopped. "Well, it's a while back now but they put me under when they took me into the Hostile compound. They said I was injected with seventh-level Green."

"Beautiful!" Sergio exclaimed at the same time as Ko said, "Wait, did you say this is a *lethal* combination?" and Elliot breathed, "You think I feel like this on account of *Colors*?"

"I remember now," Madeleine said. "That combination brings out the worst of you — like, the emotions of your darkest memories sort of come to the forefront."

"They just call them 'lethal' combinations to be theatrical," Sergio reassured the others. "It won't kill him. He'll just be feeling like a horse that has been taken from a stable of his friends and placed on a prairie in a blizzard alone, knee-deep in snow without his horse blanket, a thousand packs of wolves bearing down on him. Is that how you feel, Elliot?"

"Can I cure this combination?" Elliot demanded. "Did your documentary say?"

Sergio and Madeleine squinted into their memories.

"I think it'll just work its way out of your system," Madeleine said slowly.

"Some people," remembered Sergio, "hurried the process with cold baths."

Elliot swiveled in his seat so that he was looking hard at the row of windows at the back of the room.

"Don't even *think* about it," Ko commanded. "That'll be *ice* cold; that *will* kill you."

But Elliot had pushed back his chair, and was striding, then jogging, then sprinting from the room.

"He won't do it," Keira said. "Do what?" said Sergio, and then from outside came a crash of water, a loud shout, and a series of curse words from the farthest reaches of the Kingdoms and Empires. These were hollered so loud that the breakfast room fell into startled silence.

A few moments later, Elliot was standing in the doorway again. A waiter, seeing him, rushed away, returning with armloads of towels. He began to drape these around Elliot.

Water streamed from Elliot's hair and clothes. He was shivering like someone with a fever. His face was translucent white, his lips a vibrant purple. But his eyes were so bright, and his expression so astonished, that the room burst into laughing applause.

PART 16

1.

$\mathcal{T}$he clock on the wall outside the ticket office said twelve noon.

"And we have until five o'clock?" Elliot asked.

Madeleine nodded.

They were sitting on a bench on a railway station platform, just inside the border of the Undisclosed Province. The light was dim, poised in shadow.

"It's always twilight here," Madeleine remembered. "Even in the middle of the day."

BASALT STATION said an illuminated sign on the wall. Otherwise, the platform was a collection of hazy shapes.

"So we're *at* Philosopher's Stone," Madeleine recited. "We've got a magic weaver and a truth seer" — Elliot made a small sound of objection, but let it go — "and now we just have to make Gold."

Elliot smiled — she saw his smile glinting in his eyes.

"Gold comes from the stars," she said.

"It does?"

They both looked up at the tiny darts of starlight in the dusky blue.

"I read that in a book once," Madeleine explained. "My mother used to practice trivia when we were in the World. She had this memory of having won a quiz show once? Which I guess was translated from a real memory of a charity trivia night. Anyway, one of her practice questions was: *Where does gold come from?*"

"And it comes from the stars?"

"Kind of. It comes from neutron stars colliding, I think. Or supernovas exploding."

Elliot studied the sky. "Easy, then. We just head on up."

Madeleine laughed. "It might be more convenient to find some in the ground."

"Easy again," Elliot said promptly. "Find a gold mine."

They both smiled.

After a moment, Elliot said, "Isn't the idea that we *make* gold?"

"You're right. I got offtrack. I blame you."

"Fair enough."

Madeleine drew her knees up onto the bench and concentrated. "Okay, this is what I know about making gold," she said. "Princesses weave it from straw, or bake it from flax."

"I'm quite a good baker," Elliot said.

"You are. You gave me cinnamon cookies once."

There was a silence. Elliot scuffed the heels of his boots on the platform.

"So I did," he said eventually.

I baked you freaking cookies, he'd screamed the night before.

"Alchemists used to try to make gold," Madeleine said to cut through that memory.

"They ever succeed?"

"No. Well, I don't think so. See, they thought they could turn base metals into gold using chemistry, but chemistry won't change the number of protons in an atom. You need physics for that. You need a particle accelerator and a lot of energy. Then you get your base metal, and you smash atoms around until you tear some protons off, and if you're lucky, you get gold."

"Huh."

They both gazed around the platform. Now that their eyes were adjusting to the light, they could see that some of the shapes were people: bags on shoulders, hands in pockets, watching the rails, lost in thought.

"You know what I just remembered," Madeleine said. "We're meant to be making Gold, the *Color*, not the metal."

"You're right."

She thought for a while. "Color comes from light."

"So we're back to the stars?"

They looked at the sky again.

"Stars are where *everything* came from, originally." Madeleine studied the sparks of light, then lowered her eyes and looked at Elliot again. "And alchemists thought they could make gold if they could just get some original matter. Like the substance that everything comes from. They thought, if we take that substance apart, we get back to the essence of everything, then we can piece it together to make whatever we want. I think you have to go to the ether to get it."

"What's the ether?"

"It's kind of everywhere and nowhere. It's all the light and dark. It's finely spun chaos. It's outside of everything, but also inside."

Elliot scratched his neck. He looked at Madeleine. "That kind of sounds like the space between," he said.

She looked back at him. His eyes seemed like a city nightscape. All the gleam and light of them.

"So how do we get back to the space between?" Elliot said eventually.

Madeleine let her eyes fall from his. She saw that her shoelace was coming loose. "Remember how Samuel said that the Cello Wind is translated sadness from the World? If that's true, if he's right about that, then the Wind must come through the space between."

"So if we go to the place where the Wind is mined," Elliot reasoned, "maybe we find a way to the space between?"

"The Wind is mined right here in this province." Madeleine tied her lace and stood. "Let's find out exactly where."

"We make a great team," Elliot said, also standing. "You do all the figuring, and I relax and listen."

"Well. You asked questions. The right questions."

2.

$\mathcal{I}$nside the ticket office, train destinations were listed on a swinging board. A woman sat behind a counter. She was examining a pale green pear.

"Can you tell us where the Cello Wind is mined?" Elliot said to her.

The woman set the pear onto the counter. Her eyes flickered, and she blinked three times.

There was a pause.

"We were wondering," Madeleine tried, "if you can tell us where the Cello Wind is mined?"

Now the woman frowned. Again her eyes flickered and there was another series of three blinks: This time each slow and emphatic.

"In the Undisclosed Province," Elliot recalled, looking at the woman's face. "People speak with their eyes." The woman looked right back at him, then inclined her head in what might have been a sideways nod. Her arm reached up at the same moment so she could massage her neck.

Elliot studied her a moment more.

"Can you tell us one more time," he said, "where the Cello Wind is mined?"

The flicker, and three blinks.

Elliot looked at the board of station names. He looked back at the woman.

"Cobalt?" he said. She gazed at him.

Elliot paused. "Two tickets to Cobalt," he said.

On the train, Madeleine said, "How did you do that?"

"Her eyes kind of flew toward the station board," Elliot explained. "Then she blinked three times, so I counted three from the top and that was Cobalt."

"Are you saying it was just a *guess*?"

"Sure. But then, the way she looked at me when I said Cobalt, I knew I had it right."

Madeleine breathed in deeply, and then shrugged. "You're the truth seer."

Elliot turned his head away.

The carriage was half full. Other passengers sat in silent pairs or groups. Eyes were darting, blinking, widening, staring, and sparking.

"They're all talking," Madeleine realized. "It's like some kind of elaborate code."

The train ran smooth and quiet, with occasional jolts or bumps. Outside, the landscape was like the outskirts of any town: warehouses and factories, hulking silhouettes against the deep blue sky. Junk-yards and overgrown vacant blocks. Then a slide into a flatness of fields.

"I think it's more than just a code," Elliot said, watching the other passengers. "I think they let their thoughts reflect in their eyes, and other people read the thoughts there."

"I don't know." Madeleine was skeptical. "They might *think* they're reading each other's thoughts but actually they could be just invent-ing them. Kind of projecting their own thoughts into the other people's eyes?"

"Could be." Elliot shrugged. "But I feel like people are always speaking with their eyes, their bodies, their hands, gestures, intona-tion, *and* their words — only mostly all we hear are the words. And the words get in the way. So if we just spoke with our eyes we might get closer to the truth."

Madeleine thought about it. "I guess."

Elliot focused on her.

"I want to say how sorry I am, for betraying you. And nearly get-ting you killed."

Madeleine half laughed. "These things happen," she said.

She looked down at her hands, held them up before her, spreading out the fingers. She looked at the spaces between her fingers.

"Well, it hurt a lot," she said. "Because I trusted you completely. And it hurt how angry you seemed with me *after* it had happened. Which, when I'd just saved your life, didn't seem all that . . . polite."

Elliot watched Madeleine's outstretched hands. "It wasn't. You're right. I can't tell you how grateful I am to you for saving me from those Colors. You're my hero. You're a goddess. I see that *now*, but after it happened, all I could see — all I could see was . . ."

He turned to the window. The landscape that had stretched into flatness was beginning to rise again. It was experimenting with bumps and slopes and then, as it gained confidence, soaring into strange and formidable shapes.

"What are those?" Elliot said. "Limestone pinnacles? And what are those arches? Sandstone, you think? I guess I remember learning that about the Undisclosed Province: that it's got a lot of canyons and gorges. Forests made of stone. Mostly red."

"All you could see . . ." Madeleine prompted.

"Well, it's like this." He turned back from the window. "I thought you'd stolen Madeleine from me. Madeleine was everything, the point of it all, and it seemed like Princess Jupiter had killed her. That's all I could see. That's why I was mad."

Madeleine snapped her hands closed. "No. Princess Jupiter. She's me."

"I know that now. I'm sorry."

"And I'm also Madeleine."

They looked at each other steadily.

"You know what I just realized?" Madeleine said. "This is the first time we've really met each other. When I was in the World, I wasn't myself. And when you were in the World, you weren't yourself. And yesterday, when I saw you on the lake . . ."

"It wasn't me either. But I feel like myself again now. For the first time in a long time."

"Well. It's good to meet you, Elliot Baranski."

He smiled. His eyes fell back to her hands.

"Do you remember," he said, "when we held hands in the night?"

Madeleine was silent. The train swayed and bumped and rushed along. Their bodies swung close, without touching, and then away again.

Elliot's voice was low. "You said something like, *Let's just believe in each other and close our eyes*, and I thought you were crazy, but I did it anyway, and next thing, we were reaching between worlds, and I was holding your hand. To me, it was like I met you right then, like we said everything there was to say. Like all of you was there in the feel of your palms, and the way your fingers wound around mine."

The window rattled. Outside, the landscape had flattened and emptied again, so mostly what they saw now was a great, big star-studded curve of blue sky, pieces of night blending with day.

3.

It was 4:35 P.M. when they reached the town of Cobalt.

From the station, they could see the silhouettes of wind turbines lining the crests of distant hills. They walked a path to the town's main street. It had an unassuming feel. Shops, cafés, a bank on the corner, everything low and still. Some shops were dark, others boarded up. A car passed them, driving slowly. They watched as it stopped at a crosswalk. A man stepped in front of the car, dropping a cigarette to the road, and reaching a foot back to stamp it out. He missed. He shrugged and walked on to the other side. The car carried on down the road. The cigarette was still rolling rapidly, along the gentle slope of the road, the tiny, tiny glow of it eventually extinguished.

"I guess the Wind hasn't blown much in a while," Elliot said. "Which explains why it's all so empty here."

Madeleine was looking down the road to where a chalkboard stood outside a chocolate shop. *SPECIALS* said the chalkboard, a quick sketch of a fire-breathing dragon alongside the word. Her eyes ran farther downhill. A flag jutted out of a wall, inscribed with the name of a pub: the Three-Headed Eagle.

"I guess we ask somebody where the Wind comes from?" Elliot said. "I mean, if there's a specific place?"

"I just want to check something." Madeleine was drifting down the road. Elliot followed.

At the Three-Headed Eagle pub, she stopped, looking around. There was an intersection ahead, and around the corner she could just make out a café with tables outside.

"Is that . . ." she murmured, and she crossed to the café. A pepper grinder in the shape of a frog stood in its center. The other tables also held frog or toad grinders.

Madeleine smiled. "This way," she told Elliot.

"How do you know? Is this a magic-weaving thing?"

"Nope." She was still smiling. "I've just seen a fire-breathing dragon, a three-headed eagle, and a bunch of frogs and toads, so I'm following their path."

"Well. Sure."

"There's a garden of roses!" She picked up her pace.

"This is fun," Elliot said mildly, "but —"

"They're all symbols from alchemy. Alchemists use this secret language when they tell you how to make gold. I think this is like a treasure hunt, following the clues. Although I can't actually see . . . ha. There's a fiberglass unicorn in that front yard."

She started to run.

At the next crossroads, a car was parked at an odd angle to the curb. A sticker on its rear window showed a three-headed serpent. Farther along, she laughed at a billboard advertising a Royal Spa Treatment with a picture of a king in a purple cloak and golden crown.

"The king clad in purple with a golden crown!" she called to Elliot, who was running just behind her, bemused, but happy, watching how her hair flew wild behind her, and how, when she turned, her eyes dazzled with laughter.

The path wound them past a butterfly farm and a fountain in the shape of a phoenix. They found themselves alone on an empty street that ran between fields. They were jogging side by side. In the hazy light, the road seemed to roll itself out grudgingly, just ahead of them.

"I dreamed this once," Madeleine said. "You and me running on a twilight road."

Their feet thudded to the same rhythm.

Then Elliot remembered, "I dreamed it too."

They turned to each other, eyes surprised and something more than surprised, then turned back just in time to see the road before them vanish, replaced by deep-night black.

4.

*T*he Council of the Jagged Edge Elite met regularly in Conference Room 11, Level 27, the Amelia Shields Tower, Tek.

Tonight, a laser-beam display signaled that this was an Extraordinary Meeting. Outside, warning bells rang, alerting the city to an approaching Color storm. Inside, tins of celery sticks and bowls of green apples lined the large table. Reclining chairs had been adjusted. Men and women moved about, speaking in low, urgent voices. Some had already taken a seat at the table and were leaning over portable computing machines. Cameras were being checked; sounds and angles tested. Transparent security shutters rippled into place at all the windows. A technician was busy reinforcing the soundproofing.

"Just about ready to go?" someone called, when a voice boomed: "Not without us!"

The King of Cello stood in the open doorway. He wore jeans. His shirt was buttoned low so his tattoo was visible.

Dismay and uncertainty rolled back and forth across the room.

The King stepped inside, turned, and beckoned at shapes in the corridor.

"The Queen and my daughter Princess Ko wished to accompany me," he said, ushering them inside.

The people in suits glanced at one another. Certainty returned, along with soft, mocking smiles.

"By all means," said a voice, low and reasonable. A man with a head of bristling curls stepped forward, hands open in welcome, cheeks rounding pinkly with a smile. "Super that you're here. Brilliant."

"*President* Stanhope! Looking dapper as ever!" The King shook the man's hand vigorously, slapping him on the back. "Listen, word is, you plan to make an announcement of some import tonight?"

"Indeed. And with you here, we can formalize things at once, the Kingdom as our witness." The President jutted a shoulder in the direction of the camera, then squinted thoughtfully at the table. He beckoned at a young man who was tossing an apple from one hand to the other. "Ensure we have sufficient seats for the royal family here, will you?"

*T*heir bodies still trembled. They'd almost stumbled right into a syrup-black chasm. It stretched the width of the road and the length of a football field.

"There should be warning signs," Elliot said.

The blackness of the chasm was as brutal as the sun. They had turned side-on to it, measuring it out of their peripheral vision, and catching it in quick, sharp glances.

After a moment, Madeleine said, "I guess that must be it. The way through to the space between?"

"I'm not going anywhere near that," Elliot said.

"Me neither. But that's it, right? There's no Wind blowing from it right now, but it looks like — it kind of looks like that total darkness of the space between. It's more than just a cave, I mean. It's more than just a *hole* in the road."

"It's not your ordinary hole in the road," Elliot agreed, smiling faintly.

There was another pause.

Elliot breathed deeply and when he spoke, his voice still held that faint smile. "So, what we do is, we assume that there's the *ether* down there, and we've gotta *get* some of it out and turn it into a Gold."

"Which will save the Kingdom," Madeleine confirmed, also smiling.

"Fishing rods?"

"Fish it out. Brilliant. So we need a net, I guess. Or maybe some kind of *scoop*? 'Cause the darkness might just slip out of the holes in the net."

"A scoop with a really long handle."

They both laughed suddenly. There was another long pause while their eyes roamed the fields and the languid dark blue sky, avoiding the darkness right ahead of them.

"I just thought of something," Madeleine said.

"Shoot."

"Something important about alchemy."

"Okay."

"It's this. Making gold is not just about the material. It's about the alchemist as well. You have to become *part* of the process. Blend yourself into what you're doing. It only works if you become *one* with the material that you're making into gold."

"You mean really *believe* in what we're doing? Like when we believed and held hands?"

"Partly," Madeleine said doubtfully. "But I'm getting the feeling it might be more than that. I'm thinking maybe . . . I'm thinking . . ."

Elliot looked at her. "I'm going to ask you to stop that thought right there."

"I'm thinking maybe it's more literal than that. Maybe we need to go *into* the ether and kind of become one with it?"

"I'm pretty sure I asked you to stop that thought. Politely as I could."

Madeleine said, "But I think I might be right."

Elliot kicked at a pebble on the road. He watched it tumble, turned it over with the toe of his boot, and kicked again. He turned and faced the blackness for a steady moment. "You might well be."

*T*he Conference Room had stilled to a shuffling quiet.

Everyone but the camera operators was seated around the table. Some played with paper clips or shifted the tins of celery sticks about, but most sat calmly waiting. Everybody glanced at the windows now and then: Through the transparent security shutters, the giddy swirls of a Color storm were visible.

Derek Stanhope sipped from a glass of water, smacked his lips together, glanced toward the camera with a questioning eye, then nodded firmly and spoke. "As President of the JE Elite . . ." he began.

"Hang on," a voice chimed.

Surprised frowns turned to the end of the table where Princess Ko was waving. "It would be a rainbow of fantastic," she declared, "if *I* spoke first."

Everyone rippled their gaze at once toward President Stanhope to see his reaction. His lower lip folded downward in an amused, indulgent smile. "By all means," he said, smile deepening. "But you understand we're on a tight schedule here? So just for two minutes."

Around the table, the camera operators were busy rotating their equipment and adjusting angles and focus.

"Am I on camera now?" the Princess asked.

"Go ahead."

"And this is being sent out, live, to the entire Kingdom?"

"It is."

From his seat beside her, the King leaned toward his daughter. "Ko?" he stage-whispered. "What you up to?"

This sent a wave of quiet laughter through the room.

Princess Ko hushed him with a wave of her hand, eliciting a second wave of laughter. She reached into a saddlebag on her lap, drew out a tall, slender stamp, and placed it on the table. Next, she dragged out a pile of papers and set these also on the table.

"Tight schedule?" the President reminded her, throwing a beseeching look at the King, going for a laugh himself. The King returned the look with a helpless shrug. There were snorts.

Princess Ko straightened, ignoring the others at the table, and faced the camera.

"It is a cloud formation of wonder to be here. It is I, Princess Ko, addressing my Kingdom with delight." She paused. Around the table, the men and women in suits sat back, smiling at one another.

"Incidentally, under regulation 46(b), sub (ii) of the Charter of Provinces, any member of the presiding royal family has the right to address any Provincial Council meeting for as long as that royal family member so pleases." Princess Ko shot a look toward the President, scratching her shoulder as she did. "Not as a favor. And not for two minutes."

Eyebrows were raised. The President allowed her another paternal nod, this time both amused and impressed.

"Furthermore, I am not simply a member of the presiding royal family, I am *the crown*. Here's why. The King, my father, has been officially declared incapacitated by the Royal Surgeon."

"Ha!" The King shouted in surprise. He swiveled right around in his chair and grinned at his daughter. "He has *not* been so declared, my dear!" and again there was a movement of laughter around the table, only this time it was touched with confusion.

"He has," Princess Ko said, not looking at her father. She held up the top paper from the stack beside her, then placed it before her father.

"What . . . ?" he said, his face seeming to stumble over its frown. On his other side, the Queen, who until now had been silent and still, placed a hand on the King's shoulder. "Just wait," she murmured. "Just wait."

"Temporarily incapacitated by reason of drug and alcohol addiction," Princess Ko continued, at which the King roared, and his wife — Holly Tully, as she liked to be called now — tightened her hand on his shoulder and said, "Shush now. And wait."

"My brother Prince Chyba was heir to the throne, of course, but I regret to inform the Kingdom —" She paused, then tried again. "It is my sad duty to inform you that Prince Chyba, recently, passed away."

Complete silence descended.

"So!" The Princess spoke rapidly, wrapping her hands around the stamp and raising it into the air. "I am officially in charge, which is lucky, as there are things that I wish to do with the Royal Stamp! These" — she indicated — "are *all* official documents." She took the next paper in the pile and placed it carefully onto the table before her.

The President spoke in a low mutter to the woman seated beside him.

"Hush now," chided Princess Ko. "I realize you think I'm just a twittering gnat and you were hoping I would provide the perfect prelude to your announcement. I realize my father still believes he can sort things out by being *friendly* with you — that he shook your hand and slapped your back, President Stanhope, even though you and the Jagged Edge Elite *placed me, his daughter, under arrest and sought to have her executed.*" Her eyes had narrowed to fierceness. "Well, President Stanhope, I will *never shake your hand.* In fact, your organization — the Jagged Edge Elite — are now, hereby, formally" — she paused, raised the stamp into the air — "disbanded."

The stamp fell with a crash.

"Hang on. What?"

The Princess spoke over the low clamor. "Yes. That document officially disbanded the Jagged Edge Elite. And I am now disbanding" — she fanned out the next few documents — "the WSU!" The stamp fell: *ker-clamp.* "I am *disbanding* the Hostiles! All branches of Hostiles! Wandering Hostiles! The Hostile Registration system!" Her arm lifted high, and the stamp came down, again and again, crash, crash, crash.

The room was bursting with chatter. The Princess shouted over it, "I will now disband the Circle!"

There was a rush of total silence. It held: poised and suspenseful. The Princess addressed the camera. "The Circle is an organization that has existed for centuries," she said. "Its members are immortals from the World, whose sole purpose is to maintain their immortality. They do this by ensuring that the cracks between here and the World remain sealed, and by abducting Cellians and banishing them to the World. They influence every branch of government, every organization of note, here in our Kingdom." She raised the stamp. "But not anymore they don't!" And brought it down with a mighty, reverberating boom.

7.

*E*lliot was standing on a road in the middle of a bunch of fields. In the Undisclosed Province. A province he'd never given much thought before. Those rock formations they'd passed in the train, they'd seemed cool. Maybe good to come here on vacation sometime, and do some hiking.

"But in a lot of other ways," he said to Madeleine, "this place is kind of —"

"Creepy? I know. It's the light. It can't make up its mind. I want to push something aside and say *what?* What *are* you? Night or day?"

"Exactly."

"Even though I'm kind of opposed to labels. They're too restrictive. But there's something sort of self-satisfied about all the mystery here."

"I like your mind, Madeleine."

She laughed. Then she stopped. "I think we have to be sure of ourselves," she said, "before we go into the ether."

Her voice: It was certain, or it was wicked humor, or it was tentative, but it always had that resonance, or whatever it was you called the thing her voice did to his spine. Soft fingers or feathers running down his spine.

"I have this sense," Madeleine said, "that we'll get lost in the ether if we don't believe in ourselves."

Her face: You could look at it all the time. Or take short breaks from looking because it was such a treat when you turned back and saw it again. Expressions just sprinted across her face, one after the other, running into each other, meeting up, turning into brand-new expressions. Also, the shape of her, and the way her body moved when she was running, and the way her neck fell into the collar of her jacket, and how she skated in circles on the ice — and how he'd almost gotten her killed.

"You're a good person, Elliot, you were trying to save the Kingdom."

Also, she was a mind reader.

"And you're a truth seer."

His thoughts stopped all at once. "No."

"The first time I saw you, you were in your high-school grounds, and I saw your eyes, and I thought: *He has eyes that see the truth*. That's exactly what I thought when I saw you." Madeleine paused. "I think we should make Gold out of the ether."

His thoughts started up again, high-speed: I'll never do it. Never. But what if she's right? Maybe I *am* a truth seer.

And then he saw the truth: that they were going to do it.

He took her hand, and they stepped into the ether.

8.

*M*adeleine knew right away that they'd made a mistake.

They were holding hands and stepping forward and she was wildly, fiercely happy — because Elliot was beside her, and he'd taken her hand and they were going to save the Kingdom — and then, instantly, none of those things was true.

Elliot was gone. She was alone in a rushing tumble, terror shoving her from all sides, a silence that was splintering, a blackness that blazed, and the Kingdom's chances were shot.

She was falling into nothing. It was dark, the nothing, and it felt damp, close, and clammy, but also inestimably vast. The nothing crept around her, slowly and steadily. She had stopped tumbling and was falling in a slow, misty way, while the nothing wound around her shoulders and her chest, stomach, arms, legs, face. It felt like multiple ribbons of cold tea. She had stopped descending, and now she was suspended, held up by the nothing. It wound further, then began twisting right *through* her, taking pieces of her as it twisted, and weaving these into itself. She herself, Madeleine, was unraveling into long, fine strands. Fragments were being pried away. Her voice was coming loose: She ducked, grabbed it back, furious, and shouted: "This is *ridiculous*!"

Somewhere, Elliot chuckled.

It was his deep, throaty chuckle. She'd heard that chuckle before, a long time ago, and now it swooped right through the nothing, and looped into her belly — a summer party dress, a thrumming dance beat — the sound of Elliot's chuckle and her memory of that sound.

9.

"*I* know what you're thinking!" Princess Ko glared around the room and then back at the camera. "That I can't do this! I can't *dismantle* these organizations with a stamp!"

She held up her palms. They were ink-stained.

"Well, you're right about the WSU actually. The royal family *can't* disband that, not without the consent of the Kingdom of Aldhibah. About an hour ago, I offered them a share of the Cello Wind in exchange for their consent. They gave their consent. So, actually, you're wrong. I *can* disband the WSU and I just did!"

"As for the Jagged Edge Elite. The crown may dissolve any such Provincial Council as it chooses. It's reg fifteen of the Charter of Provinces. Look it up.

"As for the Hostiles, well, are you kidding? Of *course* I can outlaw them! They commit treason before *breakfast*, those guys! And the Circle? They're just a rainbow of fantastic when it comes to felonies and capital offenses!

"So *now* you're thinking that I might *technically* be able to disband the Hostiles and the Circle, but that none of that matters because they've got the *power* and the *force*, and there's nothing I can do. But I'm doing it anyway. You know how? I'm about to *remove* the reasons they exist. *Just watch.*"

She leaned closer to the microphone and spoke sternly: "And as for the huge and mind-blowing battle-to-end-all-battles between Hostiles and Loyalists that you're all expecting — as for the special forces, the spies, the code breakers, the Circle and Elite pulling puppet strings from conference rooms, the Kingdom next door assembling its troops, maps on walls, tables marked with drawing pins — as for soldiers lined up, row upon row, bows and arrows poised, rifles at the ready — as for the rainfall of arrows, the gunfire like drums, cannons blasting, the fireworks display of falling bombs — as for all *that*? It's not going to happen! And let me ask you this: *Why does every story have to end with a mighty show of force?* Why? Just explain to me *why!*"

Everybody stared.

10.

*E*lliot's chuckle faded. Everything paused.

Madeleine called, "Are you okay?"

"No." But he laughed again. "Not sure what we were thinking, stepping into this."

His voice was not far, but the darkness was absolute. She tried to edge in his direction, but she was too tightly caught.

"Are you caught up in the nothing too?" she asked.

"Seems like a whole lot of something to me. I'm trying to — get out of — it — now."

His voice stopped and started; it was distant, then close. He must be rolling about, trying to get untangled. Madeleine tried to do the same. She picked at the edges of strands with her fingernails, peeling them away from her body, turning herself slowly as they unwound. They were sticky and fine, seaweed or cold noodles. Each time she pulled a strand loose, she felt it hover right beside her, brushing against her skin. The air around her was dense with the tendrils and ropes.

"I'm going to try braiding some of these strands together," Madeleine called. "To stop them coming after me again."

"Good idea. Me too."

There was a short silence, then Elliot called again. "We should keep talking."

"So we don't lose each other," Madeleine agreed.

"Or our minds."

"What shall we talk about?"

"Ordinary things. Like, are you a cat or dog person?"

"I'm the kind of person who doesn't like having to make a choice. Cats and dogs are both great, in their own way. Do you like to read?"

"Sure."

"If you're reading a book, do you use a bookmark or turn down the corner of the page or leave it lying open?"

"Or you could just close it," Elliot said, "and then find where you're up to again."

"Is that what you do?"

"A mix."

"Same."

They folded themselves out of strands, rolled, turned, stopped, felt for the ends of loose strands, gathered handfuls of these, and braided these together. Sometimes they felt the strands tugging or twitching away from them.

"When I say I use a bookmark," Madeleine clarified, "I mean, like a leaf, or a tissue, or the edge of my bedsheet, say I've left the book on my bed."

"Huh," Elliot said, then he chuckled.

"So what was it like?" Madeleine asked. "Being in the Hostile compound?"

Elliot told her about stirring giant pots of tomato sauce in the kitchen, the sounds of water dripping night and day, and the board games with faded print and missing pieces.

Madeleine told him about living at Gabe's farmhouse, with the Color storms outside, and the various storms between the people in the house, and how she thought Gabe and Keira might have hooked up.

Elliot thought that was the funniest thing he ever heard, Gabe and Keira together, then changed his mind and said it made perfect sense. He told her about Chime, and Ming-Sun, the Assistant Director, the attack of the Grays, and how he shouted through the night. Madeleine told him about the day her memory had come back when she'd seen the photo of her brother and had known that he was dead.

"Before that, I used to think the worst day of my life was when —
well, you know I used to run away a lot, and my dad always told me
that was selfish."

"It makes sense why you ran away. Sergio explained it."

"But what if he was wrong about all those noble reasons? 'Cause I
think sometimes I just ran away to go dancing."

She could hear the smile inside Elliot's words. "I might not like
you as much as I do," he said, "if you were nothing but noble. It's
good you like to party. So do I."

She smiled back into nothing, but then her smile fell away.

"The day those two guards were killed," she said. "When I ran
away to the Swamp of the Golden Coast and they came after me.
That used to be the worst day of my life."

"You can't have known," Elliot said, "that that would happen."

"I knew they'd come looking. I knew the Swamp was dangerous."

His voice came steady through the darkness toward her. "If you'd
known that would happen, you wouldn't have gone there."

He sounded so sure, so close, so warm.

"I feel like you're getting nearer," Madeleine said suddenly. "Like
braiding this nothing is sort of pulling us together?"

"You keep calling it nothing. You don't think it's that original matter you were talking about? Like the stuff that everything and everyone
is made from?"

"Well, doesn't everything come from nothing?"

They carried on working. Now and then their hands reached for
the end of the same strand, and they pulled at both ends, without
knowing the other was doing the same, then they wound their pieces
together, weaving the invisible.

"What should we talk about now?" Elliot said, and Madeleine

said, "Well, I like it, in books, when the characters wake up and eat breakfast. How about you?"

11.

*P*rincess Ko held up another set of papers.

By now, people had stopped leaning to whisper to one another or sending urgent messages on computing machines. Everyone was quiet, watching. The King, beside Ko, leaned sideways, chin on his hand, a quizzical, amused expression.

"Now that I've dismantled the Kingdom, it's time to do the same to the royal family!"

The King's chin slipped from his hand.

"The Royal PR Department! Disbanded!" *Ker-clamp!* "The Royal Marketing Department!" *Ker-blamp!* "Security! Protocol! The Myth of Superior Royal Blood! Canceled! Discredited! *I* don't know the word!" *Ker-clamp! Ker-clamp! Ker-clamp!*

She flourished the next document. Her eyes gleamed.

"This one gives away all our palaces! Except for the White Palace, as that's where we live. But the rest can go to orphans! Or schools maybe? Homeless people? Anyhow, that can be worked out."

She stamped the document, blew on it, and took the next in the pile.

"This one dismantles royalty itself. From this point forward, the authority of the royal family ceases."

A zing hurtled through the room, the King straightened, his face grim, and Princess Ko looked up, pleased.

"Don't worry," she said. "There's fine print here, says I get to stay in charge until certain further steps are taken. Once complete, I step down. At which point, of course, *royalty* will cease to exist, along with the reason for the Hostiles' existence. What did I tell you?" She spoke through the muttering and exclamations. "Ah, now *this* paper says that, if he wishes to continue as part of our family, the King will undergo treatment at a registered substance abuse facility."

The King's face shone with disbelief. He turned to his daughter, but on his other side, the Queen placed a hand on his shoulder. "That was my idea," she murmured. Everyone strained to hear. "This is what you need to do." She shrugged. "Or not. It's up to you. But if you don't, there's no chance for you and me."

Princess Ko slid the paper toward her father, along with a pen.

"Sign it if you like," she said. "Whenever you're ready."

The King fell back in his chair, arms dangling over the chair arms, his face defiant and miserable.

The room waited. Nothing happened. Hesitantly, heads and cameras turned back to Princess Ko.

"Something is broken, you take it apart," she said. "That's what I've just done. Now I'm putting it back together again." Another stack of papers. "These set up a committee to implement democracy. We'll have a constitution. A bill of rights. This establishes a new World-Cello Harmony Institute, to deal with relations with the World."

Confusion broke out again. "Yes, relations with the World. As we speak, a Gold is being made. It will provide an elixir for our bruised and broken Kingdom. It will do that by permanently opening the cracks between Cello and the World. As a consequence, of course, the Circle will cease to have reason to exist. See that? I did it again.

Furthermore, with the cracks open, the Colors should fade and the Wind return."

The Princess lay the stamp on the table. "That was exhilarating," she said, "but strangely exhausting." She stretched her arms above her head, then leaned toward the camera again. "And now," she said in a low, urgent voice, "I am speaking to all the people of Cello. If you agree with what I have done here tonight — if you don't want to be ruled by the corrupt Elite, or the ruthless Hostiles, or the flawed royal family — if you don't want war, but peace, shelter, food, and democracy — if you want the same privileges and rights for every town and city, regardless of its political position — in that case, when the Colors *do* ease off — when the all clear sounds — I invite you, please, to come out onto the streets. And . . ." She looked vaguely around the room. "What should I ask them to do to show their support?"

"Wave their hands in the air," her mother suggested.

"Their arms might get tired."

Her mother laughed. "There must be a way around that."

"Right." Princess Ko nodded. "My fine people of Cello, when the all clear sounds, I hope you will run into the streets and wave your hands into the air, allowing them to rest when they get tired, then waving them again."

She paused.

"At any moment," she said, "the all clear will sound."

Faces turned from Ko toward the windows.

"At any moment," she repeated.

12.

$\mathcal{A}$ girl and a boy floated in separate boats on a lake in the darkest night, close enough to talk, a tangle of soft thread in the air between them, which, blindly, they untangled and wove, all the time drawing the other boat closer toward them.

This is how it seemed to Elliot and Madeleine. Moon behind a dark cloud. The night still, the water silent. They talked and talked. Their voices untangled their own sad secrets and serious tales, peeling threads of these away, looping them around into tiny thoughts, ideas, funny stories, then back again.

Their voices, as they talked, drifted closer and closer. Sounds close enough to touch.

"These pieces," Madeleine said, "do you think some of them might be pieces of ourselves from when we fell into this and started to unravel?"

"Could be. So we're winding pieces of ourselves into this, winding them into each other."

"Maybe we're just doing that by talking."

"Do you think," Elliot said, "that we're making a kind of bridge?"

"Like between magic and truth? If you're truth and I'm magic, or whatever."

When Elliot spoke next, his voice was so close she felt it on her skin. "I think there's plenty of truth in you," he said, "as well as magic."

They caught each other's eyes. The spark and reflection of eyes, the hint of silhouettes, shoulders, arms, under faltering, distant light, softer than moonlight.

They let the strands fall from their hands and reached for each other. Elliot's fingertips touched Madeleine's wrist, the touch sliding down and then away. Golden glow of dragon fire swooping overhead. His arms found their way around her body, and she reached her arms around his. She felt the seams of his shirt, the buckle of his belt, the smooth and muscle of him. His hand slid to the back of her head. That was Elliot's hand on the back of her head, Madeleine thought. It felt warm. It was the palm of his hand on her hair. The pressure and the warmth of Elliot's hand, just there, perfectly still, not moving, just there, holding her head — that was the best thing that anyone, anywhere, in all time, had ever felt or would ever feel. She was clear about that, but then Elliot leaned closer and kissed her.

13.

A cross the Kingdom, people watched TVs, screens, visual parchments, and projections of Princess Ko while the warning bells jangled and the Color storms raged. Princess Ko stared out and said, "Any moment now."

In Bonfire, the Farms, a crowd had gathered in the living room of Gabe's farmhouse. It was a hot summer night, and a fan stood and spun in a corner. The TV was turned loud over the noise of the Colors that crashed around outside like an angry person stumbling among trash cans.

The room was crowded with chairs that had been dragged here from all over the house. Gabe had found a pack of raspberry ice pops in his freeze box and handed them around, so people were sucking or biting at these, turning lips vibrant pink, catching pieces that broke away and slipped toward the floor.

There were the farm kids — Shelby, Nikki, Cody — strewn about on the floor. Abel and Petra Baranski shared an armchair, their hands intertwined. Agents Tovey and Kim, who always wore suits, had loosened their ties and undone their top buttons. The Sheriff and Jimmy sat on kitchen chairs, alongside Isabella Tamborlaine, who kept breaking into tears. She was the only one not watching the TV: She was gazing at her long-lost son, Jack, who himself kept glancing sideways at his mother uncertainly. Belle, on Jack's other side, spun slowly in an office chair, her eyes roaming the room.

On the couch, Gabe and Keira sat side by side.

"If it does happen," Gabe said in a low voice. "If she's right and the all clear's about to sound."

"Seems unlikely."

They listened to the thuds and screeches of the Colors outside.

"It does. But if it happens, you know what the first thing we'll do is?"

"Well," Keira said. "We're supposed to run outside and throw our arms in the air for Princess Ko."

"Yeah, okay, but after that."

"What?"

"You'll take me for a spin on your bike."

Behind them, Jack had turned to Isabella and was also speaking in a low voice. "I'm just wondering," he said, "if you could tell me who my father was?"

"Of course!" Isabella said, her eyes filling with tears again.

There was a beat.

"Well?"

She considered him. "He was not a good father. But I think, somehow, he *could* have been. He was a poet. I believe he is still famous in the World. George Gordon —"

Belle skidded her spinning office chair to a halt. "You have *got* to be kidding!" she shouted. "Not Byron! Don't *tell* me that Jack's the son of Byron! This Kingdom gets *better all the time*!"

"Byron. Yes, he was trouble. Byron." Isabella's narrow eyes turned dreamy. She twirled the pendant she always wore on a chain around her neck. Beside her, Jimmy's brow furrowed.

"I wouldn't worry," Belle told Jimmy. "He's not a serious competitor. Been dead a couple of hundred years."

Agent Kim was sketching as usual. Tovey watched over his shoulder.

"Like another ice pop?" the Sheriff asked, holding up his empty stick. "I'm going to get me another. It's so darn hot in here."

Agent Kim shook his head, eyes still on the sketch pad.

"This is a very good likeness of you, he's drawing," Agent Tovey told the Sheriff. "You're a fine-looking man, Sheriff Samuels."

"Well, you're not so bad yourself, Agent Tovey."

Agent Kim smiled almost imperceptibly, adding shading.

On the couch, Gabe murmured: "We can take it to Sugarloaf Dam."

"You're still going on about my bike," Keira said.

"I am. We can take it to Sugarloaf Dam — there's a full moon tonight. You can teach me some about your bike, and I'll teach you how to swim."

Keira looked toward the farm kids. "Shelby told you I can't swim?"

"Nope. Figured it out myself."

"In the Crimson?"

Gabe smiled. "In my head."

She reached up with both hands, touched his ears, and loved them.

On the screen, Princess Ko whispered, "Any moment now."

14.

$\mathcal{I}$n the Conference Room, almost everyone, including the camera operators, was standing at the windows. Foreheads and hands were pressed to the glass.

At the table, the King and Princess Ko remained seated. The King still sat back in his chair, arms hanging loose, staring vacantly. The paper and pen lay at angles on the table before him.

"How did you do all this?" he said, not turning. "All this . . . paperwork?"

"I've been having secret meetings with people since we got to Gabe's farmhouse," she said, flicking her nail down the pile of papers. "Those two agents — Tovey and Kim — were helpful at getting me in touch with lawyers and so on. I finalized everything today, once I knew about the Circle and the Gold."

"And they're all valid? Legitimate?"

"A sparkleshine of whirldust."

The King glanced at her.

"That means yes. Yes, they are."

He looked down at the stack of papers. "Impressive."

"There are more," the Princess said, sliding a document in his direction. "This one provides for the regular feeding of the dragons at the Bay of Munting."

The King cleared his throat. "The Bay of Munting," he said. "That's where dragons go when they've lost their hunting eyes."

Princess Ko closed her eyes.

Outside, the Color storm continued.

15.

*I*n the strange glow, they could see that most of the strands had now formed braided ropes. There were only a handful of loose ones left.

"I guess we just finish working on these last ones?"

Elliot followed her gaze. "I guess."

The kiss was still there, touching their skin, filling the ether.

"And when we're done with this weaving," Madeleine said. "I guess we'll be able to go back."

"I guess. But how?"

"Well, I have this intuition that, eventually, light will surround us and we'll walk right through it back to Cello."

Elliot smiled. "You're the magic weaver. I trust your intuition."

"But I don't know what will happen to us once we're back."

"We'll be people."

"Like, I'm not a princess or a runaway girl, and you're not a farm boy or a hero? We're not talking through a crack between worlds? We're just us?"

"Exactly."

"Kind of scary," Madeleine said. Then she thought about it. "Ah, we can drink coffee, and listen to music, and walk through fallen leaves."

"Not scary in the slightest."

"I want to find the girl I was writing to in Berlin — the wrong Princess Jupiter. And the wrong Queen. See if they're okay. Keep in touch."

"I want to check on Chime and Ming-Sun too," Elliot agreed.

"And I want you to meet Belle and Jack properly. You've forgotten meeting them in the World, haven't you?"

"Yep."

"Well, I want to visit the World all the time and show you around."

They braided silently, hands trembling with leftover glints of the kiss.

"The ends of the braids are sort of frayed," Madeleine said. Elliot looked.

As they watched, a tiny piece, the size of a whisper, an illuminated speck, broke away from a frayed end. It drifted into the darkness. Another piece loosened and darted.

"How long has that been happening for?" Elliot asked. "Is that where that pale light is coming from?"

More pieces broke away, one at a time, and then a cluster, a spray of sparks.

"Do you think it's Gold?" Elliot said.

"I have no clue, but I like it. It's kind of like we're weaving stars."

They continued.

16.

𝒥n the Kingdom of Cello, the night sky was clamor and discord. Warning bells clanked madly. The loudest Colors tore and ripped at the air. Tumbling Colors careened down streets and pounded buildings. Shutters rattled, voices rose in shouts or shrieks, animals howled, children cried.

Darts of Gold began to drift high. Nobody saw these. They drifted low. They sank, spinning, fell at a twirl, and touched grass, snow, brickwork, bark, cement. They dusted play equipment and tractors. On the Cat Walk, the animals strode through swarms of it. The darts soared high again, tangling with stars. Moonlight caught them. They dashed away.

Muffled bristles and snappings sounded. A sound like paper tearing, neat and sharp, over and over. Across the Kingdom, invisibly, the cracks were opening like swift, sharp zips. Nobody heard this.

The Colors began a slow roll, like waves. Some faded, or wilted. Colors rose like steam on tea. Some turned in languid circles, picked themselves up, and sailed away. One by one, then in clusters, then crowds, the Colors dissolved, dissipated, disappeared.

Pieces of noise began to lift away in turn. Large slices of noise left behind smaller noises, then fragments of noises, a briefly clanking bell, a gate slammed, wheels turning.

The crumbs of noise ceased.

The moon breathed silence. The specks and touches and blinks of Gold dust drifted with the stars, blew like pollen or like seeds, slid down window glass like hints of dew.

In one fine moment, the Kingdom waited. The silence stole about, exploring.

It was an unknown silence, majestic, and then abruptly it capsized as, all across Cello, the bells sounded a vigorous all clear. From town to village to city, along rivers and inside ravines, the bells sounded. They met one another. Their echoes met their echoes. A great weave of echoes patterned the land.

Right across the Kingdom, shutters shot high and doors flew open. Along canals, on beaches, in university dormitories, hotel corridors, apartment high-rises, farmhouses, and barns, doors opened and opened. People poured out onto the streets and laneways in their dressing gowns or ball gowns. The bells sang and sang, the people waved their hands and laughed so the waving and the laughter tangled with the chiming.

Something ruffled collars, skirts, and hair like a summer breeze. Nobody knew it yet but, in a moment, the bells would dim and quiet, and all across Cello, the first notes of the Cello Wind would sound.

17

*I*n the World, meanwhile, time drifts oddly, so some places were night, and some day. The globe spun as usual, but now a sprinkling of light and color infiltrated. Those who were sleeping and those who were awake, and those who were drifting, or drowsing, or staring, or watching TV, or tapping on their phones, or switching on the kettle, and those who were bright and alert — all of them, every one, woke up.

18.

$\mathcal{E}$lliot and Madeleine watched their own hands, and each other's hands, working in the pale, reflected light.

They were almost done: There were only a few strands to go.

Now and then they glanced at the flying, breaking pieces, the fraying ends, the darts of light.

"You think this is making a single bit of difference in the Kingdom?" Elliot asked.

Madeleine shrugged. "I doubt it."

"Ah, well. It's kinda fun."

"It is."

"In fact, it's a sparkleshine of — what was it again? That expression of your sister's? Anyhow, that's what it is."

Madeleine smiled.

They carried on weaving, and at every twist and turn, the light grew stronger.

THIS BOOK IS DEDICATED TO MY DAD,
THE BEST DAD IN THIS AND ALL
ADJOINING UNIVERSES.

Library of Congress Cataloging-in-Publication Data

Names: Moriarty, Jaclyn, author. | Moriarty, Jaclyn. Colors of Madeleine ;
bk. 3.
Title: A tangle of gold / Jaclyn Moriarty.
Description: First edition. | New York, NY : Arthur A. Levine Books, an imprint of
Scholastic Inc., 2016. | Series: The colors of Madeleine ; Book 3 | Summary: In Cambridge,
England, Madeleine Tully is still working to gather the Royal Family, and get them back to
their parallel world — but in Cello, Elliot Baranski is being held captive, the Hostiles are
working against the Royal Family, and the World Severance Unit is trying to stop all contact
between Cello and the World for good.
Identifiers: LCCN 2015027754| ISBN 9780545397407 (hardcover : alk. paper) | Subjects:
LCSH: Magic — Juvenile fiction. | Missing persons — Juvenile fiction. | Royal houses —
Juvenile fiction. | Interpersonal relations — Juvenile fiction. | Colors — Juvenile
fiction. | Cambridge (England) — Juvenile fiction. | CYAC: Magic — Fiction. | Missing
persons — Fiction. | Kings, queens, rulers, etc. — Fiction. | Interpersonal relations —
Fiction. | Color — Fiction. | Cambridge (England) — Fiction. | England — Fiction.
Classification: LCC PZ7.M826727 Tan 2016 | DDC [Fic] — dc23 LC record available at
http://lccn.loc.gov/2015027754

10 9 8 7 6 5 4 3 2 1   16 17 18 19 20

Printed in the U.S.A.   23
First edition, April 2016

Book design by Elizabeth B. Parisi

Acknowledgments

I have exceptionally bright, brilliant, and beautiful publishers, and have been consistently amazed by their talent and patience throughout the writing of this trilogy. To everyone at Scholastic (especially Arthur A. Levine, Emily Clement, Weslie Turner, Elizabeth Parisi, Elizabeth Krych, Sheila Marie Everett, and Lizette Serrano), and at Pan Macmillan (Claire Craig, Samantha Sainsbury, Danielle Walker, and Charlotte Ree), my heartfelt thanks. I'd like to express the same level of enthusiasm and gratitude for my marvelous agents, Tara Wynne and Jill Grinberg.

Many books were helpful, inspiring, or entertaining-yet-completely-irrelevant as I researched and wrote this trilogy. Some of my favorites were: James Gleick, *Isaac Newton*, (Fourth Estate, 2003); Michael White, *Isaac Newton: The Last Sorcerer* (Fourth Estate, 1997); Edna O'Brien, *Byron in Love* (Weidenfeld & Nicolson, 2009); Johannes Itten, *The Elements of Color* (Van Nostrand Reinhold, 1970, trans. Ernst Van Hagen); John Gage, *Colour and Meaning: Art, Science and Symbolism* (Thames & Hudson, 1999); and Carlos Prieto, *The Adventures of a Cello* (University of Texas Press, 1998).

For answering questions and for thoughts, ideas, and expertise (on motocross, farming, England, airplanes, physics, and many other topics), thank you so much to Michael Kalesniko, Oliver Sellers, Patrick Nielsen, Darryl Fain, Adam Gatenby, Alistair Baillie, Steve Menasse, and Bernard Moriarty.

For reading drafts and/or for suggestions, inspiration, conversation, emails, music, visits, or helping out with Charlie, thank you so much to my mum and dad, to Liane Moriarty, Kati Harrington, Fiona Ostric, Nicola Moriarty, Suzy McEvoy, Joanne Webb, Melita Smilovic, Stephen Powter, Elizabeth Pulie, Laura Bloom, David Levithan, Justine Larbalestier, Michael McCabe, Katherine Mair,

Rachel Cohn, Corrie Stepan, Erin Shields, Jane Eccleston, Lesley Kelly, Gaynor Armstrong, Libby Choo, Henry Choo, Hannah Kelly, and Henry Stabback.

Much of this trilogy was planned, researched, or written in the Kirribilli Village Cafe and in Coco Chocolate Kirribilli, and I have a powerful sense that I could never have done it without the welcome, the warmth, and the cinnamon and cardamom hot chocolate.

Thank you to all the readers who have sent such delightful messages, and a special thank-you to those who have followed and written Colours of Thursday blog posts on Tumblr.

For his patience when my mind drifts far away, and for his imagination, enthusiasm, and lively conversation, thank you so much to Charlie; for exactly the same things, and also for suggestions and encouragement, thank you to Nigel Wood.

This book is dedicated to my father, Bernard Moriarty, who, among many other accomplishments, has fixed my shelves and bathroom taps, taught my boy how to ride a bike, and understands the value of chocolate.

This book was edited by Arthur Levine
with assistance from Emily Clement,
and designed by Elizabeth B. Parisi.
The text was set in Adobe Caslon Pro
and the display type was set in Carolyna Pro Black.
The book was printed and bound at
R. R. Donnelley in Crawfordsville, Indiana.
Production was supervised by Elizabeth Krych,
and manufacturing was supervised by Shannon Rice.